The Children of Nyx

The Nickelville Novels
Book 4
by Tom Barnett

Books by Tom Barnett

The Nickelville Novels

The Haunting of Nickelville Academy

The Goatman of Guarded Wood

Within the Silver Mirror

The Children of Nyx

Table of Contents

Chapter I: Unhuntsman-like Conduct

Megan McGeehee felt as if the past year and a half had been no more than an instant of stolen time while someone had pushed the pause button on her flight from the Wild Hunt. Now it had begun to play again. Pain blossomed at the base of her neck as the old terror returned, twisting thorny vines down into the pit of her stomach. Her heart raced, and her thoughts turned to her mother as they always had when the faceless Huntsmen caught her scent. But Emelia wouldn't be coming this time, and even if by some miracle she did, Megan had no intention of ever running again.

The dank cave felt smaller than it had before the closing of the gate, as if some vitality had drained away, leaving nothing more than a hollow scar that would finally fill in and heal. The musty air left a film on her skin, and for the first time in months, she remembered the apartment. For a few seconds she panicked, worried that all of this might have been a dream and she would wake any moment to find herself still there in that horrible place. Then Bruce squeezed her hand and brought her back.

"I think we just broke Nickelville," he whispered, his voice echoing off the stone walls.

Her stomach clenched in a quick, hysterical blurt of laughter that bounced back at her from the confined space, shrill and unpleasant in her own ears.

"What should we do?" he asked.

"We've got to go find out what happened to Sam," she said, sounding far more confident than she felt.

"He's at the Baker," he said. "If those shields are strong enough to break our bond, then they're strong enough to hide us."

"Bruce," she said, shaking her head even though he couldn't see it in the dark, "I have no intention of living the rest of my life in an abandoned hotel. I know who they are now, and more importantly I know who I am. It's time for me to face them."

"Are you sure?" he asked. "I'm with you no matter what you decide to do, just don't forget. Where you go, I go."

"I won't forget," she promised.

Gripping his hand tight, she took them back into the uncomfortable brightness of the Baker Hotel's roof where the massive tree had somehow been grown high above the town. Although they could see their big friend's legs, his upper body remained hidden behind the massive trunk of the tree.

Thunder rolled in the distance, and clouds began to gather. Sunlight fled before them and Megan worried that being on top of the highest point in Nickelville might not be a good place to meet the Wild Hunt.

"We've got maybe four minutes tops," Bruce said, pushing through the underbrush. "Sam's thoughts feel like he's just been knocked out, but I'd hate to think of anything strong enough to do this to him. Maybe there's something hidden here that we missed."

"I don't want Sam here when the Huntsmen come," Megan said, looking around. The wild tangle of foliage could contain almost anything.

"Damn that's a big bird!" Bruce exclaimed when he drew close enough to see the huge raptor that draped Sam's upper body protectively with its wings. It had a red crest of feathers atop the white of its head.

"Get away from him," Megan yelled, running toward their friend.

With an indignant huff that seemed far more human than avian, it leapt into the air and circled the depression where the tree grew before settling on a branch several yards above their heads.

"Do you think that thing is what knocked him out?" Bruce asked, never taking his eyes off of it as he joined her by Sam's side.

"I don't know," Megan said. "But we are running out of time."

"We can pull him inside where the shields will hide him," Bruce suggested.

"No," Megan replied, shaking her head. "He brought the elevator up with him. If it turns out that he's hurt worse than we think, no one else will be able to reach him up here. I can't take him home, or I'll lead the Wild Hunt to your family."

The two of them cast about frantically for a solution.

"I think I've got a way to send him there in case you and I don't make it back. Mr. Bob?" she called.

The Cat Sidhe appeared instantly, looking up at her with his luminous green eyes.

"Please take him to the Grimbles," she said. "And try to keep them all safe until we can join you."

Mr. Bob nuzzled her hand before putting his paw on the big man's hand and fading from sight with him.

"I can't believe he actually did what you asked," Bruce whispered in awe, rising quickly to his feet. "Hurry, let's get up to the top level where we have room to fight if we need to."

Megan pulled him back on impulse and held him close, wrapping her arms around his waist and laying her head on his shoulder the way she had during the slow dances at the Academy that night.

"Or we can just hold each other until they get here," he said, surprised by the unexpected show of affection. "I'm pretty okay with that too."

"Thanks for staying," she whispered, then she kissed him quickly on the cheek and walked the shadows with him to the center of the observation deck above.

A thin mist of rain had begun to fall. Lightning struck somewhere out in Guarded Wood and the thunder that followed shook the rooftop beneath

4

their feet.

Pressure continued to build at the bases of their skulls as more and more of the Huntsmen caught their scent. Bruce winced when several more locked on simultaneously, moving his hand to massage the back of his neck. She turned to where her back rested against his, and then, closing her eyes, she sought out the shadowy outlines of the huntsmen as they drew closer.

"If we have to fight," she whispered, trying to stay calm, "Get Jade's competition sword from her room, and I'll take the one on the wall from the dojo. Neither of them is particularly sharp, but the iron in the steel will wreak havoc with Tuatha dé magic."

"That is so cool," Bruce said, his senses radiating out past the town. "They've been stationing themselves in a grid around the area where they think you're hiding. When they lock onto you, they start walking the shadows closer by increments, which allows them to triangulate."

"How can you tell all of that from this pain?" she asked, realizing that he must be sensing the approaching huntsmen differently from the way she did.

"I don't know," he murmured. "But there's one getting really close. She'll be here in a few seconds."

Over the years Megan had painted some fairly detailed images in her mind of what the Wild Hunt might look like should they ever find her. Most centered around a picture she'd seen in a library book when she'd been seven or eight. She still remembered the way her skin had prickled when she'd seen the caption, *Wild Hunt*, below an illustration of men dressed in an assortment of furs and armor riding on horseback, blowing hunting horns and waving swords over their heads.

The pain crested with the arrival of a young woman who appeared before them, looking nothing like a savage barbarian at all. Little more than a teenager herself, she wore a cloak that could have easily been mistaken for a trench coat. But the rest of her clothing wouldn't have looked out of place in a typical high school. Were it not for her short, jet-black hair and her alabaster skin, Megan wouldn't have even considered the possibility of her being Tuatha dé.

Standing in a wide-footed crouch, the girl looked as if she were preparing to jump over some hidden obstacle that only she could see even though her eyes were clenched shut in concentration. She stayed like this for several seconds, muttering under her breath in what sounded like Gaelic.

Bruce turned to look over his shoulder at this newcomer, puzzled by her appearance and lack of reaction to their presence. Megan shot him a puzzled look and he turned away from the defensive position he'd taken up to better watch this stranger.

"Excuse me," Megan finally called out. "What are you doing?"

The girl backpedaled a few steps, violet eyes opening wide as she looked at them.

Megan giggled, unable to help herself. Was this really what she'd spent her whole life dreading?

"Who are you?" the girl asked in flawless English, although she spoke with the speed of someone whose words often overtook their thoughts.

"I think I'm the one you're looking for," Megan answered, smiling. "Is there any way you can tone down whatever it is that you're doing that's giving us such headaches?"

The young woman continued to stare at them in disbelief, but the pain diminished instantly.

"You know," Bruce added when it looked like their strange companion might have become stuck in her own thoughts, "the heir."

6

"I can't believe it!" the girl yelled, pumping her fist into the air in a very, un-huntsman-like manner. "No one is going to believe me! Wait," she said as if remembering what she was supposed to be doing, "I have to tell Cian." She closed her eyes in concentration, and then opened them quickly. "Don't go anywhere!"

I'm so confused, Bruce sent.

August did say that the Tuatha dé were a race of children, Megan sent. *Almost all of the adults were killed at Mag Tuired. But this is just...*

Absolutely insane.

Am I about to meet my real father for the first time?

He shrugged next to her, unable to take his eyes off the strange young woman in front of them.

Three young men appeared, and though young like the girl dressed in the popular fashion of the time, they at least gave off an air of professionalism. Others began to appear, slowly filling the empty places around the open rooftop until the two of them were surrounded by several dozen men and women. Wind whipped their cloaks around them as the storm matured, but they seemed not to notice as they studied the heir in silence.

Only one member of the fabled Wild Hunt looked anything like either she or Bruce had expected. Dressed in a pallet of blacks and grays, the grizzled Huntsman wore a leather breastplate emblazoned with a tree whose branches and roots twisted into a seamless pattern of knotwork. His gray hair fell to his shoulders, fading to white at his temples, but his violet eyes were clear. Now that they were locked on her, he seemed to dare her to try and run again. As he held her gaze, the pain at the base of her skull began to increase.

Megan could feel Bruce shift uncomfortably next to her, and the realization that the pain the two of them felt originated from this man allowed her to focus her will on its mechanism. Lifting her hand in a gesture of defiance, she snapped her fingers and severed the tether that bound them. The pain faded instantly.

Gasps of surprise from the Huntsmen who surrounded them broke the silence as he tried to reestablish whatever bond he'd used to track them.

Bruce understood the mechanism of this method almost instantly through his smith's senses, allowing him to capture the wisp of energy with ease. Then he used it to lock on the old Huntsman the same way he'd tracked Megan, bringing the full force of his mind behind it. The man's knees almost buckled in pain, but he managed to hold himself erect by sheer force of will.

"You found us here because we wished it so," the Morrigan said through Megan's lips. "Do not presume us your quarry. I am Megan Mackgahe, Heir to the throne of the Tuatha dé, and you will treat us with the respect we are due."

The man nodded, and Bruce released his hold.

The atmosphere on the rooftop changed perceptively during this exchange. Megan couldn't help but notice the grudging respect that grew in the eyes of her father's subjects. The seconds ticked by on her antique watch while they waited there on top of the tallest building in Nickelville. Down below, the town remained ignorant of the supernatural events taking place overhead.

Five heavily armored men and one woman appeared, none of which looked like gangly teens. Each of them swept the rooftop for signs of potential threats. But there was something familiar about the woman...

"Captain Adair?" Megan called out.

The woman froze in her survey of the rooftop, her violet eyes coming to rest on Megan. Then the armored figure pulled off her helm, revealing Cara's wife from the runestone visions.

"How do you know my name?" she asked, frowning.

Without warning, all of the Tuatha dé, except Adair, dropped to one knee. Then the man Megan had dreamed of meeting since she'd been old enough to notice his absence from her life appeared. He looked almost exactly as he had in the runestone memories. That meant he must have spent most of his time in Tyr Sgodl since they'd fled.

Still dressed like a businessman from the past, he didn't stand out among his subjects as much as the woman who appeared next to him a few seconds later. With the exception of the old Huntsman and the king's guards, the rest had made attempts to blend in on Earth. This woman had brought the royal court of Tyr Sgodl with her.

She wore a black velvet floor-length dress accented with white that perfectly matched the contrast between her hair and alabaster skin. The heavily embroidered bodice left her shoulders bare beneath a jewel-encrusted collar that encircled her neck in gold and violet just the shade of a Tuatha dé's eyes. On her brow sat a crown-like headdress.

"Nimue," Megan whispered, recognizing her from the runestone visions.

But the king took no notice of the pompous newcomer, staring instead at Megan, likely trying to find the child he'd lost in the young woman before him. He barely spared Bruce a glance as he walked toward his estranged daughter. His guards rose to fall in behind him and Adair moved into position at his side, displacing the sour looking Nimue who clearly thought it her own right to be there.

"So the pretender has been caught at last?" Nimue called out in a husky, seductive voice. The King flinched at the word, but still said nothing. "Where is her treacherous mother?"

"Still angry about being his last choice, Nimue?" a familiar voice sang from behind where Megan and Bruce stood, making them turn

9

quickly.

Relief flooded through Megan, a feeling Bruce echoed through their bond.

Emelia stood near the edge of the roof with two male strangers, one of which might have been the illusive trench coat stalker. The other was a middle-aged man with black curly hair and skin that would have looked pale anywhere outside the company of the Tuatha dé. He wore a sweater, jeans and an expression of absolute horror to be in the presence of so many violet eyed warriors.

"Well done, Dougal," Nimue called out. "You're proving to be less useless than we thought."

"Be careful," the captain of the guard growled, glaring over her armored shoulder at the noblewoman. "Lest your big mouth catch an errant breeze and send you over the side. It's a long way down."

"They are not my prisoners," the trench coat stalker replied, clearly not liking the situation any more than Emelia's other companion.

"Then you're a traitor as well," Nimue replied coldly, holding Adair with a cold stare.

Throughout this exchange, the King's eyes traveled between Megan and Emelia as if trying to puzzle out how they'd all come to be there.

"Surrender the Scathlahm's Blade, witch," Nimue spat, losing her lofty composure.

"Even if I were to start listening to you, Nimue, which I assure you will never happen," Emelia said with a taunting smile. "I cannot do so. I have already passed it on to my successor that he might better fulfill the oath of his office."

"What of this abomination you've dared to bring before your king?" Nimue spat. "Even had you not stolen the heir, consorting with the Children of Nyx is forbidden."

10

Megan noticed that the man in the sweater was staring at her with an inordinate amount of interest.

"His name is William," Emelia replied quietly. "And he is indeed a Child of Nyx. But he is not our enemy. He wasn't even born yet on the Night of Many Goodbyes. He is here as my guest."

"How dare you…" Nimue growled.

"That's enough," the king said, finding his voice at last. "Dougal, surrender the blade until we have the measure of this."

The young man at Emelia's side strode forward and laid the wicked looking knife at the King's feet.

"Emelia," the King said, and Megan could feel her mother's shields waver.

"It's been a long time," she said, walking up and searching his face as he did the same with hers. His hand started to move of its own volition, looking as if he intended to touch his wife's face. Then it froze in place for an agonizing moment before dropping back to his side.

"Why have you done this?" he asked softly

"It doesn't matter…" the unpleasant woman blurted out.

"I was under the impression that it is I who am King, Nimue," he snarled, his voice finally taking on the edge of command, even as his eyes softened under Emelia's gaze. "And until I say otherwise, you will give my wife the respect due to your Queen. Need I remind you that without her, none of us would be here?" Then he waited for his wife to answer.

The pause stretched out uncomfortably. In the silence of the Baker's rooftop, the wind cut through, driving the rain that grew steadily heavier into their eyes.

"There are no words to describe why I had to take our daughter and raise her away from you, my love," Emelia answered at last, never taking her eyes from his.

He took a hesitant step toward her.

"There is only one way for you to understand," Emelia said loud enough for those gathered to hear over the growing storm. "I offer myself up to your judgement so that you may see for yourself the will of the Morrigan, by whose command I acted. Only then will you understand my reasons for leaving as I did, and what has transpired since."

Gasps of surprise rose from all present.

"Yes!" Nimue exclaimed. "Judge her!"

"No!" Megan yelled, and Bruce hardened his shields and started to gather power. His thoughts meshed with hers, preparing to fight their way free. Now that he understood the ways in which the Huntsmen had tracked his friend, he felt confident that the three of them could disappear permanently this time. He only wished he could have said goodbye to his family.

"Trust in the voice of the Morrigan," Emelia commanded without looking over at them. "Bruce, I did not train you for this. All is exactly as it was meant to be." The weariness in her voice was almost more than her daughter could bear.

"Are you sure?" Daragh asked in no more than a whisper, and although Megan could see pain in his eyes, she could also see the love he had for her mother. She'd seen that sort of love often in...in... The thought faded from her thoughts as she watched.

"I am eager to prove my innocence, and if you will have me, return to your side," Emelia answered, looking up into his face with the hint of a smile playing around the corners of her mouth.

"Not while I live," Nimue spat.

Emelia took off her coat and dropped it on the ground next to her, revealing a sleeveless halter beneath that allowed the knotwork across her shoulders and back to show. Megan wondered if she'd planned this from

12

the start to remind the Tuatha dé of the bond she shared with the King.

Emelia knelt before her husband, and he gasped at her touch when she took his hands in hers when he hesitated to do so. Then she placed them on each side of her head.

"I've never stopped loving you," she told him as she looked up into his glowing eyes.

Megan stood rigid with worry, afraid that the first memory she'd have of her own with this man might contain her mother's murder. Minutes stretched out while they waited. Nothing of the judgement's progress showed where the spectators could witness.

Nimue became more and more agitated, pacing in small circles and muttering to herself. Megan and Bruce watched the woman while she circled around the King and Queen with her ornate dress trailing behind her as she moved. Something in the jerky movements of her hands and the way her jaw muscles spasmed from time to time suggested to Megan that Nimue might not just be selfish and mean. As the judgement dragged on, she began to worry that this beautiful woman might actually be insane.

Then the King returned to himself, drawing Megan's attention away from the noblewoman nearby. His eyes focused on the woman before him and he smiled.

"Can you ever forgive me?" Emelia asked.

"Forgive you?" he replied tenderly, "It is I who should be asking for your forgiveness. I never should have doubted you."

The tension on the rooftop broke as he pulled his bride to her feet. Relief moved outward in an invisible wave from the reunited couple, and Megan allowed herself to relax. Her eyes fell on the odd young woman with the short black hair who'd found them. Now that the stress of the situation had largely passed, she noticed that the girl was wearing the same

"live long and prosper" elf shirt that Sam owned.

When the young member of the Hunt found the heir looking directly at her, the girl froze and faded partway into transparency before Megan smiled as disarmingly as she could at her.

"I like your shirt," Megan told her.

In an instantaneous transformation from fear to joy, the young woman started toward her.

This should be interesting, Bruce sent, as curious about this strange turn of events as she was.

Without warning, Nimue wailed in despair. Then, moving faster than Megan could have anticipated, she snatched the Scathlahm's Blade from the ground. The folds of her black dress flowed around her as she spun away from Adair's grasp and hurled it at Emelia's unprotected back.

Before Megan or Bruce could react, the King pulled his wife into his arms and partway into the shadows as he turned his back on Nimue. The artifact passed smoothly through his back to the hilt, narrowly missing his heart though not the arteries that fed it and continued deep into Emelia's shoulder.

He looked down into her eyes as his lips moved silently. When he exhaled, blood dripped down his chin. His fingers tightened on his wife's arms, then he sagged against her with his blood flowing from his wound down the Scathlahm's Blade and into hers.

"Daragh, no," she cried, his blood reawakening the power of the Tuatha dé in her and causing her eyes to glow. "Hold on. I've got you...please, no...please don't go." Oblivious to the knife that connected them, Emelia struggled to hold him up as if by doing so she could hold him above the dark waters that rose to claim him.

"I've waited so long to feel my name on your lips again," he sighed happily with his head nestled against her neck. Then he went limp, making her stagger under his full weight.

His eyes sought those of his daughter in the last seconds before they closed, and he whispered something softly in her mind that she couldn't hear above the roar of her mother's grief.

Emelia found Nimue staring at her in horror. Gone was the refugee waitress who'd spent the last decade and a half hidden in the shadows. Gone was the quiet, bullied girl who'd lived in the shadow of Guarded Wood. The woman who stood before them, holding her dying husband in her arms, was nothing less than the Morrigan Reborn and the rightful Queen of the Tuatha dé.

You, her thought echoed through the minds of everyone on the rooftop with such venom that all winced with her power. Her eyes glowed violet and the knotwork of his blood began to smolder across her back.

"Judge not lest ye be judged," Emelia snarled as her hand shot out, clotted with blood and twisted into a claw.

Nimue rose several inches off the ground, her head thrown back in agony as she struggled feebly in the Queen's grasp. Emelia tore through her shields and began to feed the traitor's life force directly into her husband's failing body, trying to heal him even though she knew she lacked the gift to do so. But his life drained away faster than she could hope to replenish it. The knotwork began to evaporate from her exposed skin, disappearing in a slowly spreading fire that left her skin whole and unblemished in its passing. As it faded, so did the violet glow of her eyes as she raced to finish the judgement. But in the end, Emelia's eyes turned gray and Nimue fell back to the ground, gasping with relief.

As one the Tuatha dé on the rooftop went rigid then seemed to wither and fold in on themselves as if trying to follow their king into whatever lay beyond.

Realizing that her stay of execution might only last seconds since the Queen still had other, less merciful weapons in her arsenal, Nimue shook off the death of her king and prepared to flee.

Seeing that she would escape, Bruce reached out with his mind, and with a screech of tortured metal, ripped one of the decorative iron rails from the awning that protected the tree beneath. This he flung at Nimue, twisting and forging it as it moved toward her faster than the eye could follow and bound her in its glowing mass, anchoring her to this world and cutting off her escape.

She screamed as she tried to flee through the shadows, fading into transparency before the floral designs of the metal's forging glowed red and burned into her alabaster skin. Over and over she tried, her eyes rolling back into her head as she convulsed in agony.

Adair knelt next to the traitor, her eyes unreadable as she looked down on her adversary's pain. Then, without any emotion at all, she slipped the knife at her side from its sheath and drove it directly into Nimue's heart.

With a sigh of relief, the proud woman died.

Cries of anger erupted from the Tuatha dé as they woke from the death of their king and turned on Bruce. Megan stepped before him protectively just before her mind exploded with foreign thoughts.

A sound like the flood down that desert arroyo filled her mind, growing steadily louder as sights, sounds and images flowed into her. They filled the portion of her mind that had puzzled both Bruce and Sam, flooding her soul with a chaotic jumble of conflicting sensations that threatened to carry her down into the depths of insanity. The memories of the Morrigan and her descendants filled Megan's mind and answered the question of what was happening. She was ascending.

But the memories made up only a fraction of the wave that threatened to drown her. Beneath that, connections formed between Megan and every single one of her people. No matter the distance, her ascension forged bonds so complete and binding that the Tuatha dé would never be free of her while she still lived. Likewise, their consciousness weighed on her, layering over her and anchoring her to some fate she could not yet understand. They pressed in on her from all sides within and without her mind, threatening to crush the person she'd been only a few short moments before.

She could feel Bruce calling to her, but he was little more than an offered hand, far out of reach in the flood. Faster and faster the memories came from the cooling brain of the father she'd never know. But even that wasn't completely true. As soon as she thought it, his memories came unbidden to the surface of her mind's churning cauldron, attempting to show her every thought and feeling he'd had all the way up to the sound of her mother's voice begging him not to die.

Terrified, Megan tried to dig in and hold onto herself as she'd been. But the power of the ascension was too much, and she felt herself begin to slip. Just before she lost herself, her mother caught her and held firm, not because she was more powerful than Bruce, but because Emelia was not alone. The two separated portions of the Morrigan merged within McGeehee women and rose from the dangerous waters in which Megan swam, giving her a safe harbor in which to ride out the storm.

Ancient, powerful and determined, the Morrigan stood like a cliff-shored island from the tumultuous waters around her. With one hand she sheltered Megan and helped her to protect the endangered pieces of her identity. With the other, she began to organize and settle the chaos within the girl's mind. Memories settled into their places, ready to return should they be called, no longer vying for Megan's attention, jumping on her from all sides like a pack of young dogs. As the last of the Tuatha dé bowed to the young Queen's will, they settled over her mind like armor, and she found that she could breathe once again.

You have both done well, the Morrigan told them, *but our work is not yet complete. Megan, you must earn the crown before you can be Queen in more than name.*

How will I do that? she asked.

18

You must lead the Tuatha dé back to what we once were. You must take your friend to Haven, the stronghold of our enemy, and learn what they would teach. The path begins there, but it will lead you to a place where even I was not strong enough to walk. You must set forth before this day ends.

Emelia, you have suffered for my children and sacrificed all that you held dear to bring my heir to her ascension. Your trials are almost at an end. But now you must take up the mantle of the dowager queen and lead my children past this day. Lay your husband to rest and protect your daughter's throne until she has finished with the Children of Nyx.

After making them chase me for the past fifteen years? Emelia asked. *That should go over well.*

My children will follow you. They have not forgotten what we did for them on the Night of Many Goodbyes. Not all will like the part you play, but you and I have weathered far worse together. Our quest nears its final hours. But even so, what transpires inside the gates of Haven will determine the fate of the world in the millennia to come. You must not lose faith.

When Megan opened her eyes and returned from the new world she'd discovered within herself, she found Bruce kneeling directly behind her, holding her by the shoulders and ready to follow anywhere she might go.

Something swelled within her, reaching out to him as she'd never been able to before, but she met with a wall of resistance, something that interacted with the memories and gave her a second longer to fight it, holding on to something dear to her before it slipped away once again.

Her mother knelt before her, looking deeply into her eyes and soul with such pride that Megan blushed a little before remembering where she was and what it had taken for her to get there. One side of the former Queen's body was soaked with blood, likely a mixture of her husband's and her own. Her shoulder sagged on that side as well, and her skin was almost pale enough to be mistaken for Tuatha dé.

Adair reached out to help the former Queen as she stood, swaying from side to side as she did so. But Emelia politely pushed her hands aside and took a deep breath before calling out loudly in a voice that echoed throughout the Tuatha dé.

"Rise Megan Mackgahe, Queen of the Tuatha dé!"

Those assembled on the rooftop with her, except for the reluctant Child of Nyx, dropped to one knee, and began to call out her name as they struck their fists against their chests in the ancient rite of fealty. In the newly opened part of her mind, Megan could hear echoes across Tyr Sgodl, just as she could feel Bruce's worry about her and what this might mean for their friendship.

Overwhelmed, Megan looked out over the broad expanse of the town visible below toward Guarded Wood where she hoped Sam was okay. She felt Bruce start to move back from her, but she reached out and caught his hand and kept him by her side.

"I really don't want any of this," she whispered.

Chapter II: References Available on Request

A short time later, Bruce found himself in the living room of his house with the oddest combination of people. Like Megan, he'd had many expectations of what might happen when the Wild Hunt caught up to them, and also like her he'd been completely unprepared for the reality of what came to pass. At the very least he'd thought that the events would center around her and not the internal political tensions within the Tuatha dé themselves. Instead of the mythological, and also, he now realized, stereotypical figures he'd expected, he found himself keeping company with ghostly rejects from a failed rock band. The girl that found them had even been wearing a Star Trek shirt!

Then there was the matter of Adair who stood off in the corner in full armor, holding her helm under one arm and looking exactly the way he'd pictured the Valkyries when he read about them in another lifetime at the Academy library. Her eyes scanned the room, looking for any possible threat to either the Queen or her mother. Bruce noticed that even though she changed position from time to time in order to look out of windows, she never turned her back on the Child of Nyx in their midst.

The guy in the trench coat now lurked around the edges of the room while the others talked. Apparently, he'd been keeping watch over Megan since they'd driven Big Bertha through the shadows. Sometimes Bruce really wished he'd left that damn car to rot in the woods. Not only was this guy muscular and exotic model handsome, from the sound of it he was oathbound to follow and protect her for the rest of his life. *Joy.*

Sam still lay unconscious on the couch where the Cat Sidhe had unceremoniously dumped him after they'd found him at the Baker. And it was toward him that Emelia's eyes repeatedly turned as she spoke with Dora Grimble.

Bruce knew nothing about the unremarkable looking William who'd come with Emelia from Haven. Except of course, that he looked more comfortable now than he had with all of the Tuatha dé at the Baker.

"Absolutely not," Bruce's mother said flatly. "Bruce isn't going anywhere. First Paul…well, I still don't understand what's happened to Paul, but I'm not going to stand by and let my other son run off to the other side of the country without any supervision whatsoever."

"Megan can't do this without me," Bruce explained, trying to find a path in which this worked out. "If we don't follow the prophecy, then we run the risk of everything falling apart."

"And what happens if this prophecy fails?" she asked, making Emelia look quickly his way.

"Things that would be really bad for all of us," he answered evasively.

"I was under the impression that she had an entire kingdom of people she could take with her," Dora said, folding her arms over her chest as she always did when she dug in and refused to give ground.

"We're not going to be in her kingdom," Bruce said. "We'll be with the Children of Nyx."

"Who are they?" she asked.

"Technically, they're my enemies," Megan answered, finally entering the discussion.

"And they're the ones who stabbed my best reporter and killed her

22

husband?" Dora asked with a bit of the hysterical tone her daughter sometimes used.

"No," Emelia explained quietly. "Nimue was one of our people. Sort of the Tuatha dé version of Paula Jones."

"I thought the hunter people were your enemies," Jade said, trying to keep up.

"No," Bruce explained, glancing uneasily at trench coat guy. "They're friends, but we don't really know them very well yet."

"So let me get this straight," Dora said, her frown lines starting to resemble the fissures in ice shelves just before they broke loose and went crashing into the water. At the rate the conversation was deteriorating, Bruce feared part of her face might slide off any second in an avalanche of motherly concern. "Your people attacked you so now you're going to live with your enemies. None of this is making me feel any better about sending my child away from home. Why don't these people like you, Megan?"

"That's a really long story," she answered.

"Then you'd better start talking if you want to take Bruce with you," Dora said.

"About seven thousand years ago a powerful magic person came here from a dying world," Megan began irritably.

"Like Superman," Paul said from where he and Nita joined them from his sister's phone.

This at last brought a chuckle from Emelia, although it was clear from the way she winced that it jarred her shoulder.

"How do you like that comparison, Adair?" she asked.

"I cannot say I've ever made the comparison myself," the warrior answered without even cracking a smile, "But I would say it is apt. I have always been more partial to the Marvel Universe though."

Bruce took a moment to try and figure out when he'd been drugged.

"This isn't funny," Dora whispered. "Get on with the story."

"His name was Dagda, and he and his people lived here in peace for a really long time until the Romans rose to power," Bruce said, trying to help tell the tale. "Then the goddess Nyx tried to kill him, but only succeeded in wounding him. He tricked her into going to his birth world where they killed each other."

"Ever since then, the followers of Nyx have been trying to wipe out my father's people, the Tuatha dé," Megan added.

"And how did you get mixed up in this?" Dora asked Emelia, who had returned to watching Sam sleep with an unreadable expression on her face.

"I met her father when I left for college, although he wasn't King yet," Emelia answered in a distant voice, sounding like she was telling a fairy tale. "We fell in love, got married, and then moved to Tyr Sgodl where time moves much slower than it does here."

"Then while she was pregnant with me," Megan continued, "The Children of Nyx tried to invade our world. They killed my grandparents and most of our adult population."

At this point, trench coat guy, who had been listening with interest from the hallway, spoke up, drawing the wicked-looking blade to emphasize his words.

"Then Queen Emelia donned the Morrigan's armor, and with this blade single-handedly turned the tide of battle, saving her husband, the newly ascended King and laying waste our enemies by the thousands. Before they could flee, she judged their cowardly leader and used his life force to burn his son and generals alive!"

Bruce had never seen his mother look more horrified.

"Dougal!" Adair scolded, "The Scathlahm's Blade is not a

24

plaything."

Bruce enjoyed the sudden look of shame on the young man's face as he sheathed the blade and returned to the hallway.

"I knew I should have asked for references before hiring you!" Dora muttered, shaking her head angrily.

"Dad's home," Bruce announced, feeling his father pull up in the driveway and get out of his car.

"Good," Dora said. "Let's see what he has to say about this."

Bruce reached out and plucked his father from the sidewalk leading to the front door and walked him through the shadows to the middle of the room where he dropped his duffle bag in shock.

"Bruce," Mr. Grimble cried, shuddering. "You've got to warn me before you do things like that if you want me to live long enough to see my grandchildren." Then, catching sight of the Scathlahm he added, "Who are you and where did you get that coat?"

In the entire course of his life, Bruce would never fear for his father's life more than he did at that moment.

"Why do I even bother pretending I have a say in this?" Dora screeched, throwing up her hands in disgust and turning back to Bruce. "If I say no you'll just teleport away and follow her, won't you?"

He nodded.

"When did I lose control of my life so thoroughly?" she asked with a defeated sigh, sinking down on the couch and resting her face in her hands.

"I will always come to Megan's aid when she needs me," Bruce said, sitting down on the couch next to his mother and putting his arm around her. He pulled her closer and she put her arms around him and hugged him possessively. "But my family means the world to me and I'd really prefer to have your consent."

"Because he wants you to keep doing his laundry," Jade explained.

"Come on guys," Paul called from the phone. "Don't embarrass him in front of the Kryptonians."

Bruce looked up to find everyone grinning at him.

"You can call him anytime you want," William said, joining the conversation. "We have a dedicated cell tower on site and the best internet connections available."

"That's better than we have here," Bruce prompted. His mother took a deep breath.

"And we can both bring you to him in an instant should the need arise," Adair added.

"And I can return home the same way," Bruce added.

"Okay then," Dora said at last. "I want at least one call a week. And, William, is it?"

The Child of Nyx nodded.

"Can I get your number as well for when he gets busy and forgets to call?"

Chapter III: The Dowager Queen

Emelia sat in the Grimble living room after everyone else had left, watching over Sam while he slept. Adair stood guard outside, neatly joining both halves of the strange life she'd led up to this point. Exhaustion had settled over her in a stain she doubted she'd ever be able to wash away. What she wanted most was to lay down next to him and sleep for the first time in weeks. But she stayed where she was, numb from the events of the day which had turned out so differently from what she'd hoped.

So there she was, sitting next to a man she'd loved since childhood, worrying about what could have possibly happened to put him in this state. But even as she did so, she still had her husband's dried blood under her nails. Wretched with guilt, she felt she didn't deserve the love of either of them.

Just a few hours ago, she'd been ready to return to her husband and resume the life she'd left behind, the one in which she reigned Queen as her daughter would after her. She hadn't lied when she'd told Daragh that she'd never stopped loving him. And even though she could no longer return to his side, Megan still bound her to the Tuatha dé.

She was so tired. She'd lived the last decade and a half for everyone but herself, giving every ounce of her life to this end. But her reserves had flown out of her like her husband's blood, leaving her an empty shell. She was tired of the running, the danger and the intrigue. What she really wanted was right in front of her.

At last Sam began to stir, and she walled off the part of her that wanted nothing more than to be with him. She hardened herself, willing her heart to turn the pain into armor. She had to stay the course she'd set, even if it hadn't turned out the way she'd hoped. Because when it came down to it, she had chosen. And Sam deserved someone who would always choose him first.

Opening his eyes, he immediately saw past the mask and into her pain, her shame and her guilt. But none of that mattered to him. His love for her still flavored every part of who he was, and she would never believe herself worthy of it.

"How was your trip?" he asked quietly, as if she'd only just stepped out to go shopping or pay some bills.

"Not too bad," she answered quietly, knowing as she did so that none of her shields would ever hold him out. He saw straight into her heart, just as he'd always done.

"You're not staying, are you?"

"I'm afraid not," she answered, reaching out to cup his face in her small hand, and then stopping herself and putting it back into her lap. "Paul and Luminita will fill you in on most of it."

"So you've met the bard?" he asked.

"I have," Emelia answered, holding onto the awkwardness as a way to keep from seeking the comfort she knew he'd happily give. "It's funny. We saw her dozens of times over the years at the Jubilee and never suspected a thing."

"Why won't Megan and Bruce be filling me in?"

"They're going away too," she said, hating what the words did to him.

"It sounds like I missed something important," he said, his eyes taking in her gaunt face, still thin from her months out in the wilderness.

28

"How long was I out?"

"Just a few hours," she answered. "What happened to you?"

"I talked to the Fates," he said. "Megan was right. They somehow transferred themselves into the tree when they died."

"Back up," Emelia interrupted, "Fates?"

"Do you remember the nightmares Bruce started having when Megan disappeared?"

"Who could forget?" she asked, happy to move away from the subject of where she was going.

"In order to work through them, he started going to the Baker in the middle of the night and exploring it in total darkness," Sam explained.

"You're kidding," she exclaimed, shaking her head. She wasn't sure if that spoke more of bravery or suicidal inclination.

"He discovered that the place isn't what it seems. None of us had any idea what he was up to until he got into a heavily shielded elevator and accidentally broke his bond with Megan."

"I know when you're talking about now," Emelia said. "I would have come back to investigate if I hadn't been knee-deep in dire wolves at the time. Knowing my daughter, she didn't take that very well."

"She almost leveled his bedroom and fried his computer," Sam chuckled. "And then they had their first big fight."

"Bruce finally stood up for himself?" she asked. "It's about damned time!"

"I agree," Sam said, trying to sit up. "I couldn't understand what they were saying, but I could feel their anger all the way out to my place."

"I'm not surprised," she said. "I had no idea they'd grow so much stronger in such a short time. From the sound of it, Megan severed the tracking enchantment cast by the Master of the Hunt as if it were wet newspaper. And then Bruce, after only being exposed to it for a few minutes, figured out how it worked and snared Cian with it."

"Is that hard to do?" Sam asked.

"No one could find those two now unless they allowed it," she answered. "I just wish Bruce had stayed out of my fight with Nimue. He bound her with iron. While I'm not going to say the woman didn't deserve it, I'm not sure the Tuatha dé will ever trust him after that. But tell me about these Fates."

Sam spent the next several minutes explaining what they'd found and why Bruce went there by himself. While he did, Emelia finally began to grasp all that she'd missed while off on the Morrigan's mission. Although she still didn't understand the necessity of her absence, she did take comfort in seeing that it all still seemed to be in keeping with the path laid out before them. All she had to do now was leave the few people she had left behind and go off to run a kingdom that didn't really want her there.

"So you're talking to trees again?" she teased, smiling a little in spite of the pain. He deserved so much more than this. "And what did they say?"

"Not a lot yet," he answered with a grin. "I got greedy and asked what was at the heart of Guarded Wood. They're the ones who created it, by the way."

"And?"

"Apparently it was too much for me. I remember something about a really big tree, and something asleep under it. Maybe a wolf?"

"That doesn't sound so bad," she said.

"There was more, but the rest is all muddled. I've never been so afraid of something in my life. How long are you going to be gone this time?"

"It might be a while," she answered, trying to memorize the lines of his face. She'd spent too much of the last few months trying not to look at him too closely lest she begin to dream of what wasn't meant to be. "I'm returning to Tyr Sgodl."

"With Megan's father?" he asked quietly, now attempting unsuccessfully to block his own feelings from her.

"No," she whispered, realizing she shouldn't be having this conversation with him, not while Daragh's body was barely cold. "He died a few hours ago."

"I'm sorry," Sam said, and it was worse for her that he really was. No matter how much it hurt him to do so, he'd always choose his path based on what was best for her.

"Sam," she said, steeling herself. Of all the things she'd had to do, and of all the things she'd had to give up, she dreaded this the most. "You can't keep waiting for me. I don't know how long this will take. You deserve much more than this."

"What makes you think I'm waiting for you?" he asked, gently reaching up to cup her face in his bear-like hand as she'd wanted so badly to do with his. "Maybe I've just got high standards, and you're the only one who has ever met them."

She almost stayed. She almost told the voice of the Morrigan that she'd had enough, and that nothing could ever make her leave again. But then she realized that all of her internal blustering was just that. As long as the Morrigan needed her to guide the Tuatha dé and support Megan on whatever quest the Morrigan had given her, Emelia would do her own part.

"I shouldn't have left without letting you explain," he whispered.

"And a part of me will always wish that I'd stayed in Nickelville like you wanted me to," she whispered. "But neither of us did what we wished we had."

"I love you, Emelia," he whispered, and even without using his voice it was still one of the most pleasant sounds she'd ever heard.

"And I will always love you," she said, holding his gaze longer than

31

she should. "Paul will know how to contact me. Luminita told me about the ruins they're renovating for her people. I'm sending Tuatha dé craftsmen to help them."

She hadn't meant to say that. She'd meant to cut this off completely so he could begin to heal. But of all the things that she'd been able to do, letting go of this man had never been one of them. She kissed him on the forehead and left before either of them could say goodbye.

A short time later, Emelia walked down one of the paved paths that branched like a web through the Nickelville cemetery. Or maybe it was more like the tree Sam had mentioned at the heart of Guarded Wood. Even though the town had never been anything grand or even important, it had stood hidden from the eyes of the world far longer than almost any other in the state. As such, the graves spanned many different styles from the simple stone markers with only the initials of their occupants to a few sculpted crypts complete with angels and columns.

A young woman of the Tuatha dé walked with her, helping to carry bouquets of flowers. Dressed in the traditional garb of Tyr Sgodl, her young companion wore hunter green to show that her family descended from the old-world city of Falias before the Dagda had brought them here. A dark leather cloak, which could easily be confused with a trench coat from a distance, hung from her shoulders. Her tunic had been embroidered with the image of the world tree in support of the royal family and protective knotwork. Made from a heavy, coarse fabric that Emelia personally had never liked against her own skin, it provided protection from most blunt impacts. Her pants were simple black, woven from the same pliable yet durable material as the tunic. Her boots were of black leather as was the belt that held the dirk-like knife that all of the Tuatha dé

carried.

    Without being asked, the young woman had assigned herself to the former Queen, and it galled Emelia greatly that she would have to depend on others to walk the shadows for her. If she'd felt more like talking, she would have asked her if she was related to Cara, as there was more than a passing resemblance between the girl and her husband's previous

Scathlahm.

But she had no words left after walking away from Sam. Even though her weariness took root deep within her, she didn't want to sleep in Tyr Sgodl where a full night's rest would devour almost seven days here on Earth. All too soon, time would fly by on fast forward, taking everyone she loved further and further down a future of which she would no longer be a part.

Ivy had overtaken most of the graves where her parents had been laid to rest. Mountain junipers hung low over them, covering surfaces with a thin layer of tiny blue berries. But her mother's grave had been well kept by the man who now rested beside her. Questing tendrils of grass had only just begun to invade the small rectangular patch of fresh soil. Below that, her father laid in the baby blue casket he'd picked out some years back.

She'd never visited her mother's grave by herself before. She'd stood there dutifully by her father's side on many occasions for things like Mother's Day and Christmas. But even then, she'd always harbored the childlike guilt that she'd somehow been responsible for the hole that her mother's death had left in her father's life. As an adult, she knew this was completely irrational, but when she'd been younger, that guilt had been her constant, silent companion.

Kneeling down, Emelia laid the first bundle of flowers beneath the tombstone where several others had already begun to wilt. She wondered who had brought them now that the tight-knit circle of friends had almost gone extinct.

"I'm sorry," she whispered. "I wanted to be here with you at the end more than anything…but I saw you both. Mom, you were so beautiful. My girl looks just like you, but you already know that, don't you? Dad, I'm sorry for all of the time I missed, and for how much I made you worry. I think I'm about to get a taste of that for myself. I've prepared her as well as

34

I could. She's so much stronger and smarter than I ever was. And I would bet everything I've ever held dear that Bruce will protect her. But all I can keep thinking is that they're only sixteen!"

Emelia looked up and noticed that her Tuatha dé shadow was trying very hard not to listen, but with the sharp senses that the Dagda had bestowed upon his people, she had little choice in doing so.

"I'm a little out of practice with acting like a Queen," she said.

"I've come to like you better in the last few minutes than I ever did from the stories of your valor," the young woman replied quietly. "I still have my father, but my mother died on the Night of Many Goodbyes. My aunt as well. Even after all of this time, I still expect them to come back sometimes."

"I think I knew your aunt," Emelia said.

"Yes," the woman agreed. "She was your predecessor…as Scathlahm, not Queen."

"What is your name?"

"Brighid Breathach," she answered with a bow.

"Well met," Emelia said. "I promise I won't be much longer."

"Take as long as you need, My Queen."

"Thank you," Emelia said before turning back to the grave before her. "I guess what I'm trying to ask is for you to help watch over our girl while she lives within the shadow of our enemies. I know she's not alone, but I've never felt so helpless before in my life."

In the silence that followed, the wind carried a familiar voice to her ear, and Emelia stretched out her senses. Sitting several rows down and closer to the end of the cemetery, she found Kate sitting before a grave with a scrapbook in her lap.

Stopping only to put flowers on the graves of the librarian and his wife, Emelia made her way down to where the old woman was currently engaged in lively conversation with her late husband.

"I wondered when you'd get back," Kate said when she noticed her. "We were all worried. Did they tell you what happened?"

"They didn't have to," Emelia said, sitting down on the ground next to her. "I could see it from where I was."

"It was so beautiful," Kate said, smiling.

"You all were," Emelia said, smiling back and for once, not feeling guilty about it.

"I missed it when Alan stopped bringing you and Sam to the movies," the old woman said, pointing to a ticket stub in the scrapbook that Emelia did, indeed remember seeing with him. "You don't look too much worse for wear on the outside."

"I'm not too bad," she answered, not particularly wanting to discuss the bandages across her shoulder that were hidden under her coat.

"They're wrong," Kate said, looking closer at her eyes. Emelia wondered for a moment if there were still hints of violet there.

"About what?"

"They say you can't see the deepest scars on the outside. But they're wrong. If you take the time to look, you can always see the deep ones, the ones that damn near broke us. They're always there in the eyes."

Later still, Emelia walked down a different path leading from the tree house into Guarded Wood with Luminita at her side. Paul had gone off somewhere nearby with his sister, sensing that they needed time to talk but unwilling to be more than a quick sprint away.

"I felt you when they passed," the bard said quietly.

"I know you did. I had no idea that Paul…" Here she made a confused motion with her hands and Luminita laughed. "I mean, I think we all knew that there was something special about him, but wow. It's funny, I've spent so much of my life thinking that I had all of the answers to everything going on, when right here where I grew up there was all of this. There's just layer after layer after layer and no matter how deep I go and how often that happens, I always think that this is it, and I don't need to look any further. Why don't I ever learn?"

"Don't look to me for answers," the bard replied. "I might have been born two centuries ago, but for all that I'm still not that much older than Megan. I still don't really think of myself as an adult, which is probably why I get so mad when they call me Eldest."

"I'm not sure any of us ever really feel like adults," Emelia replied. "Thank you for what you did for my father and the others. I have seen magic enough to awe the limits of human imagination, but none of that compared with the beauty of what you and Paul did that night."

"They were family," the bard said with a shrug. "And as your wise daughter told me not so long ago, we take care of our family. Speaking of which, I believe Sam Wise is up ahead."

Emelia stopped in the path, wanting more than anything to go further.

"We've already said our goodbyes," Emelia explained. "It's time for me to go. Don't forget, any of the Tuatha dé craftsmen can contact me in an instant. We have pledged our aid and support so that you will never have to worry about facing things alone in Guarded Wood again."

A short time later, when she took Brighid's arm and returned to her husband's kingdom, Emelia couldn't help but notice the empty place in her senses where her childhood friend had been.

Chapter IV: Nyx Hospitality

Megan took them to the cliff overlooking the gates of Haven where she'd once watched her mother outwit those who sought to find her. Although she'd seen it from a certain perspective in the dreams that the Cat Sidhe had given her, she wasn't prepared for how picturesque it was to stand there. A cold wind cut through their clothing, making her companions shiver. It wouldn't make any difference to her, but she knew Bruce would probably need warmer clothing here in Wyoming than he usually wore back in Nickelville.

"I could really get used to being able to travel like that," William said. "I wonder if it's something that could be learned or if it's genetically specific to the Tuatha dé."

"I don't know," Megan said, still trying to get the measure of their new companion. "I'm willing to try and teach you though."

"You can leave your things here," he said, nodding toward the bags they'd brought with them through the shadows. "Someone will come up and get them."

"You seem anxious," Bruce said, watching their new companion who'd already begun to descend down the steep trail.

"I want to see my wife and boys," William called back. "We haven't spent this much time apart in years, and it's been the strangest day of my life. I can't wait to tell her about it."

"Can't you reach her from here?" Bruce asked.

"The shield gate blocks out almost all inbound magics," William answered, slightly out of breath from his exertions. "It doesn't stop empathy though. My wife knows that I'm here and that I'm excited, but she doesn't know why. Likewise, I can feel her curiosity and impatience for me to tell her."

"So what is it exactly that you hope to get out of this?" Megan asked. "I can't imagine that your people are too excited about having us stay with you."

"Honestly, I haven't asked them yet," William admitted.

"Wait, are you telling me that the stronghold of my enemies doesn't know that I'm about to show up on their front doorstep?" Megan asked.

"Not exactly," William admitted sheepishly. "There wasn't any time to call a meeting of the High Council after I spoke with Queen Emelia. But I'll go before them as soon as I get you two settled in."

"I'm really not feeling good about the big blank spot in the future right now," Bruce muttered under his breath.

"I can't say that I understand why your mother felt the need to taunt Haven the way she did," William admitted, "but it was pretty funny. That woman has an absolutely wicked sense of humor. As for what I hope to learn, I'm most interested in the way the ruling monarch of the Tuatha dé communicates with his or her subjects no matter how far apart they are from each other."

"There's something else you're not telling me," Megan said, narrowing her eyes and looking at him closely. "It's nothing bad, but you have extremely strong feelings about it."

"You've got some pretty strong empathic talent as well," he observed. "I have twin sons. About a year ago they were afflicted with a condition that has left them in a semi-catatonic state. There's no reason that we can find for them to be this way. I've come to believe that they have

39

somehow traveled outside of their bodies and require help finding their way back."

"And you think the way Megan communicates with the Tuatha dé may hold the key to reaching them and bringing them home," Bruce finished.

William nodded, then started to take them down the steepest part of the slope, using many switchbacks to slow their descent.

Distant mountain peaks surrounded the lands that the Children of Nyx called home. Although the wind couldn't reach them down this far, it still whistled through the rocky crags overhead and merged with the sound of a nearby river that ran somewhere just out of sight. It took Megan a moment to realize that she had subconsciously assumed that they were somewhere in Guarded Wood when confronted with this new terrain. Who knew? Maybe there was an entrance nearby and the space between two boulders might come out somewhere near the beach or the desert plateau where August had once enjoyed eating his lunch during the winter. Now that she thought about it, she wondered how far they were from the place where Paul had until recently hunted fossils.

When they reached the bottom, Megan looked closer at the gate before them. In the vision she'd had of her mother, the mouth of the cavern had been sealed shut with blocks of black stone and a great iron gate. Although the actual gate had been removed, the black stone remained.

"This has changed," she said. "It wasn't like this a month ago."

"No, it wasn't," William admitted. "Did Emelia tell you about it?"

"No, my cat gave me a vision of my mother being chased here by wolves," she answered.

"I remember that day," he said, probably not knowing how to decipher the part about the cat. "My sister and I had a bet going on how long it would take for Emelia to lose them. Priscilla was in a full-blown rage by that point."

"Priscilla?" Bruce asked.

"The Great Oracle herself," William said, not even trying to hide his dislike.

"The one who figured out how to wake the Nine and send them after my people," Megan said. "I wouldn't mind meeting this woman."

Bruce looked suddenly concerned.

"If I have my way, the two of you will never cross paths," William said, reacting much the same way Bruce had. "She's a powerful force among the Children of Nyx though. Most of us are afraid of her."

"We've had some experience with people like that," Bruce said.

Now that they were closer, Megan could feel an extremely powerful barrier of energy stretched from one end of the cavernous opening to the other, and just inside of it stood a desk where a young man with short dark hair sat.

"This must take enormous power to maintain," Bruce said, then after closing his eyes for a second and testing its properties, "And it isn't from just one person."

"You're right," William said proudly. "That's why my wife and I created the Dark Crystal to power it."

Bruce chuckled, and Megan cast him a curious glance.

"Someone's got a Sam Wise kind of humor," Bruce explained. "The Dark Crystal was an old movie. It was live action and had a lot of puppets."

"You know your fantasy," William observed, pleasantly surprised. "My wife is going to like you. She's the one who named it. I don't think anyone else realizes what it's referring to though. The Children of Nyx almost exclusively prefer nonfiction. My wife, Catherene, is always pestering me to talk about those books of hers. And in addition to loving to read, she's also an amplifier like you."

"So let me get this straight," Bruce said. "You were created to counter Megan, and you both just happened to pick up an amplifier. What are the odds of that?"

"We live in strange times," William agreed with a shrug.

"And you built this shield for the sole purpose of keeping my mother out of your city?" Megan asked.

William nodded.

"How well did that work out for you?" Bruce asked.

"We never had an opportunity to find out," William replied, walking up to the shield wall, just opposite the gatekeeper. "I found her nearby that same night, and I think you know the rest."

"Who are these strangers?" the gatekeeper asked.

"Think of them as exchange students, Cassius," William answered. "They're going to be staying with us for a while. We need someone to go up to the overlook and collect their things."

"By whose authority?" the sour looking young man asked.

"By my authority, Cassius," William answered, becoming annoyed. "We've had a long day and I want to see my family."

"You're welcome to enter any time you want, but until I hear from someone on the council, these two stay outside. She looks like she could be Danann."

"I'm on the council," William reminded him.

"Not the part that matters," Cassius countered, crossing his arms stubbornly.

"Enough of this," William said, reaching out and opening a hole in the shield before motioning to Megan and Bruce. "Follow me."

Cassius jumped up from the chair with an angry hiss and ran off into the cave like a mistreated cat.

42

"He really hates it when I do that," William said with a grin. "But it's one of the perks of being the one that created it. I can't be locked out if I don't want to be."

"That seems like a pretty bad design flaw," Bruce said. "What if something happens to you?"

"It uses cascading ownership," William explained. "If I die or in some way become cut off from it, it shifts to my wife and then my sister. If anything bad enough happens to take out all three of us then the shield has probably already been breached anyway. But for now, it's mine, and I can bypass it as I please. It's rather fun annoying Cassius. He wasn't one of my favorite students when he was younger, and I find a great deal of enjoyment in being as much of a pain in his backside as he was in mine."

Megan could feel Bruce panic as the shield closed behind them, cutting them off completely from the outside world. For the first time she noticed the way that her sense of her mother faded from the link they shared through the stone necklace around her friend's neck.

This is like the shields on the Baker elevator, Bruce sent. *I can barely see shadows of the future in here. We're completely cut off from the outside world.*

I promise not to nuke your bedroom this time, she sent.

He shot her one of his quirky grins, and she felt something rise and fall in the back of her mind, gone almost as soon as it started. She had the feeling that whatever it was had happened a lot lately.

The cavern stretched out before them, growing taller as it went further back. Curtains of stalactites disappeared into the darkness further out, lit only by the structures that the Children of Nyx had built within the gut of the mountain. Similar to the cliff village where Luminita's people had settled, Haven possessed the haphazard organization that resulted when a small settlement in a confined space grew outward and upward.

But unlike the one in Guarded Wood, these dwellings had been designed in the style of Roman villas, complete with stone columns supporting the undersides of buildings that had grown larger than the crevices in which they'd been constructed. Statues occupied niches and everywhere throughout Haven, people bustled with activity.

Megan heard the waterfall before she noticed the light that came from the cavern roof high overhead. Blue witchlight poured with the water from an opening, looking almost like an opening to the sky above.

Several stories of galleries rose against the far wall of the cavern, supported by rows of Corinthian columns. At its peak, near the place where the water likely pooled, a huge statue of the goddess Nyx raised her arms to welcome her children to Haven.

"This reminds me of the things that August created in the lands surrounding his cottage," Bruce said.

"I was surprised to hear that he'd only died recently," William said, leading them into an open space over which they could see a huge amethyst crystal, roughly the size of one of the ground sloths.

"He didn't think anyone would remember him here," Megan said.

"No one would if it wasn't for my sister," William explained. "She stumbled across his writings in the archive several years ago. She's the foremost expert we have on his works."

"You have someone who specializes in August's writing?" Bruce said. "Don't get me wrong, but I never expected his writing to be particularly awe inspiring."

"I've read some of them and you're right, they're not always interesting, but the man was ahead of the rest of us by several centuries," their guide replied. "He was an absolute genius."

"He was an artist," Megan corrected him quietly. "And his magic was beautiful."

William looked at her speculatively for a moment, looking as if he were weighing his next words carefully. At last he leaned in close to be sure that only the two of them could hear.

"You were fond of him," he said, "I can feel your sorrow when you think of him. But I gave my word to both of your mothers that I would try to keep you out of trouble. So I want to make sure that you understand how rare people like Augustus are among the Children of Nyx. He had his reasons for leaving, and most of them are still relevant." An awkward silence followed.

"Is that the Dark Crystal?" Bruce asked at last, trying without success to keep from laughing at the name as he pointed at the huge purple crystal that rose from the buildings below on a huge pedestal of black stone, making it look as if it was floating until one was close to it.

"The one and only," William said proudly. "It gathers small amounts of power from each of us and uses it to power the shield. That way, none of us are unduly taxed by its existence."

"Smart," Bruce said, looking it over. "Is it a natural crystal?"

"No," William answered. "It took Catherene and I three days of non-stop effort to create it. We don't usually work on things that scale, but it needed more mass to handle the energy needs of the shield. If you were closer, you'd notice that it has a flaw running through the center. It doesn't really affect the functionality of the crystal, and it was an accident, but I do enjoy the way it annoys some of my adversaries on the council."

"Did it have to be amethyst?" Megan asked, recognizing the mineral from Jade's last birthday.

"No," William said sheepishly.

"Your wife did that on purpose too, didn't she?" Bruce asked. William nodded in reply.

"What?" Megan asked.

45

"Using amethyst made it look like the one from the movie," William admitted. "Now if the two of you don't mind, I'd like to have you stay with my wife and I while you study here. I'm eager to see them, but if there's anything else you'd like to see…"

"Do you live in one of those buildings?" Megan asked, pointing to the ones that climbed the cavern walls. Each gave out pinpricks of light in the darkness from their windows, like a few hundred will-o'-the-wisps.

"Not even close," William chuckled. "That's where the rich and powerful gaze down in disdain over mere mortals like me. They may look small on the outside, but each one of those continues deep into the cavern wall and represents a fortress in and of itself. And don't walk under any of them during festival days. They like to urinate and vomit off of those balconies when they get drunk."

"Lovely," Bruce said, starting to hope that their business would be done here soon. "So where does your family live?"

"See those tunnels?" their guide asked, "There are four of them that cut deep into the mountain. That's where most of the Children of Nyx live and work. My home is close to the school, which works out well since I teach there."

It was clear from the reactions of those around them that Haven did not normally attract visitors from the outside world. Like the gatekeeper, many of them seemed to find an inordinate amount of concern in Megan's alabaster skin. For the most part, the Children of Nyx dressed in toga-like robes that certainly wouldn't have been warm enough to protect them from the Wyoming weather outside.

The longer they walked, the happier William seemed to become, sometimes laughing for no reason at all. It took her a moment to realize that he must be speaking mind to mind with his wife, Catherene.

A young woman dressed in a stylish modern blouse and jeans turned the corner of a corridor and walked directly toward them. Unlike the others they'd passed up to that point, the girl's dark eyes slid over both Megan and William as if they didn't exist to rest on Bruce. Then she smiled, boldly holding his gaze as they passed.

47

Something stirred in the back of Megan's mind, like a wild animal slowly swimming back to consciousness after being hit with a tranquilizer dart. But it faded quickly, leaving behind only a faint sense of unease.

Shortly afterward, they rounded another corner in the maze of tunnels and found their path blocked by nearly a dozen men and women. Unlike the others they'd encountered, these weren't outfitted in classical attire. Instead, each wore tactical body armor and carried an assault rifle.

An old woman with long and elaborately braided white hair stood at the rear of the heavily armed company. She wore flowing robes reminiscent of those worn by the Children of Nyx in the runestone memories from back when the two opposing Beloved still lived. Only these were made with purple and black silk. She carried herself with an air of authoritarian disdain that made Megan dislike her at once. Beside her stood Cassius.

"What is the meaning of this?" the old woman asked in the raspy voice of a lifelong smoker.

"What is what, Priscilla?" William asked, giving an air of boredom that didn't match the level of agitation Megan could feel coming from him.

"You dare to sneak our enemy into the very walls of Haven," she snarled.

"I would hardly call walking in through the front gates in the middle of the day sneaking," William explained. "And neither of them wishes the citizens of Haven any harm."

"You do not have the authority to bring outsiders inside the protective shield without consulting the High Council," she snarled, irritated by his lack of respect.

"As I was in the process of doing before you accosted me with your personal guard," William said. "I fully intended to call you all together as soon as I cleaned up and changed into attire less offensive to your high

48

station."

"You had no reason to bring them inside before we met," she said with quiet menace.

"We would have frozen to death out there before the council finished deciding what they should eat for their evening meal," he taunted. "And there are no laws about bringing anyone inside the shield wall because the thing has only been there for a few days. So if you'll go get your people ready, we'll be along shortly to put all of this right."

"They will leave at once," Priscilla said with an air of finality.

"What are you talking about?" William asked. "The High Council..."

"Would require a unanimous decision to allow them to stay," she finished for him. "And I will never vote in favor of that. I've had visions concerning her."

"Dearest Nyx," William spat in exasperation, "More of them? I've only been gone for a little over a day!"

"Fool," the old woman spat, "You have invited our destruction in by the front door!"

"Speaking of visions," William said pleasantly, making Megan realize that contrary to what he'd said about keeping Priscilla and herself apart, he'd been looking forward to this confrontation. "Emelia shared two of her own with me. In the first, you and yours mistreated Queen Megan and she responded by tearing down Haven around us. In the second, Megan and Bruce became my pupils. In time they forge new and peaceful relations with us and eventually become our greatest ally."

"Why would you listen to anything that woman says after all that she has done?" Priscilla demanded. "Particularly in light of her recent interactions with our city?"

"She allowed me to view them directly from her mind," William answered, enjoying the sharing of this bit of knowledge. "As I'm sure you

49

know, it is not possible to lie in this manner."

Oddly enough, the great seer apparently hadn't seen that coming.

"So you trust her vision of the future more than mine?" the woman said in a deadly quiet voice.

"It seems appropriate to remind you that she has never led us into a war that not only wiped out half of our population, but also led to the deaths of her own brother and nephew," he said.

"How dare you suggest that the actions of that bloodthirsty witch were my fault!"

"Perhaps you'd like to set the precedent that the Children of Nyx should no longer be guided by visions of the future? As you may recall, I've made this argument before the council on several occasions already. I would happily pledge my vote to such a purpose."

The Morrigan rose up into Megan's conscious mind, lending her own interpretation of the verbal sparring match. What she had first taken to be poor planning on the part of the man who'd brought them here now looked to be part of a well-planned attack on the seer's power within the Children of Nyx. She could feel Bruce come to the same conclusion at her side, and they both wished William would have warned them before dropping them in the middle of this.

"You owe your very existence to me!" the seer snapped.

The pleasant mask William wore disintegrated at these words. Megan could feel him tighten his shields and begin to gather power.

"Be careful that you attach yourself too closely to my conception, Priscilla," he whispered, making even the armed guards look concerned. "Lest I decide that you should bear the blame for what was done to my mother."

Priscilla looked at him with loathing while she tried to find an argument that didn't undermine her own power with the council. But he'd maneuvered her into an unfavorable position, and it was clear when she realized that she'd lost this battle.

"Very well," the old woman said with exaggerated sweetness. "You are welcome to teach her as you see fit, but I stand behind what I've said. She is henceforth barred from our city and may never return. They can stay in one of the old farming cottages that remain in the neighboring valley while you teach them whatever it is that you intend. The minute their studies are finished, they will return to where they came from."

"But those buildings haven't been lived in for over a century!" he protested.

"Then she's quite welcome to leave," Priscilla replied. "And you do not have permission to shirk your duty to teach our own children in favor of this..." She looked at Megan in disdain.

"Go ahead," Megan said pleasantly. "I'd love to hear you finish that sentence. Oh, and where are my manners? My mother, you know, the bloodthirsty witch, sends her regrets that she couldn't be here to give you the same *warm* regards she's presented other members of your family with in the past."

Everyone assembled went silent and Megan knew that Bruce was trying to figure out if those words came from her or the cranky old woman in her head. Honestly, she wasn't sure herself. Something about this woman really pissed her off.

"You don't frighten me," Priscilla whispered. "I have foreseen my own death at the hands of a green-eyed man of your clan. There is nothing you can do to me."

"But the Tuatha dé all have violet eyes," Bruce said without thinking, which made the ancient seer look at him closely for the first time. She paused as if meaning to say something more, then walked away.

"I guess the tour is over," Megan said, turning back the way they'd come.

"That probably could have gone better," William agreed. "You never had much of a chance to win her over given who you are. But if I had any doubts about taking you on as students they're gone now. I can't wait to tell Cat about that. *Warm regards...*"

His eyes went distant before he started to lead them back the way they'd come.

"My wife will meet us outside of the gates with an ATV so we can get your things. I'm really sorry about the boarding situation. I haven't looked in one of those cottages for years and they weren't very well kept then. We may have to take you to the nearest town and get rooms for you there."

"The cabin will be fine," Bruce said. "I'm really good at fixing things."

Chapter V: Poltergeist and Paradox

Megan knew that their expulsion from Haven had been intended as an insult, but it felt more like an escape. The only place where she'd ever felt more confined had been that last apartment, and she could think of nothing that would ever tempt her enough to return. The air outside was clean and cool, once again bringing back images of Guarded Wood. She realized she was already homesick.

"If the ATV's are too much trouble, we can just walk the shadows now that we're free of the shields," she said.

"That probably won't work," William said. "There are iron spikes driven into this field at four-foot intervals for about a quarter of a mile in every direction."

"And?" Megan asked.

"Iron has no effect on either one of us," Bruce said.

"Really?" William asked in surprise. "I knew Bruce was obviously immune after what he did to the woman who killed your father, but Megan is too?"

In answer, Megan held up her right hand and showed him the ring Bruce had made to dampen her nervous energy.

"What does it do?" he asked, sensing the power it radiated.

"It keeps me from frying electronics when I'm angry or frightened," she answered.

"Then I should probably be thankful for it," William said, reaching out to touch it. "Otherwise you might have sent Haven back to the pre-industrial age while you were talking to Priscilla. It might be best to keep anyone else from knowing that you're immune to the effects of iron. They'd be much less likely to accept your presence here, even outside the city, if they knew you weren't muzzled as they'd hoped."

The three of them heard the sound of the approaching vehicle before they saw it. When it pulled up, Megan found herself looking not at a toga-clad, dark-haired and pale-skinned clone of all of the other women she'd seen inside the cave, but rather at a tan blond with short, spiky hair and an oddly eclectic collection of tattoos on the exposed portions of her arms. Her sweatshirt sported a picture of a tower topped with a single red eye and a caption that read *Mordor Fun Run 2017*. Belted into the seat next to her sat two motionless young boys with their mother's hair and Williams black eyes.

"You must be Catherene," Megan said.

"And you are my favorite person in the world right now," the woman said. "Did you seriously threaten Priscilla?"

"News travels fast here," Bruce said, glancing over at William.

"We haven't stopped talking since you entered the city shields," Catherene said. "Hop in and I'll take you up to your stuff. I think I know which cabin is in the best shape, too. The boys and I used to hike up there sometimes, before...Well, William has already told you."

"Is there any way that one of you can take her through the shadows?" William asked, making his wife blush. "She's been jealous ever since I told her that I got to."

"I'll bet we can make that happen," Megan said, climbing into the back seat of the big-wheeled vehicle with Bruce and William.

The drive up to the cliff overlook felt like Jade was driving, and it was clear that Catherene was likely far happier outside of Haven's shields

54

as well. When they reached the top, she unbuckled the boys and took them over to where Bruce and Megan had left their gear.

"I know there are several cottages closer," she said, pointing to one that was nestled into the tree line in the distance. "But that one was in much better shape than the others when we were there last. It's going to take some work to get it habitable, but at least it's got a roof."

Megan picked up her bag and held out a hand to the woman.

"Pick up one of your boys and I'll take you over there," Megan said.

"Are you sure it's okay for Owen and Ethan?" Catherene asked.

"We've never had any problems with walking the shadows," Bruce said, "And I don't see any problems with them in the future."

"I didn't know you were seers," Catherene said.

"Just me," Bruce said.

"But how is that possible?" Catherene asked, holding one of the twins on her hip. "You're an amplifier. You shouldn't have any abilities on your own that Megan doesn't have herself."

"So we've been told," Megan said. "He's also really good at building and repairing, but unless you count my wondrous ability to break stuff, I don't have that either."

"I'm going to want to study that," Catherene said. "I guess anything is possible since we don't really have much information on amplifiers. We're incredibly uncommon, so much in fact that it's a bit of a miracle that there are two alive at the same time."

"And Megan can look into the past," Bruce added. "I've never had any luck with that. The clock only seems to run one direction for me."

"Stranger and stranger," William said, picking up the other twin.

"But we're sure it won't hurt the boys?" Catherene said, returning to the previous subject. "I know I'm just overprotective, and I've probably watched too many episodes of Star Trek."

55

"We're not actually being broken down and reassembled somewhere else," Bruce said, understanding her concern now. "We open a very short-lived opening into a parallel universe and then move from here to there and then back to the location where we want to be in this one."

"That doesn't sound much safer," William said.

"You won't even know you've been to Tyr Sgodl," Megan explained. "Unless you want us to pause there before coming out by the cabin."

"What's it like?" Catherene asked, interested by the possibility of visiting another world.

"It's extremely cold and windy," Bruce answered, hoping they said no. "We got stuck there the first time Megan did it, and I almost froze to death. She can handle extreme temperatures much better than I can."

"Okay then," Catherene said, no longer able to contain her enthusiasm, "Just the non-stop flight though, at least this time."

Megan reached out and took all of them into the shadow of the cottage, which on closer inspection, looked much worse than it had from a distance. From what they could see of the stone structure that wasn't covered in ivy, it looked sound. Only a few of the slate tiles, at least as they could see through the ivy, looked like they needed repair. The roof had a steep pitch, probably to help it shed snow, and the windows on this side at least still had glass in the panes even they were too dirty to see through.

"That was too cool," Catherene said when she realized they'd already arrived. "William, why couldn't you have been one of them? They seem a lot cooler than the Children of Nyx."

"I don't recall being given a choice," he answered, "But I think I'd have to agree. Aside from camouflaging ourselves and the crystal stuff, we didn't really get much from our Beloved."

The hinges on the door had rusted shut since the last time it had been opened, but Bruce made short work of them, and soon they stood just inside. Motes of dust drifted through the places where the sun shone in through the windows and missing roof tiles overhead.

At one point the interior had likely been quite nice by the standards of its time, but sometime over the past decade or so the roof had begun to leak, ruining the furniture which still remained. Only the heavy wooden table and the two benches pushed beneath it could be saved.

Bruce was happy to find the broken pieces of the window glass just below the sill where it had fallen. Laying them all flat on the table, he reassembled them in short order and began to fuse the pieces back together.

"How are you doing that?" William asked in interest.

Bruce allowed both he and his wife to enter his shields while he worked, but they both only shook their heads in dismay when it was done.

"It's not as easy as he makes it look, is it?" Megan asked from where she was gathering up the remains of old bedding to take out to the pile of rubbish they intended to burn.

"Did August teach you how to do this?" William asked. "I've never seen anything like it."

"No," Bruce answered, putting the pane back into the window and making it whole again. "I learned how to do it from looking at the visions of myself doing it."

"So you're saying that you can learn new skills, by watching a future version of yourself do them without anyone actually teaching either of you how to do it in the first place?" Catherene asked in astonishment.

"Don't think about it too hard," Bruce warned. "The only things I've ever managed to accomplish when I try to figure it out are headaches. But it absolutely works. When Megan tried to figure it out she said it was an incredibly complicated set of actions. From my end I'm just asking the glass to remember what it once was and returning it to that state."

57

"I hope the rest of the things we try to learn from the two of you don't turn out to be like this," William complained, putting one of the twins down on the bench next to his brother so they'd be out of the way while everyone else worked. Then he stepped back and looked at the two of them, staring off into the cluttered interior of the cabin.

"They used to be very active," he said quietly.

"What exactly happened?" Megan asked.

"Before this," Catherene began, sitting down next to her boys and running her fingers through the hair of the one closest to her. "They were perfectly normal. I've wracked my brain for any hints that could have warned us that this was coming, but I can't think of a single one. The two of them were inseparable. They played, they laughed and they got into so much trouble together."

"And then one night," William said, picking up what was clearly a story that had been repeated often, "after we'd put them to bed, I heard one of them say something about a big bird. I'm not even really sure which one of them said it, they both sound so much alike."

Megan noticed Bruce tense at the mention of big birds, and she placed her hand over his to calm him.

"But they didn't say anything else, and I just assumed they'd gone to sleep," their new friend said miserably.

"In the morning," Catherene said quietly, "they were like this. I'd been up for a while, but mornings when they slept in were so rare that I just left them."

"There's no way you could have known," Megan said, feeling sorry for the couple. "Have you taken them to a doctor?"

"Several," William answered. "As far as anyone can tell, there's no reason why they should be this way. And when we try to probe their minds, it's like they're gone someplace else. The weirdest part is that they

58

don't exhibit the signs of true catatonia. They chew and swallow if you put food in their mouths. They even go to the bathroom when you put them on the toilet. But they do all of those things like robots."

"Do you really think that the way I communicate with the Tuatha dé might help them?" Megan asked.

"We've tried everything else we can think of," Catherene said. "At this point we're willing to try just about anything to get them back. But for now, we need to get all of this stuff out and see what we can find for you in the way of furniture and bedding."

"I can just borrow some camp cots from the garage back home," Bruce said. "My family has enough camping gear to get us by until we work out something better. I'd rather not ask too much from you guys if we can help it. Otherwise I have the feeling Priscilla would become involved. Would you guys mind if I fix the roof while you carry things out? It's going to rain tonight, and I'd rather not get wet."

"Sure," Megan said, picking up the remains of a chair that was eaten through with rot.

He disappeared at once, and they could hear him moving across the roof overhead.

"Our friend Paul would love to get his hands on some of this cast iron," Megan said, moving a large rusty pot out the door with Catherene's help. "I know we can re-season this, but blowing everything out will be easier if most of the stuff is out. I'm sort of surprised that there's so much iron that has been left behind."

"That wasn't accidental," William said. "Our ancestors kept a lot of iron on hand in all of their homes."

"To keep the mean old Tuatha dé away," Megan said, nodding her head in understanding.

"That's part of the reason why they were so worried about you," he said carrying the last of the wood debris from a cupboard that had collapsed sometime in the past. "They understood from the beginning that there was a possibility that you would not share the weakness that we exploit with your people."

"But you said I shouldn't let them know that it doesn't affect me," Megan said, confused.

"And there you have stumbled upon another trait of the Children of Nyx that drives me nuts," Catherene said with a relieved sigh when they'd placed the cauldron-like pot outside. "They seem to have this inborn ability to believe multiple conflicting things at the same time and act as if they all must be true. I mean, they were worried enough at the possibility that you might be immune to the effects of ferrous metals to create their own version of you. And I'm not complaining about that, I'm rather glad my husband was born. But then they make an entire defense system based on the belief that you would be hindered by iron. The only reason we have the shield is because of your mother."

"If we're being completely honest," William added. "Now that I've had a chance to experience what Megan can do, I think I'm something of a failed experiment. I'm a powerful practitioner compared to any of the Children of Nyx, but her power dwarfs mine in every way that matters. I doubt the two of us would stand any chance at all against the two of you should it ever come down to hostilities."

"All fixed," Bruce said, appearing in the doorway. "I have to say, whoever built this place did a good job. I know it's ugly, but almost all of the damage was minor. Of course, it might have survived the elements better than the others due to its proximity to the trees. It's protected fairly well on the side most of the storms come in from. None of the holes were over any rafters, so everything is still structurally sound up there. I'm going to go get some camping cots and sleeping bags for us to sleep on

60

tonight. Want me to pick up pizza from Gordon's while I'm there?"

"Sure, and get something to drink too," Megan said. "By the time you get back we should have the inside blown out and the trash burned. Would you guys like to stay? Gordons has the best pizza you'll ever eat."

"You're just going to pop over to Texas for takeout?" Catherene asked.

In response Bruce faded from existence, waving goodbye theatrically as he went.

"Let's get the boys so I can blow the dirt out and get the cobwebs and bird nests down from the ceiling," Megan said, following them back inside.

Inside they found Mr. Bob sitting in the lap of one of the twins, purring loudly.

"Should I be concerned about the cat poltergeist that's sitting in my son's lap?" Catherene asked.

"Its shields are like a black hole," William observed in amazement.

"I was wondering how long it would take you to find your way here," Megan said, walking over to scratch him in his favorite spot behind the ear.

"That's not really a cat, is it?" Catherene asked, still unsure how comfortable she felt with this new development or its proximity to her children.

"Not really," Megan said, "But he's really sweet."

"Life is going to be interesting with you around, isn't it?" William murmured.

The ancient Cat Sidhe purred even louder.

Chapter VI: Monumental Morrigan

Bruce woke in silence, punctuated only by the sound of birds chirping outside. His breath steamed in the interior of the empty cabin as he lay there on one of the camping cots he'd borrowed from home. Sunlight poured in through the east facing windows behind him, casting ivy shadows across Megan's sleeping form.

Her own cot sat on the packed earthen floor just out of reach next to his. She'd tossed around quite a bit during the first part of the night and at some point, she'd come out of the sleeping bag which was now lying on the floor between them. She was clearly comfortable in spite of the cold and her breath didn't even steam as he watched the slow rise and fall of her chest as she laid on her side, facing him.

It was the longest he'd ever been able to look at her without her catching him. He took full advantage of the opportunity, committing each line, curve and angle to memory even though he already knew it better than his own. With her alabaster skin she could have been cast in marble.

Waiting until he sensed that she'd soon wake, he reached out and set the wood they'd left in the stone hearth ablaze so it could begin to warm the air. After several minutes in which the snapping and popping of the resin pockets in the wood filled the previously silent room, she finally began to stir.

"I'm afraid we missed the sunrise," he said when he felt the last of her dreams fall away. "We must have been pretty tired since we are still about two hours behind Texas time."

"We did have a pretty long day," she said quietly. "What do you want to do about food? I know we could mooch off any of our friends, but I'd rather not impose."

"That's exactly what I was just thinking," he lied. "You know, when I was a kid, there was this little mom and pops restaurant in New Mexico that we always went out of our way to stop at while we were on vacation. They had the most amazing pancakes. Now that we're not confined to Nickelville anymore, maybe we could explore the world a little."

"I'd like that," Megan said, sitting up and stretching. She cast her eyes around the room with neither hope nor dread, and then settled on him where he was huddled in the confines of his sleeping bag. "Are we doing the right thing?"

"We're not going to start questioning the voice of the Morrigan now," he said, trying to sound surer than he felt.

"I'm sorry about yesterday," she said.

"I can't think of anything that you should be sorry for. But just out of curiosity, which part are you talking about? There was kind of a lot going on."

"I should have kept my temper with the seer," she said.

"Why are you sorry for that?" he asked, finally daring to unzip the bag. "That was by far my favorite part."

"I could have escalated things while we were in the middle of their stronghold," she said.

"Even cut off from the outside as we were, I'm pretty sure we could have taken them."

"What happened to the quiet boy who was afraid to fight?" she asked.

"He met a princess and decided he needed to up his game," Bruce answered playfully. As soon as he stood up, Mr. Bob appeared on his cot and curled up in the warm spot he'd just vacated.

"Is it my imagination or is his fur a lot longer than it was in Texas?" Bruce asked.

"I'm good with what I'm wearing," she said with a shrug, pulling on her shoes. "You?"

"Same here," he answered. After looking through several visions of his immediate future, he picked one in which no one noticed their arrival, took her by the hand and started walking, knowing that she'd fall into step with him without question.

He'd intentionally picked a place where a footbridge crossed a small river tributary, knowing the way that the newly risen sun would reflect from the gently churning waters as they flowed over and around the stones in their path. All was exactly as he'd seen except for the old woman fishing with a crude bamboo pole at the water's edge, dressed in jeans and a blouse that had last been in fashion several decades before in spite of the cold.

"Enjoying your morning?" the woman asked, seeming unsurprised by their abrupt arrival, though still not looking up from the water.

"So far," Megan replied. "And you?"

"Can't complain," she answered. Bruce noticed then that although her shadow moved the same way that she did, its shape suggested she was something else altogether.

"What are you?" Megan asked, echoing his thoughts.

"Nothing you need to worry about," the woman answered, looking up to reveal reptilian eyes. "Enjoy your pancakes, Your Highness. Now if you don't mind, my own breakfast will be returning shortly from an evening of gambling away his daughter's paycheck again, and I prefer to dine in private."

"Happy hunting," Megan said, leading Bruce away. Surprised, he allowed her to do so.

"Are we seriously going to let her kill someone?" he asked.

"She's a water nymph," Megan explained. "The memories tell me that the Tuatha dé leave them alone because they only prey on the truly depraved. If a nymph has targeted that man then he's likely abusing his daughter as well as taking her money." Then, changing the subject, she added, "I think I might have been through here with my mom several years ago. It's hard to tell. We drove through so many places over the years, and I was usually distracted."

He tried to put it aside, but encountering something like that outside of Guarded Wood made him uneasy. Over the past year he'd come to realize that Nickelville was far more than he'd grown up thinking, but this new development suggested that the rest of the world might be hiding things as well.

How did she know who you are? He asked just as the sleek chrome outline of the diner came into view.

They're psychic, Megan answered, apparently still consulting her memories. *They can see a short distance into the future and past of anyone who comes close to the water. Which not only tells them who is worthy of their attention, but who won't be missed.*

"I'm just going to apologize in advance for all of the stuff I'm going to be asking you about," Bruce said, opening the diner's chrome and glass door for her. "You are seriously better than a search engine."

Inside, the diner sported a black and white theme from the chess board floor to the black vinyl upholstery on the booths and bar stools. Bruce led her to the counter where a bored looking girl brought them menus and coffee.

"I've always wanted to sit up here," he confided. "But Mom and Dad always made us sit in the booths."

"Mom worked at a few of these places," Megan said, glancing

around.

It was hard to think of the previous Queen of the Tuatha dé waiting tables, but that was probably why she'd done it. Their food came out quickly, and his hunger was such that it took him a few minutes to notice that Megan wasn't eating."

"What's wrong?" he asked.

"The last time I ate pancakes was a few days before we found out they were dying," she whispered. "It's so hard to believe that they're all gone."

"I know," he agreed, reaching out and taking her hand. She squeezed it and then started to eat in earnest.

"You're right, these are really good," she said. "We should bring my mom sometime."

"We can actually do things like that now," he said, glad that her dark mood seemed to be passing.

"So what do you see us doing next?" she asked. "World tourist attractions?"

"You know," he said, finally pushing away his empty plate. "I've been thinking about that."

"Uh oh," she said, pausing with a bite halfway to her mouth. "Nothing good ever comes from that."

"I mean, is there any place where we could go that's better than Guarded Wood?" he asked, ignoring her comment. "What beach is better than the one August showed us? If we want to explore ancient ruins, there are about a dozen more that we haven't looked at yet. Any type of geography we'd like to visit exists there where we don't have to share it with rude tourists."

"So what do you suggest?" she asked.

"Let's go to Tyr Sgodl."

"You're serious?" she asked, putting down her fork.

"Why not?" he asked. "With the exception of that rocky outcrop where I almost froze to death, we've never been there."

"But, shouldn't we be dressed more formally? I don't know any of their customs or the way they do things. I mean, I'm starting to get flashes of things here and there, but it's not completely reliable yet."

"What better way to start?" he asked.

"I don't know," she said, frowning.

"Let's just go to where Emelia is. That way she can help us get going in the right direction."

"But how do we know where that is?" she asked.

"With this," he said, pulling his necklace and the stone it held out of his shirt. "The three of us are bound by this. I can follow it back to her."

"Why didn't we just do that when she was gone?" Megan asked.

"I tried to find her several times," he said. "I'm pretty sure she was intentionally hiding her location from me. She's not doing that anymore."

"Why didn't you tell me?" she asked.

"I didn't want to get your hopes up unless I could deliver results," he answered with a shrug. "I'm also pretty sure that's how she tracked us to the top of the Baker."

"Okay," Megan said, finally allowing herself to get excited. "Let's do it then. But what about the time difference?"

"We'll ask your mom how long we can stay. I'm betting she's pretty good at time conversions between our two worlds by now."

After leaving a good tip for the waitress in honor of all the times when Megan and Emelia had depended on such generosity, they retraced their steps to the footbridge. They found no sign of the nymph, but a red baseball cap lay close to the water's edge now that had not been there before.

Trying not to contemplate what might have happened there too deeply or the fact that neither of them could see what might be happening under the bridge on which they stood, he took her hand in his and left the Earth behind.

When they arrived, they found Emelia in a large room at the head of a long table, speaking with several dozen men and women who were all dressed in formal attire. As one, with the exception of Emelia who smiled brightly at their arrival, they all rose from their chairs before dropping to one knee and bowing their heads.

"You may rise," Emelia said happily, "How has your day been?"

"We met a water nymph," Megan said when nothing else came to mind.

"Many of your allies will likely come to pay their respects," Emelia said. "To what do we owe the honor of this visit?"

Megan and Bruce looked at each other in concern. Neither of them had considered the possibility that they would be interrupting something that looked this important.

"I was wondering if you'd like to take a break and show us around," Megan answered quietly, trying not to let her voice break in her nervousness.

"I'd love to, my dear, but I only just got here a short while ago," she explained, "And we've only just begun. This will take several hours."

"I'm so sorry," Megan said. "I keep forgetting about the time difference. Would it be okay if we look around for a little while before we go back?"

"That's a wonderful idea," Emelia said out loud and added, *I really am happy to see you*, where only the two of them could hear her. "Dougal, stop skulking in the hallway and come in."

Bruce and Megan both turned to find the Scathlahm stepping guiltily into view, still wearing the clothing that Mr. Grimble so liked.

"Please give our Queen a quick tour of the castle. But keep a close eye on the time," she said. "Megan, when do you have to be back?"

"William won't be able to work with us again until Friday," Megan answered.

"And what day was it when you left?" her mother asked.

"Oh," Bruce answered, realizing that wasn't readily apparent here, "It was Monday."

"Chamberlin?" Emelia asked one of the older men at the table.

"To arrive at roughly the same time of day four days hence, Your Majesty, they would need to leave in slightly less than five hours," he answered.

"Excellent," she said, "Dougal that should be plenty of time to give her a proper feel of her castle. And remember, keep close watch on the time. We've found that it works best if you try to go back at the same time of day as when you left to eliminate jet lag."

"Excuse me your majesty," the Scathlahm said uneasily, "I'm not sure if I'm the best person to do this. I was raised on Earth."

"Oh, that's right," Emelia said, frowning, "they would have sent you back after your selection so you'd be closer to Megan's age and better able to protect her. Do you know where the monument is?"

"Yes, your majesty," he answered. "And we could go through the throne room afterward."

"That should do nicely," Emelia said, and unable to help herself, she stood, walked over and embraced her daughter quickly, wincing at the movement to her injured shoulder. "I probably won't see you again until Thanksgiving. But don't hesitate to come back anytime you like. It is, after all, your kingdom."

The three of them hurried out so Emelia could get back to what she'd

70

been doing before they arrived. Once out in the hall, Bruce turned to Dougal.

"You've been following us, haven't you?"

"My oath of service to the Queen requires that I be near her at all times," he answered, leading them down a series of stairs and corridors.

"Why haven't we seen you?" Megan asked.

"You made it fairly clear at the time of your ascension that you did not want my services. But that doesn't excuse me from my vows, so I watch from a distance."

"What do you mean?" Megan asked. "We've never even spoken."

"You said you didn't want any of this," he answered.

"You heard that?" she asked.

"We all did," he answered.

Horrified, she realized that her first act as Queen had likely alienated all of her subjects.

"That's not what I meant," she whispered.

"What about when we entered Haven?" Bruce asked.

"I could not follow you there, and I cannot say I am unhappy that you will not be returning," he answered. "It was one of the worst half hours of my life, knowing that she was surrounded by her enemies without allies to turn to."

"What do you mean without allies?" Bruce demanded. "I was there the whole time."

"I apologize," the Scathlahm said in a most unconvincing manner, "I did not mean to impugn your ability to protect our Queen. I saw how you dealt with Lady Nimue."

"And you didn't approve," Bruce said.

"She was evil and deserved the death she received." he said coolly, stopping to face Bruce as he spoke. "But none of the Tuatha dé deserve to be shackled in iron."

"I didn't see any of you trying to stop her," Bruce snapped. "She'd just killed your King."

"And for that we thank you," Dougal said, trying to calm himself. "What you do not understand is that the Children of Nyx do the same to those of us that they capture."

"But they remove the iron eventually," Megan asked, frowning as she tried to make sense of the memories. "Right?"

"No, my Queen," he whispered. "Eventually we either die from their torture or from the strain on our bodies as we try over and over to escape the pain through the shadows. Sometimes, if there's not too much iron present, the reigning King or Queen is able to end our suffering through the bond we share. I'm sorry for leading our discussion to such a dark place. After all, you came here for exploration. Prepare yourselves," he said with a flourish and opened the door.

Megan gasped when the door opened, but not from the frigid wind that cut through Bruce like jagged splinters of ice in his veins. Completely distracted by what she saw outside, she followed Dougal out the door.

Bruce reached through the shadows and brought his coat and gloves to him from the hallway closet back on Beverly Road. But even though they'd proven more than adequate for winter in Texas, he still had to supplement his body heat with magic before he could step out into the open.

Disappearing into the barren lands on either side of the horizon, the likeness of the Morrigan stretched her arms toward the gray sky. Her face tilted upward as if looking for a sun that would never shine in this desolate place. In defiance of the millennia during which it had stood and the laws of physics it broke, its delicate features remained as perfect as they'd been the day that the Dagda had created it, for none but one of the Beloved

could have crafted such a beautifully monstrous thing.

"It's magnificent," Megan yelled over to Bruce when he joined them.

"I need to get closer," he yelled back.

Realizing that he'd likely freeze to death before he walked halfway there, he walked the shadows, arriving at the base of the massive sculpture. He ignored the pain of the cold in his curiosity for what the thing could tell his smith's senses of its construction. He reached out with his hand and was almost overwhelmed by the power within it.

Megan and Dougal appeared instantly on either side of him. The Scathlahm looked at him in horror.

"What have you done?" the young man yelled over the roar of the wind which was much worse away from the castle. "It is forbidden to touch the likeness of the Morrigan! We must go before anyone sees what you have done."

Megan reached out and took them with her back to the cottage.

Bruce glared at them both, deeply annoyed at being scolded for something no one had warned him about. It was, however, nice to be able to feel his face again. Never before had a few degrees above freezing felt so warm.

"It's not like the Queen is going to have me executed," Bruce growled.

"Dougal," Megan said, still smirking at Bruce's remark. "There's no reason for you to hide out in the woods. Why don't you come and stay with us in the cabin?"

A wave of completely irrational anger surged through Bruce.

"I must respectfully decline," the Scathlahm said. "I fear I cannot watch for danger from the inside. And if I cannot do that, then I cannot fulfill my vows. I have made a small shelter within the tree line for when I must sleep."

"But you'll get cold," she insisted, to which he gave her a puzzled look.

"I will be near should you need me, but I will remain out of sight. May I ask a favor of you, should I be so bold?"

"What is it?" Megan asked.

"Please call out to me if you plan to travel," he asked. "I can track you when necessary, but it is much easier if I don't have to."

"I can do that," Megan said.

"Thank you, my Queen," he said and then faded from sight.

Up until that point, Bruce hadn't particularly liked Dougal. But now he truly hated the man and the way Megan acted when he was around.

"So this isn't the same day that we left?" she asked. Bruce checked his phone.

"Tuesday," he answered, then noticed something strange. "Did we have curtains when we left?"

"No, we didn't," she answered, looking over at their temporary home. "And I'm sure we put out the fire before we left, but there's smoke coming out of the chimney."

"And all of the iron cookware was definitely inside," he added, noticing that it was all currently piled out by the small barn that stood adjacent to the cabin.

Cautiously the two of them approached and opened the door to find out if it was indeed Goldilocks that had invited herself in for dinner.

Flagstones had been laid over the dirt floor and the interior walls sealed with mortar and plaster as they would have been when the cottage had first been built. Furniture upholstered in dark fabrics and carved with knotwork filled the interior space. Tapestries of scenes Bruce suspected to be Mag Turied covered the walls, and thick rugs covered the flagstones where they were most likely to stand.

Megan noticed a piece of parchment laying on the sturdy table, which had been the only furniture in the cottage when they'd left.

Megan and Bruce,

The Queen of the Tuatha dé does not sleep rough on a cot in the land of her enemies unless she is having a great deal of fun at their expense. Breakfast, lunch and dinner will be provided for you each day. Your cooking staff will send meals directly to your table. Should you need anything else, simply call to your Scathlahm and he will make sure that you have it. Hopefully your "hosts" will not mind the improvements our craftsmen made to this dwelling. If they do, well, let's be honest. We don't really care if they do or not. I look forward to seeing you at Thanksgiving.

Emelia Mackgahe

Before Megan even began looking for the other improvements that her mother had mentioned, she was struck by how different her mother's handwriting looked. It wasn't quite calligraphy, but it was certainly more sophisticated than her mother's normal handwriting. Even her signature looked different, and not simply by the use of her real married name.

Then she looked up and noticed a door where there had not been one before. With Bruce following closely behind her, they entered a completely modern bathroom complete with a shower.

"How does this even work?" she asked, turning on the hot water tap at the sink and finding it scalding hot.

"Magic my dear Megan," he answered pleasantly from where he had gone to lay down on an incredibly soft-looking bed. "Magic. I take back every bad thing that I've ever said about Emelia. I positively love that woman."

She came over and dropped down next to him, making him happier than he'd been all day.

"I'm sorry I forgot about how badly the cold hurts you," she said. "I was just so surprised by the monument, I guess."

"Not a big deal," he said in reply, "but...I'd better go move all of that cast iron inside the barn so it won't get wet and rust even worse than some of it already is. Otherwise Paul might send the scouts after me."

"You're sure it will be okay out there?" she asked.

"Well, there are already tons of iron rods in the shed," he answered. "I wonder if they're the same as the ones that William said were in the ground closer to Haven."

"Need help?" she asked happily.

"No, I have no intention of doing it manually, it should only take me a few minutes," he said, then turned back as if remembering something. "Remember the monument?" he asked.

"It's kind of hard to forget," she answered.

"I know why no one is supposed to touch it," he said.

"Why?"

"It's one of the Dagda's artifacts," he answered.

"You're kidding," she said. "How can something that huge possibly be an artifact?"

"I guess anything is possible with the kind of power that the Beloved have at their disposal," he answered. "I know why he made it so big too."

"And?"

"The artifacts made by the Beloved can't be destroyed, but they can be badly damaged. When that happens, their power turns toward repairing themselves, and for a brief time, they stop fulfilling their purpose. With an artifact that large, you'd almost have to be a Beloved yourself to cause enough damage to take it offline for even a short time."

"What purpose was so important that he made it too massive to damage?"

"It binds the entire race of the Tuatha dé to the oldest living descendant of the Morrigan," he answered thoughtfully. "And now it binds their lives to yours."

Chapter VII: Welcome Disappointment

Sam Wise stood in the prep area at Gordon's, cutting off pieces of warm pizza dough and rolling them into balls to rise for another round. He had plenty of help who were more than capable of doing this menial task. And to be honest, he really didn't have time to be spending on activities such as this. But compared to all of the other things that demanded his attention now, this was a slam dunk every time and always turned out exactly the way he wanted it to. Furthermore, it took his mind off of things he'd rather not think about, such as how little progress he'd made with the Fates.

He didn't think that they intentionally tried to hinder his attempts to understand what they had to tell him. In fact, they seemed almost desperate to lead him toward the knowledge he sought. But after living for what appeared to be several hundred thousand years, their perceptions had evolved to the point where they could barely be considered human. Or maybe the differences could be explained as nothing more than the byproduct of being imprisoned in a tree for nearly a century. Furthermore, as Paul had suggested, the Fates might be different by the virtue of being from so far back in the evolutionary history of the human race. Whatever the cause, Sam found it difficult to make them understand the full scope of his questions and even more so to decipher the vastness of their answers.

Once again, he found himself wishing that he could sit down with August one more time and see if the old hermit's long life full of experiences might hold the key to understanding what the women had to say. At least he wasn't thinking about someone else for a change…

"Mr. Wise?"

"Patty," he said patiently, "You've been working for me since you were barely in high school. Please call me by my first name."

"Yes…Sam," she said, just as uncomfortable with it as she always sounded. "There is someone out front who wants to speak with you."

His heart raced, trying not to think about the diminutive, yet fierce woman he hoped it would be.

"Thanks, Patty," he said, quickly washing the dough residue from his hands and heading for the door to the dining area.

Silhouetted against the front door waited several strangers, none of which looked to be his childhood friend. He knew it had been a long shot, but the disappointment was still real. As he drew closer, he could tell that there was an old man, a couple likely in their mid-twenties and three small children. However, his disappointment faded quickly when he noticed the familiar skin tones and facial structures of his childhood. He'd barely hoped to ever see their like again.

Before he had a chance to approach them, the elder caught sight of him and moved forward in greeting. As the language Sam had so longed to hear again began to flow from the old man's lips, Sam wrapped his great arms around him and greeted him like a brother.

It was then that he noticed the quiet woman standing just outside the door as if unsure of receiving the same welcome as the others. He motioned for her to join them, and she reluctantly entered. The toddler in her arms looked as if she shared Black heritage as well as his own, and she lunged toward him with outstretched arms so suddenly that she might have fallen had he not happily taken her.

And in words that sounded like thunder laughing, he told his new

80

friends that a home had been prepared ahead of their arrival. When he realized that only the old man understood, he turned to the others and welcomed them to Nickelville.

Chapter VIII: Interdimensional Taxi Service

Megan dozed beneath a tree near the cottage. Bruce had been walking the shadows over and over again with William in tow, fading in and out of existence all over the valley. It had been Bruce's suggestion that he be the one to show their friend the inner workings of instantaneous travel, citing what the Morrigan had done to Sam the last time he'd tried to enter her mind. Given that Sam had been a friend, he thought they should avoid having an actual Child of Nyx try to enter her thoughts. While she'd slept, snow had begun to fall in large, heavy flakes to accumulate in the shady places and around the edges of the slate shingles on the roof. For that matter, it had begun to collect on her as well in slightly lighter patches against the alabaster of her skin.

For most of this apparently fruitless exercise, her thoughts had returned to the Morrigan's monument and Bruce's discovery. Perhaps it was only the side effect of a childhood so dependent on secrecy, but she abhorred the thought of someone being able to look into her deepest and most private thoughts. This ability that had settled over her unwilling mind violated every rule of decency and every concept of right and wrong that defined who she was. And yet, ever since her ascension, even as she promised herself that she would never take advantage of the Tuatha dé in such a way, knowledge of them still flooded her thoughts whether she wanted it or not.

"How do you not feel that?" Bruce asked from in front of her, making her open her eyes. "I'm still freezing, and I swear I'm wearing almost everything we brought with us."

"I feel it," she answered, stretching her arms and back. "It just doesn't bother me. Are you guys finished?"

"Even with Bruce completely unshielded I can't feel a thing," William complained as he had already done many times before. "As far as I can tell he's not doing anything at all."

"And yet I can feel what I'm doing just fine," Bruce added, helping Megan to her feet and gently sweeping snowflakes out of her hair. Then, in the midst of brushing away the ones that had caught in her eyelashes with his thumb, his fingertips gently grazed her neck and cheek.

Warmth filled her, awakening something as her hand rose to overlap his. In many ways it felt like the early days of moving things with her mind. But instead of a single object she'd locked onto, she sensed a thousand shrouded parts of herself that she could feel shifting imperceptibly, trying to come at her call. But whatever they were, once again like the early days of her training, they merely rocked slightly in her direction before settling again and fading from her thoughts like snowflakes landing near a fire. An ache settled into the base of her skull and she pushed his hand away.

"You don't have to do that," she snapped. "How many times do I have to tell you that the cold has no effect on me?"

"I know," he said with only the faintest hint of hurt in his voice, "But they'll melt when we go inside and you hate it when your clothes stick to you."

She nodded in apology, grudgingly admitting that he was right.

"It's like nothing else I've ever seen," the Child of Nyx said, likely confused by what he'd just felt passing between them with his empathic senses. "Bruce doesn't expend any energy that I can see or detect that he applies to any task. The closest way I can think of to describe it is that it's like he hails some sort of interdimensional taxi, and it takes him wherever he wants to go."

"Sorry," was all Megan could think of to say. She couldn't remember why, but it felt like she'd been working hard to try and accomplish something, and the fatigue merged with her thoughts about the Tuatha dé, further souring her mood. So far none of their studies into the ways their power worked had yielded any results. She began to wonder if the Morrigan might not have some ulterior motive for keeping them in Haven even though she and Bruce would have both been much happier back in Nickelville.

"Oh well," William said regretfully. "We can pick this back up after you return from the holiday."

"Are you sure you wouldn't like to come with us?' Megan asked, trying to snap herself out of this dark mood. "You don't have to go back to the classroom until Monday. I know the Children of Nyx don't celebrate Thanksgiving, but I'll bet Catherene would like to."

"I'm not one to turn down good food, but I don't think we need to take the boys so close to Guarded Wood in their current state. Maybe when they're better."

Megan looked at him hard for a moment, sensing more than he'd said out loud.

"What?" he asked.

"What's the real reason?" she asked, drawing a laugh out of their friend.

"I guess I should know better than to try to hide things from you by now. Don't take this the wrong way, but this is the first holiday you've all celebrated since the deaths of so many of your friends."

"So?" Bruce asked.

"I'm an empath," William reminded them. "Your mother's grief when her father passed was so strong that I felt it all the way past the shields in Haven and came out to investigate. I have no desire to spend the next few days around people who will unintentionally make their personal pain into mine."

"I can't say I blame you for wanting to avoid that," Bruce said thoughtfully.

"If the offer is still open next year when you've all had time to process these feelings," William offered, "I'd love to bring my family to spend the holidays with you."

"Catherene shares your empathic gift, doesn't she?" Megan asked.

"Yes, and the boys too," he said, catching himself. "Or at least they did. Please send your mother my regards."

"Not warm regards?" Bruce asked.

"I'm not that foolish," their friend said, grinning before turning to leave.

"I didn't think we'd be done this early," Megan said, looking at her watch. "But I'm excited about seeing everyone."

"Me too," he agreed. "Who would have thought that I'd actually miss Jade and Paul? I wonder what kinds of trouble they've been into since we left. Are you just about ready?"

"I think so, I packed up everything last night. Oh, I almost forgot," she said, turning away from him. "Hey, Dougal!"

The Scathlahm appeared at once, immediately kneeling before her, "Yes, my Queen?"

"You have seriously got to stop doing that," she said irritably. "You have no idea how self-conscious it makes me."

"But this is the customary way to greet the ruling monarch of the

85

Tuatha dé," he said, looking up at her but still staying on one knee. "Others would think me acting above my station if I did otherwise."

"How about a compromise?" she asked. "You only do it when there are others of the Tuatha dé around. Otherwise, you don't kneel and you just call me Megan."

The Scathlahm frowned.

"And now you've put him in the position of needing to decide whether he should do what custom demands and disobey his Queen, or do what you want and fly in the face of tradition," Bruce said sympathetically.

Dougal nodded.

"Just relax a little," Bruce advised, and Megan was pleased that he was trying to help instead of sulking about the Scathlahm's presence the way he usually did. "Megan was never raised to be Queen. She learned at an early age to hide from attention so she could blend in and avoid the Wild Hunt. When you do what you've been taught, it makes her feel exposed and vulnerable. Just give her some time to grow into this. Doing what she asks is the best way you can serve her right now."

"Is this true, your Majesty?" Dougal asked at last.

"Absolutely," she answered.

"Then I will do as you ask," he said, rising to his feet and then adding her name though it clearly pained him to do it.

"That's definitely a step in the right direction," Bruce said, trying not to enjoy the other man's discomfort. "But what will really help, if you want to stay close to her without drawing attention to yourself like you do now, is to get rid of the trench coat. In spite of what my father might tell you to the contrary, people don't actually wear those anymore."

Dougal shrugged and let the coat slide from his shoulders. Upon doing so, Megan was surprised to find that in addition to the Scathlahm's Blade, he also carried a short sword.

"Are you wearing chainmail under your shirt?" Bruce asked, noticing the odd bulk.

"Yes," Dougal answered. "And a heavy vest of something underneath that."

"Kevlar," Bruce murmured respectfully, running his hand an inch or so above Dougal's shoulder. Then, getting a better look at the sword, "May I?"

Dougal shrugged again and drew its length, handing it hilt-first toward Bruce, who whistled in appreciation.

"I had no idea that the Tuatha dé were working with titanium alloys," he said reverently. "The craftsmanship is exquisite."

"There are very few of them," Dougal said. "The materials are hard to come by and they are of questionable use now."

"What do you mean?" Megan asked.

"Because they," he said, nodding toward Haven, "prefer to shoot us from great distances. We seldom get close enough for hand to hand combat."

"The same way Nyx wounded the Dagda," Megan added. "So the trench coat is for hiding that sword?"

"Yes," Dougal answered. "But it is also to hide my pale skin."

"You're pale," Bruce said, "But lots of people are."

In answer, Dougal pulled his shirt, mail and vest over his head, revealing the whitest expanse of flesh that Megan had ever seen.

"As you can see, my skin lacks any of the pigments that yours have. If I cover most of my skin it isn't very noticeable. But even my bare arms would draw the attention of anyone who saw me. And since I feel no discomfort from heat or cold…"

"You have no trouble wearing a coat in the Texas heat," Bruce said. "The problem is that everyone else does. The very fact that you are not dressed for the season makes you stand out."

"Maybe I'm not as pale as I thought," Megan said.

"By the standards of the Tuatha dé," Dougal said quietly. "Your skin is positively aflame with color...

"If you lose the sword, which I admit is a shame because that thing is utterly awesome," Bruce said thoughtfully, "We could get you a lower back sheath like the one Emelia used, and then you could get by with just a light jacket or hoodie. People wear those all the time, even when it's hot."

"Your skin is pretty though," Megan said, reaching out to touch the bare skin of his shoulder.

"I'm going to go get my gear," Bruce said, suddenly disappearing.

"So," Dougal asked when he'd gone, "Was my choice of wardrobe the only reason you summoned me?"

"No," she said, "I promised you we wouldn't go anywhere without telling you first. We're returning to Nickelville for a few days."

"That is good to hear," he said, pulling the last of his gear back into place. "It would be nice to be away from this place."

"You don't like them very much, do you?"

"*Latha nan iomda beannachd.*"

"The Night of Many Goodbyes," she translated, once again surprised that she could understand Gaelic.

"I was very young, but I remember. The people who hide down there were responsible. I do not like that you, who are so precious to us, spend so much time among those cowards. Cowards who kill us from afar and bind us with the same iron collars they use on their dogs. But I know that the voice of the Morrigan speaks to you, and who am I to question her will?"

Chapter IX: The Dancing

Emelia sat at her late husband's desk, running the tip of one finger across the fuzzy leaf of the African Violet her father had potted for her. While she did so, she stared at the things Daragh had left unfinished and unaware that he would never return. His chief advisor, one of the few adults to survive the battle of Mag Tuired, never voiced aloud the opinion that Emelia should not be making decisions concerning the well-being of the kingdom. After all, here in Tyr Sgodl, only a year had passed since she'd stolen the heir and led the Wild Hunt on a chase spanning two worlds.

Perhaps he was right. Try as she might, she couldn't keep her eyes from the clock that took up most of one corner. Daragh had told her once that it had been made centuries earlier by a master clockmaker. Using only non-ferrous gears and springs, it told not the time in Tyr Sgodl, but on Earth. Over and over, no matter how hard she tried to concentrate on the documents before her, she found herself gazing at the unsettling speed with which the hands spun around the face.

Each time that happened, a chasm opened in the pit of her stomach. This was so much worse than it had been during the months of her early marriage and pregnancy. Back then she'd known what she was doing. Dedication and purpose had bound her here, even though it meant that she'd had to leave her father behind. But this time it was she who had been cast adrift while everything she loved sped on without her. Back then she'd never truly understood what she was losing. This time she understood it all too well.

At some point during her last morbid contemplation of the clock, the chamberlain had come in and begun to speak. She couldn't remember if she'd acknowledged his presence or not. He droned on and on, making her feel like she was back at the Academy listening to lectures about things she'd never do while the Dark Man competed for her attention. Now she found herself haunted by the specter of the life that would pass back home while she governed over a people who no longer wanted her there.

Then the chief advisor was standing in front of her, offering his arm. She looked at him blankly for a moment before realizing that it was time to go home, even if it were only for a little while. And after that, the preparations for her husband's funeral should be finished.

An instant later, she stood on the front porch of the house on Beverly Road. He said something she couldn't recall and then he was gone.

When she found that the door had been locked, Emelia finally understood that she'd never see her father again. The emotions she'd locked away began to seep around the stones she'd piled around them, walling herself off from the moment when she'd have to feel.

She almost melted the locking mechanism in her haste to get inside before the dam broke and she drowned. Once inside, she slammed the door shut and staggered to the stairs, where she collapsed in a shivering heap.

A part of her waited for his voice, for the concern and the consolation that she would be okay, that this wasn't the end. She let the breath she hadn't realized she'd been holding out in one long hiss, trying to force the pain out with it as it went. But the ache had taken root in her soul and she doubted anything would ever ease its presence.

She still hadn't slept, fearing what ghosts might walk her dreams. They'd suggested she sleep when she first arrived in Tyr Sgodl, but she'd shrugged them off and allowed them to bathe her instead.

It was a different experience from the one she'd shown her daughter. The old women had since learned more about the limitations of her frail human body. The numbness probably helped as well while she'd watched them clean the last of his dried blood from her skin and hair, thus leaving her bereft of his presence for the first time since the laughter over Kermit. Had that really happened?

Now that the numbness had finally lifted, she hurt so deeply that she hardly noticed how stale the air had grown in her childhood home. But she noticed all too well how much his presence had begun to fade from the home where he'd lived for the better part of a century.

Oddly enough, the house also smelled like brownies.

She felt her friends and loved ones nearby, but didn't want to greet them in the Celtic gown her handmaidens had dressed her in upon her return to the castle. She felt no desire to be Queen of the Tuatha dé, even though she'd dreamed of it often while they were on the run.

She realized now that she'd been two women living in the same body for all of these years. Well, three if you counted the Morrigan. On one side she'd been Queen Emelia Mackgahe of the Tuatha dé, and on the other she'd always been the quiet girl who'd left Nickelville looking for answers. Each of those women had fallen in love, but with different men. When the King had died in her arms, the Queen had faded with him, leaving only the girl from a forgotten Texas town to continue. But even though the Queen had died, the need for her had not, and thus the quiet girl was left to carry on in her place, an imposter to sit on the throne of the Morrigan Reborn.

Emelia slowly climbed up the staircase, her gown dragging the steps as she rose, trailing her fingertips along the worn banister. She knew something had changed before she reached her childhood bedroom. Her daughter's lingering presence coated the stale air like perfume, and she felt

at peace for the first time since… She wasn't ready to think about that yet. After all, her shoulder was still bandaged, and the wound had not yet begun to heal in the two days since it had happened for her.

She hadn't expected yellow.

At some point Megan had apparently taken it upon herself to do what her mother had not. She'd unpacked and made it look like someone really lived there. Like someone real lived there. It was a shame that Emelia never would.

Dropping the gown on the floor near the foot of the bed, she went to the closet and pulled out a pair of her high school jeans. Still gaunt from months of living in the wilderness outside of Haven, they fit her looser than they had when everyone had still been alive. But that was another thought she wasn't ready to think about. After a short search she discovered that her favorite shirt wasn't there.

Following a suspicious wisp of intuition, she walked down the hall to her daughter's room, ignoring the pictures that whispered to her from their frames. She avoided looking through the open door across the hall, not ready to see the bed where she'd fled from nightmares, thunderstorms and where she'd played games of hide and seek with Sam. She wasn't ready for a lot of things yet, it seemed. And there, hanging in the front of Megan's closet was the shirt she'd stolen from Sam so many lifetimes ago.

"I love you girl," she whispered, "But this one is mine."

It was a splash of warm sunshine across her skin, which hadn't been warm since returning to the castle. It was the embodiment of broken promises made on moonlit walks as well as the betrayal of the man she'd pledged her life to. But it was also the memory of happiness that now lay beyond her reach. The pain of moving her bandaged shoulder gave her focus, reminding her that she couldn't just collapse on her daughter's bed and sleep. She also pulled one of Megan's sweatshirts out, not only because she wanted a reminder of why she'd chosen this path, but also to prevent any misunderstandings about what she longed for most but would never deserve.

Downstairs, she found that her father's porch-bound garden not only lived but thrived. Sam's essence lingered, letting her know that her big friend still came to the house often, if not inside.

"I didn't know you were back yet!" Ben Grimble called from her father's brick smoker. The smell of pecan smoke and turkey filled the air as he pulled out the first of two birds.

"Only for a few minutes," she called back, happy to see him but not enough to think about the previous year when her father had cooked the main part of the meal.

She'd intended to go straight to the tree house, but her feet had other ideas and took her instead to her mother's grove. She'd avoided the place when she'd last returned to Nickelville, unwilling to see it stripped of the power and beauty it had once held. But now it was a perfect place to pause, a perfect place to poke and prod at the hurt in her heart so she'd know her boundaries before she put on a mask to hide her pain from the ones she loved.

On some level she'd known that Kate would be there, sitting on the bench where her husband had passed, humming the haunting melody with which the bards had, for a short time, bridged the present with eternity.

"You and I seem to be bound together by the love we held for these old men," Kate observed when she noticed her.

"It would appear so," Emelia replied warmly. "How have you been?"

"Some days are better than others," the old woman said with a shrug. "Sometimes I wonder why we had to wait so many years to start living. I'm sure he had his reasons for not making his intentions known. I must have had reasons for not ignoring the way my generation felt about women who pursue the men they want. But for the life of me, I can't remember what any of them might have been."

Emelia came over to sit next to her and put her good arm around the old woman's shoulders.

94

"Do you know what I do during the nights when I can't sleep?" Kate asked, "I go back in my mind to that first time he noticed me there at the concession stand."

"Sam and I were only kids, but even we knew that there was something between the two of you," Emelia said. Some of the muscles that had been clenched around her lungs and heart began to relax as she sat there.

"Alan had been coming every week for a year before he started using the two of you as an excuse," Kate said with just a hint of laughter in her voice. "No matter how bad the movie was, or how many times he'd seen it. But in the daydreams, I have during those early morning hours, I come outside after my shift and he's there waiting for me. We go to that diner that used to be out by the old water tower."

Emelia smiled, remembering for the first time in years how her father had taken her there with his friends. More often than not, Sam had come with them too. Maybe it was the happiness he'd found there that led him to start Gordon's.

"And being the impatient kind of person that I am…" Kate continued.

"You waited on him for at least seventy years, Kate," Emelia laughed. "I'd say you're probably the most patient person I've ever known."

"Only where he was concerned. But anyway, I usually fast forward to the part where we get married. Then he's not the odd one out with your father and their friends. Somehow us being together changes what happened to your mother so that she lives, and all of us have babies that grow up together here."

"I think I like your version of our lives better than the one that we got," Emelia offered when the old woman went silent.

"This one isn't all bad," Kate said at last. "I've gotten to see such amazing things. And we did find each other in the end, even if it was for only for a little while."

"I know how you feel," Emelia said at last. "I only got to spend a year with my husband. And then we had to be apart for almost sixteen."

"Did you want to be away from him?"

"Not at all," Emelia admitted. "It was one of the hardest things I've ever done. And when I finally got him back, he loved me like we had never been apart."

"What happened to him?" Kate asked.

"He died in my arms before Megan could even speak with him."

"Then I'd say you do know something about how I feel," Kate said, putting her own arm around Emelia's slight frame and hugging her close.

"Do you know what else I know?" Emelia asked.

"What?"

"One of the best feasts this side of Tyr Sgodl lies just beyond those trees," she said.

"What place is that?" Kate asked, frowning. "It seems like I should know it."

"It's a name that probably speaks to your Irish blood, which never really forgets where we come from. It's the place that our ancestors called under the hill…the place where the fair folk lived for thousands of years."

"Have you been there?" the old woman asked in awe. "The place where one day is a hundred years here?"

"Time does move slow there, but not quite that slow," Emelia laughed.

"And did you eat or drink?" Kate asked. "Is that why you had to stay and why you were gone for so long?"

"I did," Emelia answered. "But it wasn't the food or the drink that held me there."

"What was it then?"

"I think it was the dancing," she whispered.

"Oh yes," Kate agreed, holding Emelia close as she stared ahead with unseeing eyes out over the grove. "I know all about the dancing."

The aromas that filtered through the trees while Emelia and Kate walked toward the others brought on the first hints of appetite she'd had since that day at the Baker. The treehouse bustled with activity, and notes of violin and piano rained down over them while they walked, dancing around one another like flights of birds diving from the heavens. As Emelia listened, her grief retreated enough for her to look forward to the familiar foods of Thanksgiving.

Emelia dropped the shields she'd held close about her, hiding her presence from the others lest they come upon her before she was ready. At once the awareness of her daughter and the bard embraced her senses, along with the seemingly paradoxical aura of Paul which was made up of equal parts young and ancient.

Then she could feel Sam's head turn in her direction with a smile that matched her own.

The conversation she'd just had with Kate echoed in her mind, and the smile withered on her lips.

Jade and Andrew looked happy as they carried loads of catering boxes up the stairs, unwilling to make Paul stop playing long enough to man the pulley. Their laughter lent itself to the music, all the more beautiful for its lack of magic.

Sam strode up from the woods, too big to fit into any mortal tale. He had a sack of what looked like bread fresh from August's oven. For just a second, she found herself back in that moment when he'd woken on the

Grimble's couch to find her kneeling over him. She thought longingly of Kate's fantasy game of what ifs. Was there a world out there where she'd told her father to bring her back home to this underappreciated paradise?

But her situation wasn't the same as Kate's. It wasn't as simple as one woman loving one man. No matter how the events of that winter had played out, she would have hurt someone she loved. Even in daydreams she couldn't imagine making a choice that would have erased her daughter from the world. She had left Nickelville behind. She had fallen in love with someone else. She'd been a Queen, and she'd been a refugee. Now she'd be whatever Megan needed her to be in order to avoid the dark path shown to her by the Morrigan so many years ago.

So they ate too much food, and they drank too much of the meade that she'd sent the previous day. But sometimes the long pauses deepened like snow drifts as if, by common consent, they all paid homage to the voices absent and for the stories left untold.

Megan surprised them all with brownies that she'd cooked from Esther's recipe. And even though they tasted exactly the same, they all missed the laughter that had always come with them.

Finally the bard and the man who looked at her as if she held within her all the beauty of a newborn day soothed their souls with a magic so rare that it had been thought lost forever. When they asked Kate to play with them, her pride at how far her only pupil had progressed was evident to all assembled there among the branches of the Sentinel tree. And in the ghostly transition between dusk and nightfall within Guarded Wood, while the last echoes of bardic magic drifted through the trees, Emelia noticed several faint but familiar shapes there among them, one of which wagged his tail happily.

Chapter X: The Morrigan Remembers

Bruce could tell that something was bothering William when he knocked on the cottage door shortly after they returned from their time in Nickelville. They hadn't expected to see him at all today, since it was one of the days that he was obliged to work with the children of Haven.

"What brings you all the way out here on a workday?" Megan asked when Bruce let him in.

"The council has decided that Bruce can enter and study in Haven," William answered reluctantly.

"That's great," Megan said, "But the invitation only extends to him, doesn't it?"

William nodded.

"You mean like right now," Bruce asked, "Don't you?"

"I'm not sure what this is all about, but it would certainly make it easier since you could study with Cat while I'm teaching," William said. "Sorry, Megan."

"Don't worry about me," she said, nestling down into one of the armchairs that the Tuatha dé had brought to the cottage. "I never intend to set foot in there again. You and your family are great and all, but putting me in the same city with Priscilla probably isn't a good idea. She doesn't bring out the best in me."

"You're sure?" Bruce asked.

"Absolutely," Megan replied, pulling out the next book in the series that she'd been reading from her mother's bookshelf. "I'm more than happy to read in peace and quiet for a few hours."

"I'm not that loud," Bruce said defensively.

"No, but you feel the need to entertain me," she said, already starting to read. "Seriously, you're good."

With a shrug, he turned toward William and left.

Bruce asked him about what sorts of things he taught the youngest Children of Nyx, and the discussion still continued when they reached the shield gate. This time, the gatekeeper opened without comment or interest, returning to whatever he'd been reading before their arrival.

"Sure," William muttered under his breath, glancing back at the gatekeeper, "Now he starts to read."

Although Bruce wouldn't have voiced his interest in front of Megan, the smith in him was eager to see how they did things here in this place that had been largely cut off from the rest of the world for centuries. What alternate paths had they discovered from the mainstream?

The citizens of Haven still stared at him when he passed them in the corridors, but without his pale-skinned companion, none of them showed fear or hostility. He suspected that even the curiosity would soon fade as they became accustomed to seeing him.

As William had suggested, the city of Haven became a great deal less grandiose the deeper they traveled into the mountain. Furthermore, it also seemed as if they were traveling back in time. The polished marble of the cavern proper gave way to brushed steel panels and institutional fluorescent lights. Then the panels ended and the bare stone of the tunnels were broken only by riveted iron supports. They even passed by one side tunnel that was nothing more than a circular hole into the darkness beyond. By the time they reached the school, the dimly lit corridors felt more like mine tunnels than places for education.

"This is my little slice of Haven," William said when they arrived at the door to his home, chuckling at his own joke. He turned the doorknob without resistance and motioned for Bruce to enter before him.

"No lock?" Bruce asked.

"When you live in a city full of people who can manipulate the physical world with their minds, locks don't serve much purpose," William answered. "It's well warded though."

Had Bruce not just walked through Haven to get there, he'd have had no reason to think they were anywhere other than the living room of just about any home in the United States. The first thing he noticed was the fire in the hearth, which of course made him wonder how they vented the smoke so far underground. The furniture was fairly common by American standards, largely chosen for comfort over fashion, but everywhere he looked, he saw pictures and knick-knacks with fantasy themes that he recognized from his own readings. Bookshelves had been tucked into just about every available space, and as he glanced over them, he recognized most of the titles.

"I like your home," Bruce said. "This looks more…"

"Normal than you would have thought?" Cat finished from where she sat feeding one of the twins. The boy chewed mechanically when she put a spoonful of food into his mouth, but with the exception of those actions, he might very well have been an extremely lifelike doll.

As Bruce looked at him, he realized he'd seen the two before.

"I think your sons were in my very first vision," he said, getting down eye level with the one that was sitting on the couch.

"They were?" Cat asked in surprise. "Were they moving or were they like this?"

"Like this," he replied.

"How long ago was that?" William asked.

"Over a year ago," he answered before adding, "I don't usually have premonitions of the future that far out though."

"But that's before they were even like this," Catherene said thoughtfully.

"That's usually how visions of the future work," William said sarcastically, smiling at his wife who glared back.

"Here," Bruce offered. "Let me show you."

Reaching out to the fire, he cast the memory of the vision across the flames.

"How are you doing that?" Cat asked.

With a shrug, he lowered his shields so she could see for herself.

After watching for a few seconds, she took control of the flames which showed a memory of the boys laughing as they ran down a slope outside of the city on a warm day. William froze, listening to the sound of his children's happiness.

"I'd almost forgotten what they sounded like," he whispered.

"Thank you for being so trusting with us," Cat said softly, still staring at the flames. "This must be hard when William and I were meant to be your adversaries."

"The Tuatha dé and the Children of Nyx don't seem to be that different from each other," Bruce said with a shrug.

"You must not be lulled into thinking you can trust all of the Children of Nyx," William said, repeating his warnings from before. "We are not all good people. Most would happily take up arms against your friend and her mother."

"And don't forget that you and I are neither," Catherene added. "Of course, that's not as much of a problem for me. My husband's people seldom pass up a chance to remind me that I'm an outsider."

"I know what you mean," Bruce said. "What I did to Lady Nimue didn't help matters either."

"Who is that?" Catherene asked. "And what happened?"

"She's the noblewoman who killed the King," William answered. "Bruce bound her with iron to keep her from escaping justice."

"What were you thinking?" Catherene asked, horrified by the implications. "Even I know better than that."

"But I didn't," Bruce explained defensively. "Dougal explained it afterward though. I just hope the Tuatha dé will eventually forget about it. But while I'm thinking about it, I've been wondering this ever since I found out about you guys. If you're a Roman culture, why do you call your Beloved by her Greek name? Shouldn't you be calling her Nox?"

William laughed, but his wife was still looking thoughtfully at their two sons.

"As I understand it, she did call herself Nox," William explained. "And until a few hundred years ago that's what my ancestors called her as well. Then they decided that Nyx sounded better and changed it."

"That doesn't exactly scream religious devotion," Bruce observed, frowning. "I thought the people of Haven were filled with religious fervor."

"Only when it suits them," Catherene answered. "They actually tried to tell us that I couldn't have tattoos because their religion forbade it. Back then the only thing I had was this Deathly Hallows symbol," she said, showing him the inside of her wrist.

"I take it you didn't listen," Bruce laughed, taking a closer look at some of the others. "Do you have to leave Haven to get them?"

"No, William learned how," Cat explained. "He was always a good artist, so I just put him to work."

"You're very talented," Bruce said. William gave a mocking bow in response.

"But moving back to trusting the Children of Nyx," Cat continued, "Their actions at Mag Tuired were much more in keeping with what I've come to expect from them. Can I ask a totally unrelated favor of you?"

"Sure," Bruce answered without hesitation.

"Would you take their hands the way you did in the vision that you showed of them in the fire?" she asked.

Bruce moved over and took two small hands in his own. Each of them closed over his fingers. Looking up in excitement, he found both parents looking sadly down at the two boys.

"They always do that," William explained. Catherene looked heartbroken.

"I'm so sorry," Bruce whispered.

"Well," Cat said, collecting herself. "That's not what you came for. Let's start off by seeing if you can sense the messy energy flows you're creating."

Bruce left their home an hour and a half later with a horrible headache. During that time he'd begun to understand some of the frustrations that William and his wife had experienced with trying to figure out how the Tuatha dé worked certain magics. Energy flows that were perfectly obvious when he shared Cat's senses utterly disappeared when he tried to sense them on his own.

He didn't understand why his precognition didn't help him in any way as it usually did. It was almost like the instruction manual that had taken him this far was missing a chapter and he was going to have to muddle through just like everyone else who had to learn a new skill.

"Are you okay?" a pleasant voice asked.

He looked up to find the attractive woman who'd smiled at him in the corridor on his previous visit. She was dressed in designer jeans and a pale silk blouse.

"Who, me?" he asked.

"You are the only other person here," she answered, smiling boldly at him again.

"I'm sorry," he stammered, "You caught me off guard. Yes, I'm okay. I've overworked myself and gotten a headache."

"Would you mind?" she asked, moving closer to reach out and place her hand on the back of his neck.

"Uh, sure…"

Her hand was warm, but the sensation of cold moved briefly up the back of his neck and skull and the throbbing in his temples receded to a dull ache.

"Are you a healer?" he asked.

"Not even remotely," she laughed. "I just cooled the blood passing through the artery enough to reduce the inflammation and pain. You could have done the same thing yourself with a cold compress."

"Well, thanks," he said awkwardly. "It feels much better now. I'm Bruce by the way."

"I know," she said, letting her fingertips slide lightly down his spine. "You and your friend are the only outsiders, beside Catherene, that have been inside Haven for a very long time. You should come to the festival tonight."

"I don't think we're allowed," he said.

"The council has given you permission to come and go as you please," she explained. "It is only your friend who has been forbidden."

"Well, we're sort of a package deal," he said regretfully. "Maybe I'll see you another time."

"That's a shame," she said, pouting slightly. "It isn't often that I have an opportunity to speak with anyone new. If you change your mind, ask for Antonia."

Megan had been sitting in one of the cabin's armchairs for quite some time, turning her senses inward. It was the first time she'd tried to intentionally access the memories that she'd inherited from her late father.

At first, she'd wanted to learn more about him, but if her experiences with the runestones had taught her anything, it was that memories involving herself could be difficult. Furthermore, it seemed almost disrespectful to flip through his memories like a magazine she had no intention of buying at the grocery store. If she was truly honest with herself, she wasn't ready to feel the pain she and her mother had caused him.

Her thoughts turned to learning about the origins of the Tuatha dé. What had their previous world been like, and what had led them to leave it behind? The more she thought about it, the more curious she became about the Dagda.

Please don't, the voice of the Morrigan spoke in her mind.

Don't what?

I feel and see everything that you do. Please don't take me there, the voice whispered.

But aren't they your memories too? Megan asked.

I am a portion of a soul that was trapped in a suit of armor for millennia. I've had all of that time to come to terms with the fact that I will never be allowed to move on and return to his side. Please don't reopen those old wounds. I don't need any more reminders of the love I took for granted for the sake of winning a battle that was lost before it ever began.

So you can't ever move on? Megan asked.

The parts of me that exist within you and your mother will end when you die, and that is a small bit of comfort. But as long as that cursed armor remains whole and functional, a part of me will remain trapped within and I will remain.

I don't want to cause you pain, Megan thought.

Would you like for me to guide you through my memories? You want to know what we once were and there are pieces of my past that can show that to you without summoning the love I can never join again.

I'd like that.

Megan found herself within the body of the Morrigan and she smiled at the reversal. They sat astride a horse at the head of several dozen of her Tuatha dé. The land was lush and green in the valley toward which they rode.

Faint cries of recognition rose from the collection of huts and longhouses below and let her know that her party had been seen. As they neared, many lined the worn trail to greet their arrival with awe, curiosity and fear.

For the ones who considered the Tuatha dé to be nothing more than exaggerated stories meant to keep the young out of trouble, The Morrigan could see the hope for entertainment and distraction from the difficulties of their lives.

For the ones who believed them to be the actual offspring of the gods, there was religious zeal and the euphoria of finding proof in a divine plan that would deliver them from the evils of the world.

And for the ones who profited from the suffering of those weaker than themselves, there was fear for the reckoning to come.

Down past the livestock pens they rode, onward toward the center of the village. There the signal fire had been lit, asking for the Tuatha dé to bring judgement for those who deserved it. When they reached the place where most had gathered, the Morrigan and her retinue dismounted.

A chair had been brought out on which she was expected to sit, most likely from the longhouse of the chieftain himself. So she sat, even though she'd have preferred to walk for a while following their long ride. Perhaps it was time for the Tuatha dé to ignore the fear that walking through the shadows caused among the superstitious commoners of this world.

Three men, each dressed in rags, were brought before her and it was clear that each of them had been recently beaten. The chieftain came forward to speak.

"The body of a girl was found last night at the base of the cliffs," he said.

"This is a sad thing," The Morrigan remarked. "But that is not why you have summoned us."

"No, it is not," he agreed. "They lit the watchfire to bring you here because the young woman was promised to the druids and was expected to follow in their teachings."

"And they are afraid that whoever has committed this murderous act will bring down the wrath of the dark-robed mystics on this village," she added.

The collected villagers cried out in agreement.

"Bring them forth," The Morrigan ordered to the enthusiastic cheers of the villagers.

Fearing what might happen, the three men began to struggle in spite of their injuries. Her people forced the accused to their knees where they were approached by two men and a woman who had been selected to carry out judgement. Then The Morrigan's servants reached out and took the men's heads between their hands. Each of the three stilled at once.

The eyes of all the Tuatha dé present began to glow violet, and the villagers bowed their heads in supplication. The first man whimpered *softly as his judge partook of his memories. After a few moments, the male Tuatha dé declared his innocence. Shortly afterward, the man on the other end did the same.*

But the woman of The Morrigan's clan declared that although the man was innocent in the murder of the druids' apprentice, he was guilty of stealing from his neighbors even when doing so caused a child to starve. "What is your sentence, My Queen?"

"Only death can assure the end of his predatory ways," The Morrigan answered.

Then the eyes of the Tuatha dé glowed brighter as the man's life force was drained to feed the power of those present. When it was done, he slumped to the ground, an empty husk where an evil man had once been.

"Our village owes you our thanks for rooting out this criminal," the Chieftain said.

The Morrigan walked the shadows to stand directly before him.

"Our judgement is not yet complete," she said, looking up into his face and reaching out to grab him by the throat. "The one responsible for the girl's murder remains unpunished."

Then her eyes began to glow even more brightly as she held the large man helpless before her.

"You coveted her not because you truly wanted her for your own, but because she was forbidden to you. She was not the first of your victims, und you did not act alone," she added.

The chieftain's son broke from the others and tried to escape into the woods nearby. Her faithful Scathlahm reached out and threw the young man through the shadows high into the sky overhead. Then the chieftain's son fell screaming to his death in the signal fire that had summoned them, throwing an explosive burst of charred wood and embers across the green grass.

109

The chieftain whimpered, but her hold over him was otherwise complete.

"Now you understand a portion of the pain you have caused the parents of that young woman. You understand the way you have robbed not only them but also the parents of all the others. Your line dies this day and the world will be better off without it.

"Then kill me and have done with it!" the chieftain whimpered when she finally allowed him to do so.

"Kill you?" The Morrigan asked. "And drink in the poisonous essence of your soul? I think not."

One of her men brought a dark robed man through the shadows to stand before him. And then the once brave chieftain began to struggle in earnest, shaking his head violently.

"You're strong," she observed. "Perhaps you'll be able to impress the gods enough to grant you a good afterlife. A man strong enough to take whatever he wants from those weaker than him should have little difficulty enduring the Blood Eagle."

Megan came up from the memory, horrified by the hunger that the judgements had evoked in her.

Why did you show me that?

So you could understand the purpose we were created to fulfill. We were meant to be impartial instruments of justice. We were meant to weed out corruption before it could evolve into the kind of sickness that consumed the world of our birth.

Why did you stop? Megan asked.

We functioned thus for thousands of years until the jealousy of Nyx put an end to it.

Why did she do that?

110

Because we held off the legions when they attempted to invade the lands we had claimed for our own.

It's so weird that history remembers the Romans, but not you, Megan thought.

History has not forgotten me. I was no longer known by my true name in the days of Nyx.

What did they call you?

Boudica.

Chapter XI: Caer Sidhe

Bruce walked the shadows to the outside of the cottage as soon as he was clear of the shield gate and found the utterly amazing sight of Megan, sitting on the steps, unaware of his presence for a moment as she stared at her phone.

"Did I just fast forward into the next century, or are you using your phone for something?" he asked.

"Hey Bruce," she said, glancing up at him and smiling. "How were things with Cat?"

"We made progress," he answered, wishing she'd acknowledged the phone comment. He really was curious about what she was doing. "I can at least feel the energy flows sometimes. Which is more than I could do when I got there. I never expected learning this stuff to be so hard. I did discover that she's read even more fantasy than I have, and I swear that she's got tattoos of everything from Allanon to Zelda."

"Hey," Megan said, looking up in surprise. "I just finished the last one with Allanon. Any idea why the amp abilities don't just come to you in visions the way everything else seems to?" she asked

"Still no clue. How did you spend the afternoon?" he asked, hoping that the pale skinned Scathlahm wasn't part of the answer.

"I had a long talk with the cranky lady," she answered.

"You're kidding," he prompted, coming over to sit next to her on the steps. She was looking something up. "And?"

"She doesn't want me to look at her memories of the Dagda," she answered. "She says it's too painful when she will forever be trapped in the suit of armor she made, unable to join him."

He felt his stomach lurch at the thought of being trapped inside of a barbeque pit for eternity.

"Are you okay?" she asked, looking up from the phone.

"Just hungry," he lied. "What are you looking up, anyway?"

"Boudica."

"As in the one that turned back the Roman legions?" he asked.

"That's the one," she replied, putting the phone down. "And why do I need to use technology when I've got you?"

"Why are you looking up ancient Roman history?" he asked, afraid that he already knew the answer. "Doesn't your memory bank have everything you could need?"

"The cranky lady said that was one of the names she'd been known by," Megan answered. "From what I can tell the stuff in our history is like all the rest of the stuff from back then. They've got hints at the truth that have been distorted by all of the retellings before they were recorded. The historians got the part right about her being married to someone important, although they probably weren't ready to admit that he was something just short of a god. She wasn't captured like the records show, but she did die shortly after the battle from one of the only sicknesses that could touch the Tuatha dé."

"Let me guess," Bruce said. "Something that sounds a lot like tuberculosis?"

Megan nodded.

"Let's go eat," he said. "I don't think I'm ready to think about that too hard right now. My lessons gave me a headache. Any idea what they sent us this time?"

"I don't know, but it smells good and as usual, there's enough to feed us for several weeks."

Inside, the long wooden table was laden with food of so many types that the two of them often didn't eat the same things. Each of them picked up one of the plates that always appeared with the food and began to pile them up.

"Did she tell you anything else?" he asked, sitting down to eat.

"She showed me a memory from way back." Megan answered. "Apparently the Tuatha dé were intended to be judges. She and a bunch of others were called to a village to find out who'd murdered a girl who was supposed to become a druid. They judged the suspects that the village had rounded up, but none of them turned out to be the murderer. Then the Morrigan herself judged the village's leader and discovered that he'd been the one that killed the girl with the help of his son. Her Scathlahm killed the son and she turned the leader over to the druids."

"It would have been kinder to kill him," Bruce said with a grimace. "It sounds a lot like the Tuatha dé were vigilantes."

"She was able to see that he and his son had done it to several other women before the one that was supposed to become a druid," Megan added. "And I thought about the vigilante thing at first too. But is the modern way any better? How often do people like Tony Jones escape punishment because they're powerful? How often do we punish the innocent because we can't find out what really happened?"

"Good point," he agreed.

"And since we can see directly into the accused person's mind," she added, "there's no chance of making a mistake." They both ate in silence for a while after that.

"I wonder if this is the normal sort of thing that the Tuatha dé eat or if it's normally reserved for royalty," he said, eating the last of the food from

114

his plate and thinking about going back for more. One thing was certain, he'd already put on several pounds since Megan's people had started feeding the two of them. "I should probably start running in the mornings again."

Megan froze in mid-bite.

"None of my people go hungry," she whispered, looking over the table. "But most of them will never eat anything like this, not even during their holiday feasts. And here I am shoveling it into my face without a thought of where it comes from."

"In your defense," he said, trying to make up for upsetting her, "I've done a fair bit of shoveling myself."

"I never asked for any of this," she whispered, putting down the bite she was about to eat. "The worst part is that I've got all of this information in my head."

"But it doesn't come to you unless you actively look for it," he finished. "I know exactly what that feels like. That's how I missed everything that happened with Paul. At least you don't have weird blank spots that have a nasty habit of trying to kill you or the people you love."

"Are there any of those coming up?" she asked absently, still staring at all of the food.

"Everything inside of Haven is one big blank spot," he answered. "I just keep telling myself that your mental houseguest knows what she's doing, and I don't need to worry. I haven't felt anything bad while I'm inside either. For tonight, at least, they should be too busy with their Haven founding day party."

"I wonder what that would be like," she said, picking up another plate and beginning to fill it with food.

"They invited me to attend," he said, puzzled by her change of heart where the food was concerned. "But I told them that we are a package deal.

I won't go unless you can."

"That's sweet," she said distractedly, still piling on food. "You should go though. I'm going to make a plate for Dougal. He's never eaten this before. I can't believe I've been sitting here with so much food going to waste while he's living off rabbits outside."

"How do you know that he's never eaten this before?" Bruce asked irritably.

"When I access the collective knowledge of the Tuatha dé, I get more information from those nearest. He's sitting in a tree across the clearing, watching the cabin."

"Maybe I will go," he said on impulse, wanting her to focus on him instead of the man who increasingly seemed to be his rival.

"I think you should," Megan said, not even looking at him. "It might help us to understand their customs better. And we both know it's unlikely that they're ever going to invite me to a party."

"If you're sure," he replied, almost begging her to ask him to stay.

"Just be prepared to tell me all about it as soon as you get home," she said before walking out the door.

He almost turned back several times on his long cold walk down to the gate. He'd decided not to walk the shadows in hopes that she'd only been distracted by the realization about the food and that she'd come to her senses any second and come to stop him. After all, it wasn't exactly safe for him to be going alone into Haven. But while he walked, it wasn't the danger or even the cold that made him almost turn back. He didn't want to leave them alone together.

Just before he came into sight of the gate, which wasn't lit in any way that would allow it to be seen at night, someone appeared before him.

"I was starting to think that you wouldn't come," Antonia said quietly.

"I'm pretty sure that I told you I wasn't going to," he answered, surprised by her sudden appearance.

"And yet you are here," she purred.

The gatekeeper bowed respectfully as they passed. Antonia didn't seem to notice.

Apparently the shield also muted the light that passed through from the inside, because the dimmest glow from the outside gave no indication of the near daytime sunlight within. Looking up to find its source, he saw that the dark crystal wasn't so dark any more.

"We talked William into diverting some of the energy into light for tonight," she said, when she noticed the object of his gaze. She wore a fairly traditional Roman stola, although he doubted many back then were made of black and gray silk. Before she dragged him on, he wondered if the choice of materials had been for its slight resemblance to moonsilk.

"I'm not dressed for this," he whispered in her ear. "I should go."

"Not to worry," she said, taking him through a door into a sort of claustrophobic changing room that barely held the two of them. "I came prepared." She pressed a bundle of clothing into his hands and stood there, watching him.

"I don't suppose you could give me a moment?" he said awkwardly when he realized she intended to stay.

She smiled wickedly in reply, but did step out of the room, closing the door behind her. The garment turned out to be a sort of toga-like robe. He remembered hearing that the Romans didn't wear undergarments, and he made the decision that this was indeed not Rome, and he had no intention of doing as the Romans did. A few moments later, he left the changing room feeling extremely uncomfortable.

117

"Not bad!" she exclaimed, "I may be able to steal you away from the Danann and make a proper Child of Nyx out of you yet. Have you eaten?"

"Yes," he answered.

"But this is a feast," she pouted. "Are you sure you can't eat more?"

"Probably," he said with resignation that he hoped didn't show where his seductive host would notice.

"Wow," she said when she slipped her bare arm through his, shuddering when their skin made contact. Laughing lustily, she pressed her silk clad body against him as she led him toward the wealthiest part of Haven.

He knew it was just the sensation of amplifying her abilities, but it was still hard to think about anything with her so close. He found her perfume pleasant, although it would have probably put him in the hospital before he'd bonded with Megan. The mere thought of his friend made him feel guilty just long enough to remember that she was probably eating with Dougal at that very moment. But as warm as Antonia's skin felt against him, she remained shielded so tightly that he could barely sense her presence with his extended senses.

As they moved deeper into the cavern, simple tile floors gave way to elaborate mosaic scenes, most of which depicted a dark-haired woman in armor. In some, she led armies from a chariot pulled by hellhounds. In others, she presided over the sacrifices her children brought her from a jewel-encrusted throne of black stone inlaid with gold.

Murals covered the walls, portraying what Bruce suspected to be the history of the Children of Nyx. He tried to ignore how many depicted the subjugation of those with black hair, pale skin and violet eyes.

At last they arrived at a tall, intricately carved wooden door that reminded him of the ones at the Academy library until he noticed what the multitude of entwined bodies that made up the scene were doing. Blushing, he averted his eyes, But Antonia didn't even hesitate as she opened it with a wisp of thought, revealing the decadence within.

The music caught his attention at first, played by a trio of musicians in one corner. Though not unpleasant to hear, it sounded utterly unfamiliar. Several women danced in the center of the room, dressed in silks more to accent their movements than cover their bodies.

Antonia led him past a heavily laden table to sit on a sort of low backless couch. No sooner were they seated than young men and women dressed in simple white robes placed heavy golden plates and goblets laden with food and wine into their hands.

Thick rugs covered the floor and loosely draped fabrics painted the walls in riotous color. Heady incense filled the air, making it hard for him to concentrate on any of his normal senses.

As if that weren't enough, Bruce noticed that not only were he and Antonia the youngest people in the room by at least two or three decades, but everyone in the room also seemed to be watching him with an inordinate amount of interest. Becoming even more self-conscious than he'd been before, he couldn't seem to find a way to juggle the food, drink and Antonia all at the same time.

She, however, appeared to have no such difficulty. At any moment it felt like she had at least half of her body in contact with his. Given that he'd never had a woman show anything close to that level of interest in him before, he thought he handled himself fairly well. Now if he could just make it through the meal without falling off of the couch or dumping the heavy plate on his extremely friendly host, he'd be happy.

"You don't drink wine," Antonia whispered with her lips brushing his ear and neck as she spoke.

"Not usually," he admitted quietly. "And I don't think it would be a good idea for me to get drunk and make a fool of myself in front of your people."

"You don't have to play the diplomat tonight. Festivals are meant to make fools of us all. But to be honest, I'm not particularly fond of strong drink myself. Would you like to see my workshop?"

"I think just about anywhere would be more comfortable for me than this," he answered hopefully.

"Then let's get out of here," she suggested, rising gracefully from the couch and pulling him with her.

"What about our dishes?" he asked, glancing back at the plates and goblets.

"That's what servants are for," she giggled.

Drunken couples staggered down the hallways, barely casting a second glance at Bruce as they passed. More than anything, he wanted to get out and return to the cabin.

"What is it that you do in your workshop?" he asked, trying to keep track of all the twists and turns in the underground passages so that he could find his way back later.

"I unlock the secrets of the ancient artifacts that come into our possession," she said importantly. Then she giggled and added, "At least that's what I try to do. I'm unsuccessful more often than I would like."

"You're kidding," he said, noticing the transition between decadence and utilitarian as they moved back into the area near the school.

"Why would I kid about that?" she asked, looking at him strangely.

"Sorry, poor choice of words. That sounds very interesting."

"Much better," she purred as she led him through two very large and stout iron doors. The cavernous space beyond held machines and devices that he'd have liked to spend more time exploring, but Antonia had other ideas. Leading him into the next chamber, she stopped at a workbench and stool.

"I take it that this is it?" he asked, looking around in interest. All around the room were tables and shelves which were piled high with seemingly random collections of things that looked to the untrained eye to be completely unremarkable.

"This is where I spend almost all of my time," she admitted, picking up an old amulet. "This is my current project."

"Can I see it?" he asked, and she happily passed it to him. "This isn't an artifact," he announced after a moment.

"How can you tell?" she asked, frowning.

"It was originally enchanted to allow someone who isn't gifted to communicate over long distances with someone who is. I made something similar for my brother and sister. It was created by a very powerful...woman, I think. Yes..." he said with more confidence after studying it for a moment, "It was definitely a woman. It's just a necklace now that its creator has died. She must have really been something when she was alive for it to still have this much memory of magic so long after she passed."

"Now who's kidding?" she asked in astonishment. "You're serious?"

"It's all there," he said, enjoying her reaction.

"I've spent the better part of three months working with that damn thing, and you unravel all of its secrets within seconds of touching it for the first time." Then, taking his face between her hands, she kissed him.

The amulet came back to life in his hands, and he worried for an instant he'd turned it into a true artifact.

"What did you just do?" she asked, taking it from his hands. "It practically radiates magic now. You've reawakened it!"

"It's not too hard to do that with something that's been enchanted before," he said, trying to figure out how to escape with the least amount of embarrassment.

121

"Are you sure you're not just trying to impress my niece?" a voice came from the doorway behind them.

Bruce turned to find the old seer watching them closely. She was still dressed in the same traditional robes she'd been wearing the first time that he'd seen her.

"I knew I'd find the two of you here," Priscilla said.

"You wouldn't be much of a seer if you didn't," Antonia observed. "Bruce just saved me months of research. He says it's a communication device for the ungifted and that it's old."

"Probably French then," the old woman said, picking it up and turning it over in her hands as she looked closer. "There was a coven there in the sixteenth century that worked with a fair number of norms."

"Well," Bruce said, feeling awkward. "I've had a lot of fun tonight, but I should probably be going. Thank you for inviting me."

"Thank you for saving me several more months of work," Antonia said, smiling at him in a predatory way that made him extremely uncomfortable.

"Please accept my apology for the cool reception you received upon entering our city," the old woman said.

"I understand," he said. "Megan is a good person though. She'd never hurt anyone."

"Even when she judges them?" Priscilla asked quietly.

"I should be going," he said, really wanting to leave now. "Thank you again for a wonderful evening."

"Bruce," the old woman persisted. "Would you allow me to show you my visions so that you can interpret them for yourself? Perhaps you will see hope where I could not."

He didn't relish the idea of having this old crone in his head. However, he was extremely curious about seeing the visions of another seer. After all, wasn't it possible that he would be able to see something that she'd missed and by extension lift the persecution of his friend? Maybe this was the whole reason the Morrigan had brought them there.

Rather than speak and risk having his voice break out of sheer nervousness, he nodded, stepped toward her and lowered his outermost shields. He did, however, keep the other parts shielded lest she try to take liberties with what he knew about the Tuatha dé.

The touch of her hand on his shoulder was gentle, but instead of that reassuring him, it put him in the mindset of insects crawling over his bare skin. But her thoughts, in utter contrast to her touch, bludgeoned him with the force of her mind and left him reeling.

The Children of Nyx danced by the light of cold green flames. The festival field raised misty tendrils of fog around and between the revelers. Strange music compelled them, stirring them into a frenzy of movement. Enraptured by the lust of their movements, they remained unaware of the strangers in their midst until the shadows themselves came alive. Helpless, they watched as the Dark Queen reached for Antonia, her eyes glowing in judgement.

The young people of Haven fled the field, seeking the safety of the gates. Two men carried a woman on a stretcher. When they tried to take her to the infirmary, she whispered that their only chance to survive could be found in the workrooms.

Explosions ripped through Haven, collapsing corridors and leaving huge open spaces where there had not been any before. Afterward, the citizens of the city searched frantically for survivors. None of the children could be found.

Dressed in moonsilk, The Dark Queen demanded entrance to the city. When they refused, she shook the very mountain around them with her anger. When lashing out with her magic failed to gain her admission, she summoned an army thousands strong to lay siege to Haven.

Bruce carried a sword in his hand as he lashed out at something down one of the corridors, sending a wall of flame toward an unseen assailant with William at his side. Behind them, several dozen frightened children followed Catherene. A loud hyena-like cry split the air and prompted them to run.

An explosion ripped through the uppermost levels of the mountain, sending clouds of smoke and dust through the lower tunnels. The Dark Queen raised her head and smiled.

A blinding flash of light preceded the fall of the shield gate. The Tuatha dé swarmed through corridors with unconscious children from the city in their arms.

The Children of Nyx lay motionless across the field that lay before the once great city of Haven. A vortex of clouds swirled in the sky overhead. A storm the likes of which Wyoming had never seen brewed overhead.

Deep within a vast and unnatural space that had opened within the mountain, The Dark Queen stood with her arms outstretched in triumph. Her army knelt by the thousands around her as the dim light of her creation bathed them all in violet. Energy arced between her body and the cave around her. With a smile of victorious glee she caught fire and began to burn from within.

Megan sat at the edge of the cliff, puzzling through why the Morrigan had brought her and Bruce to Haven. Why had her mother been sent to harass the Children of Nyx and stir up a virtual hornet nest of animosity right before Megan would come? Surely that hadn't been the only path along the future in which she made contact with William? Below those thoughts lay the real reason why she sat in that particular spot. Why had she encouraged Bruce to go?

Dougal appeared at her side, and for once he didn't drop to one knee.

"You shouldn't be alone out here," he said, before quietly adding, "Megan."

"I'm safe enough," she replied. "Did you enjoy the food?"

"The food was wonderful," he answered. "But you misunderstood me. No one this side of the gods has the right to exclude you. You should be surrounded by others like yourself, not exiled by hedonists who have forgotten their heritage in favor of modern amusements."

"What if I happen to like modern amusements?" she asked playfully. "What then?"

"I know just the place," he said, extending his hand to help her up.

Then, without warning, he walked the shadows with her.

Unprepared for the jackhammering bass that reverberated through not only her chest, but the floor beneath her feet as well, Megan ripped her hand from his and covered her ears. They'd traveled to some dark cavernous room in which lights clawed through the darkness, raking through frozen instants of chaotic movement and revealing a sea of alabaster skin.

Before her mind began to unravel the chaotic thread before her, the Tuatha dé felt her presence and froze. The crowd turned toward her in one seemingly choreographed movement and dropped to one knee. The lights came up, and the music stopped, leaving an echoing silence in its wake. She couldn't help but notice when they did so, that a sprinkling of others with wider varieties of skin color and dress remained standing like the cast-offs in some monumentally strange game of musical chairs.

Megan almost fled back to the cottage, or maybe to the familiar comfort of Nickelville. But a woman who bore a striking resemblance to

125

her father's first Scathlahm rushed forward in a nearly obscene dress and took her by the hand.

"Forgive us, My Queen," she said, her voice echoing through the vast silence. "But my idiot brother did not warn us that he would be bringing you here to join us."

"Please stand," Megan called to them. "I really don't expect everyone to do that when you see me. I just wanted to meet others like myself."

It took them a moment to start moving, and the sudden burst of mental chatter almost overwhelmed Megan with so many of her people this physically close to her. Eventually they started to rise.

"If you're anything like this degenerative lot," her Scathlahm's sister muttered, "Then the kingdom is probably doomed." Then, turning to the crowd, "You heard her, pretend everything is normal and stop staring at her like it's the first time you've seen a royal!" The lights went off and the music resumed.

"But it is the first time," Megan said quietly, where only her Scathlahm and his sister could hear. "I can feel it from all of you. I've never been around so many…"

"Of your faithful subjects?" the woman finished for her. There was something in the way she held herself that reminded her of Jade. "Please don't think badly of them. They just come here to let off steam and…"

"Be young," Megan said. "You've all had to grow up fast after Mag Tuired."

"This is so weird," the woman said. "I mean, I've always been told that your family knows everything that we do, but it's strange to see it in person."

"I'm sorry," Megan said. "I'm eavesdropping on your thoughts without your permission. I really should go."

"Please don't," the bold woman pleaded, holding tightly to her hand.

126

"The only thing you've done wrong is fail to burn my inconsiderate brother alive, and there's still plenty of time to remedy that mistake." Then she turned to Dougal. "Did you even warn her that you were bringing her someplace like this before you dropped her in the middle of a mosh pit?"

"No," he admitted sheepishly.

"I'm not dressed for this," she said, looking around. "You're Brighid... Sorry, that just popped into my head."

"Probably from this jerk," the woman growled, punching him in a way that made her resemble Jade even more. "Everyone but him calls me Bri."

At last the majority of the club's inhabitants began to return to what they were doing before she'd arrived. Once again, she noticed the others.

"Some of them aren't Tuatha dé," Megan observed. "Who are they?"

This earned Dougal another hard glare from his sister.

"I was rather hoping that you wouldn't notice them. They're the children of some of the other Beloved. We're not really supposed to hang around together."

"Why not?" Megan asked.

"The elders from all of our tribes want to avoid the kind of conflict we have with the Children of Nyx, who incidentally are not allowed here," Dougal explained.

"All of the different groups are just supposed to keep to themselves," Bri continued. "Which isn't too bad for the Tuatha dé. Even after Mag Tuired, there were still a few thousand of us. But some of the others have either declined to the point where no more than a few dozen remain or they were never numerous to begin with. It's hard on their young because there isn't anyone similar that they can talk to. We never intended for this merging of the different tribes to occur, but when they heard that we'd created Caer Sidhe, a few of the bolder ones asked if they could come too."

127

"This is great!" Megan said, thinking immediately of how much she'd like to bring Bruce.

"So you're not going to shut us down?" Bri asked.

"Why would I do that?" Megan asked. "As far as I'm concerned you're providing an important public service."

Bri relaxed visibly.

"Where are we anyway?" Megan asked.

"This is the basement of a building in a failed Chinese mining town." Bri explained. "No one comes within miles of here."

"The locals think it's haunted," Dougal added.

Bri looked extremely guilty.

"You've got something to do with that, don't you?" Megan asked.

"Just some strategically placed wards of misdirection that make people feel extremely paranoid. Their own imaginations take care of the rest."

"Can the others walk the shadows too?" Megan asked. This was the most fascinating situation she'd ever encountered.

"Teleportation seems to be unique to our crowd," Dougal answered. "We have a system worked out where they contact us and we pick them up."

As Megan watched the dancing crowd before her, she noticed a familiar face. The short haired woman of the Wild Hunt danced past in jeans and a t-shirt, making Megan feel a little bit better since that's what she was wearing as well. The girl's partner, a dark-skinned man with brightly colored clothes, looked as if he'd have preferred to avoid Megan's gaze. When the girl noticed Megan looking at her, she squealed with delight and dragged her reluctant partner toward where her Queen stood.

"Greetings, Your Majesty," she said, almost taking a knee until she remembered she wasn't supposed to do that. "Do you remember me?"

"Of course I do," Megan said, unable to keep from smiling at the enthusiastic girl. "You're the member of the Wild Hunt that found me."

"You were serious about that?" her dance partner asked, looking horrified.

"I told you I was," the young woman said proudly. "I'm the youngest member to ever be admitted to the order. And they're lucky to have me because they would have never found you without me."

"I'm sorry, you know who I am, but I don't know your name."

"It's Maeve," the young woman answered uncertainly, looking at Bri as if something might be wrong.

"Our Queen believes that we should have our own privacy," Bri explained.

"Oh," Maeve said, "That is such a relief. I mean, like just a few minutes ago, after I knew that you were here, and I was trying to only think good thoughts, I looked at Okay here, and let me tell you, what I was thinking about him when he was dancing was so not okay." Then she covered her mouth in horror.

"I think we've all got a pretty good idea of what you were thinking," Bri laughed.

"Everyone calls me Okay," the young man at Maeve's side said by way of introduction, managing to keep his dignity in spite of his companion's inability to keep her thoughts to herself. "And I honestly prefer it that way. Our language is an old one and there are nuances not usually noticed by people from outside of our small group. I would also prefer that others not know my true name since I am most certainly not supposed to be here."

"Maeve," Megan said, trying to get the girl's attention before she drifted off into the crowd again. "How exactly did you find me? Something changed a little over a year ago. Was that you?"

"Yes," Maeve said happily. "I can't believe you noticed!"

"We couldn't catch a break," Megan explained. "We'd barely get settled before you guys were after us again. That's why we ended up in that apartment in New York."

"That place was awful," the girl said with a shudder. "I couldn't even go up to your floor. I don't know how anyone with any sort of empathy could spend more than a few hours there without losing their mind."

"It almost killed me," Megan admitted. "But what did you start doing that changed how you found us?"

"In the beginning I hacked into the security footage of all the places that faced where you and the former Queen had been staying. That's how I found out about the old truck you were using. Nice idea by the way. As soon as you got inside that thing, we totally lost our lock on you. But once I knew you guys were keeping the same vehicle, I started using the traffic cams to track where you went. That way, we didn't have to start off with the big grids we'd used before. As soon as we lost track of your truck, we'd go to that area and start searching with a much smaller target area."

"We had no idea the Tuatha dé had started using modern technology to find us," Megan said in exasperation. "So you weren't even tracking me most of the time? You were following the one thing we always took with us because we needed its iron frame to disguise my presence!"

"Right up until you disappeared out where there are no traffic cameras and into the black hole that is Nickelville, Texas."

"It was good to meet you, your Majesty," Okay said when Maeve paused to breathe, "But I must go."

"I don't think I'm ever going to get used to being called that," she admitted. "It was nice to meet you as well."

"You probably should soon," he added. "Like the rest of us, you and yours must remain hidden from the modern world. But among all the children of the Beloved, you and your line are known and respected. I offer my condolences on the death of your father, and I pray that your reign will be long and peaceful, Queen Megan."

"Thank you," she replied, touched.

"Maeve," he said, "Would you please?" In reply, she placed her hand through the crook of his arm as if they were going to take a stroll and disappeared.

"Megan," Bri said, "I've got an idea. You've never experienced dancing as one of the Tuatha dé, have you?"

"I couldn't," Megan answered, panicking at the thought, "I mean, I don't want to exclude the others just so you can all entertain me."

"A chance to see the fair folk dance is the main reason why they come," Dougal said. "Trust us, they won't mind."

"I'm not dressed for this," Megan said, casting around for another excuse.

"I have dresses that will fit you," Bri offered.

"No," Megan whispered, mortified by the thought. "I'd look like an adolescent boy in something like that. I doubt I could pull off your tamest clothing."

"You are the most beautiful woman I've ever seen," Dougal said. "It doesn't matter what you wear."

"What is it that you truly fear?" Bri asked, moving closer and looking closely at her eyes. "You know everything that we know. The knowledge is in your head, and dancing with us is in your blood."

"But what if I didn't get that part of being Tuatha dé? What if that part of me is human?" Megan asked and at last they understood.

"Then you'll learn," Bri answered with a dismissive shrug. "You will never disappoint us. You are our heart. Just give us one dance, and then I'll raid the bar for meade so we can go to your cottage and tell stories around the fire."

"Just about anywhere would be less stressful than here," Megan said, unknowingly echoing the words Bruce would use a short time later.

The lights came up and both of them each took one of her hands, leading her between them to the dance floor. She realized Dougal hadn't been exaggerating when he'd said that the outsiders wanted to see them dance. When the music began to play, running through her soul like fire, she realized she had nothing to fear at all.

Chapter XII: Separate Ways

Megan woke in the midst of an earthquake with her head pounding and an all-consuming hope that she'd just die soon. Light from the window burned directly into her soul.

"Here," Bruce's voice boomed from nearby, "Drink this."

The world stopped moving and two pills dropped into one hand and a glass of water into the other. She gratefully accepted both and then gave him back the glass before trying to pull her pillow over her face.

"Sit up," he commanded, and she complied just to get him to stop talking so loudly. A hot cup was placed into her hand and she took a greedy sip.

"Ugh," she complained. "You never put enough sugar in it."

"I'm oh so sorry," he muttered before adding, "Your Majesty." She risked the brain damage of sunlight to crack an eye open and get a better look at him.

"Are you mad at me?"

"Gee," he sneered, walking toward the door. "What gave it away? I'm gone for a few hours, and I come back to find you drunk off of your royal butt, singing Gaelic pub songs with two of your loyal subjects."

"I don't speak Gaelic," she muttered, closing her eyes again. Why was he talking so loudly?

"Well then maybe it was the grumpy lady. If so, her tongue gets pretty loose after a few beers."

"It wasn't beer," she whispered. "Do we really have to do this right now?"

"I know," he said coldly. "It was meade. I got a long good smell of it while I was holding your hair back while you puked. Funny how your new friends didn't stick around for that part."

"Why are you so angry?" she asked.

"That's why you were so eager to get rid of me last night," he said, suddenly quiet. "I was in the way. Well, that won't be a problem today. Enjoy your breakfast."

Then he stormed out the door with his laptop, and the energy of him walking the shadows made a little explosion of light inside her head where she couldn't block it out.

In his anger, Bruce came out further from the gate than he'd intended. As soon as he arrived, he was overtaken by the strong sense that he was not alone. Casting his senses out over his immediate surroundings, he looked for the eyes that watched him. When he found none, he wrote it off to lack of sleep and continued on toward Haven. Perhaps it had been some sort of ward, he thought.

Not particularly wanting to go back inside, he sat down just outside the gate and opened his laptop. If he was lucky, the signal would be strong enough to update Sam's portfolio without going inside where the shields interfered with his foresight. It began to lag at once and he knew he'd have to go somewhere else.

"I thought I might find you here," a familiar voice drifted from the empty space before him. Then Antonia, dressed a bit more on the fashionable side of normal, appeared before him. "Why are you sitting down here?"

"I needed both the internet and my foresight at the same time," he said. "And I can't get the latter inside the gate."

"What for?" she pressed.

"Just helping a good friend back home."

"Have you broken your fast yet?" she asked.

"No," he answered and got an idea, "You?"

She shook her head.

"You've been away from Haven before, right?" he asked.

"Yes, but not often."

"Is there anywhere you've eaten breakfast that you'd like to return to? Distance isn't a problem."

"There was a place in the French Quarter…"

"I could definitely do New Orleans this morning," he said, remembering one of the courtyard gardens that they'd visited while on vacation several years previously. Then he reached out, took her hand and walked the shadows with her.

With a gasp of surprise, she pulled closer to him, and he was once again aware of the way she smelled.

"It must be so wonderful to be able to go anywhere you want without needing to rely on anyone else," she marveled.

"It does have its uses," he replied, utterly distracted by the closeness of her. Then, trying to focus, "Let's see if we can find the place you were talking about."

It wasn't far, and they talked while they walked. She wanted to know everything he could tell her about what it was like outside of Haven. For just a second, he was back on the school bus asking a certain dark haired and pale skinned girl many of the same questions. But he really didn't want to think about his friend right now.

After a while, he got tired of lugging the laptop around and sent it back to his bed at the cottage. He'd have plenty of time to update the portfolio later.

He tried repeatedly to turn the discussion around toward her, because he really was very interested in what life was like among the Children of Nyx, but she always steered it back toward him. Truth be told, it was nice to have someone take such an interest in him for a change.

From there they walked the French Quarter, and he couldn't help but notice that she never passed up an opportunity to touch him. Whether it was a brush of her hand against his or the way she'd rest her leg against his when they sat down somewhere.

"It's a bit addictive," she admitted while they ate lunch. "The way it feels when you amplify my power that is. But that has nothing to do with how much I've enjoyed this time with you today."

He told her felt the same way, and if she'd held her shields less rigidly, she might have identified the lie as he spoke it. No matter how beautiful he might find her, or how much he might enjoy her company, he'd have much rather been there with Megan.

After Bruce's loud departure, Megan did indeed go back to sleep. She wasn't sure how much later she woke, but she did at least feel as if she might live through the horrible prospect of leaving the bed. When she did, she spent a while alternating between anger and guilt in equal measure before finally stepping back and trying to see how things had looked from Bruce's point of view. She grudgingly admitted that it didn't look good and that she'd have been terribly hurt if he'd ditched her to spend time with other people, particularly since he'd left everything behind in his life just to be with her.

Furthermore, they were in foresight blank spot territory, which always made him tense. He was probably concerned that last night's behavior was going to become a frequent occurrence.

She ate breakfast alone, once again horrified by the amount of food on the table. She thought briefly about taking some out to Dougal. But then she remembered that was what she'd been doing when Bruce had suddenly changed his mind and left. She'd have to be more considerate of his feelings in the future.

Hearing a commotion outside. Megan looked out the window and found Dougal and Bri sparring.

She doubted Bruce would be back any time soon, so she pulled on her shoes and refilled her coffee cup to go sit on the steps and watch. Just a few yards away, her Scathlahm and his sister circled each other with the dirk-like utility knives that all of the Tuatha dé seemed to carry. Megan couldn't tell that the previous night's drinking had much of an effect on Bri. Dougal, however, was in trouble.

While Megan watched, his eyes darted to her and Bri took advantage of his momentary lapse in concentration to sweep his legs out from under him and pin him to the ground with her blade against his throat.

"You're not going to be much of a protector if you lose concentration every time she looks at you,' Bri scolded. "We've got a lot of ground to make up."

"What do you mean?" Megan asked.

"Given the unique nature of your, um, absence," Bri explained. "His weapons training wasn't as dedicated as it normally would have been."

"My time was split between combat and tracking," he added, accepting his sister's hand as she pulled him to his feet. "I spent more time training under Cian than any of the Wild Hunt."

"He's the older guy, right?" Megan asked.

"He's the only member of the order that survived Mag Tuired,"

Dougal said.

"And he was actually being prepared for burial when they realized he was still bleeding," Bri added. "Even though my idiot brother isn't the best fighter, he did manage to track you to Nickelville several weeks before the rest even came close."

"Cian isn't very fond of you or Bruce," Dougal added.

"Then he should have released the lock on us when I asked him," Megan replied.

"Did your friend actually dare to place a trace on the Master of the Hunt?" Bri asked. "I've been wanting to know about that since I heard."

"Yes," Dougal answered. "It was most impressive. I might not agree with what he did afterward, but Bruce is certainly a force to be reckoned with."

"So is this an open lesson?" Megan asked.

"What do you mean?" Bri asked, suddenly uneasy.

"I haven't had any time in the ring for weeks. I don't want to get rusty."

"Your Majesty," Bri said hurriedly, her accent thickening in concern. "We can't bring arms against you. T'would be treason."

"No it wouldn't," Megan said, putting her cup down on the steps and walking closer. "But don't go easy on me or I will be angry."

"She was trained by one of the greatest warriors to ever live," Dougal admitted to which Bri rolled her eyes.

"I'm surprised he didn't wet himself in sheer adoration when your mother passed the Scathlahm's Blade to him," Bri confided. "I think the only reason he ever learned to read was so he could read all of the accounts of her battle with the Children of Nyx for himself."

"But would it offend you if we asked to fight with blunted weapons until we have the measure of your abilities?" Dougal asked.

138

"I notice you all carry those," Megan said, nodding toward the knives they held.

"They're damned useful for everything from carving your meat to a weapon of last resort," Bri explained.

"Where can I get one?" Megan asked, to which Dougal reached out and plucked one from the shadows.

"The armory is full of them," he explained, "Unless you'd prefer one from your personal stash?"

"I have a personal stash of weapons?" Megan asked.

"Eventually you're going to realize that you're a Queen," Bri said with a pained sigh.

"This will do fine, I'll get a belt later," she said, walking over to put it on the step next to her coffee. "But if we can't use knives, how about staves?"

"Your mother's preferred weapon," Dougal observed with a sagely nod. Both he and his sister summoned matching lengths of brass capped wood.

"We should probably teach you how to summon your own," Bri offered.

"Why?" Megan asked.

Before they could react, she reached out and snatched Dougal's weapon with her mind and flew into action, delivering a series of blows that drove his sister back until she finally managed to dig in and return some of what she got. Then Megan walked the shadows to just behind Dougal, who'd only just managed to summon a replacement. Allowing Bri to think her focused on him to the point of forgetting the more lethal opponent, she faded into transparency and jumped through him to attack the surprised warrior and shove her directly into him, taking them both down in a heap.

As she stood there looking down on them, Bri burst into laughter.

"And we were worried about hurting her, Dougie!" she gasped, pushing him over as he tried to rise.

"I hate it when you call me that," he complained.

"Don't take this the wrong way little brother," Bri continued, "But you might very well be the most unnecessary Scathlahm in the history of the Tuatha dé!"

Without warning, Bri disappeared.

Megan spun to look for her in case she intended to continue the exercise. But then Bri appeared next to a tree at the edge of the woods, reached out and plucked a woman dressed in a sweater and jeans from the air.

"I know your kind don't have any manners," Bri growled, drawing her knife once again and holding it meaningfully close to the woman's abdomen, "But we consider it rude to spy on the Queen."

"I'm sorry," the woman stammered loudly enough for Megan to hear before she walked the shadows to her friend's side. "I wasn't trying to spy on you."

"She's scared to death," Megan said, "I don't think she meant any harm."

"But why is she here?" Dougal asked.

"I was trying to work up enough courage to come and talk to you," the woman said, looking at Megan while she spoke. "My brother told me that you knew the scholar Augustus."

"Oh no," Megan said, reaching out to pull the blade back from the frightened woman. "You must be William's sister."

"Yes," she agreed, nodding vehemently.

"Let her go, Bri."

The Scathlahm's sister did so reluctantly, but she didn't return the

140

knife to its sheath.

"August didn't think there would be much of anyone left who remembered who he was," Megan said, finally getting a better look at the frightened woman. Like all of the Children of Nyx, she had dark hair which partially covered the left side of her face. Her dark eyes traveled between each of them, but as she calmed, they came to rest most often on the Scathlahm's sister. Likewise, Bri had looked nowhere else since the woman's appearance.

"Let's start over," Megan said, extending her hand. "I'm Megan, this is Brigid and this is her brother Dougal, who apparently hates being called Dougie."

The look he gave his sister was truly menacing.

"I'm Mariana, and like Augustus, I'm a scholar," she said, extending a hand covered in dime-sized scars which matched the one Megan could just see under the woman's left eye. "I found his manuscripts a few years ago, and they've become the foundation of my work. His ideas were so bold and innovative. No one except William is supposed to be outside the walls with you. But I couldn't pass up a chance to speak with someone who actually knew him."

"That still doesn't explain why you camouflaged yourself," Dougal said.

"When I heard you fighting, I became frightened," she explained apologetically, "I know it was cowardly, but I grew up with the worst sort of bully and that's what I learned to do when she was around."

"I have to admit that there are times when that skill would have come in handy with my own bullies," Megan conceded.

"I'd be honored to teach you how. I'm surprised William hasn't done so already. It is the one skill in which I surpass him.

"Your bully sounds kind of familiar," Megan mused. "She doesn't have red hair, does she?"

"No," Mariana answered, confused. "The Children of Nyx all have black hair, just like the Tuatha dé Danann. Why do you ask?"

"Just wondering," Megan answered. "So yes, August was one of my closest friends. He passed away several weeks ago. I owe my very existence to a kindness he performed for my family a long time ago."

"It breaks my heart that I missed meeting him by such a short time," Mariana said sadly.

"I think he would have loved to meet you. And I know what you mean about his innovation. I had the pleasure of working with him several times, and his magic was nothing short of art."

"Do you know if he continued to write after he and his wife, Aurora, escaped from this place?" Mariana asked.

"His cottage is full of hundreds, maybe even thousands of journals," Megan answered.

Mariana swooned with the thought, swaying on her feet until Bri reached out to steady her.

"I wish I could read them all," Mariana whispered.

"Perhaps I could take you there sometime," Bri offered.

"I would be forever indebted to you," the Child of Nyx said.

"Be careful," Dougal said, looking knowingly at his sister. "She's not someone you want to be in debt to."

"Somehow I don't think I'd mind it at all," Mariana said boldly, holding Bri's eyes. "But I regret that I must return."

Until then, Megan hadn't realized that the Tuatha dé were capable of blushing.

Mariana backed away slowly then faded out of sight as she cloaked herself again.

"Brighid," Dougal scolded quietly. "She's a Child of Nyx. Father would die of shame!"

"Then you'd better say your goodbyes to him," Bri muttered under breath as she tracked the occasional indention in what foliage still remained as Mariana returned to Haven.

Chapter XIII: Not All Remain Lost

Emelia woke with her entire body sore from the exertions of the previous days, still sitting in the rocking chair they'd bought for Megan's nursery. Without thinking, she moved her shoulder and was rewarded with a spearhead of agony that passed clean through from the front to her back, just as if she were reliving the death of her husband all over again.

When she shifted her weight to try and ease some of the pain, something fell from her lap. Then she remembered the Kermit doll. Not wanting to bend over and start the painful wound throbbing again, she reached out with her mind and brought it to her hand. Megan had loved it well. The felt covering was worn through in places, and one of the plastic eyes had been scratched so badly that it didn't really look like an eye anymore. Perhaps Bruce would be able to restore it like he'd done with so many other precious things.

At some point during the night she'd started dreaming about Rip Van Winkle. As a child, her father had read her many childhood stories, and she'd done the same with Megan even when they'd often had to leave the books behind. A favorite they'd shared was the story of dear Mr. Winkle. She could remember many discussions about what it would be like to jump a hundred years into the future. Now, probably after her talk with Kate the previous afternoon, she'd dreamt that she was him and it filled her with despair.

She didn't really want to return to her husband's study yet. But she also didn't want to spend any more time sitting there. She was tired enough that she'd start to drift off again if she did, and she wasn't ready to burn any more time on Earth dreaming of things that could never be here.

So she rose to her feet, still dressed in the previous day's clothing. The Tuatha dé didn't set much store on changing clothing unless it was soiled, and given that only the hottest or coldest temperatures affected their pale skin, they had never evolved the need to sweat. She was glad the trait had manifested in her daughter.

She walked down hallways familiar to the person she'd once been. To be honest, she hardly remembered who that silly girl had been all those years ago. Then she had to remind herself that she'd been gone from here less than a year to those who had remained behind.

The throne room remained largely the same as it had been when she sat there next to him, and it wasn't much different than it had been when she'd been introduced to court.

"I miss you Cara," she whispered. "I wish you were here to help guide me through this mess."

Her armor still stood on display behind the thrones, but the voice of the Morrigan had since moved into her mind, and the delicate lines of the unnamed metal no longer beckoned. When she reached out to rest her palm on its perpetually warm surface, she felt a tiny bit of the Morrigan stir within.

Daragh had replaced several of the paintings closest to where he sat on the throne. All of the new ones were of her, only one of which was a portrait. The rest were unpleasantly realistic renditions of Mag Tuired. She turned away in guilt and disgust.

Then there was the throne. Her hand slipped of its own accord to her abdomen out of habit. She'd been pregnant the last time she'd sat there.

"You would have been a good father," she whispered.

145

"Here you are, your Majesty," the chamberlain's voice came from behind her. "Your breakfast has been placed in your sitting room as you asked."

"Thank you," Emelia responded without looking back at him. "I'll be there shortly."

When she couldn't hold off her responsibilities any longer, she walked slowly back the way she'd come. But she knew there wasn't really any going back, at least not in the way she wanted.

A short time later she sat, picking over a dish that she'd missed often during the years when food had been so scarce. She hoped Megan and Bruce were enjoying the meals she'd planned for them during their time in Haven. It was nice to know that Megan would finally get to sample some of her father's favorite foods.

So far Emelia had discovered that her husband had, for the most part, left the day to day running of the kingdom to others. This might have seemed foolish anywhere else, but given that the Tuatha dé were unanimously tied to the ruling monarch who could see even the most guarded secrets in their hearts, he'd had no reason to fear disloyalty.

But Tyr Sgodl was sparsely populated. After the deaths of almost all adults at Mag Tuired, her husband had made the decision to create enclaves all across Earth where the young could mature at an accelerated rate. Had he not done so, there still wouldn't have been any new generations on the horizon. The down side was that there was now a strong generational gap between the old and the young that eclipsed anything they'd experienced before. The old worried what the future might hold when so few of the Tuatha dé felt truly bound to the world where their ancestors had lived for millennia.

When she returned to the study again, she couldn't help but think about how fast things were moving back home. During the next eighteen days in Tyr Sgodl, a year would pass back in Nickelville. A year from now Sam would be well into his years as a senior citizen, and he would likely be gone the year after that while she still remained.

Sam intended to go home to a well-deserved rest when he locked the doors at Gordon's. But he was lost in thought when he passed his car and not terribly surprised to find himself standing in the middle of the quiet dojo. Sometimes his rebellious feet knew what he needed more than his overworked brain.

He'd only been able to make it in twice over the past week, and even though Mr. Wallace and Jade would never complain, he still felt like he was shirking his responsibilities.

Much of the way he'd come to define himself relied on maintaining order in all the parts of his life. He maintained the time he spent as a martial arts instructor, and he did it well. His pupils left with a better understanding of the world around them and with the confidence to protect both themselves and the ones they loved. He maintained the time he spent at Gordons, providing the town he loved with good food at affordable prices. In return, they gave him something that had been sorely missing after the death of his grandfather: a place where he belonged. And that had been enough for him, at least until she'd wandered back into his life.

He wasn't sure who he was anymore. For a little while, it had almost felt like he had a family again. Watching over Megan had been one of the greatest honors of his life, but now she'd left him behind as well. And as much as he'd like to just go back to the way things had been before, they'd changed not only the man he saw in the mirror, but the rest of Nickelville as well. Furthermore, over the past year and a half, his responsibilities had grown exponentially while his time to fulfill them had not. Instead of

147

maintaining the dojo and the restaurant to the high standards he'd set forth, now he was stretched too thin between too many different responsibilities. He didn't know how much longer he could keep them all afloat.

He changed into his full gi, feeling the need to pay more respect to the dojo after his long absence. He warmed up, letting the familiar movements lull into slumber the restless thoughts that his mind refused to release. Then he moved through the dancelike forms, allowing him to separate from thoughts of friends lost, the growing number of people that depended on him, and also from his slow progress with the Fates. But most of all, it helped to distance himself from how much he longed to see *her*. And on that last account, it took him a long time to clear the ledger.

When he finally reached a place where he just felt like himself, he cued up a song for which he'd been choreographing a competition piece before she'd walked into his restaurant that night, and for a brief time, back into his life. When the music started, he was pleasantly surprised that his body flowed with the familiar movements as if he hadn't put his entire life on hold.

"You've been holding out on me," Jade said from one of the chairs that lined the side of the mat, making him jump.

"How long have you been there?" he asked.

"Long enough to be glad that I came over," she answered. "I just locked up over at the Palace and I wondered why the dojo lights were still on."

"How is Kate?" he asked.

"She only comes in for matinees now," Jade answered, searching his face as she spoke. "She hasn't said it yet, but she'll probably retire sometime in the next few months."

"She's earned it," he said, coming to sit down next to her.

"Can I ask you a favor?" she asked.

148

"You know you don't even have to ask."

"Will you teach me that one?" she said, nodding to where he'd just been practicing. "I really need something that makes me remember the way things used to be."

"Is everything okay?" he asked, concern flavoring both his voice and expression.

"Compared to some of the things we've been through, it's an absolute paradise," she answered.

"But?"

"But now that things are settling down, I need to go back to being more like I used to be," she whispered, revealing at last how lost she felt. "Too much of who I used to be relies on empty places where so many of my favorite people used to be. For a little while I'd like to be just a martial artist learning a really cool kata from the most amazing sensei in the world."

Then she hugged him, and he realized he'd come here looking for exactly the same things.

Chapter XIV: A Snowball's Chance in Haven

Bruce woke alone in the cabin with a huge fire roaring in the hearth. Blissfully warm air greeted him when he climbed out of the bed and hurriedly changed into fresh clothing. Then, hoping that he wasn't expecting too much, he looked over at the coffee pot and saw that it was full.

"My life is dangerously close to perfection," he whispered, pouring himself a cup and sitting down at the table to drink it. It was nice to wake up slowly for a change and without any real responsibility. It was one of the days when William couldn't come down, and Catherene had given Bruce the day off. So he sat there in the grandeur of the most lavishly decorated stone cottage in history, wondering where his friend was and hoping that the awkwardness of the previous day had run its course and they could just be like they were before.

When at last he could stand the curiosity of what Megan might be doing outside no more, he bundled up and opened the door. Outside, the world had turned white and the snow seemed to absorb the normal sounds, making it eerily quiet. He squinted against the unexpected brightness.

A snowball hit him in the side of the head, sending cold mushy lumps down his collar. The last of the coffee in his cup left an ugly brown stain in the snow.

Megan's laughter danced in the cold air, and he wondered, for the second it took for the next snowball to hit him just below the ear, if all of the women in the McGeehee line might not have just a bit of the bardic power.

Dropping the now empty cup into a snowdrift where it wouldn't break, he snatched up a handful of snow and hurled it at his best friend. She faded out just before it reached her and reappeared next to him, tackling him into the same snowdrift where he'd dropped the cup. It didn't cut either of them when it broke, but he made a mental note to find the pieces and mend them later since it was his favorite one.

Realizing that revenge was at hand, he snatched up a handful of snow and forced it down the back of her sweater. She smiled at him in mild amusement.

"It's so not fair that cold doesn't affect you," he said, gasping in the cold air.

Megan looked up at the line of the roof overhead and smiled. When he followed her gaze he found Bri and Dougal watching from where they sat comfortably on the peak of the roof.

"I was just telling Mari how regal our Queen is," Bri called down to them.

In response, nearly a cubic yard of snow disappeared from the drift, including his broken cup to drop on the Scathlahm's sister, dislodging the young woman and sending her sliding down the steep pitch of the roof.

Bruce reached out and plucked the broken shards of the cup from the falling snow and sent them to the kitchen table. His best friend really seemed to have it in for that cup for some reason.

The Tuatha dé landed lightly, turned her fall into a roll while snatching up a handful of snow and sending it flying toward her Queen. Dougal found this profoundly funny until his sister knocked him from the summit with a flick of her hand and sent him tumbling down the back of the cottage, only to reappear a few feet in front of her with a snowball in hand that he fired point blank into her face.

The snowball fight that followed was probably unlike any that had ever occurred before with its participants winking in and out of existence and snowballs following their targets like missiles.

Although Bruce had fun it, no one seemed to enjoy themselves as much as Dougal, making him think that his rival might not have had much of a childhood.

Mariana appeared a short time later, appearing as usual out of thin air as she uncloaked herself.

"Is this open to anyone?" she asked, smiling broadly at Bri who had just been tackled into a snowdrift by her brother.

"You are always welcome," Bri said, kicking her brother in the side as she passed him and making him laugh even harder.

"Can we build a snowman?" Bruce asked. "We never get snow like this in Nickelville."

"I tried a few times as a kid, but Mom didn't know how," Megan said.

"Because it never snows in Nickelville," Bruce repeated.

"We grew up in the Florida enclave," Bri said, her eyes still on the Child of Nyx. "This is as new to us as it is to you."

"That's okay," Mari said. "I know how. I spent a lot of time outside of the walls as a kid. It was the best way to avoid bullies that wanted to take away my books."

"It sure beats a hole in the bushes," Megan said, smiling at Bruce who had stopped to blow the moisture out of his clothing. One of these days she needed to get him to show her how to do that without tearing them to shreds.

"It sounds like you and I had similar childhoods, Mariana," he said when he was done. "One of my bullies tried to kill me with ragweed."

"Mine set my shoes on fire," Mari said with a smile that didn't reach her eyes.

"That was most unkind," Dougal said, noticing the change in her mood.

"My feet were in them at the time," she added.

Even Bruce could feel the anger rise in Bri, and he wasn't bound to her the way Megan was.

"After I started walking again, I got so good at cloaking that she could never find me," Mari added.

"You should show us how," Bruce said.

"To cloak?" Mariana asked.

"No," he said with a grin, "the snowman."

"But we would like the other sometime soon as well," Megan added. "Let's all step inside and eat the oversized breakfast that was just delivered. Then, when we get Bruce and Mariana warm again, we'll come back out and see what we can make."

"I've never eaten Tuatha dé food before," Mariana said.

"We really haven't either," Bri commented. "For some reason my aunt has this fixation with Hamburger Helper. I've eaten that far more than any of our native dishes."

Chapter XV: A Letter from Beyond

Andrew of no known relation was lying on a packing blanket that he and Jade had dragged up to the roof of the Palace Theater. They'd wanted to do something like this ever since she'd discovered the space a few weeks earlier. There was supposed to be a meteor shower that night, and they were both lying side by side, gazing up at the night sky.

It was a nice change, he thought as they laid there. He'd been overly stressed as of late with the looming specter of graduation hanging over all that he did. His parents had both expected him to have a plan in place by now, but he still didn't know where he was going to apply.

"I hope prom is better decorated than the fall dance was," Jade mused.

"It might have been ugly, but it sure was fun," he said in reply. It had been one of his best school experiences so far. "My stomach muscles hurt the next day from laughing so much."

"That was a great night," she said quietly. "Everything changed after that though."

He moved to where he could kiss her. It was still hard for him to believe that she'd chosen him.

"I'd say things are still pretty good," he whispered between kisses. He took the noise she made to be one of agreement.

Just as he leaned back again, a big meteor crossed the sky, leaving a green tail in its wake.

"So we've talked about me taking online courses so I can keep working at The Palace while getting a business degree," she said. "But what do you want to do? You never talk about your dreams."

"You are my dream," he said.

"You are the sweetest boy alive," she said, nuzzling up to him. "But stop evading."

"You'll think it's stupid," he answered quietly.

"When have I ever told you that something you liked was stupid?" she asked.

"My favorite shirt," he said.

"Sorry, but that shirt is stupid," she said. "I just didn't want to lie to you."

"When I mix mustard and catsup together and dip my fries in it," he continued.

"That's not stupid," she giggled. "Just gross."

Another shooting star crossed the sky and he hoped it would distract her from this line of discussion. This time it was she that sat up to see him better.

"Andrew, I'm sorry if I've ever made you feel self-conscious. My mouth has been getting me into trouble for most of my life. The only thing that would be stupid is if your dreams took you away from me, because I'm not all noble and self-sacrificing like the rest of my family. I would hunt you down and drag you back."

"Aww," he said, hugging her close. "That's the sweetest thing you've ever said to me."

"I'm serious," Jade said. "I'd even leave Nickelville for you if I had to. But I'd really like to take over the Palace. Now that I know more about our town, I would really like to be a part of its history."

"We already are," he chuckled. "Probably not the part that anyone will ever be able to print, but we've definitely been a part of its history."

"And I'm still not distracted," she said. "I really do want to know."

"I want," he said, pausing to take a breath and get the courage to tell her something that he'd never even voiced aloud. "I want to take over being the Academy librarian."

She didn't say anything at first.

"But they'll probably fill the position before I can get a degree, "he added quickly. "My grades aren't good enough for a scholarship, and my parents definitely don't have the money to send me."

His phone beeped.

"That's weird," he murmured, "Who could that be? You're the only person who ever messages me." Then, reading aloud: "Congratulations, you've earned a full scholarship for an online degree in Library Studies from Wise Industries."

"I didn't even know they gave scholarships," Jade said suspiciously, taking his phone to look for herself. "That's Bruce's number."

"So it's just a joke?" Andrew said, trying not to feel disappointed.

"No," Jade said, frowning, "That means he's seen it in your future, and he's going to streamline the process to make sure that it will happen."

The phone beeped again.

"And he just sent a note telling you that Sam will make a motion to have you work part time until graduation. After that, you will work full time until you have your degree and get a raise up to the full salary."

"You don't seem happy," Andrew said.

"I'm having trouble figuring out if I should be grateful or irritated that he's snooping around in our futures," she said.

"I kind of like the idea that he's still watching over things here. It's been too quiet since..."

"Everyone died or left town?" she prompted when he paused.

157

"Not exactly how I planned to put it, but yes."

"Let's pack a picnic and go horseback riding in Guarded Wood tomorrow," she suggested.

"What about school?" he asked.

"We already know we're both going to pass and get the jobs we want to grow old and retire in," she answered. "Let's steal a day together while we're both young enough to appreciate it."

Andrew started to chuckle.

"At least he didn't appear out of nowhere, screaming about what we'd done this time."

Paul and Luminita doubted they'd ever be able to move into the hermit's cottage. It just didn't feel like they were meant to. However, they weren't particularly happy with living in the treehouse with its limits on what they could and couldn't do, either. Both of them were more than capable of providing for themselves and living off the land, but the need to bring things up and down into the treehouse wasn't ideal. And as much as Paul might enjoy cooking over a campfire from time to time, it wasn't nearly as much fun if he had to do it every day.

So there they were, poking around in the hermit's home, trying to envision a path that would lead them to making it their own. It wasn't that the place was cluttered or dirty. The old man had been meticulous in maintaining his living space right up until the very end. There was, however, the accumulated things that came from having lived alone there for centuries.

Then there were the books. Paul and Luminita both cherished them, not only for their sentimental connection to August, but also for the valuable information they contained. Or, more accurately for the value they would hold once they learned to decipher them. Furthermore, a door that they'd thought led to a food larder turned out to be a room lined with bookshelves that were all filled with yet more books.

Paul was ecstatic over the cast iron their friend had accumulated over the ages, and he looked forward to cooking in them. But once again, that would be after they moved in, and right now there was still too much of August there.

Luminita walked over and sat down on the bed, which didn't give very much. Reaching over, she pulled up the edge of the worn bedding to expose bundles of reeds that had been organized to create a fairly flat surface on which to sleep.

"I guess he liked his mattress extra firm," Paul said, picking up yet another journal from the table that stood next to the bed.

She moved closer to look at the pages as he flipped through it, both of them thinking that this was probably the last one that he'd written. Apparently, their friend had been quite an artist too, for there were many drawings of Paul and the others in its pages along with scenes they recognized, like the last big meal they'd shared when Alan had proposed to Kate.

Then, when they found a rough sketch of the rocs, Luminita reached out to touch the page and found herself drawn into one of the book's memories taking Paul with her.

August was stirring something in the pot that hung over the hearth, with the big wolf stretched out in front of him on the floor. Then Fang looked up at the door and August smiled, feeling them too.

"Keep them away from the marsh," he said, opening the door so his friend could leave. "The bog hag has been stirring again."

"I wonder which day that was," Paul said wistfully. "And we never had any idea he was watching over us."

159

"He loved you guys," she whispered, leaning her head on his chest while he continued to flip through the pages.

Then, near the end of the writing, he found a loose piece of paper that had been folded in half. When he opened it, they saw that their names were written across the top in August's even script.

My Dear Friends, Paul and Luminita,

By now I have moved on and left the enormity of Guarded Wood unto your capable hands. I should wish that I'd met the two of you sooner, but I can't bring myself to do so. I have watched the births of so many, and even though I only watched over them from afar, they still took bits of me with them when they passed. Then all of you showed up. I knew it was somehow different than all of the times before, but I no longer understood how to be with anyone other than Fang. When Paul got lost in the woods, everything changed. It wasn't easy talking with any of you at first, and if I seemed angry at times, it was only with myself. I'd promised many years ago that I would not allow myself to love anyone because it hurt too much to lose them. But Guarded Wood didn't let me down this time like it did with my Aurora. It brought all of you here to me at the end, and this past year with you has more than made up for the ones I spent alone. Even though I hate that the others will have to pass on with me, it is a blessing that we didn't have to live to see any of you go before us.

Paul, I need to confess a few things that I have not been entirely honest about. First, I don't think that the siren had anything to do with you running out into the woods that night (but she still deserved to be sent back to sleep for what she did to

Azarich and the others.) As soon as I started to track you, I realized that you were not heading in the direction of her lair. But where you went was so strange that I allowed you to believe she was the cause if for no other reason than that I couldn't give any explanation for what really happened. Fang and I had no trouble tracking you. At no point during your travels that night did you leave the paths I maintain. Furthermore, you moved with a certainty that implied that not only did you know exactly where you were going, but that you were desperate to get there quickly. Your tracks showed that you sprinted the entire way on the balls of your feet. And Paul, you traveled several miles before we found you. I have no idea how you made it that far so fast. It almost looked as if something had been chasing you. In several places we found horse tracks even though to my knowledge, there had never been any there before you told Sam to bring them. But the strangest thing was where we found you. When Fang and I finally caught up to you, you were standing at the same cliff where your brother saved Megan that day. And you were crying, "I'm so sorry, I can't run as fast as you do," over and over. But then you noticed me there with you and you said, "Why did he send me, August?" as if you knew who I was. Then you collapsed, and I had to carry you all the way back to the treehouse. I don't understand what happened that night, but I do know that there is no way you could have known my true name before then.

Do with this knowledge what you will. Don't be shy about reading my journals. I wrote them for the two of you even though I didn't know it was for you that I did it at the time. You'll need the information they contain in the years to come. Hopefully, with the boundary repaired and the siren sent (perhaps unfairly now that you know that she was innocent of what I accused her) back into hibernation, the two of you will have a decade or two in which to have the honeymoon you so richly deserve. There are maps rolled up on one of the shelves that show places you should go often and others you should probably avoid at all costs. I've also marked the gateways that lead to the center as far as I was brave (or foolish!) enough to travel. But most of all, don't ever feel as if you are trapped here. Within your grasp are forgotten worlds of such beauty that none but the two of you will ever travel. Try to remember me with even a portion of the love that I felt for all of you, and Fang and I will take this well-earned rest.

Augustus

Ps- Paul, I'm sorry about your library books.

"Library books?" Paul asked, looking at her in confusion.

Reaching out to touch the letter, the bard let the old man lead her to a box under the edge of the bed. Inside were several Nickelville Academy Library books, each of them on paleontology. Many were dog-eared from frequent reading as the old man had puzzled through the creatures he'd found inside of the boundary over the years. But best of all, one of the cover's bore clear puncture marks from the claws of the eagle that had stolen it.

Chapter XVI: So Many Promises

The snow had largely melted by the afternoon when Bri and Dougal stood out at the edge of the tree line while Megan and William remained close to the cabin. As usual, Bruce was working with Catherene within the warm confines of Haven.

They were close enough to hear each other when necessary, but hopefully far enough away to avoid the stray thoughts that leaked past even the best of shields. Megan wasn't particularly eager for this exercise, because it involved conscious exploration of the bond that she shared with all of the Tuatha dé.

She'd already had experience with reading them accidentally, but she'd never zeroed in on someone personally like this before. Buried somewhere within all of these new abilities that she'd inherited lurked the ability to kill with a thought. Even though what she knew from the memories of those who had gone before her implied that such an execution had to be intentional, she still remained nervous about what she might accidentally do to one of them.

"Is everybody ready?" William called out, to which the siblings at the edge of the clearing both waved.

Megan lowered her shields so William could better see what was going on. Then, still nervous, she reached out and cautiously looked into Bri's thoughts.

"Bri is thinking about Mariana and how much she'd like to take her to look at August's books," Megan called out, surprised with how easy it had been.

"That doesn't mean anything," Dougal called out. "She's always thinking about that girl."

"And you were just thinking about how you dropped the Scathlahm's Blade on your foot this morning and that it still hurts," Megan called out.

"That is amazing," William called out.

"I assure you it's not," Bri yelled. "He does that fairly often."

"Come on back in," William called. "I can tell something is happening, but I can't figure out how Megan is sending or how you two are receiving."

The two appeared next to where Megan was standing, looking out over the sprinkling of white that still remained on the open ground. She wondered how much longer it would be before Bruce came back.

"Could either of you feel Megan touch your minds?" William asked.

"Not at all," Bri answered. "That's what's so unsettling about the whole royal to subject bond. You never know if you're completely alone inside your head."

Megan noticed that her Scathlahm was staring at her, and without intending to, she entered his thoughts. His feelings for her washed over her like a disorienting flood, and she pulled back in a panic, causing him to cry out and reach up to his head.

"I'm so sorry," Megan blurted out, realizing what she'd done. Had she just come close to killing him? She didn't realize she was walking the shadows until she found herself looking down from the cliff at the gate far below.

A few seconds later, Bri stood next to her.

"What's wrong with me?" Megan asked in despair.

"What do you mean?" the young woman asked.

"There's something broken inside of me that keeps me from being able to love anyone," she whispered.

"Now I know that's not true," Bri answered, sitting down on the ledge and motioning for Megan to join her. "If anything, you probably love too much. It's quite frightening at times."

"But that's not real love," Megan insisted. "You know…"

"Do you mean romantically with physical attraction?"

"Yes,"

"Has no one told you about the promises that bind the descendants of The Morrigan?" Bri asked.

Megan turned to look at her.

"You mean the one that makes it where I can only fall in love once?" she asked.

"Yes," Bri said, "But that's not the only one. I don't know how many there are in total, but there's at least one more that might be your problem here."

"I wish there was some sort of an instruction manual for me," Megan said. And of course, as soon as she thought about it, she knew the answer. "One of my ancestors fell in love with someone who was completely unsuitable for becoming king, someone who could never love another person more than he loved himself. So she made a promise that the rest of us would never be able to fall in love until we were old enough to make a better choice."

"See," Bri said, "you've got nothing to worry about."

Megan wasn't at all convinced, but she also didn't really want to talk about this anymore.

"So you seriously can't feel it when I'm in your head?" she asked.

"Not at all," Bri answered.

"Doesn't that bother you?"

165

"It doesn't matter if it bothers me," Bri answered without emotion. "It's that way whether it's fair or not. Nothing can change it. Our parents raise us with the knowledge that either the King or Queen can see and judge all." Then she started laughing.

"What did you do?" Megan asked, smiling in spite of her mood.

"I used to tell Dougal that the King was going to burn him alive at any second when he did something that made me mad," she confided. "It used to make him cry so hard."

Megan could see Jade doing something like that if she'd had the opportunity. And thinking of her friend made her miss Nickelville so badly it hurt. Then the worry she hadn't wanted to speak came out anyway.

"But what if the promise isn't the problem?" she asked miserably. "I'm a lot older now than most of my ancestors when they came of age. What if it really is something broken inside of me?"

Bri frowned and searched her face for several seconds before she spoke, choosing her words carefully.

"Then you won't love someone like that," she answered with a shrug. "Even among the Tuatha dé there are individuals who feel no physical desire for another. There are those like me who prefer the intimate company of their own sex. But being different does not make us broken."

At last, Megan started to feel a little bit better.

"However," Bri continued during a pause in which Megan suspected she'd thought about not finishing what she had to say. "Being different is not without its own difficulties, particularly for you as our Queen. It's okay if I never bear children. But our very survival will one day depend on you producing another heir. That would be much more pleasant for you if this is indeed the result of your ancestor's promise."

"None of this is fair," Megan whispered, shaking her head and throwing a rock down at the gate below.

166

"No, it isn't," Bri agreed. "I'm sorry for not realizing it."

"What do you mean?" Megan asked. "I'm not the one who could have some stranger kill me because they were bored or distracted. No one is snooping around in my head without my permission."

"And yet you are still just as trapped as the rest of us," Bri whispered.

"Please get my mind off of this," Megan said at last.

"Can I ask you something?" Bri asked at last.

"Anything."

"Why did your mother run away from us?"

"And why did my father forgive her before he died?" Megan prompted.

"Yes."

"Can I just show you?" Megan asked.

"You can do anything you want, My Queen."

"Stop that," Megan said, irritated until she realized Bri was teasing her. "Are you going to lower your shields so I can show you or not?"

"I am incapable of shielding you out," Bri answered. "My Queen."

"Okay, if you don't stop doing that I'm seriously going to see if I can burn you alive."

"As you wish," she replied with a grin.

Hoping that this didn't somehow hurt her, Megan shared her memories with Bri, starting with the Morrigan's armor calling Emelia to battle and ending with the purchase of the old truck which apparently had been not only their best protection against detention, but also the thing that eventually got them caught.

"So you and the dowager both share your bodies with the living essence of The Morrigan herself?" she asked when Megan was done. "No wonder Dougal and I were no match for you. Not even The Dagda himself was her equal in battle. What's it like?"

"She's rather cranky most of the time, and only comes out when she feels like it," Megan said. "Now that I think about it, she's an awful lot like Mr. Bob."

"And who is that?" Bri asked.

"Here kitty, kitty," she called out with a shrug.

The Cat Sidhe faded into existence at her side, his irritation at being summoned thus palpable. Bri gasped.

"Sorry boy," Megan apologized, reaching out to scratch behind his ear the way he liked. "I really didn't think you'd come just because I called."

"The Cat Sidhe hasn't been seen in centuries," Bri said reverently.

"He sleeps a lot," Megan suggested.

"Where did you find him?"

"Chasing the fish in an aquarium at my school's office," Megan answered. "He's a bit of a kleptomaniac, although Bruce thinks he was only stealing stuff to make sure I got into trouble and ended up in detention with a ghost that turned out to still be alive."

"I don't think I understood any of that," Bri said.

"He wants you to pet him," Megan told her.

The fearless woman who lacked any modesty whatsoever when it came to dance apparel didn't know how to respond. At last she raised one hand to gently stroke the black fur.

At once, Mr. Bob moved over to her lap and began to rub the side of his head against her jaw, purring loudly as he did so.

"But resist the urge to squeeze him," Megan suggested. "He won't scratch you, but he usually disappears when I try to hug him. Although he has let me do it a few times when I was really sad. He also showed me visions of what was going on after my grandfather died. I slept for two days straight without eating or drinking while I held him, and I didn't even need to go to the bathroom when I woke."

"Even by our standards you've had a strange life," Bri said, becoming more relaxed with him.

Then Mr. Bob, the Cat Sidhe, happily sat between them where they could both pet him at the same time. His purring became even louder as he looked down at the stronghold of their enemies with interest.

Chapter XVII: Deep Learning

A short time later when Megan had collected herself, she and Bri returned to the cottage and discovered that Mariana had joined them. Bruce hadn't returned yet, and they still had an hour or two in which they could try to work out the mystery of how Megan communicated with her people.

"I have an idea," William said, eyeing Mariana. "Why don't you try to teach Brighid how to cloak herself. If that works, then I can trace the familiar information back to Megan in much the way a tracking program identifies the path it travels through on a computer network."

"Even if it doesn't work, I'd still like to know how that's done," Bri admitted.

"You're lucky to have such a good teacher," William added. "I don't think there's a single one of us that's as good at camouflage cloaking as Mari."

"Aw, shucks," Mari said, feigning bashfulness.

"Speaking of which, Bri, how did you manage to catch her that first time?" he asked.

"I just happened to be looking in the right direction when she slipped," the Tuatha dé answered with a shrug.

"That's the part I don't understand," he said, looking at Mari who was for some reason blushing. "Mari never makes mistakes with cloaking."

"I guess I was too shocked by the way they were fighting and lost my concentration," she said, looking at Bri guiltily.

"Now I understand," he said, looking slowly from Mari to Bri with a knowing smile.

Mariana hit him hard in the shoulder.

"Okay," Megan said, "How are you two related exactly?"

"My parents took him in because they didn't think they could have children," Mari answered.

"It was a pretty sweet gig until she showed up several years later," he added. "But yes, we are actually related distantly. I mean, all of us are. We don't marry outside of our own city, so there are an awful lot of interrelationships as time goes on. Just like the Tuatha dé probably are."

"Yes, we keep close records that are consulted before a couple is allowed to wed," Dougal agreed.

"Not that it's been an issue for a while now," Bri said. Her brother glared at her.

"What do you mean?" Megan asked.

"Your father made the decision that none would be allowed to bring children into Tyr Sgodl as long as the status of there being an heir was in doubt," he explained. "No children have been conceived among the Tuatha dé since your mother left with you."

"Why would he do that?" Megan asked, horrified.

"Because he said it was cruel to bring children into the world when it would be so easy for something to happen to him and to you," Bri explained. "No one really agreed with him, but we have no choice. When the royals command, the Tuatha dé obey."

"So you became a race of children after Mag Tuired," Megan said, "And now you're on the verge of being a race without children?"

Bri and her brother both nodded.

"That's not fair," Megan said, gritting her teeth, to which they both shrugged in muted agreement. Then she closed her eyes in concentration.

171

"Wow," Bri said, looking surprised.

"What?" Mari asked.

"Our Queen just informed all of the Tuatha dé that they could uh…go forth and multiply," Dougal answered.

"I really wish I could have tried to follow that one," William said. "Oh well, let's try this again. Bri, would you take my sister to the other side of the clearing?" They faded out and reappeared where he'd directed.

"Okay," he yelled to them. "Show her how it's done, Mari."

Even from that far away, Megan could feel when Mariana dropped her shields and invited Bri in.

"Can you two please tone the lust down a bit?" William yelled. "I really don't want to be in the middle of those emotions, especially when they're coming from and centered around my sister! Okay, go ahead and start."

They watched from afar as his sister disappeared from view.

"What I'm hoping to accomplish here is a different approach from what we've done before," he explained. "As far as I know, this knowledge isn't possessed by even a single one of your people. That means that when you try to learn it, it will only be coming from one place. Furthermore, this is knowledge with which I am intimately familiar. I should be able to recognize it as it passes into you."

Bri disappeared for a few seconds and then reappeared.

"That's really good for a first time," William observed.

Then she did it again and remained hidden for almost a minute before she came back.

"Okay," William said, preparing to open himself to anything resembling this knowledge.

Megan lowered her shields so he could follow and allowed him to search her senses while she reached out for the knowledge of how to cloak

172

herself and felt it instantly merge with her own. Before William could even comment, she cloaked herself and stayed that way until she wanted to reappear.

"Is that seriously all there is to it?" she asked. "William, did you get that?"

"I think I did," he said, cautiously excited. "There's not a word for this so I'll just…" he paused for a moment, making hand motions that meant absolutely nothing to them.

"He's really bad at charades too," Mari observed from where she still stood with Bri.

He made an unfamiliar gesture with his thumb between two of his fingers.

"You remember what happened the last time Mother saw you doing that," she warned with a contagious grin.

"For lack of a better word, we all communicate at a kind of frequency," he said. "The information that just came from her to you is at a much, much deeper frequency than anything I've ever felt. I had no idea that there was even anything down there. That's why I could never sense it before."

"So what does that mean?" Megan asked. "Will you be able to talk with your sons?"

"I might," he said, allowing himself to become more excited by the prospect. "But I think I can already see something useful we could do with it."

She winked out and returned, thinking about how much Bruce was going to love learning to do this.

"Please don't ever let Priscilla see you do that," he said as his sister and Bri returned. "I'm not her favorite person as it is. Mari, would you mind if I placed a sort of receiver in your mind that should allow you to hear things in this new frequency? You'll be able to remove it without any problems afterward."

"I can't say that I have any desire to let you," she said, "or any other man for that matter, put anything in any part of me."

Everyone laughed except for William, who commented that she was worse than the students sometimes.

"Mari," he said, trying to be patient. "If you let me do this, I'm almost positive that I can get you over your fire summoning block."

"You're serious?" she said, suddenly interested.

"Completely," he answered before explaining to the others. "She's always had a problem with fire. She can barely summon it and she can't control it at all."

Mari glanced at Bri with a little bit of embarrassment.

"What do you say?"

"If this has any chance of lobotomizing someone, I think we should try it on Antonia first."

"Who is Antonia?" Bri asked, "The same one who set your shoes on fire?"

Mariana nodded.

"Our childhood bully." William answered. "As much as I'd like to run amuck in that woman's mind, I'm pretty sure I couldn't get within a dozen yards of her without her bodyguards stopping me."

"I've had a fair bit of experience with bullies myself," Megan said. "What is her problem with you?"

"Pretty much our existence in general," Mari said unpleasantly. "Well, that and the fact that I prefer women to men."

"How about you William?" Bri asked with an edge to her voice. "Does she hate you for liking women too?"

"That and the fact that I'm a half-breed abomination," he answered.

174

"She may have a few new names by now. That was her favorite when I was about nine. Although sometimes she fell back on her aunt's which was "the unfortunate necessity.""

"Nimue called you an abomination," Megan recalled.

"He gets that a lot," Mari added. "Okay, I'll let you do it, but if you plant any weird obsessions in my mind again…"

"I will make him miss the days when it was this Antonia that he worried about," Bri finished for her.

Mariana grinned and lowered her shields to let him in. Before any of them even knew that he was doing something, it was over.
"That's it?" Mari asked, frowning.

"That's it," William answered, leading her over to the fire pit where there were still some logs left over from the night of drinking.

"Ready?" he asked and she nodded in reply.

Then he focused for a second and her eyes went blank as if she'd slipped into a state similar to that of his sons. Reaching out to the wood, he summoned a small fire and then built it into an inferno before snuffing it out.

Mari came instantly back to herself, frowning.

"It can't be that easy," she muttered before reaching out and summoning an inferno disproportionate to the amount of wood there. Then she quenched it with an overly theatrical flick of her fingers.

No one cheered louder than Bri.

"I don't understand how that was any different from just showing her normally," Megan said with a puzzled frown.

"When he did whatever it was that he did, I didn't just see him summon fire. I actually *was* him while he summoned it. So when I came back to myself, I just did exactly what I'd just done as him."

175

"Do you have any idea how much easier this is going to make teaching?" he asked, giddy with the possibility. Before long, they were all laughing around the fire. Megan couldn't help but notice how different Mari seemed from the first time she'd met her. As William's sister looked at Bri in the firelight, she looked whole for the first time.

In the middle of that unplanned celebration, Bruce walked the shadows to them and managed a smile that didn't reach his eyes.

Chapter XVIII: The Voice of the Fates

Sam knelt between two of the three graves he'd carved out between the massive roots of the tree. In those graves he'd laid to rest the remains of the Fates in the manner they had shown him from their earliest days. His hands rested easily on the strangely warm bark of the tree as he spoke to the women within.

It had been a fairly productive session. He'd discovered that the town of Nickelville sat within what the three women had called a wellspring, a place which, due to an indefinable quality in the earth's energy, called and drew in people with gifts like his own.

There had once been three such places, but this was the last. Even the Fates had never discovered what caused them to become dormant, and they had never successfully restored one that had dried up.

At some point in the distant past, the three mysterious women had made plans to create a society centered around the wellspring and thus concentrate within the area people of magical ancestry. And their plan was going well, right up to the point when that damnable preacher tried to open a gate in the middle of it. Not even they, with all of their experience in such matters, would have attempted what he had done.

Moreover, a temporal anomaly had centered itself over a nearby field at the same time that he'd failed in his attempt. This further muddled the energy that should have been drawing the gifted to this place as it had for thousands of years, forming the base of Sam's people.

When they'd first arrived at the wellspring, they'd gone in search of the disturbance. Much to their surprise, the foolish man who had created the breach in the veil between worlds had not only survived the act, but was now trapped within it. Worse yet, they recognized the world he'd touched to be none other than the one where The Dagda had killed the Beloved Nyx. This represented the most dangerous of all possible scenarios.

The things trapped in that realm had mutated with the ability to cross through damaged portions of the veil. Should they ever make their way into this former Eden, all of the Fate's work would have been for naught. Because not even they, who had watched over this world since it had been new, would be able to stop this plague once it took root.

Knowing that they must proceed with caution lest the preacher open the rift any further, they approached slowly and found him in a sort of dream state, neither fully awake nor asleep. Unable to rouse him enough to communicate what must be done, they surrounded the partially formed gate and prepared to close it with him inside since removing him would release what lay within.

Unfortunately for all, he chose that moment to come back to himself, forcing them to retreat lest he further damage the veil. Realizing his vulnerability, he created a massive ward to surround his church so he would never be caught unaware again.

This brought them to an impasse.

In order to better monitor the problem, the three women erected a stronghold in the center of the wellspring where they could watch from afar. They raised shields strong enough to insulate them from the wild energy that the gate emitted. But while it kept them safe from the outside, it also blinded them to it, which would eventually prove to be their undoing.

For a short time they watched from their lofty perch, looking out through telescopes for changes at the church which had now been converted to a school. Likewise they monitored the festival field with the temporal anomaly, and the edges of Guarded Wood where the old hermit unknowingly did their bidding.

When Sam asked the Fates how they had died, they took him far back into the past, but even then, they had already lived for years beyond his ability to imagine. In the millennia since their creation, the three Fates had amassed power, wealth and glory. Which in turn led to the pride that was eventually their downfall. For pride gave birth to envy among those who owed their existence to the Beloved. It was one such group, known best for their practice of necromancy, that created the weapon that eventually destroyed the Fates. Using the blood of their own fallen Beloved, the Fates' enemies had devised a weapon of such power that it turned on its own makers before spreading out into the world. Since the time of its creation, the three women had stayed one step ahead of it, creating rituals and habits to protect them from exposure. Although this disease had been tailored to the Fates, it killed without purpose, striking down all in its path. At the time of their infection and death it had been called consumption. But now it was known as Tuberculosis.

As curious as he was, Sam's knees had reached their limit. He reluctantly let his hands fall away. His body ached from kneeling for so long, but only through such sessions would he understand all that the women in the tree had to teach him.

He'd already learned much, but doubted he had enough days left to do more than glimpse the knowledge gleaned from what appeared to be hundreds of thousands of years' worth of memories and knowledge. But he suspected that he would soon be able to share this task with others, because now that the wellspring was functioning as it was meant to, there were indeed gifted men and women drifting into his previously hidden home.

He'd also been overjoyed to solve one mystery that had plagued him these many years, even if he'd never be able to share it with the world outside. From the beginning of his research and preservation of the language his people had spoken, he'd been painfully aware that their words, phrases and conjugations were nothing like any other language in the world. There was no clear evolutionary path from one group to another where this was concerned, and now he knew why. When the earliest of his ancestors had been drawn to the wellspring, they had found three women waiting for them there. And since each newcomer brought tongues indecipherable to the others, in the end they learned the sacred language of the Fates, a language with origins so far back in the history of mankind that nothing remained of what it had once been.

Chapter XIX: The Bard's Christmas Wish

The adze felt familiar in Paul's hand as he finished squaring off the beam that would replace the rotten one his brother had identified a few months back. It had taken weeks of backbreaking labor to clear away the debris from the keep, but now it was almost ready for Nita's people to move in. And it wouldn't be a day too soon. The wind had changed direction a few hours ago and it carried with it the scent of snow.

Not that cold seemed like a problem right now. Paul's shirt dripped with sweat, and his muscles held the pleasant heat of hard work. Now that he'd finished, he allowed himself to sit down on this massive length of squared timber that would soon hold up the entire roof overhead.

Sprinkled through the varied, olive-skinned people of Nita's clan were a score of Tuatha dé craftsmen that Emelia had sent. Without them, the keep would never have been restored in time. Seeming to need little or no sleep, they were a tireless force of order and creation. No task was too big or small to draw their full attention. Things that he wouldn't have even noticed needed work transformed under their experienced hands, leaving the ancient building stronger than when it had first been built.

It had taken a while for Nita's people, who'd always been private and mistrustful of outsiders, to accept these pale phantoms who made no attempt to hide their supernatural nature. But in the end, it was impossible not to warm up to the excitement the Tuatha dé had for just being in a place that needed their skills.

Apparently, there wasn't much to do where they were from. The castle and surrounding structures in Tyr Sgodl had been designed to last for multiple lifetimes, and due to the war that had decimated their population, many stood empty. Thus, there was no need for new building or opportunity to ply their considerable skill.

"Is everything in readiness, my lord?" the Tuatha dé foreman asked. His speech still held a hint of the Gaelic these men and women spoke amongst themselves, but given that he hadn't spoken anything else a few weeks ago, that was more than impressive.

"I'm definitely no lord," Paul chuckled, and the serious man smiled, likely influenced by the unconscious power in the young bardic amplifier's voice. "But yes, I think we are ready."

Knowing that what came next lay outside the abilities of any but the alabaster skinned craftsmen, Paul ordered everyone else out of the way. He'd liked to have made them clear out entirely, but like himself, they were too curious about what came next. So, backed against the edges of the room, they watched as the Tuatha dé positioned themselves around the new beam.

Working in unison, most of the craftsmen used the force of their minds to lift the load of the roof off of the rotten wood. The ancient timbers groaned in response as everything moved, ever so slightly, away from the massive timber which responded by cracking and twisting as the forces that had held it for so long disappeared.

Without pausing, lest their brethren tire unnecessarily, several of the craftsmen walked the shadows to the supports surrounding the rotten beam and sent it back through to the floor next to its replacement. Then, just as miraculously, the new beam was in place, and the craftsmen returned to the ground. The weight of the castle roof settled into place with alarming creaks and groans before holding firm.

The following whoops of excitement brought Luminita from wherever she'd been working. They all understood what this meant. Preparations for the winter that even now bore down on them could begin in earnest. It was time to make this place into a home.

"Not bad," Luminita said, smiling at Paul, an act which never failed to make him wonder if all of this was truly real.

"Do you think the Queen will approve?" the foreman asked.

"I know she will," Paul said, thumping the man on the back in excitement.

"This calls for a celebration!" Luminita yelled, and the excitement in the room magnified through the sound of her voice.

"The dowager Queen has already been apprised of our progress, and she wishes to provide a feast," the foreman added. "Which would also allow us to fine tune the way the kitchens function."

"I don't know how we could have done all of this without you and your craftsmen," Paul said happily. "Now if we could just get you to stay on for the renovations in the town itself."

The Tuatha dé within earshot all perked up at his words.

"I'm just kidding," Paul said quickly. "You've already done too much for us. We couldn't possibly ask you for more."

"May I speak freely?" the foreman asked.

"Of course," the bards answered in unison.

"We have trained our entire lives to be able to fight at a moment's notice, and to be able to rebuild afterward. We live in Tyr Sgodl, where there are more than enough stout dwellings to house the survivors of the Night of Many Goodbyes. This may very well be the only chance we will have within our lifetimes to do what we love most. We were already planning to ask if we could stay on and work through the winter. We promise you'd barely even notice that we were here. And in the spring when you emerge to plant your crops, we should be finished."

"But it's too cold to work during the winter," Luminita argued.

"In the old days we bathed in the water of the salty seas even after the ice formed," he said with mirth in his eyes. "Cold does not affect us the way it does you. The only hindrance I can foresee is that it might sometimes be too cold for mortar to set properly."

"I still feel like we'd be taking advantage of your people," Paul said and Luminita nodded in agreement.

"Would you really cast us out into the frigid lands of Tyr Sgodl without any work to help pass the long hours?" one of the younger craftswomen asked, clearly much more comfortable with the nuances of English than her mentor.

"What do you say?" the foreman pressed.

"I say we'd be fools not to accept!" Luminita laughed and a ripple of happiness passed outward from her in a wave.

That night, full of food that he couldn't even identify, Paul tried unsuccessfully to stifle a yawn. He was quiet about it when he finally gave in lest it send half the room deep into slumber.

Nita looked up at him from where she was laying on a bench, resting her head on his leg. They'd only finished playing for the crowd a few moments before in the warm glow of the great hall. Outside the snow fell, traveling on strong winds.

Nearby a little girl played with a toy bird, making it fly around the hearth. Something about the way it moved mesmerized him.

"I want one of those," Nita whispered.

"A toy bird?" he asked. "I'm pretty sure I could make one for you."

"A daughter," she said, reaching up to touch his face. "A bard that will be able to leave Guarded Wood and bring our magic back into the world."

"I'm pretty sure I can help you make one of those too," he chuckled.

"I want to marry you," she pressed.

"I gathered that much when you said yes," he teased.

"On Christmas Eve," she added.

"As in the one that's less than a week away?" he asked, no longer sleepy.

Chapter XX: A Long, Cold Walk

Bruce told himself that if it was okay for Megan to have other friends, that it was okay for him as well as he walked down the corridor with Antonia. As usual, she had her hand resting on his arm as they walked, and he could feel her power increase with their closeness.

"Wasn't it hard living somewhere where you constantly had to hide what you were and what you could do?" she asked.

"At first it wasn't too hard since I couldn't really do much of anything that could give me away," he answered, "but it got harder as time went on, particularly when the kids who used to bully me were around."

"Did you ever get even with them?" she asked.

"I beat the main one in a town race, and then we bleached their hair. We never used our gifts against them, though. As time went on they just stopped being important and sort of faded into the background."

He thought she'd say more, but he couldn't sense much of anything behind those shields she always kept up.

"Will you come see me again before you leave?" she asked.

"Of course," he promised as she kissed him chastely. Then he sensed someone behind them.

When he turned he found William and Mariana standing just a few yards away, both of them looking at him in bewildered horror. Without another word, Antonia slipped away from him so quickly that he might have thought she'd walked the shadows.

"Hey guys," he said uneasily. When they didn't answer, he continued on to where Catherene waited.

Later that same night when his lessons were over, and he had kept his promise to see Antonia, he stepped outside the shield gate and walked the shadows to the cabin. Megan was sitting as she often did on the steps wearing only a t-shirt and jeans even though he was partially frozen after only being outside for a minute or so.

"I don't think I'll ever understand how you do that," he said, helping her to her feet and hurrying through the door where she'd already lit the fire. "I know you can feel both hot and cold."

She shrugged in response.

"Are you okay?" he asked. "You look down."

"Sorry," she said once they were inside. "I'm having a lot of trouble accepting the fact that whole generations of Tuatha dé children will be raised worrying that I might burn them to death if they displease me."

"And that's why it's going to be okay," he said, making sure that she made eye contact with him. "You're a good person, and you'd never do something like that. That sort of power would corrupt just about anyone but you."

"How about you?" she asked. "Did you learn any new amplification skills?"

"I'm not sure I'd say it was a new skill," he answered, going over to the table to see what they had tonight. He had worked up an appetite. "I can now reliably identify and control the flow of power between me and the people I strengthen. I never really noticed the drain when I'm with a group of gifted people, but now that I'm aware of it, it's hard not to notice."

"Am I doing it now?" she asked, concerned.

"Always," he said. "But it's different with you because there is a cycle of energy exchange between us. I draw from you all the time too. Catherene also thinks I might not be able to walk the shadows by myself. That's why William couldn't ever feel anything when I did it."

"That can't be true," she said skeptically. "I would literally be dead if you couldn't walk the shadows."

"She thinks you do it for me on a subconscious level," he explained.

"But what about when I was unconscious?" she asked just as a loud knock came from the door.

"Come in," Bruce called out.

The door opened to admit William and his sister, followed shortly by Bri and Dougal.

"Excellent," Megan said. "You guys can help us eat some of this food."

"We need to talk," William said.

"Can we eat at the same time?" Bruce asked. "Your wife is an absolute taskmaster. I'm famished."

"How well do you know Antonia?" Mariana asked.

"Wait," Bruce said, remembering their odd reaction in the corridor that morning. "You know that Megan and I are just friends, right?"

"How much time have you been spending with her?" William pressed.

"She showed me her workshop after we ate at the festival," Bruce began.

"You ate with the high council?" Mari asked in shock.

"Maybe," Bruce said, starting to feel uncomfortable with this discussion. "I don't know who they were. Then her aunt showed me her visions of the future."

"You let Priscilla inside your defenses?" William blurted out. "Are you insane?"

When the man put it like that, it didn't seem like a particularly smart thing to do. Bruce didn't like it when people made him feel anything less than intelligent.

"It wasn't that big of a deal," he said in his defense. "They were pretty much just the darker side of the Morrigan's prophecy."

"And this Antonia was nice to you?" Bri asked, making Bruce wonder what business she even had in this discussion.

"She's a nice person," he answered. "Of course she was nice to me."

"Not even remotely," William said, shaking his head vehemently.

"I think I'd know if she wasn't," Bruce countered, starting to get angry. Then, in spite of what he'd said about not being in a relationship with Megan, he didn't look at her when he added, "We've sort of been seeing each other."

For just an instant he saw the conflict within Megan and braced himself for her anger. And even though he knew it would hurt, he found himself eager for the jealousy that would prove at last that she loved him and wanted him for herself. But then the familiar fog of confusion passed through her and she sighed with relief. Her reaction was the same in all of the possible futures as she realized he'd be focused on someone else for a change.

"Priscilla has been trying to get the council to attack Megan," Mari almost shouted.

"She's just frightened of the visions," he said, "particularly the green eyed Tuatha dé warrior that throws her from the cliff."

"Come on," Dougal said. "None of us have green eyes by the very virtue of what we are!"

"We should get some of those things that make your eyes turn

191

different colors," Bri said, "I'll bet we could have a lot of fun with those."

Everyone smiled at this except for Bruce, who still was still looking at Megan, feeling the echoes of that relief radiating from her.

"How could anyone take that seriously?" Bri asked.

"Megan's own mother feared the dark side of her prophecies enough to go on the run for fifteen years. I'd say she took the possibility rather seriously, wouldn't you?" Bruce said.

The room went silent, and he finally felt the hurt from Megan that he'd hoped for before.

"That isn't you talking," Megan whispered.

"How would you know?" he asked. "You barely even talk to me anymore. You're always out drinking meade with your loyal subjects."

"That was one time," she growled. "Bruce Grimble, I know you better than any person ever has or ever will."

"And yet you still can't love me," he said, feeling numb. Was this what it was like when The Morrigan took over for her?

"She's just trying to seduce you in order to get back at me for what my mother did all those years ago," Megan said quietly.

The only time he'd ever felt her this angry was when she'd argued with her mother that first Thanksgiving. And he hadn't been able to see them then.

"So you admit that you know me better than anyone else," he said, so deeply hurt that he didn't care what damage his words caused any more. "But it doesn't even occur to you that it's possible for someone else to love me for who I am and not just as an extension of you."

He reached into his collar and pulled out the stone and lifted the leather cord over his head. It was a hard thing to do since it had actually become a part of who he thought himself to be.

"I don't want you to think that I regret anything," he said quietly, feeling almost as empty as he had during that week after the Baker. "Nothing we've ever done or been through together. I owe you so much. But I deserve better than this."

Megan recoiled from him as he held it out, realizing what was happening.

"It's not my fault," she stammered. "My ancestor promised…"

"I know," he said calmly. "And your one person is never going to be me."

He caught her hand and placed it in her palm then closed her fingers around it. He grabbed his backpack, shoved his laptop and some clothes into it and then slung it over his shoulder. When he turned and tried to walk the shadows back to the gate, nothing happened.

"I guess your wife was right," he said to William. "It was Megan doing the work all this time, and I was just along for the ride."

He barely noticed the cold as he walked down the slope. Someone might have called his name at some point, but he'd given up on things like that. By the time he reached the gate, his body was almost as numb as his heart.

Chapter XXI: The Rottweiler Queen

A chill had set into Emelia's body, and her shoulder was stiffer than it had been before. But no matter how much she amplified the fire in the hearth, the room never seemed to get any warmer.

She'd also discovered that no matter how much she tried to stop thinking about it, her thoughts were split between the years she'd lost of Sam's life already, and how each hour she spent in Tyr Sgodl was roughly twenty back home. Then she'd remember why her shoulder hurt, and she'd cycle back between the self-recriminating hypocrisy of such thoughts and the guilt.

"That's it," she said at last, dropping the reports she'd been reading on her late husband's desk.

"I'm sorry, Your Majesty," the old woman who was cleaning the room stammered, running over to see what she might do, "Do you require anything?"

"Yes, if I'm going to be stuck here in the cold, I'm going to be comfortable while I do it."

"I don't understand, Your Majesty."

"Take me to my childhood home on Earth," Emelia said.

"But I've never been away from Tyr Sgodl," the woman whispered, terrified by the thought.

"Then it's high time you did," Emelia said, taking her arm. "This is where I want to go."

Realizing that there was no way out of this command, the woman reluctantly did as she was asked. When they appeared by the back porch of the house on Beverly Road, the poor woman shielded her eyes from the cloudy sky, which was still far brighter than any part of Tyr Sgodl. Furthermore, the woman's terror at the sheer openness of the space made Emelia realize that she'd seldom if ever been outside of the castle.

Quickly dragging the woman along behind her, Emelia was pleased to see that Sam was still taking good care of her father's plants. The back door to the kitchen was locked, but opened easily at her touch.

"This won't take long," she assured the frightened Tuatha dé.

The air had grown even more musty with disuse, and she was tempted to open the windows and blow everything out. But she also realized that this was a trap. If she allowed herself to start, one task would beget a thousand until she lost any desire to ever go back. Not that she had that much desire in the first place.

The house was too quiet, and for the first time she felt like an outsider there. *If this place was no longer home, what was?*

With the old woman following close behind her as if afraid that some monster might burst in at any moment, Emelia walked down the hallway, trying not to look at anything too closely for the same reason she'd avoided opening the window. She took the stairs slowly, avoiding the memories of laughter she'd heard there and finally arrived at her bedroom.

She didn't realize that her daughter had warded this room until the girl appeared in front of her. The moment she saw Megan, Emelia knew two things. The young Queen's power was still growing, and something was horribly wrong.

The woman behind her dropped instantly to one knee.

"I really wish everyone would stop doing that," Megan snapped.

"My daughter will bring me back to Tyr Sgodl," Emelia said

formally. "You may return if you would like."

The woman was gone almost before the words were spoken.

Too upset to speak, Megan flooded her mind with thoughts, knocking her shields aside as if they were little more than tissue paper. She'd known that her daughter's power had grown, but this was an order of magnitude beyond what she'd expected. And there was no longer any scent of Bruce in her magic. In seconds she knew all that had transpired, including the relevance of a second promise of which Emelia herself had been ignorant.

"I'm sure he'll come back around," Emelia said, although she had to admit that there was an air of finality in the way he'd left that suggested otherwise.

Before Megan could reply, they both felt Luminita call them to Guarded Wood. And the ease with which the girl snatched Emelia up without contact and walked the shadows once again showed her how far her daughter's power had evolved.

"I'm so glad you're both here!" the bard said, gathering them into her embrace and holding them there. "Paul and I have decided to…how does he say it? Oh, make it official."

"That's wonderful," Megan said, and Emelia was happy to note that her daughter's grief receded a bit. Of course much of that stemmed from the fact that Luminita had already ascertained the nature of the girl's sadness and laced the sound of her own voice with a soothing poultice of happier emotions.

"Hey guys," Paul said, sticking his head out of the treehouse door. "Where's Bruce?"

And just like that, the happiness left Megan's eyes again.

"They've had a falling out," Luminita said, wrapping her arm around her.

"What has the idiot gone and done now?" Jade yelled from down

196

below where she was quickly climbing the steps to reach them.

"He hasn't done anything wrong," Megan said quietly when they were all together. "It was my fault."

"Somehow I doubt that," Jade said. "Unless it involved a bunch of water falling out of the air on him. Then it's your fault, but once again, perfectly understandable."

"Not this time," Megan said. "I don't really want to talk about it."

"So what are your plans?" Emelia asked, changing the subject. "I would kill for a chance to plan something that doesn't involve Tyr Sgodl."

"Thanks again for lending us the craftsmen," Paul said. "We couldn't have gotten the great hall done before winter without them."

"Well," Luminita began, returning to Emelia's question. "Our choices are limited to the treehouse, one of the more pleasant places in Guarded Wood, or maybe the Castle at Roanoke."

"Wait," Megan said, coming back to herself, "Is the missing colony inside of Guarded Wood?"

"No," Paul answered with a grin, "That's what we named the ruins." Emelia could feel the power in his voice change as he began to soothe Megan as well.

"That was your idea, wasn't it Paul?" the young Queen asked.

His grin was answer enough.

"What if the restriction of Guarded Wood wasn't a problem?" Megan asked, looking serious for a moment. "Where would you want it then?"

"Jacob's church," the bard answered without hesitation. "But it would kill us to go that far from the boundary."

"What are you thinking?" Emelia asked.

"I might know a way around the boundary restriction," she answered. "It would be temporary, and we'd probably have to limit your time there to the actual ceremony, but it should be possible. Wait here for a minute."

As soon as Megan disappeared, Luminita turned to Emelia.

"She's in such pain," the bard whispered. "Should she be alone?"

"I'm sure her Scathlahm will be here momentarily," Emelia assured her. "She forgets to tell him where she's going when she's troubled or excited, and it takes a few minutes for him to track her."

"She practically radiates power now," Paul said quietly. "She's changing, isn't she?"

"She is the living nexus of all the power held by both the Tuatha dé and Crina's clan as well," Emelia explained. "And it's not just their power. She has the memories from her ancestors spanning back thousands of years. But even so, I didn't expect her to change this quickly. I suspect Bruce may have been anchoring her in place in his desire to keep her the same. Now that she is no longer bound to him, the process has accelerated."

The possibility of further explanation ended when the Queen of the Tuatha dé returned, holding two parts of a stone in her hands. It looked as if there was a piece missing that would make it whole.

"Okay," Megan said, placing a piece in the hands of both Paul and Luminita. "I'm going to take you to the Academy in a minute. The third piece of this rock is sitting next to the fire pit with the big armadillo things."

"And you've bound them all together so that they think they are still whole," Emelia exclaimed, "and as long as they're in contact with Paul and Luminita, Guarded Wood thinks that they're still within its boundaries. That's genius!"

"I wish I could take credit for the things I find in my head these days," Megan said with a shrug. "I just hope it works." Then she reached out and took the five of them to the isolation room at the Academy.

"Is everyone okay?" she asked, ready to whisk them back at the first

198

sign of trouble. But aside from the fact that Paul and Luminita clung to each other and breathed a little harder than they had a few seconds earlier, they seemed unharmed.

"It's a little bit uncomfortable," Luminita said, frowning. "More like a sense of unease than actual pain."

"Did you seriously have to bring us to the spot where I died?" Paul complained, looking at the wall uneasily.

"I'm so sorry," Megan said quickly. "I didn't even think about that. I just always use this room because hardly anyone ever comes here."

"I never had to come here as a student," Emelia agreed, looking around.

"I've lost count," Jade said pleasantly. "That table doesn't look comfortable, but I've had some pretty good naps on it."

"We didn't have time to fix it properly," Megan said, noticing that Paul was still looking at the wall with morbid curiosity. "The doorway is still open. It's just an illusion."

"Can we go down?" Luminita asked quietly.

"Of course," Megan said, dispelling the illusion so they could see the opening.

The rest of them followed the bard down into the dark and Emelia summoned a light for them at the bottom.

"I can still feel Jacob here," Luminita whispered.

"Me too," Emelia added.

"And that's where I died," Paul said, pointing to the rubble.

"I'll get the craftsmen to come and rebuild the wall properly in the original style of the school. Paul, would you like to have your remains moved to Guarded Wood Proper?" Emelia asked.

"Every time I think things can't get any stranger, something like this comes up," Paul said, still staring at the collapsed portion of the cave.

"Megan, can you cremate them where they are? I don't really feel like seeing anything that belongs on the inside of me anywhere on the outside."

"You're sure?" Megan asked to which he nodded.

It happened so quickly and with so little effort on her part that the rest of them were still waiting for her to start when she asked them if they needed anything else.

Luminita glanced at Emelia again, and it was impossible not to understand its meaning. When Megan had left for Haven, she'd already been the most powerful being that Emelia had ever encountered, and she'd always thought that was largely in part the result of Bruce's amplification. At the very least, having his ability removed from her own should have diminished her for quite some time. Yet here she was, powerful in ways that Emelia couldn't even comprehend.

"Speaking of craftsmen," Paul said. "Is there any way your guys can stay a while longer? They keep asking if they can restore the whole city. I'll understand if you say no, but I think they're afraid of how badly we'll mess stuff up if we do it ourselves."

"Of course they can," Emelia said, not at all surprised considering how excited they'd been when she'd first sent them to help. "Just make sure you give them clear parameters, or you'll wake up one day with a full-blown bona-fide fairytale kingdom on your hands."

"I can think of worse things to have happen," Luminita said. "Sam told us that we don't have to worry about influencing the past any more. The only places where Guarded Wood opens into the real world are in the present."

"What about that time August told us he was going to work on something that looked like Medieval Germany?" Megan asked.

"He made that up so we could work on the runestones," Emelia said.

"I didn't think you could lie mind to mind," Luminita said.

"It wasn't technically a lie," Emelia explained. "He did know of such a place, and that is where he'd planned to go before deciding to help me. He just postponed it a bit."

"You were sad that day," Megan said, reading her mood. "That's when he told you they were all dying, wasn't it?"

Emelia nodded.

"I'm so sorry that I didn't trust you more," Megan said, coming over to hug her while they stood there.

"No one likes to feel like they're being lied to," Emelia said, hugging her back and wincing at the pain in her shoulder.

"It still hurts?" Megan asked.

"For me, that was only a few days ago," she reminded her. "Do you feel any better now that you know all of the things you wanted to know?"

Her daughter shook her head sadly.

"Can we go back now?" Paul said. "The longer I stay here the more I remember."

"Of course," Megan said, reaching out to them and crossing back into Guarded Wood. "Before I forget, Luminita and Paul, would you mind if a Child of Nyx comes to study August's journals?"

"Can she read them?" Paul asked.

"Yes," Megan assured him. "She's a scholar who specializes in his works, at least the things he wrote before coming here. She's positively dying to read the rest."

"Wow," Jade said, "I don't know if that's impressive or incredibly sad. I mean, I loved him like a grandfather, but I never would have expected him to have a fan club back home."

"She's more than welcome," Luminita said, sitting down on one of the benches. "It would be nice to meet someone new that we didn't have to kick out."

"Is that still a problem?" Emelia asked.

"There are a handful of kids who've built a clubhouse just inside the boundary where my GPS says it touches the Washington State and Canadian borders. They're all about ten or so," Paul said, chuckling as he thought about them.

"I'll bet they remind you of us, don't they?" his sister asked.

"I should probably start working on my grumpy old man costume in case I ever need to warn them off," he answered.

"No costume," Luminita said, pulling him down by the collar of the coat he always wore now. "This is too tasty to hide under a costume!"

"Stop…" he managed to say before she was kissing him again, and he finally gave in and sat down, pulling the bard into his lap.

"We don't really have to do that," Luminita said when they stopped. "We can make people avoid the woods on their own with our music if we need to."

"Yeah," Paul said grinning hard, "If they get too persistent, I just do my imitation of Jade singing in the shower!" Then he jumped up so fast that he almost dumped the bard on the ground and started to run while singing in an eerily accurate rendition of his sister's voice before taking off with her hot on his trail.

"I've missed that," Megan said, watching them go.

"Then come home," Luminita said. "This will always be where you belong. And that goes for you too Emelia."

"As much as I'd like to stay, I have a kingdom that requires my attention," Emelia said. "But there will be people to see you before the day is out to start making plans. And tell Paul that I will need the craftsmen back for a few days to get the Academy ready for the wedding and then to put it back together afterward. Then they are yours for as long as you can stand them."

"Of course," Luminita replied. "Thanks again."

"What did you come back for anyway?" Megan asked.

"Comfortable warm clothing," Emelia answered. "The rest was just an amazing bonus."

"Same here," her daughter replied. Then she walked them through the shadows back to where she'd found her.

It only took a few minutes to gather what she needed and then they were back in the study. In the moments that had passed since she'd left, a young man had entered with yet another stack of papers.

When he noticed them, he dropped to one knee so fast he hurt himself.

"Are you okay?" Megan asked, rushing over to him.

He nodded furiously, rose to his feet unsteadily and backed out of the room. Megan looked after him when he went, a mixture of emotions playing over her face as he went.

"They'll get used to you in time," Emelia offered.

"It's not that," Megan said quietly. "I can hear their thoughts, especially when they're upset like he was. They've been raised to fear me."

"I don't think anyone's actually burned someone alive in centuries," Emelia said.

"They've all done it at least a few times," Megan replied sadly.

"Not your father," Emelia said, shaking her head in denial.

"After we left," Megan explained. "He had a nightmare. After that he took some sort of potion that blunted his power while he slept to keep it from happening again."

"I didn't know," Emelia said, feeling sick.

"And I should have let it stay that way," Megan said wearily, making Emelia worry about her all the more.

"So you're going to be the one that keeps the secrets now?" Emelia whispered, reaching out and taking her daughter's hand.

"Growing up sucks," Megan said, looking around the room.

"I want to show you something," Emelia said, pulling her toward the door. A few minutes later they were in the nursery.

"Was this supposed to be my room?" Megan asked, her eyes scanning everything until she noticed the doll. "Kermit!" she squealed in delight and snatched it up, hugging it tightly. Then she noticed the posters and started to flip through them, making little sounds of recognition as she went.

"He collected everything we left behind, didn't he?" she asked at last.

"It would appear so."

In the midst of holding the worn stuffed animal, Megan's expression changed and Emelia knew that she was connecting the doll to the memory from the runestone.

"What about your room?" Megan asked, still holding the stuffed animal possessively.

"I haven't been in yet," Emelia admitted.

Megan looked hard at her for a moment then put the doll down and hugged her tight, remembering to go easy on the shoulder this time. Emelia stiffened at first, but finally relaxed and rested her head on her daughter's shoulder.

"I've missed you so much," Emelia whispered.

"Me too," Megan admitted. "So why haven't you gone in and where have you been sleeping?"

Still enjoying the hug too much to answer, she pointed to the rocking chair.

"Then we'll do it together," Megan said, taking her by the hand and using her father's memories to find the way.

As soon as Megan opened the door, Emeila knew that nothing had changed since the morning she'd left. The bed remained unmade, and given the devotion that the castle servants gave to every task, that could only mean that Daragh had commanded them to leave it alone. The clothing she'd changed out of was still on the floor at the edge of the bed, and her jewelry box still stood open as she'd left it.

"I guess I wasn't the only one who couldn't bear to sleep here alone," she whispered. "Oh Megan, he never did anything to deserve this."

"Neither did you."

"That's not the same," Emelia said, walking over to the bed. Sitting on the pillow was her wedding band, repaired and restored, waiting for her to return. But for all its outward perfection, its power had faded like his blood beneath her skin leaving behind nothing more than a hunk of pretty metal.

"You see," she said, picking it up and holding it in her hand, thinking that maybe she should put it back on as a reminder of the choices she'd made. "I always understood why this had to happen. No one betrayed me."

"Mom," Megan said, reaching out to her. "You never..." She struggled to find the words to explain.

"And I had you," Emelia continued. "He was so alone. He didn't even have Cara any more. For a little while I even had my father back."

"And Sam," Megan added.

"And Sam," she agreed, looking around. "I wanted all of this back for so long. I spent so many years wanting to be Queen again, to rule by his side the way I promised I would when he gave me this ring." Here she clenched her teeth against the words that she needed to say, yet afraid of what her daughter might think. "But all I want now is to go home."

"Then why don't you?" Megan asked.

"I don't deserve that life anymore," Emelia said, trying to explain. "I made my choice, and now I need to keep my vow."

"Why shouldn't you deserve to be happy?" Megan asked.

"Because I'm sitting here, wanting to run back home when I just buried my husband!" she said through teeth clenched so hard that it hurt her jaw.

"It wasn't your fault."

"He died protecting me," she cried, "I dishonor his memory by even thinking about…"

"Sam?"

Emelia sat down on the bed and rested her face in her hands.

"You hadn't seen my father in fifteen years, and yet you remained faithful to him, even when your daughter was throwing temper tantrums on rooftops to make you start dating again."

"That was so much fun," Emelia giggled, although it was dangerously close to a sob.

"It's okay to love more than one person in your life," Megan said, kneeling in front of her so she could see her face and make her look into her eyes while she spoke.

"Even though you'll never be allowed to?" Emelia asked sadly.

They were both silent for a moment before Megan shook her head almost angrily.

"Maybe you can have the freedom for me," she suggested.

"I'm not just anyone," Emelia replied. "I'm a widowed Queen, a dowager."

"That is such a weird word," Megan said. "It was the first thing I looked up on my phone by the way."

"I know," Emelia agreed. "It makes me think of rottweiler every time they say it."

"Go home mom," Megan ordered.

"No," Emelia said, shaking her head. "The Morrigan said I had to do this. I need to watch over your kingdom while you're away."

"Mom," Megan said, taking her hand in her own. "I don't think the Morrigan sent you here to fix anything. And with all of the stuff my father dumped into my brain, I'm actually starting to be rather wise."

"Then why did she send me here?"

"To make you realize how little this all means to you," Megan explained. "That way you can go home and live happily ever after with Sam. Otherwise you would have always wondered what you'd left behind."

"So you think I should go home to that horrible yellow color you painted my room?" she asked, smiling genuinely at last.

"I thought you liked yellow," Megan said defensively.

"I like sunflowers," Emelia explained. "I even thought about buying a yellow car once. But I never said I wanted to live inside a glass of lemonade."

"Then move into Grandpa's room," Megan suggested.

"No," her mother said, sobering at once. "He…"

"Would want you to have the room where he spent the best part of his life with Grandma Josie," Megan interrupted. "He'd want you to sleep in the same room where the McGeehees have been for generations."

"If I do, you've still got to help me finish cleaning out the attic," Emelia said.

"And you have to learn how to smoke a turkey without utterly destroying it," Megan added.

"Sam will take care…," she stopped, realizing what she was already thinking. Her eyes dropped to the wedding band she still held in her hand.

"You're the best Queen they've had since The Morrigan. But even so, you're not Tuatha dé. Just because you loved one amazing man doesn't mean you can't love another. Even more so when that man would otherwise stay alone for the rest of his life waiting for you to return to him.

207

Don't you think it's time that Sam got to be happy too?"

"You don't know that he feels that way," Emelia said.

"You can't possibly believe that he doesn't," Megan countered. "Besides, he told me he did."

"When?"

"When I asked him how many cameras you fried before he got a picture of you."

"When did he manage that?"

"At Jade's birthday party," Megan answered.

"I was distracted by the power I could sense in Paul's voice," she said, nodding as she remembered.

"You could hear it even back then?" Megan asked.

"That man is incorrigible," Emelia said, smiling again.

"Then he'll fit into the family perfectly," Megan agreed. "Are you two still young enough to have kids? I'd love to stop being an only child."

Emelia fixed her with what she hoped was a baleful glare, but she was too happy to be sure.

"Oh please," Megan said, flicking her hand in a dismissive manner, "I totally outrank you now. Reigning Queen totally trumps Rottweiler Queen."

Sam, oblivious to the discussion underway between the two most important women in his life, sat at his desk, long after the last of his employees had left for home, missing the days when the occasional party or tournament made up the bulk of his worries.

He currently had two construction crews struggling to build homes on the land where his people had once lived faster than they were returning. Had it not been for Bruce's premonition and the seemingly insane request to start building, he wouldn't have been able to keep up. As it was, he'd need to hire a third crew by the end of the month or start putting the new arrivals up in lodging outside the town proper until their homes were finished. So far five families had returned, and even without foresight to guide him, Sam knew there would be many more.

At present, his growing community was willing to look to him for guidance, or rather, they expected him to guide them since he couldn't recall ever accepting the position. But as their numbers grew, they would have to decide on how to best govern themselves. Would they want to rebuild the tribal clan system that they'd used before? Or would they prefer to simply merge with the rest of the town and govern themselves in a manner more keeping with the modern world?

Whatever path they chose, it would be difficult. Many had not passed down the language or customs of the past, and the youngsters had no idea where they had come from. Even so, they'd all felt and heeded the call of the Wellspring.

His people were not the only ones finding their way to Nickelville either. Two young men had shown up during the lunch rush one day, just as hungry as anyone who'd been forced to live on roadway fare for any length of time. But unlike anyone else, they'd come in with wisps of magic trailing behind them as they crossed his threshold. Within moments he'd tucked them away into a quiet corner booth. When he'd struck up a conversation with them, they'd explained that they'd always dreamed of starting a coffee shop together. Then, a little over a week previous, they'd packed all of their possessions into a cargo truck and driven straight to Nickelville, which incidentally, didn't show up on most maps. By lunch the next day, they owned one of the abandoned shops on Main Street and were already converting the space above it into a loft where they planned to spend the rest of their lives together.

This barely scratched the surface of Sam's responsibilities. He'd long since passed the point where he needed help, but who could he ask without drawing attention to the often-supernatural aspects of day-to-day life in Nickelville?

With a weary sigh, he turned off the lights and wondered if it would be too much to ask for the Wellspring to summon a supernatural accountant.

Chapter XXII: The Hermit Fan Club

Bruce had lain on a narrow bed in the cell-like room for only a few minutes before he decided to go back. The only reason he hadn't done so already was because he'd almost gotten frostbite walking to Haven without his coat, and he wasn't entirely sure he'd survive the walk back without one. It would be warmer in the morning, and he'd have more time to work out his apology.

As for the feelings he'd felt from Megan, he knew he should have expected that. He knew that she didn't love him the way he wanted, but that was okay. He knew his feelings toward Megan put her under a lot of stress, and she felt guilty for not feeling the same way about him. So her feelings of relief that he was in a relationship with someone else shouldn't have come as such a surprise. If he'd taken the time to talk with her, he'd probably have found out that she was just happy that he was getting what he needed even if she couldn't be the one to give it.

He hadn't been a very good friend. And he really wished he hadn't said that part about her mom not trusting her.

"I heard that you'd come to your senses and come in out of the cold," Antonia said from his open doorway. Inwardly, he groaned. She was *not* what he needed right now. It was so hard to think clearly with her close, and as much as he might have denied her bad motivations to Megan, he'd seen more than enough hints that she wasn't as pure of heart as she pretended to be for his benefit.

"Sorry," he said. "I'm probably not going to be very good company right now."

"Let me be the judge of that," she said, walking in, closing the door behind her and coming to lie down next to him. She was very close since the bed wasn't meant for more than one person and her perfume almost overpowered him. "We don't have to talk if you don't want to."

So they spent the next minute or so staring up at the ceiling with him wondering what he could do to fix things and Antonia's thoughts entirely her own since she was so heavily shielded.

"I'm sorry," she said, turning on her side and looking at him. "I always got into trouble for talking in class. I'm not entirely sure that I can be quiet for more than a minute or two."

"My brother and sister are like that," he said, smiling in spite of himself.

Then she launched into a theory she had about the ways that artifacts reacted to the passage of time. It was well thought-out, and she was funny at times without intending to be so. As the time passed, he found himself thinking once again that he'd know if this was completely an act. Furthermore, it was nice to have someone who really wanted to be around him, to seek him out as she always seemed to do.

Several hours later, he woke to find her asleep with her head on his chest. It was nice enough to ignore the fact that he never really slept on his back. She shifted slightly and woke to find him smiling at her.

"I'm so sorry," she said. "I didn't mean to keep you up so late, especially after you had a bad day."

"It was nice," he said quietly, very much aware of the warmth of her against him.

"I've got to go," she said, sitting up reluctantly. Then she turned back toward him, looking down coyly, and kissed him in a way that left no ambiguity to its intended meaning. Then she was gone.

Maybe he didn't need to rush back in the morning, he thought pleasantly as he drifted back to sleep with the smell of her on his pillow.

Megan walked the shadows back to the cabin where she found Bri, Dougal and Mari waiting for her.

"I'm sorry about not telling you where I was going," she apologized to Dougal. "I felt my mother trip my wards in Nickelville, and I wanted to see her before she went back."

"I know," he said. "I tracked you as far as Nickelville, but I figured you were safe enough in Tyr Sgodl."

"Luminita and Paul are getting married," she announced. "And you're all invited. Mari, will you tell your brother that he and his family are invited." Then she paused, realizing that she had no way to get word to Bruce. "And can you let Bruce know that his brother is getting married on Christmas Eve at the Nickelville Academy."

"I didn't think they could leave Guarded Wood," Bri said, frowning.

"I found a temporary workaround," Megan explained. "And both of her sisters were married there."

Now that the necessary explanations had been given, Megan realized she had no idea what to do now. More than anything she wanted to talk to her best friend and see what he could see in the future surrounding the soon to be married couple. But that probably wouldn't be possible for a while, if ever.

"Oh," she said, remembering, "You have permission to read the journals, Mari."

"What are we waiting for?" The young woman said excitedly, standing up and grabbing Bri by the hand as if she could drag the Tuatha

213

dé through the shadows by herself.

"You mean right now?" Megan laughed.

"You can't dangle something like that in front of me and not expect me to bite," the Child of Nyx said seriously.

"You don't have to come if you don't want to," Bri said. "You just got back."

"Want to know a secret?" Megan asked, getting up. "I don't particularly like being here anymore. Dougal, you can stay if you want."

"And what have I ever done to make you think I'd want to be here a moment longer than I have to?" he asked, moving closer to them so they could all arrive in the same spot. "I hate this place. It feels like someone here has me in their sights and is just waiting for a chance to pull the trigger."

When they appeared on the deck of the treehouse, they found Luminita dancing to something only she could hear through the headphones of Paul's phone. Her eyes were closed as she moved, and Megan could feel through their bond that she was thinking about being married to him.

Then the bard felt their presence, opened her eyes and screamed.

Megan had just enough time to throw up a dampening shield before the wall of sound hit them, glad that the experience with the siren had made her think about shielding out sound. Even so, it shoved them back, shield and all, several inches before the bard recognized them and stopped.

"You're a bard!" Mariana gasped, still holding tight to Bri's hand.

"She's a quick one, isn't she?" Paul said from the bench he'd been sitting on, admiring his wife to be.

"I thought you were all gone," Mari stammered.

"Not quite," Luminita said, a little embarrassed by what she'd done. "But as far as I know, I'm the last."

"You must be the fan club for August that Megan told us about," Paul said, rising and holding out his calloused hand. "I'm Paul."

"Bruce's brother," Megan added.

"And I'm Mariana," she said, reluctantly releasing Bri's hand to shake his. "I'm an archivist as well as a teacher, and I stumbled across his work a few years back. It's amazing. I can only imagine what his later work might contain."

"From what I've been able to decipher, it contains a lot about Guarded Wood," Paul offered. "I haven't been able to find a translator that works reliably with his dialect of Latin though."

"Guarded Wood is real?" she asked, surprised. "He wrote about it right before he escaped with the Great Oracle's sister. But I always thought it was one of those early myths like El Dorado or the Fountain of Youth."

"I assure you it's real," Luminita said, smiling. Megan could tell that she already liked this woman.

"You're at the very edge of it right now," Megan said, enjoying the way that Mariana's eyes widened in response. "But you can't tell anyone. Guarded Wood isn't a place that needs any extra attention."

"No one beyond my brother and his wife would listen if I did," Mari said. "And they wouldn't understand its importance either. I'm the only person who has touched August's manuscripts in centuries, and the only reason they still exist at all is because the Children of Nyx are hoarders by nature, particularly with things that might contain secrets about forgotten magics. As for a translator, I have the only one in existence that could translate those books."

"Where did you find it?" Paul asked in interest.

"I made it myself," she answered. "He writes in an older dialect of our language. And even though you are right in thinking that it looks like Latin, it has a totally different evolutionary path than the rest of the

Romance languages. I'd be happy to give it to you. Now, I don't want to be rude, but can I see those books now?"

"And I thought Bruce was bad," Paul chuckled.

Megan winced.

"This one is more handsome than Bruce," Mariana observed as he led them to the stairs.

Luminita stopped in mid step.

"You've got nothing to worry about," Bri said quickly. "Mariana and I are seeing each other."

The bard started walking again and Megan wondered if Mari would ever realize how close she'd come to dancing off of the treehouse deck.

"Bruce is rather scrawny by comparison," the bard admitted.

"He's not that bad," Megan said, mainly to herself.

The simultaneous looks that Luminita and Dougal gave her could not have been more different.

Chapter XXIII: Dangerous Toy

Bruce felt guilty about ditching his studies with Catherene to work with Antonia, but they both knew that he'd learned everything he could from her. She was, at this point, just keeping up the pretext so he could stay there as long as he wanted.

Which brought the question to the surface of his thoughts about when he was going to go back to Nickelville. He couldn't stay in Haven indefinitely, and if he was honest with himself, he really didn't want to. Until last night, he'd never slept within the confinement of the shield wall. Cut off from his ability to see the future, he found his thoughts and dreams turning to the oracle's apocalyptic predictions with increasing frequency.

Antonia, however, made it easy to forget that he didn't belong there. On several occasions when he'd accidentally made breakthroughs that went too far beyond the possibility of luck, he'd almost told her that he was a greater smith. The potential for disaster in those lapses made him understand most why he couldn't stay. As only someone who feared the water could truly understand, the calm nature of the ocean's surface did not mean there weren't dangers lurking beneath. As much as he enjoyed having a beautiful woman pay attention to him, she wasn't the girl he wanted, and it wasn't fair to Antonia to pretend otherwise.

His hand brushed something in the bottom of one of the boxes they'd been looking through and he pulled it back in revulsion.

"What is it?" Antonia asked.

"I don't know," he said, carefully clearing the things around it away so he could get a better look without actually touching it again. As the toy boat came into view, he recognized it from the runestone memories Megan had shown him.

"Is it an artifact?" she pressed.

"Yes and no," he said at last.

"How can it both be and not be an artifact?" she asked, frowning.

"It's an extremely powerful artifact," he explained. "But it was created for a single purpose, which it has already fulfilled."

"Then how is it still an artifact?" she asked, moving closer to get a better look.

"I'm not sure," he lied. "But it's extremely unstable. It wouldn't take much to make it work, but in completely unpredictable and dangerous ways."

"Could you fix it?" she pressed.

"It's too dangerous," he said, shaking his head. "I'm pretty sure that thing could destroy the whole city."

"So that brings us up to a total of two artifacts among all of this stuff," she said with a sigh. "And as cool as the medicine blanket was, I doubt anyone is going to need it to cure tuberculosis anytime in the near future."

He shrugged in reply.

"Okay then," she said, pushing the box aside and lifting herself up onto the table in front of him. She clasped her hands together behind his neck and looked him in the eyes. "You've been distant all day. What's bothering you?"

"I'm sorry," he said. "I'm heading back to Nickelville tomorrow for the wedding."

"I love weddings!" she said.

"I'm not looking forward to talking to my family," he said. "And I'm not looking forward to explaining why I walked out on my best friend."

"I take it they like her," Antonia said, her voice cooler than it had been seconds before.

"Probably more than they like me," he admitted.

"Take me with you," she said. "I'd love to get out of here and stand behind you if they make things unpleasant."

His initial reaction wasn't a good one. It wasn't that he didn't think he'd enjoy his attractive friend's company so much as his fear of having the girl and Emelia in the same room together. However, he did like the idea of having someone with him that would definitely be on his side.

"Sure," he said against his better judgement. "I'd like that."

"And you can show me all of the sights in the town where you grew up," she added in a good imitation of excitement.

"That should take all of about three minutes," he admitted. "I've spent my whole life wanting to get away from there."

"Then you can come back here and stay with me," she offered. "Be done with this small-town business if you want."

"Do you really mean that?" he asked.

She nodded, holding his eyes with hers.

He lowered his defenses, inviting her in. And when he reached for her, he was rebounded back into himself by battle-hardened shields.

"That's as far as you get after only dating me for a few weeks," she said, playfully pulling him in for a kiss that held all the promise her shielded mind had not.

It took him a long time to fall asleep that night, and when he did, he dreamed of a combination of dark, sulfurous passages and Pricilla's visions of doom. When he woke, he showered quickly to rid himself of the night terrors before leaving to meet William, Catherene and Antonia.

219

Chapter XXIV: Two Paths Converged in Guarded Wood

By the time Megan arrived at the treehouse with Dougal, Bri and Mariana in tow, it was already a bustle of activity. People were everywhere, and the largest portion of the crowd were Tuatha dé who predictably dropped to one knee when she appeared.

"Okay everyone," she said out loud and across the entirety of her subjects. "I appreciate the greetings and the respect that they convey, but we've got too much going on to mess with this nonsense today. No more kneeling unless you're tying your shoe or picking something up off of the ground."

The response she felt through her bond with them was confused at first, but quickly turned into respect for the practicality of the command. They were pleased with her, she realized.

"It's okay," Bri was whispering to the Child of Nyx who was looking around with wide, frightened eyes.

"It's one thing to be around one or two of you," she whispered where she hoped no one would hear. "But being surrounded by a veritable hoard of the people that your parents told you would eat you if you were bad is a little bit unsettling."

"That's funny," Bri said cheerfully, "We scare our children with the reigning King or Queen."

Megan shot her a dirty look. Then she reached out, found Paul and took them to him.

His choice of clothing was eccentric, just like he was. Most of it was likely Tuatha dé in origin, which shouldn't have surprised her since he was spending so much time with the craftsman in Roanoke. But the tie and the shoes probably belonged to Mr. Grimble.

Much to her surprise, Luminita was there with him in a dress that reminded Megan of the one the bard's sister had worn in the vision of the past for its simple design. But no dress like that had ever been made of pale green silk with white lace.

"Why is Paul here with you before the ceremony, why isn't your dress white, and my mother had something to do with this didn't she?" Megan asked.

"I've been answering those same questions all day," Luminita answered. "Well, except for the one about Emelia. Yes, she insisted that there was no point in having the resources of the fair folk behind her if she couldn't give me a fairy tale wedding. My dress is green because in my time it symbolized my fertility and suitability for getting married and hopefully making lots of babies. Seriously, why would anyone want to wear a white dress when you're going to be eating, drinking and dancing all night? Oh, and Paul is here because this isn't an arranged marriage where they're worried about us running away if we know our partner is ugly."

"But it was preordained," he said, making her face soften.

"And because he won't let me out of his sight," she added.

"You look amazing," Bri said.

"And now," Luminita said, turning to Megan. "Your mother told me to send you to her as soon as you got here, and I believe her exact words were, *so she can have you dressed appropriately as befits your rank and station.*"

"I don't like the sound of that," Megan said, frowning.

"She's already had Jacob's church linked with Guarded Wood, and we both have amulets to save us from pain when we cross between the two. You're completely out of excuses. Go get dressed so I can claim this man!"

Megan reluctantly walked the shadows to a familiar room where her mother was being fitted with a moonsilk dress. As she recalled the memory, she was fairly certain that this was the same group of old women from before. Of course, that shouldn't come as a surprise since only a couple of years had passed here in Tyr Sgodl since that day.

"Perfect timing, my dear," Emelia said, stepping away from them to check her hair, which resembled something from one of the old movies she loved.

"But your dress isn't finished yet," Megan said, noticing how much skin her mother still had showing.

"What do you mean?" Emelia asked, stepping in front of a mirror. "I'm glad the wound in my shoulder has healed enough to remove the bandages. That would have ruined the whole effect." Not only were her arms bare, but the neckline also plunged far deeper than Megan would have ever imagined her mother to allow. Her mother turned for a better look at her reflection, and Megan saw that the back was utterly nonexistent.

"Wow," was all Megan could think to say.

"Your turn," she said, moving Megan into position. Then she told the old women in Gaelic, "Hold nothing back."

Fast and efficient for women who appeared to be so old, they stripped her and slid an undergarment like the one she'd seen in the runestone over her head. Then they surrounded her and began to work. She wasn't even sure which of them was working on her hair since it seemed to be dividing

222

itself of its own volition while tiny gold combs studded with emeralds embedded themselves into the intricate weave of her midnight tresses.

"I'm really glad I took a shower before I got here," Megan said to her mother.

"It took weeks before my skin stopped tingling from that washing," Emelia said. "It's so nice to be able to share my past with you. Now, before we join the others, I want to let you know that I've got everything wrapped up in Tyr Sgodl."

"You mean you're actually going to listen to me and come home?" Megan asked, surprised.

"Yes, My Queen," Emelia said formally in Gaelic, giving a slight curtsy.

The women around her froze, eyes wide as they glanced at each other. Then they continued as before.

"What just happened?" Megan asked.

"I just ceded all power to you and relinquished any claim I have to the crown," she said pleasantly. "You have no idea how good that felt."

Megan felt like her mother had just shoved her off of a cliff.

"Shouldn't that have been some sort of a big ceremony or something?" Megan asked.

"Probably," Emelia answered. "But don't forget, this is Tyr Sgodl, not Earth. The simple passing of power will impress your subjects more than a big ceremony. I know you're trying not to intrude on their thoughts, but if you were to check in on them right now you'd find that the whole kingdom is awash with discussion about what I just did. These ladies might look like they're focused on what they're doing, but each one of them is a veritable switchboard of communication right now. Within seconds every single one of your people will know that I have officially stepped aside. The speed and efficiency of the internet has nothing on the internal network of the Tuatha dé. And none of these women understand English, so you don't have to worry about what we talk about here. They love how practical you are almost as much as they love the way you put their needs above your own. You're already doing a much better job of being Queen than I ever did. My work here is done. Now that you've ascended, you can rule from anywhere in either of our worlds. I'm ready to spend the rest of my life in the tiny little town where I was born. My part in this fairy tale is complete, and before the sun rises tomorrow, I fully intend to propose to a certain giant we all love. Do you think he'll say yes?"

"Make sure that you give him a chance to get used to you in that dress first," Megan teased. "It might take him a while to regain the ability to speak."

The resemblance to the girl Emelia had been in those early pictures on the wall outside her father's bedroom was uncanny in that moment. Her smile was radiant.

"Do you think he'll like it?" she asked.

"Wow," came a familiar voice from nearby.

"Hello, Brighid," Emelia said pleasantly, looking over what the women were doing with Megan's dress in approval. "It seems like only yesterday that your aunt was here with me as I was fitted for the first time."

"She was so worried about making everything perfect for the two of you," Adair said, appearing next to Brighid. "The church is secure and everyone is in place."

"Cara made it into something out of a fairy tale," Emelia assured her.

"I've never understood that comparison," the captain of the guard admitted. "The Tuatha dé were at the heart of almost all of the stories you call fairy tales, and few of them had happy endings."

"At heart most humans are romantics, and our memories aren't as long as yours," Emelia explained.

224

"Which is why the Tuatha dé will never forget all that you've done for us, Your Majesty," Adair said, bowing slightly to her former Queen.

"I've just ceded the right to that title," Emelia said happily. "I am no longer the rottweiler Queen and you will both have to call me by my name from now on."

"As you wish," Bri said. "As soon as the two of you are ready, we will bring the bride and groom to the church."

"Thank you," Emelia said. "We just have a few touches left, so it shouldn't be more than twenty minutes or so earth time."

"Emelia," Bri said, after a moment's hesitation. "My friends all call me Bri."

"I shall do my best to remember that," Emelia said, warmly. Then the young Tuatha dé returned to the church.

Megan noted with relief that the old woman had used considerably more moonsilk to create her dress than her mother's, covering most of her alabaster skin in a molten layer of liquid night. Then the former Queen asked her daughter to take them to her bedroom where she quickly selected jewelry for them both, choosing emeralds for Megan to match the bard's dress and rubies for herself.

"What's Sam's favorite color?" Megan asked, looking at the ruby necklace that hung around her mother's throat.

"Red," she smirked. "Why ever do you ask?"

As a final touch, Emelia removed a delicate crown made of finely woven gold flowers whose vines wove in and out about each other in a series of knotwork designs that made the Morrigan stir in the back of her mind.

"No," Megan said quickly, putting up her hand in protest. "Please don't make me wear that. It's Luminita's day, not mine."

"You won't be able to put it off forever," Emelia said quietly, but giving into her wishes and replacing it in the cabinet from which it had come.

"I promise I'll wear it," she said, relieved. "Just not today."

Then she took them to the church, and even though Megan had known it would be so, she wasn't really prepared for the utter transformation that had been carried out by the skilled craftsmen of the Tuatha dé. It looked exactly like it had in the vision the bard had shown them on the night of the Jubilee except that the room had been lit with hundreds of candles. Garlands of fresh flowers hung everywhere, filling the chapel with the scent of spring promise.

"I understand that the craftsman had a blast moving all of the pews and things that you and Bruce found up in the attic," Emelia said, looking around.

"I can barely tell that I'm in the school cafeteria," Megan gasped, noticing that they'd even removed the floorboards to expose the stone underneath.

"Megan!" Jade squealed, dragging Andrew behind her. But then stopped, looking at her friend closely as if realizing that she was indeed a Queen.

"Don't you dare," Megan said. "Don't ever treat me like I'm not the same girl you used to hit in the ring!"

"Okay," Jade said in an uncharacteristically Jade way. But then she seemed to snap out of it and moved closer to her friend. "Isn't this amazing!"

"Yes, it is," Emelia answered.

Would you mind if I stay outside with the rest of the security detail? Dougal asked in the back of her mind.

If that's what you want, she sent. *But you're more than welcome to come and watch.*

Crowds are not my thing, and there are about eighty other Tuatha dé in there with you that would fight to the death to protect you should the need arise. Add my aunt to that and you've got an even hundred.

That's not exactly something I want to think about at a wedding, but thanks.

Mr. and Mrs. Grimble came over to see her, and Megan reveled in the kind of energy they'd used to have at her Grandfather's dinner parties. She asked about Sam, but they said he'd gotten ordained to officiate the wedding, and he was probably still making sure he was ready before he came out.

Then the front doors opened, and Megan felt Bruce even without seeing him. Her sense of him was muted compared to what it had been before he'd removed the stone necklace, but she still knew the feel of him better than anyone alive.

"There he is!" Dora said, disappearing from her side as if she'd learned to walk the shadows. Megan could hardly blame the woman who hadn't seen her son since Thanksgiving.

"That insufferable little brat," Emelia said menacingly, looking in the direction that Megan could feel her friend.

When she turned to look, she saw him standing in a tux, much like the one he'd thought about getting for the school dance they'd attended a lifetime ago. William had dressed similarly and Catherene wore a long-sleeved pink dress that looked good on her. Next to them, with her hand resting on Bruce's arm, stood a beautiful dark-haired woman with features that marked her as a Child of Nyx.

"That must be Antonia," Megan said quietly, realizing that this was the one who had drawn her mother's ire. She wore a long white dress in conflict with just about all wedding customs.

Before Megan knew what was happening, Emelia had taken her by

227

the arm and was walking toward the newcomers with unmistakable malice.

"William," she said regally when they reached them. "It's so good to see you again. And you must be Catherene," Emelia added warmly, reaching out to take the woman's hands in her own while she spoke. "It's an honor to meet you at last. Your husband had so many good things to say about you and your boys."

"It's good to meet you as well, Emelia," Cat said, smiling. "He's told me good things about you as well."

Megan looked away from them and found Bruce's eyes locked on hers. He smiled at her like he used to before looking back to Emelia. Something moved within her, reaching out to him in a way that she doubted he'd appreciate under the circumstances. Why did she miss him so much?

"Have your studies provided any improvements in their condition?" Emelia continued.

Antonia spat at the former Queen's feet.

Before anyone else could react, Emelia bound her in coils of power so strong that the Child of Nyx could scarcely breathe.

"Silly child," Emelia whispered with a pleasant smile. "Do you really think you're a match for me, even with poor Bruce there amplifying your paltry abilities?"

Then she stepped back, looking the girl up and down.

"Let's have a look at you," Emelia continued, "Ah, yes. I can see the resemblance now. What was he? A several times removed grandfather, perhaps? I won't even attempt to unravel your lineage. Your Nyx crowd has always bred like rodents. No insult intended to you though my friend."

"None taken," William said, unable to hide a certain amount of amusement that played around the corners of his mouth.

Unable even to struggle, Antonia turned a violent shade of red.

228

"Now, while I've got your attention, we need to talk before they bring out the bride and groom. You are lucky that she isn't wearing white. You are going to be a quiet little statue of polite perfection, because if that bride so much as frowns at you today, I will make what I did to your armies at Mag Tuired look positively cheerful by comparison to what I will do to you. Now, I hope that this demonstrates that your kind do not possess the skills necessary to save you from me should I choose such a path." The contrast between her words and the pleasant tone in which she spoke made the message all the more chilling.

When Emelia released her, Antonia shuddered with rage for a moment before William suggested they go and find their seats.

"You," Jade said reverently, eyes wide as she looked at Emelia, "will always be my hero."

Bruce marveled at Antonia's shields. He couldn't feel anything of what the foolish young woman felt, although judging from the expressions of William and Cat, it wasn't a good day to be an empath.

All three of them had warned her that she shouldn't wear the dress. None of them had even imagined she'd have the suicidal inclination to actually spit at the woman who had single handedly won a war.

Worst of all, her actions had driven a wedge between their small group and the people he'd so desperately missed. None of them had wanted this, and he deeply regretted bringing Antonia along. Furthermore, he wished he'd packed everything to return so he'd never have to go back to Haven again.

It would only be a matter of time before Antonia or Priscilla discovered what he was and tried to make him create artifacts to their own specifications. Worse, no matter how many times he recalled what the hermit had warned him, a part of him still wanted to create more.

Are you okay? Bruce finally asked her, feeling sorry for her even though she had brought it on herself. After all, she had no friends here aside from him, and she had come to support him when he'd thought no one else would.

No, I'm not okay. That witch wiped out half of my people in a single afternoon before burning two of my direct ancestors alive for opposing her. And now she's taunting me with it. I think I've got a right to be angry.

I understand that, but how was spitting at her supposed to help? Even if she wasn't one of the most powerful witches that have ever lived, she's surrounded by several scores of her soldiers. I'm flattered that you think I can handle odds like that, but let's be reasonable.

She put a dead rat on my pillow while I slept, Antonia added.

What do you mean?

Before William brought the two of you to Haven, she spent several months taunting us and showing us every hole in our defenses. She even appeared one day and welded the gate to the city shut with her magic.

Bruce chuckled at the thought.

It's not funny, she sent, pulling her hand away from his arm where it had been since they'd sat down. *Then she led our best trackers into the mountains and got them lost in the very lands where they'd grown up. Before they returned, she somehow snuck into Haven itself and left each member of my family presents on our pillows while we slept. That's why the High Council made William and Catherene create the Dark Crystal in the main cavern.*

When Luminita arrived with his brother, Bruce understood what Emelia had meant about the dress. It was similar to the one worn by her sister, yet original in its own way. He couldn't help but enjoy the work that had gone into making this place a replica of what it had once been.

He still wasn't used to seeing this adult version of Paul. Even though he understood everything that had happened as well as any sane person possibly could, he still thought of the man before him as his little brother. Then, catching sight of Bruce, Paul strode up to him with a smile that made everything alright.

"Hey Bro," he said in that deep voice that held hints of their big friend in its depths. "I never thought I'd say this, but I've really missed you." Then he reached down to where Bruce was sitting and wrapped his arms around him in a tight embrace.

"It's good to see you too," Bruce said, enjoying the hug more than he'd thought he would.

"You're going to need this," Paul said, reaching into his pocket and pulling out a delicate ring of woven gold.

Bruce could feel the power forged into it and recognized Emelia's signature in the oddly detailed wedding band. Under the scrutiny of his smith's senses he knew it was enchanted to find its mate, just like the one Emelia had given to Megan's father.

"Are you asking me to be your best man?" Bruce asked.

"Who else would I trust with this?" Paul asked.

"It's because none of your friends can come, right?" Bruce asked.

"It would have been you anyway," he answered. Then, noticing Antonia at his brother's side, "I'm Paul."

"And I think I picked the wrong brother," she replied suggestively.

"Uh, thanks," Paul replied awkwardly.

Bruce glanced over at Emelia, somewhat hoping that she'd heard.

"I guess that means I have to go up to the front," Bruce said to William, happily leaving Antonia behind to be someone else's problem.

Sam entered from the library just as Bruce joined his father and brother at the podium. Megan and Jade stood opposite them on the other

231

side. Dressed once again in the tux he'd worn just a few months earlier at the wedding between Alan and Kate, Sam had an air of concentration about him as if he was going over what he planned to say.

He paused in mid stride as if catching a familiar scent in the air, sweeping the room with his gaze, at last finding Emelia standing near the end of the aisle with the bride. Then the normally graceful giant tripped over his own feet and almost took out half of the wedding party.

Bruce's eyes found Megan, just as they always did in moments of beauty or sadness, and found her smiling back at him. The moonsilk of her dress absorbed the light from the candles even as the gemstones cast shooting stars of green light through the intricate braid of her midnight hair. He doubted anything the world had to offer, past or present, would ever compare to her beauty.

So lost was their big friend in the approach of the woman he loved, that Bruce feared he'd completely forget the words when she arrived with the bride at her side. Then she smiled and mouthed, *Silly Man Who Still Talks to Trees,* and he snapped from his trance. He took a deep breath to settle his thoughts before looking back to find her watching him with such intense interest that he almost knocked the podium over.

Would you please stop seducing our minister until after I get to kiss my husband? Luminita's thoughts echoed through their minds, bringing smirks from the rest of the bridal party.

Although the former Queen's sigh suggested one thing, the arc of that powerfully raised eyebrow suggested quite another. Bruce wondered exactly what had been going on during the few days he'd spent within Haven.

Then Luminita joined the man with the boyish smile that she'd waited centuries to see again. Although the words they repeated had been spoken by so many before, the love of the bards carried them deep into the hearts of everyone gathered around them except one.

Afterward, before the cheers of joy faded from the great hall, Emelia appeared at Sam's side with such fluid grace that Bruce wondered how he'd missed her approach. Sensing the potential of what might follow, he opened his mind to Megan, giving her an opportunity to see what he saw of their future. She caught the strand of thought as if nothing bad had happened between them, and their minds merged as effortlessly as they'd always done. In the clearest path his foresight had ever shown, they watched Emelia's tiny hand slide into Sam's and their separate futures merged so thoroughly that it took his breath away more thoroughly than a handful of ragweed on a humid day.

Thank you for that, Megan sent, and then she was gone, leaving him aching for her to return.

By the time Antonia made her way to him, he'd made up his mind. It was time to come home. He'd return to Haven long enough to wrap up loose ends. As nice as his time with Antonia had been, that was the one that needed wrapping up the most.

He wasn't sure how much longer it would take for Megan to finish up her work with William, but Bruce intended to have his apology ready when she came home. She might never love him the way he still loved her, but all of his future paths lay at her side, and he looked forward to exploring each and every one of them.

Chapter XXV: Christmas Comes Early

Megan tried not to eavesdrop while Antonia did her best to convince Bruce to return with her to Haven. And it pleased her to note that even when the beautiful Child of Nyx realized that he would not, she never offered to stay here in the lands of her enemies as Megan had.

"There is no way that my son is going to miss spending Christmas with his family," Doreen had said when Antonia persisted. Megan could tell that Bruce's mother didn't like the Child of Nyx very much at all.

At last, William and Catherene said it was time to go, reluctantly taking Antonia with them. Megan watched as Bruce carried on a conversation with his mentor mind to mind, and it was clear that Cat felt he owed her for being stuck with her husband's childhood bully on the flight home.

Right after Megan and her mother changed back into their normal clothing, Dougal appeared.

"Just so you know," he whispered with barely hidden mirth, "the entire kingdom is talking about Emelia's encounter with your friend's date." The day was turning out better than Megan could have dreamed.

Paul and Luminita, now clad in normal clothing as well, came up to her, stopping often to speak with the Tuatha dé craftsmen with whom they'd apparently become friends. That didn't surprise Megan at all. Paul made friends with everyone he came into contact with, and his fiery wife didn't appear to be very shy either.

"Can we ask a favor?" Paul asked.

"Anything that is within my power to grant," Megan answered, watching the way her mother and Sam remained in physical contact, no matter what they were doing.

"Can we all take Christine back to Guarded Wood?" he asked. "Nita hasn't had a chance to see what Nickelville looks like now."

"Of course," Megan said. "The amulets should hold up long enough to make the trip and the car's iron frame shouldn't interfere with their magic since my mother's the one who enchanted them."

"I want you and Bruce to come with us," he said.

"Oh," she said, glancing over at his brother who was currently being hugged by both of his parents. "I'd love to."

A short time later found all three of the Grimble children riding inside the great metal beast along with Luminita and Andrew. Much to everyone's surprise, Jade offered to let Paul drive since no one would suspect that he wasn't old enough to do so. But he politely declined, citing his desire to be free to point out landmarks to his new wife as they rode in the front seat.

Andrew offered to sit in the middle, having been warned in advance that Megan and her best friend weren't on good terms. But Megan knew he'd be uncomfortable, and frankly, it would be more like the old times that she so desperately wanted back if he didn't.

"I never thought we'd get to do this again," Paul said happily with his new wife sitting so close to him that she'd only be able to move nearer by sitting in his lap. "The ward is gone," he observed as they passed.

"I didn't notice," Bruce said, looking back. "I guess that means that Jacob really is gone now."

The familiar landmarks felt like a foreign land even though it hadn't been that long since Megan had been there. But time, she realized, was measured not only by the days that passed, but also by the things that had happened during them. No calendar could hope to convey even a portion of what had transpired since that evening when Jade had threatened to lock her brother in the trunk.

Megan enjoyed Paul's impromptu tour of the town, adding things that she hadn't learned during her relatively short time living there. But by the time they pulled into the Grimble driveway, she could tell that the enchantment was wearing thin and the newlyweds were more than a little uncomfortable.

Bri, Dougal and Mariana already waited for them beneath the treehouse when they got there, and Megan felt her mother arrive with Sam shortly afterward.

"Well, thanks everyone," Paul said after his parents finally arrived, "This has been amazing. We never thought we'd get to leave the woods again, let alone get married at Jacob's church."

"Don't you want to see your wedding gifts?" Emelia asked mischievously. Then she closed her eyes in concentration.

Both Paul and Luminita turned their heads toward the trees as if hearing something strange.

"What is that?" the bard asked, taking her husband by the hand and leading him into the woods.

Whatever was going on had to be Emelia's work, and she wasn't going to let anyone know before the happy couple did. After several minutes on the trail, they came to a path that Megan couldn't remember having seen before.

"I didn't know it was possible to hide things from us within the boundaries of Guarded Wood," Paul said, a little concerned by the revelation.

"Normally it wouldn't be," Sam said. "But I had a little talk with the women who made the place, and they showed us how to do it."

Like many of the impossibilities found in Guarded Wood, the simple wooded path with a clear view of the area ahead for several hundred yards suddenly opened into a narrow mountain pass that should have been visible a few steps back. Blocking their path in the distance, a gatehouse occupied the opening between the two steep faces. Complete with watchtowers and battlement encircled walkways, its pristine stonework looked like the recent construction they knew it to be, and yet the flowering vines that climbed artistically across parts of its breadth suggested otherwise. Windows of crosshatched leaded glass looked down from the heights, keeping watch over any who might approach.

"Is this where we are to live?" Luminita asked, her eyes traveling over the structure.

"No," Emelia replied, enjoying the bard's reaction. "This is what I meant by needing to give the craftsmen of the Tuatha dé clear parameters. They finished your home early and got bored."

"How did they get all of the vegetation to grow up around it?" Bruce asked, standing in the shadow of a tower. "It looks like it's been established for years."

"They didn't," Emelia answered, no longer irritated with him since his poor choice of companionship had departed. "It was like this the day after construction wrapped up."

"What is that on the flag?" Paul asked, eyeing the green banner that moved listlessly in the breeze. "It seems familiar."

"It's one of the oldest symbols for bard," Megan answered, drawing looks of surprise from those around her.

"Seriously better than a search engine," Bruce said quietly, making her smile.

When they passed through the open gate, the craftsmen of the Tuatha dé greeted them on the other side. Beyond that, a lush valley stretched out into the distance in a riot of spring color. A clear stream danced about the rocks in its winding channel, running parallel to the cobblestone path that led to a building that looked half rustic cottage, half castle and entirely enchanted.

"How did you do this without us knowing?" Nita asked. "I mean, we only told you a few days ago."

"You didn't seriously think we'd rebuild Roanoke and leave you living in a treehouse," the foreman said, walking up. "And it was such a treat for us to build something new. I hope you don't mind, but we took the liberties of naming them Guardian Gate and Guardian Castle."

"That's perfect," the bard whispered.

"Don't you want to see the inside?" Emelia prompted.

"There's more?" Paul asked, taking his bride by the hand and leading her up the path.

Built on the sloping descent down which the stream flowed into the distance, Guardian Castle backed up to the tall trees of a forest that took up over a third of the valley. The craftsmen had constructed it from the same stone as the gatehouse, and the vegetation had embraced it as well, lining the foundation with flowering bushes and shrubs.

A stone bridge crossed the stream where the path led up to the door, and Megan laughed as she watched the newlywed couple run across like schoolyard sweethearts. Then she pulled the foreman aside and let the others pass.

"What you have done here is beyond amazing," she told him. "How can we ever repay you?"

"Your majesty is too kind," he said. "All we have done is what was asked of us."

"You and the men and women under you are far too modest," she

238

said. "Is there anything I can do for you?"

"You have already granted us permission to finish the restoration of Roanoke," he answered. "What more could we want beyond the chance to do what we love?"

"So what you want most is a chance to continue working?" she asked after a moment's reflection.

"More than anything," he answered.

"Then we shall have to see to it that more opportunities present themselves in the days to come," she said.

"My Queen," he said, almost timidly for someone so confident, "If I might be so bold?"

"Yes?"

"It is not just the craftsmen who feel thus," he said. "All any of the Tuatha dé wish is to have meaningful purpose and the honor of fulfilling that purpose to the best of our ability. If we have those things, we can want for little else."

"You have given me much to think on," Megan said. "And I promise you that I will do so."

As the words left her lips, she felt something settle over her.

Inside Guardian Castle, she was pleased to see furnishings similar to the ones they had at the cottage near Haven. She caught up to the happy couple in the kitchen where Sam must have taken charge, because the combination of cast iron and modern conveniences could have come from no one else.

The bedrooms, of which there were many, had been lavishly furnished, and there were quite a few to which Megan clearly heard Luminita whisper "our children" into her husband's ear.

"I'm so moving in," Jade said.

"Me too," her father added.

But it was the music room, filled to overflowing with a variety of instruments, that brought the bard to tears.

"This is too much," she whispered, drawing Emelia and Megan into her arms.

"You're family," Emelia whispered back, "and we take care of our family. But next year you're going to have to look to Megan for the good Christmas presents. On my waitress salary you're going to be doing good to get a pair of socks."

"And where are you going to be waiting tables?" Sam asked, drawing her back to him.

"At Gordon's of course," she teased.

"I wasn't aware that I was hiring," he laughed.

"Of course you are."

"I take it you don't want your old job back at the Tribune?" Mrs. Grimble asked.

"Nope, it's a bad idea for relatives to work together," Emelia said. "Besides, my heart was never there."

"Well you were a damned good reporter, and you'll always be welcomed back if the Gordon's gig doesn't pan out," Bruce's mother added.

"Nope, I'm definitely going to Gordon's."

"Even though I still haven't made a job offer," Sam said, his happiness spilling out into the sound of his voice.

"You will," Emily predicted, looking up into his eyes. "Because we won't want to be away from each other once we're married."

The room went silent.

"Did you just propose to me?" Sam stammered.

"You really must pay attention," she whispered, "we might not have waited as long as Paul and Nita, but we still have lost time to make up, Silly Man Who Still Talks to Trees.

Chapter XXVI: Yet More Treetop Confessions

Bruce woke to the familiar sounds and sensations of his childhood bedroom. His ceiling fan was twisting long shadows across the room, and the air was on since it was so much warmer in Texas than it had been in Wyoming.

His parents remained deeply asleep, probably relaxing for the first time since Paul and Luminita had shared their wedding plans. Jade, as usual, slept so deep that he could barely sense the flavor of her dreams. Paul was, of course, absent, and Bruce spent several minutes envisioning the two newlyweds in their new home. They were probably still asleep as well after insisting to play for everyone before releasing them for the evening.

But there were other things missing as well. He doubted he'd ever get used to the absence of the Hermit at the edges of his mind when he was this close to Guarded Wood. And of course, there was still an empty place where he knew he should be able to feel Megan. From the moment she'd awoken the power within him, he'd been able to feel her at the edge of his senses, thus defining the outline of who he was and what he wanted to be.

He got up silently, not wanting to wake anyone who would feel the need to talk when all he really wanted was to drink his coffee in silence for a bit while he considered all that had happened. In the kitchen he heated the water in the French press with magic for the sake of allowing his light-sleeping father to sleep in.

Then he slipped out the back door which he'd oiled thoroughly back during his night time excursions with Megan. As annoying as those disturbances at the boundary had been during the summer, he missed them now.

He glanced over at the darkened silhouette of her house, wondering if she was already up, watching for the sun's first rays as he planned to do. He wanted to reach for her so badly it frightened him. But for now at least, he'd lost that right.

The spiral staircase winded him a little, and he vowed to start running again as soon as he was back.

The drowsy awareness of the newlyweds touched his mind as he crossed the threshold of their lands before moving on, making him smile. He only spilled a little bit of the cup on his way up the ladder, and he was overjoyed to find that someone had hung a swing like the one on Megan's porch in the tower. He sat down gratefully and started to drink as he waited for the sun to rise.

Without warning, Megan appeared in front of him, already moving toward the rail. Then, feeling his presence, she turned.

"I'm sorry," she whispered as if fearing to wake someone, "I didn't feel you under all of those shields. I'll go."

"Please stay," he pleaded.

"Are you sure?" she asked.

"More than I've been about anything lately," he answered.

"I doubt Antonia would approve," Megan teased.

"If Antonia doesn't stop antagonizing your mother, it won't matter what she does and doesn't approve of for much longer."

"Is it okay that I really don't like that girl?" Megan asked.

"To be honest," he said wearily, "I'm not exactly sure what I liked

243

about her. She's a very different person when no one else is around though."

"She is beautiful," Megan admitted.

"If you're into that whole high contrast dark hair and pale skin thing," he admitted.

The sky had lightened enough for him to see her lopsided smirk as she glanced in his direction. He was glad it was still too dark for her to see the way it touched him to see it.

"I need to tell you something," she said, exhaling hard as if trying to muster up the courage to do something scary.

"Consider me your captive audience," he said, smiling.

"You remember how the Morrigan made a promise, and all of her descendants were bound to it?"

"Yes," he answered. He hadn't expected her to bring this up so quickly and feared she might still be angry with him. If so, she had every right to be.

"There's another one that binds us where we can't fall in love until we're mature enough to do it wisely," she said in a rush.

"Your ancestors really had problems with keeping their noses out of other people's business," he observed.

"I've never agreed with anything more," she said, taking another deep breath. "I want you to know that I've thought about what you said about me thinking that no one would want to seduce you for you and only you. And I'm really sorry. That was cruel."

"Megan," he said, reaching for her hand to comfort her and let her know that he understood. But he wasn't expecting the surge of raw power that rose in response to his ability as they started to interact. "Wow, what kind of vitamins are you taking these days?"

"It's happening much faster now," she said absently.

244

"You don't have anything to be sorry for," he said as he'd intended to before touching her.

"Yes, I do. Maybe there's just something wrong with me," she started.

"No," he said firmly.

"Let me finish," she said urgently, squeezing his hand. "Maybe it's this damned promise thing. But no matter what the cause, it's not okay for me to let you think I don't care about you. I might not understand how romantic love works, and I don't know if I will ever feel the way toward you that I sense you feel for me. But I want you to know that ever since that day when you let me sit next to you on the bus, you have been the center of my world. You are the only one I think of when I want to talk. You're the one I always turn to when something happens, and I'm so very sorry that I did such a poor job of telling you…that you could ever think that I don't know how lucky I am to have you in my life."

"You might not come out and say it," he said after making sure that she was, indeed, finished. "But you still tell me. I'm just too selfish to admit it."

"Like when?"

"I seem to recall an incident not so long ago when you nuked my bedroom when you lost track of me for a little while," he said with a grin.

"But I let you think I was dead for so long," she countered.

"Because you were busy saving me and everyone that you love."

"And that was right after you jumped off of a cliff and fought a giant supernatural bird to save me!" she exclaimed, spilling some of her coffee with the gesture that accompanied it.

He winced.

"We seriously don't ever need to talk about that. I think it shaves a week off of my life every time someone brings it up," he said at last.

"And yet I would bet my life on the fact that you'd do it again if the need arose," she added.

"I don't want to stay in Haven," he said, changing the subject.

"Yes," she agreed, sitting straighter. "Can we please come home? I think William has everything he needs from me. I don't know if it's going to help his boys or not, but I'm so tired of being there. I just wish I knew what it was that the Morrigan sent us to do."

"I do too. Maybe you just had to prove you weren't going to take the path that Priscilla saw in her visions," he agreed. "How is your mom settling into the house?"

"She hates the yellow paint," Megan said. "I thought you said she liked it."

"No," he replied, "I said that was the color you ended up painting it. This was too far out for me to see how she responded to it."

"How about now?" Megan asked, "What do you see now?"

He sighed deeply. "A big blank nothing," he admitted. "There's been a lot of that lately. But as long as you're with me, I don't mind. So other than the paint, how is she doing with being back in the house after Azarich passed away?"

"I have no idea," Megan said. "As far as I know she's only been there to pick up clothes."

"What do you mean? Isn't she there now?"

"Nope," Megan said with a wicked grin. "She left with Sam last night and told me not to bother waiting for her."

Chapter XXVII: Bardic Windchimes

Megan took the turkey that Ben Grimble had just removed from her grandfather's smoker and tried not to get drawn into thoughts about people who weren't there. Paul and Nita had suggested that it would be more comfortable for everyone to meet at their new home, but no one wanted to intrude on the privacy of the newlyweds, so here they were, once again at the treehouse.

Emelia passed her on the way to the treehouse carrying a catering container with the Gordon's logo on the side, and Megan could feel the happiness radiating from her. At that moment it was hard to believe that this woman was one of the most feared people in the magical world.

Then she came up on Kate standing below the treehouse, looking up the stairs with trepidation.

"Want me to give you a lift up?" she asked, putting the turkey through the shadows onto the table next to the other two.

"You know," Kate answered. "I've always wanted to try that."

"Tell you what, we've got a little bit of time left before we're due to start eating," Megan said, "Let's take a little adventure. Is there any place you've ever wanted to go but never had the chance?"

"That's a pretty long list," Kate chuckled.

Megan offered her arm, which Kate took and they walked the shadows to August's beach. A storm was brewing on the horizon and the waves were loud as they crashed on the shore. Kate marveled at the power of it all, but she was old and it was a little bit chilly.

Then Megan took them to the waterfall from her mother's runestone, knowing that it was secluded enough with little risk of anyone coming up on them by accident. Like the beach, the falling water was loud, but at least it was warm. Birds they'd only seen in books flew through the canopy of trees that surrounded the lagoon, and Kate's face was full of childlike wonder.

Then, saving the best for last, Megan took her to the mountaintop shrine where August had told them about the fauns. Much to their surprise, one of the elusive creatures was standing directly in front of them when they appeared. However, it not only seemed unsurprised to see them, but gave a short bow of greeting before going on to wherever it had been headed before they came.

"Did we just see Goatman?" Kate asked in wonder.

"One of them," Megan answered, watching the small form disappear down the stairway.

Finally she brought them back to the deck of the treehouse, knowing that nothing she did next could possibly compare to seeing the local legend up close.

"Thank you, girl," Kate said, giggling. "That's the best Christmas gift I've ever gotten." There was something in the way she said it that made Megan realize that she and Alan hadn't even gotten to spend the holidays together before he'd passed.

Bruce paused to give Kate a hearty one-armed hug since he was carrying a loaf of bread that looked like it had been cooked in August's bread oven. Then, pulling out the package he'd held under his arm, he offered it to Megan.

"It's your present," he said awkwardly.

"And here's yours," she said. Reaching through the shadows, she pulled his from the foot of her bed where she'd left it. "I went first last year, so now it's your turn."

Moving over to one of the tables that weren't currently laden with food, they huddled together over the gifts.

"You've gotten better at wrapping," he said, trying to get into it. "And I detect my sister's hand in your use of tape."

Megan giggled. "She said that watching you struggle was half of the fun, and she was right."

"Wow," he said, finally lifting off the top. "You got me thermal underwear…that's not weird at all. And you," he paused, sensing more to the gift than first appeared, "enchanted it so that it would always keep me at the perfect temperature no matter how cold it gets."

"I worry about how cold you get sometimes," she said, waiting for him to find the other part.

"And," he paused again, this time too excited to maintain his calm facade as he pushed the long johns aside and found his necklace at the very bottom.

"I thought you might be wanting to have that back," she said quietly.

With a goofy grin that left no doubt that he was indeed Paul's brother, he lifted it over his head and came fully alive to her senses again. In response, the temperature on the deck soared as he amplified her power and the warming enchantment she'd used.

"Whoa," he said, swaying slightly in his seat.

"Are you okay?" Megan asked, reaching out to steady him.

"Just give me a second," he said, closing his eyes and centering himself. "I'm okay. You've just gotten stronger, and it's a lot to handle."

"Take it off," Megan said, reaching for it in concern. "I didn't mean to hurt you."

"Mine," he said, reaching up to catch her hand even though he hadn't opened his eyes yet. "I'm already getting used to it, and you are most definitely not hurting me. It's almost intoxicating in fact. Have you noticed any differences in your abilities?"

"Things seem to be much easier," she admitted.

"Maybe it's just that I'm sensitive to the power flow around me after working with Catherene," he said, finally opening his eyes. "But I'd guess you are four or five times stronger than you were before I stormed off like a child that night. And you were already the strongest of us all."

Megan really didn't want to talk about that right now.

"Can I open mine now?" she asked. When he nodded, she pulled back the perfectly wrapped coverings which she was happy to note had not been designed to make opening difficult to find a familiar leather-bound book. She looked up to find him grinning. "I know it's supposed to be okay to regift things, but why are you giving me back the journal I gave you last Christmas?"

"Open it," he said in reply.

"Wow," she said, still confused. "You've already filled the whole thing. Is this your way of telling me you need another one? Your gifting skills have gotten weak," she teased.

"Says the girl who gave me underwear," he said, rolling his eyes. "Read it."

As her eyes slid over the first dated entry and the familiar words it held, her eyes opened wide in recognition.

"It's every one of the stories they told us," he said proudly. "The ones they told while I was there, at least."

"How did you remember them all?" she asked in wonder. "I swear these are Grandpa's actual words."

In response he pulled out his phone and said, "Storytime." It immediately pulled up the voice recorder and started.

"I can remember wondering why you always said something about it being storytime when they'd start," she laughed.

"There are even a couple that August told us in there," he added.

"Mariana will probably want to read those," Megan said.

"She'd probably like to hear the audio since she didn't get a chance to meet him in person," he said. "I'll download all of the files to your phone so you can listen to them any time you want."

Unable to help herself, she put the book down and gave him one of her best Jade style hugs, refusing to let go until she was ready.

"I really missed you too," he said happily, making no attempt to free himself.

When she finally opened her eyes, Megan found the newlyweds standing in front of them, smiling broadly. She knew they were happy to have the tensions between them over.

"We already gave Bruce his present," Paul said as his wife handed Megan a cloth wrapped bundle.

"It's heavy," she said, hefting it in her hand. The clank of metal and something faintly melodic sounded within as she carefully removed the folds of fabric.

When it was free, she discovered a finely crafted windchime in which copper tubes hung from a burnished brass bird that looked like it had been crafted to turn in the wind when it blew.

"There's a hook at the edge of the roof," Luminita said, pointing to where Paul carried it over and hung it. "That's where we tuned it."

Then Paul made a soft hissing noise and a breeze crossed the deck, making the bird twirl in the sunlight and the sail move the striker around the tubes. A haunting melody rose in response that made everyone in the treehouse stop and look.

"I didn't know you could enchant objects," Bruce said quietly so he

251

wouldn't disturb the music.

"We can't," Luminita said, "But we can alter the way things work that already make sounds so that they mimic simple aspects of what we do with our magic."

"And the weather?" Megan asked, remembering their part with the sunrise that Bruce crafted for her.

"We can," Paul said, still looking at the windchime critically. "It's tricky business though, and it's really easy to spawn massive thunderstorms if we're not careful."

"So do you like it?" Luminita asked.

"I love it," Megan answered.

"But why did it have to be a bird?" Bruce complained.

"They were just doing what they would in nature," Paul said.

"There was nothing natural about those two," Bruce countered, looking away from the windchime.

"What are you talking about?" Luminita asked.

"A giant bird tried to eat me and Bruce," Megan said before he cut her off.

"Who is already regretting bringing it up."

"Paul forgot to mention that part," Nita said, stepping into the warmth of her husband's arm and hugging him. "He's absolutely fascinated by birds in this lifetime."

"What can I say," he replied, kissing the top of her head. "I like what I like."

"Well it's still perfect," Megan said, reaching through the shadows and producing a small bag that she handed to the bard.

"But you and Emelia have already given us so much!" she exclaimed.

"This is more of a necessity than a gift," Megan said.

Inside the bard found a new phone and headphones.

"Oh my god," Bruce cried in genuine shock, bringing Emelia over to see what was happening. "Did you actually buy technology for someone?"

"Well," Megan said guiltily, "It wasn't really me. The Tuatha dé tech department took care of it."

Bruce looked at her in utter bewilderment.

"You're going to love Maeve," Megan added. "But anyway, the

phone is loaded with just about every music service you can imagine. And if you need anything else just let me know and we'll get it for you."

"Does this mean I get my phone back?" Paul asked.

"I'm sure you guys are having fun over there," Sam called, "But can we eat now? I'm famished."

"Of course," Luminita called out loud enough for everyone to hear after she linked arms with Emelia. "We could have eaten an hour ago if someone hadn't kept pulling his fiancé back into a warm bed this morning!"

Emelia kicked her playfully and Megan realized that her mother shared the same unconscious link with the bard that she herself did.

"Oh my god!" Jade yelled. "Is Sam Wise actually blushing?"

"My people don't blush," he said, trying to muster his usual dignity and failing miserably. "It's just the heat."

"Good try, young man!" Kate cackled. "It's forty degrees out here!"

Chapter XXVIII: Misjudged

Bruce felt blissfully warm while he walked the shadows to Haven's main gate. He was wearing both of Megan's gifts, and although he wasn't looking forward to telling Antonia he was leaving, he was more than ready to leave this place behind him. It was also nice to have the ability to walk the shadows back, not so much for the actual ability but what it meant about his restored relationship with his best friend.

"If you don't want to come in just say so," the gatekeeper called, making Bruce realize that he'd paused there at the entrance, thinking about the time he'd just spent in Nickelville. He stepped through, thinking about how much he'd never liked the young man and remembering what William had said about him. As always, he felt a moment of panic as the bond he shared with Megan was severed and his view of the future diminished to shadows.

He found William in the main training hall, surrounded by a large group of his younger students and the three older teens Cat had mentioned in passing that helped her husband. One of them was a councilwoman's son, placed there to make sure that their teacher wasn't corrupting the youth of Haven. But the way the children all stared off into the distance as if in a trance was a bit unsettling. As he watched, his mentor lifted a brick from a large pile next to him with his mind, rotated through all axes and then placed it neatly into the corner of a large square that had been marked out onto the stone floor.

"What are you doing?" Bruce asked.

William held up his hand to tell him to watch. Then the students all came back to themselves, looking eagerly at the pile of bricks.

"Okay," William said. "Let's show our friend Bruce what you just learned."

A veritable cyclone of telekinesis enveloped the pile of bricks, lifting them into the air where they moved seemingly of their own volition to the square, ordering themselves in perfectly stacked rows and columns until they filled the marked space to a height of three feet.

"How long have you been working with them on this?" Bruce asked, astounded that they could do something this complex at such a young age.

"I was teaching them how to do it when you came in," he said proudly. "This is what has come from the communication work I did with Megan."

"I'm glad," Bruce said, watching the children as they begged their teacher to let them do it again. "Did any of it help your boys?"

"It's hard to say," William answered, keeping most of the disappointment from showing on his face. "Cat and I have been trying to reach them several times a day using something similar to this. It hasn't worked yet, but we're still hopeful."

"I just wanted to let you know that Megan and I are going to head back to Nickelville," Bruce said at last.

"I'm sorry to hear that," William said. "But I also understand the desire to be back home with family and friends. My wife and I will miss you. And of course my sister will miss Bri."

"I'm pretty sure those two will keep seeing each other," Bruce chuckled. "I'm certainly not brave enough to tell them they can't."

"Smart man," William said. "I'm glad they met. I've never seen Mari this happy."

"I also want to remind you that you know your way to Nickelville," Bruce said warmly, "And that you and your family will always be welcome there. Consider this an open invitation both to visit and to move there permanently if you'd like. We could use people like you. Then he handed William a folded piece of paper.

"What's this?" he asked.

"Paul figured out something while we were visiting," Bruce answered. "There's an opening into Guarded Wood about twenty miles from here. That's where my brother and sister have been hunting fossils. I suspect that's where August first gained access to the woods when he left."

"And these are the coordinates?" William asked.

Bruce nodded in reply.

"There may come a time when we take you up on that invitation," William said, touched by the offer. "Are you going to see Cat now?"

"That's the plan. We probably won't leave for a few hours yet," Bruce added. "So if you could send Mari out to see Bri that would be great."

"I'll let her know right now," the teacher said, "Take care of yourself, Bruce."

"You too," he said before heading back to the corridor.

Once outside, as he tried to figure out what to say to Antonia when he found her, his time to do so ran out when she appeared in his path.

"You're back," she said, smiling.

"Only for a bit," he replied, "We're going back to Nickelville."

Her eyes dropped to the spot just below his neck where he was sure she could see the outline of the stone necklace beneath his shirt.

"I'm sorry to hear that," she said coolly. "Before you go, I was wondering if you could look at this new piece we just acquired. It's got me completely stumped."

"Sure," he said, relieved that she seemed to be taking this so well.

Then she reached out and placed a pendant necklace into his hand. He had only a second to realize that something was horribly wrong before he was plunged into Priscilla's apocalyptic visions of Megan's destiny.

"You're making this up!" Luminita giggled as Paul tried to teach her a dance from his childhood. "People didn't actually do this in front of other people?"

"The early years of the new millennium were a scary time for dance," he answered, trying to sound serious. "Are you telling me that good little colonial girls didn't do anything like this?"

"Maybe the ones who were possessed," Nita answered, trying to replicate the strange series of motions that her husband was making.

"Did you come across possessed girls often?" he asked, trying to figure out if she was serious or not.

"No, but accusations of possession went hand in hand with those of witchcraft," she replied, sitting down for a moment, breathing heavily from their exertions. "And for some reason, my sisters and I kept a close ear out for those."

From where she sat, the bard could see out of the huge window that looked out from their tower bedroom across the expanse of the valley. A lake took up the lowest part, fed by the numerous creeks and rills that flowed down from the mountains. Even from this distance, she could see huge flocks of waterfowl.

Something changed out in Guarded Wood, and they both turned their attention toward it.

"There's an imbalance," she whispered.

"And it's pretty far in," Paul observed with a wide grin. "How would you feel about an overnight outing?"

"You're just eager to try out some of the camping gear you found in the gatehouse," she said, raising an eyebrow in an eerily accurate imitation of one of her sister's descendants.

"Guilty as charged," he agreed. "So what do you say?"

"I say I'll follow you anywhere," she said, pulling him closer and kissing him.

A while later the two of them, dressed in the forest clothing of the Tuatha dé with the exception, of course, of the leather trench coat that Paul had come to love, rode into the deeper paths of Guarded Wood. Their saddlebags held an assortment of gear that they probably wouldn't need. But as he'd said repeatedly during their quick preparations, it was always best to be prepared.

They rode slowly, enjoying the scenery and committing it to memory for times when the problems might be closer to home. But they also rode slowly because the paths in this direction weren't clear enough for Paul to ride on horseback without constant care to duck and push branches aside while he passed. She, on the other hand, could ride normally since she was so much shorter.

Over the next hour, they passed through a myriad of different landscapes, taking trails that should have doubled back on themselves any number of times, yet somehow never did.

"It's a good thing that Guarded Wood tells us where to go," Paul said. "I don't think I could remember how to get back if it didn't."

Then, without warning, they entered a vast open plain that continued out to the horizon. Paul whistled in recognition.

"Do you know this place?" Nita asked.

"Sam took pictures of it for me," he said, scanning the area. "They said it was too dangerous for Jade and me. August actually made Fang

259

keep us from following them. He had to sit on Jade to keep her at the treehouse."

"I wouldn't mind having a couple of wolves," the bard admitted.

"It would make Bruce's day if we got some," Paul said.

"So what happened here?" she asked. "I can feel powerful emotions in the past as it tries to surface for me."

"Let's cross back while I tell you," he said cautiously. "There are apparently two huge birds here that are invisible to our extra senses, the ones that almost killed Megan."

"Hence your brother's dislike for birds," she mused.

"August called them Huginn and Muninn," Paul began after they reached safety, "After Odin's ravens because they're both solid black. My brother said you can detect them with the normal five senses, but they are utterly invisible to the rest. Furthermore, they are completely immune to most forms of magic."

"Suddenly I start to understand why Emelia, Sam and August had so much trouble saving her," Luminita said, sitting down with her back against a tree while he talked. His bardic power made the images come alive in her mind, and it was nice to experience how she normally sounded to others firsthand.

"It was Bruce that saved her," Paul said quietly.

"Truly?" she said. "Don't misunderstand me, I like the lad well enough, but he's no warrior."

"You're not wrong," he said, "He'd much rather think his way around danger, and he's amazing at doing just that. But don't ever doubt his courage when it comes to protecting the ones he loves."

"And there's no one he loves more than Megan."

"He still gets scared senseless," Paul agreed, nodding. "Probably because he understands most situations better than the rest of us. And then he just puts it all aside and does it anyway. I just wish she felt the same way about him."

"We talked at length about that before they returned to Haven," she confided.

"When? I was there the whole time."

"It was too personal to share out loud," the bard explained.

"But you're still going to tell me?" he asked.

"As she knew I would. There have never been secrets between you and I," she said, "and there never will."

Paul realized that he already knew what she'd learned through the bond he shared with his wife. "Does Bruce know?"

"That she did not tell me. And it is her secret to share, not ours." They sat quietly for a moment, just enjoying each other and the sounds of the forest around them.

"I never realized there could be so much excitement living out in the woods!" he said happily.

"It certainly does beat living the same night over and over for two centuries," she admitted.

He pulled her up into his embrace and kissed her until she almost forgot why they were there.

"No," she said, "We have work to do."

Quite a while later he agreed.

"Did you see any of the honking cow things?" he asked before they returned.

"Honking cows?" she asked.

"There were thousands of these loud, honking wildebeests the last time they were here," he said. "I think that might be what called us."

"We have to go find them?" she asked.

"I'll bet they'll be on the side with the trees. That's the only cover they have from the birds. But we're going to have to move both the wildebeests and the birds. They've decimated the vegetation in this area and whatever the rocs ate before they came has probably died off. This area is going to need a good long break before anything can live here again. If we take the animals but leave the birds, they'll starve."

"Then we should probably move the birds first," she reasoned. "Otherwise we'll have to keep a watch out for them the whole time we're working, and I'd happily go my whole life without finding out what it would be like to be carried off by a bird. I'm not fond of heights."

"I agree," he said.

"Do you have a new home for them in mind?" she asked.

"My gut says they need to go to that series of valleys with the big rocky cliffs in the distance," he answered. "They probably need someplace like that to nest."

"Isn't that awfully close to home?" she asked.

"They can't get loose now that the boundary is fixed, and…" he paused. "I can't really explain why it's the right place for them, but I still know it's right."

"Then that's good enough for me," she said, kissing him once more, then pulling her violin from the case that hung on her saddlebag.

It only took them a few seconds after they returned to see the dark shapes in the sky overhead, and from the fact that they stayed close to where the sun could hide them, it was clear that they were already hunting the bard and her mate.

"Dear god," he exclaimed. "Those things are enormous. I mean, I knew they had to be big in order to carry off one of the wildebeests, but wow."

"I can see why Bruce hates them," she agreed. Then she brought her bow to the strings and started to play, hoping that the beasts wouldn't be immune to this sort of enchantment as well.

Ready to flee back into the previous part of the woods, they watched as the rocs dropped lower, becoming even larger than either of them had imagined. When they landed a short distance away, they finally got a good look at them.

"They're definitely not ravens," Paul mused, moving closer now that they were sure that the great brutes were bound by the music. "If I had to guess I'd say that they were based on some sort of falcon. As a matter of fact, I can see darker patterns in their plumage that are just about an exact match for peregrines. It's like someone took normal falcons, put them on steroids and spray painted them black."

I can control them with the music, she sent, *but unless you want them to walk all the way to the valley you mentioned, we're going to have to open temporary portals for them to fly through.*

We can do that? Paul asked. *Cool, but if Guarded Wood gave you that information and not me, then it follows that you should be the one to do it. I can control the birds.*

The two of them soon rode back the way they'd come through Guarded Wood, stirring up animals they hadn't known to be there as the massive predators traveled above. It was slow going with both of them playing as they went, but the horses seemed to know where they were going without guidance. Furthermore, their steeds seemed to understand that they were safe from the dark shapes overhead even if the other forest creatures did not.

It was a relief to release them into their new home, although the local wildlife might not have agreed.

When they returned to the barren plain, it was much easier to have a look around. The honking cows were still hiding, unaware that it was now safe to be out in the open. Great splotches of rusty red dotted the level ground all the way to where it ended at the cliff she now knew to be ahead. Large boulders of the same color littered the landscape, having possibly tumbled down from the mountain behind them.

"I wonder if this place is the reason I can't use a compass in Guarded Wood," he mused. "This whole thing seems to be sitting on top of the biggest iron deposit I've ever even heard of. That's also why the grass died off so fast. There wasn't enough topsoil to hold it in place when the wildebeests started to graze on it."

"I know that we only have to move what's left of the herd to the next zone over," Nita said, "but it's getting late. Could we wait until morning to finish it?"

"I was thinking the same thing," Paul said. "Do you want to catch something for dinner or set up camp?"

"I'm pretty sure I felt rabbits in the last zone," she said. "I'll go get us one if you don't mind."

"Sounds good," he said, "I'll follow you and get firewood. That way I can have the fire ready by the time you get back. Would you like me to set up a tent or would you rather sleep under the stars tonight?"

"It looks like it will be a clear night," she said, glancing out across the sky. "Let's sleep in the open."

"Do you think you can do the past projection thing later?" he asked. "I'd really like to see exactly what happened here that day."

"Me too," she said, heading off into the trees.

"You are so perfect for me," he called after her.

"You're more than adequate yourself, Husband," she called back, smiling in spite of herself. His pleasure at being called this made her smile even more.

By the time she returned to the plain with a good-sized rabbit, he had camp set up a dozen yards back from the cliff. The horses were unsaddled, and they were grazing on the sparse vegetation that peeked out from the rusty outcroppings nearby. A cooking fire was already burning down to the coals they'd need for spit-roasting her kill.

After they'd eaten, when the sun was low on the horizon, she summoned that bit of magic that had nothing to do with the bardic gift he shared. It was always a thrill for Paul when she did this.

Sensing that the events of that day had begun near one of the other entrances to this domain, they started there. Closing her mind to better summon the past forward into the present, Luminita took his hand and brought him with her.

A honking mass of grass-fed chaos carpeted the open space before them. She was glad that sounds didn't usually come clearly through their travels from the past, because even now the atonal din was almost too much for their bardic senses.

At first it looked like August and the others were just trying to figure out what they should do. Something had clearly gone wrong in their coming, though Luminita had no idea what that might have been, and it didn't look like they'd had the option of ducking back into the previous portion of Guarded Wood to plan.

One of the rocs dove down out of the sun, snatching up a wildebeest as if its quarter ton of struggling muscle meant nothing. Then the rest stampeded.

"I didn't realize your brother could run so fast," Nita whispered, watching as all of them tried to escape to the passage.

"Like the wind," Paul whispered back.

They were unprepared for the violence of the rampaging beast that knocked Megan several yards through the air or for her mother's savage retaliation as Bruce, without any regard for his own safety, ran straight for her.

The bards followed the ghostly images across the field until they reached the cliff. But Bruce wasn't the only one to surprise them. At one point, while Emelia's concentration was focused on clearing his path, she failed to notice one of the great beasts bearing down on her. With a speed and strength they wouldn't have believed, Sam launched himself toward it, grabbing its horns in his huge hands, and twisting its head downward to make it tumble away from the woman he loved.

August created massive swathes of fire with which he attempted to turn the herd away toward the trees.

In spite of the knowledge that Megan and Bruce returned relatively unharmed, both Paul and his wife gasped when Bruce leapt from the cliff. They could now see the wide expanse of water below them, stretching out toward the horizon.

"Have I ever mentioned that my brother is afraid of water?" he asked.

"That can't be true," she whispered, watching as he appeared high in the air before slamming into the bird with such force that it let go of its prey.

Together he and Megan plummeted into the empty space below with Bruce's arm bent back at an unnatural angle while he tried to cover her nose and mouth before they hit the water below.

"I dislocated my shoulder once," Paul said quietly. "I could barely think it hurt so bad."

"Yet all he could think of was to protect her," Luminita murmured. "I misjudged him badly."

"We all do," Paul admitted.

When at last they'd seen what there was to see, they sought the comfort of each other's embrace beneath a sky so filled with stars as to grant them a glimpse of the eternity they'd likely spend together in Guarded Wood.

"I could never do something like that," Luminita whispered just as she drifted off to sleep into her husband's arms.

Even though they both slept well, she did wake once in the night when Paul began to thrash in his sleep. Just before he woke, he cried out, asking some unseen presence for forgiveness. She didn't understand what it meant, and she considered packing them up and returning to the safe comfort of Guardian Castle. But then he pulled her close, and she did her best to chase away the terrors of the night. This time they slept peacefully until dawn's first light.

Chapter XXIX: The Queen's Hunt

Dougal seethed with anger at his inability to distance himself from the Queen. No matter how much he tried to lock away his feelings, they still came to the surface in ways that endangered his ability to protect her in a land populated by her enemies. So he'd chosen to come back out to the spot where he'd watched over her in the early days before she'd asked him to call her by her name.

He knew he had no right to even hope that she would choose him over the inconsiderate boy who had once again, from the look of things, chosen the company of her enemies over her. He could sense her worry in the way she held herself as she sat on the cottage steps, pretending to pay attention to whatever his sister and her companion were talking about.

But even as Dougal sat there, he could recognize differences between the way his sister looked at the shy Child of Nyx and the way she usually pursued the women she liked. And even though he'd vowed he would not be the one to tell their father, he liked Mariana and thought she might very well be strong enough to tame his sister's wild ways.

Clouds rolled in, darkening the valley. The wind changed direction, cutting at right angles from where it had come just a short time earlier. Megan stood up to get a better look at the sky. Lightning branched overhead and he decided he should probably move closer in case she needed him.

Something slammed into his left side, just below the armpit, with all the force of a war hammer slung by a god, knocking him down from his perch. Luckily, he fell on the opposite side of the blow, but pain still blossomed where he'd been struck, making each shallow breath an agonizing ordeal.

He had just enough time to thank whatever deity watched over fools in trees that his armor had held before someone large and heavy pinned him to the ground. Then something hard and cold encircled his neck and locked with a terrifying click.

He knew it was an iron collar as soon as he felt its weight settle on him. He also knew what would happen if he tried to walk the shadows as his every instinct begged him to do. He found the cloaked Child of Nyx's hands before the man could draw a weapon. Then he pulled his own legs up enough to heave the man off to the side, and rolled over on top of him.

Even though the smallest movements ground the jagged edges of his broken rib into his flesh, he managed to get in one good punch to where he thought his assailant's throat should be and was rewarded by a gurgling cough. Then he launched himself away in a roll. When he came up the Scathlahm's Blade was in his hand.

"Only a coward attacks from concealment," Dougal taunted, scanning the area around him for movement. But even as he did so, he realized that the bullet had hit him before he heard the report, meaning that his enemy was not alone.

The rain increased from a drizzle to a downpour and he caught the faint halo of his enemy. Diving to put a tree between himself and the cowardly assassin, he came up with his free hand already pulling the collar out as far as he could from his skin on one side. Then, knowing that he had only seconds before his invisible opponent cleared the tree, Dougal slipped the Scathlahm's Blade under the collar and swept outward in one mighty arc, turning the metal molten in the instant before it shattered.

This new pain eclipsed the broken rib and he almost lost consciousness. Free to use his abilities, he cloaked himself as Mariana had taught them and walked the shadows to another nearby tree branch where the foliage would hide his displacement of the rain. He scanned the ground for his enemy but couldn't see anything.

Realizing that the Queen might be in danger, he walked the shadows to Megan's side and fell to one knee, not out of fealty but because he was dangerously close to blacking out.

Brighid moved in front of the Queen, drawing her sword from the armory even as she cast Mari through the shadows into the cabin where she'd be safer. He took an extremely painful deep breath to steady himself and rose back to his feet.

There are two attackers in the woods, he sent, *not wanting to try and yell over the roar of the wind and rain. One of them is a sniper. They ambushed me.*

No one could get a clean shot off from any distance in this downpour, Bri sent.

In the next flash of lightning, over a dozen large dark shapes could be seen sprinting toward where they stood.

Hellhounds, Brighid sent in recognition.

The Children of Nyx are seriously starting to piss me off, Megan sent, stepping between her protectors as the creatures drew closer. Energy arced outward from her outstretched hands in a wave of pure power, shredding the turf for a dozen yards and sending the whining beasts flying through the air as if they weighed nothing.

"Don't hurt them," Mariana yelled from behind, apparently not interested in staying inside where it was safe. "Can you get the collars off of them? That's how they control the wolves."

Before the huge beasts could recover, Megan reached out and broke the locks one at a time, freeing each of them to run back to Haven.

"We need to find out what happened to Bruce," Megan yelled before getting a better look at her Scathlahm, "What happened to your neck?"

"One of the cowards put an iron collar on me," he yelled over the storm.

"How did you get it off?" Brighid asked, horrified.

"Is that a bullet hole in your coat?" Megan asked, and even though she'd spoken quietly, her words seemed to travel the length of the valley.

"That's how they got me down from the tree," he said. "It's okay though, my armor held. Feels like it broke a rib. Then I used the Blade to break the collar and came to warn you."

"Cloak yourselves and move away so they don't know where you are," Megan commanded in a way that let them know it wasn't a suggestion.

"What are you doing?" Brighid asked.

"I'm going hunting," the Queen said with a chilling smile and disappeared.

"I should have gone with her," Dougal murmured. "She shouldn't be alone out there."

"We would have only gotten in her way," Bri said from nearby.

Then Megan was back, not even bothering to cloak herself.

"What did you do?" Mari asked.

"I laid wards all over this valley," she answered with her eyes cast downward as if she were concentrating on something far away, or perhaps, Dougal thought, like a spider waiting for its prey to step into the web. "If anything out there larger than a golden retriever moves, I'll know it."

Then her hand shot out to the side as if she were reaching for something just above her head, drawing a struggling cloaked man through the shadows. Energy arched across the back of her hand and the clearing was filled with screams and the smell of burning flesh. A large man dressed in tightly bound layers of woolen cloth appeared within her grasp, struggling to free himself.

"And if anyone attempts to bend light around themselves then they're as good as mine," she said, her eyes glowing violet in the dim light of the storm.

The big man stopped struggling and looked down at her without a trace of fear in his eyes. Then he shuddered and went limp. She let him slump to the ground, wiping her hand on her wet jeans as if they'd been soiled by touching him.

"What happened?" Dougal asked, disappointed that the Child of Nyx had escaped judgement. He was rather pleased by the burns around the man's neck though.

"He's an assassin," Mariana said, looking down at him. "They have small explosive charges implanted at the base of their brain stem to keep the Tuatha dé from judging them and finding out what they know."

Frowning, Megan opened her hand and a small, jagged piece of blood-soaked metal appeared in her palm. The rain immediately began to wash the chunks of flesh and blood from it to wash run her arm.

"Did you just pull that from the inside of his head?" Bri cried in revulsion.

"I needed to know what it felt like and how it worked," Megan said calmly, looking at it with detached interest. Then she dropped it on the corpse. "None of them will escape from me that way again."

"Mariana," the Queen continued. "I need you to go and find your brother. Tell him what has happened here, and find out why Bruce hasn't returned."

When the cloaked Child of Nyx had left, Bri asked what she planned to do if Bruce had been harmed.

"Don't worry," she answered, following the girl's cloaked progress through her wards. "We'll get all of our friends out before I raze Haven to the ground."

It sounded like a joke, but Dougal knew better.

Megan moved them inside, knowing that they had nothing to fear inside of her protections. She knew she should sit down and conserve her energy for what promised to be a long night, but her nervous energy needed an outlet. So she paced around the room while Bri taped her brother's ribs with the first aid kit she'd plucked from the treehouse.

"There they are," Megan said, and then with an unconscious gesture, she reached out to where they walked and brought them through the shadows to where she stood.

"How are you doing that?" Bri asked, looking over from where she was still helping her brother don his chainmail shirt. "I couldn't even feel Mari that far out."

"Where is Bruce?" Megan asked, ignoring the question.

"He's back in the room where he was staying before," William answered with his breath steaming in the cold room. He lit the fire in the fireplace with a thought and then continued. "Which is strange because he came to tell me goodbye earlier this afternoon. Then he told me he was going to go see Cat before he went and even invited all of us to come live in Nickelville."

"He never made it there," Mari said. "I checked with Cat before we left."

"What really concerns me is what my sister said happened here," he said. "It's hard to see how someone could accidentally set an assassin and hellhounds on you."

273

"Mari told us not to hurt them," Megan said before adding, "They were being controlled with these." She reached out through the shadows and pulled one of the iron collars to her. Then she handed it to William, who stared at it gravely.

Dougal rubbed his neck gingerly.

"There's no doubt about this," he said, looking at it closely. "The council tried to kill you. Only Priscilla could have sanctioned this."

"It works in your favor that the old hag continues to underestimate your ability to work around iron," Mari said, looking at the collar in distaste.

"My Queen," Bri said, pointing toward the collar, "I don't want to criticize your actions, but every time you move iron through Tyr Sgodl it causes major disturbances."

"You caused an electromagnetic storm when you moved the car," Dougal added. "That's how I found you."

"Sorry," Megan said, distracted. "Did you actually get to speak with Bruce?"

"Yes and no," he answered, clearly not looking forward to what he was about to say. "Antonia was with him, and he didn't look very good. Very distracted. She told me that he'd changed his mind and that he wanted to stay a while longer. Then she told me to give you this."

When he held out his hand, Bruce's necklace lay in the center of his palm.

Chapter XXX: The High Council

Mariana and William waited together on a stone bench in the colosseum-like amphitheater tucked deep within the lowest parts of Haven. Although she'd never been there before, her brother had been on several occasions. What worried her most was that since this was an unscheduled meeting of the High Council, there would be no audience to witness what transpired. Given what had happened the night before, she felt she had good reason for concern.

The High Council, in spite of the facade of its elected officials, was really nothing more than an extension of the Great Oracle. That might not always have been the case, but since the death of her brother and nephew at the Battle of Mag Tuired, no one remained to rein her in. And in the days immediately following that battle there were many who voiced concerns that listening to the oracle had coincided with the death of everyone who opposed her. But in the years since, those voices had fallen silent one way or another until Priscilla ruled in all but name over the Children of Nyx.

But as much as Mariana hated Antonia, she knew that Priscilla was infinitely more dangerous. Because where the young woman was motivated by her hunger for more power, the seer was driven by the need to find and destroy the green-eyed Tuatha dé who would one day end her.

Council members began to file in, each taking one of the padded benches that encircled the front half of the circular depression in which Bri and her brother sat. Priscilla entered last and took her seat, which looked surprisingly like a throne considering that Haven considered itself a democracy.

"What emergency proved so great that we needed to be dragged from our beds?" the old seer asked.

William stood and took his place directly before the old woman, ignoring the raised platform provided for the purpose. In doing so he seemed to acknowledge the fact that she was the only one of any importance.

"A storm rose over the valley last night," he began.

"How horrible," she cackled in mock horror. "We live inside of a mountain, William. What does this have to do with the Children of Nyx?"

"It wasn't a natural storm," he continued when the laughter of the council members subsided.

This brought a deep sigh from the old woman, and it was clear several members of the council had already begun to doze off where they sat.

"What are your guests getting up to now?" Priscilla asked. "If they're disrupting the energy flows outside of the city enough to cause storms then they're going to have to go."

"Neither the Tuatha dé Queen nor her friends caused this storm," he said gravely. "It was a diversion for an attack."

"Are you saying that someone attacked the child queen?" Priscilla asked.

"Someone shot the Queen's protector and collared him, so he couldn't warn her," he said.

"How awful," the oracle said, then yawned. "So I take it your little queen has led enemies to our front door. I suppose she wants to claim sanctuary and gain entrance to the city. Come on now William, we're not that dense. She probably faked the whole thing to get inside. You know our final verdict. Under no circumstances will she ever be granted access to this city again."

"And then someone set a pack of hellhounds on her," he added. There was a second of shocked silence in the huge space before the council erupted in outrage.

"I suppose you have more than the questionable word of this child to prove this?" Priscilla asked, quietly, her tone silencing the assembly.

"I have nearly a dozen of these," he said, reaching into his robe and removing one of the iron collars. "The entire pack had been fitted with them."

Everyone in the room knew that the very presence of such a thing outside the gate could only mean that the Children of Nyx were behind the attack. Ever the politician, the seer changed her strategy.

"Diana did report that some of her charges escaped last night," the seer admitted.

"And somehow enchanted hunting collars for themselves to make them hunt the Queen of the Tuatha dé?" he laughed. "Diana is their handler, but she lacks the skill to create even one such as this."

"Then what do you think happened?" Priscilla asked, her calm voice drawing looks of concern from around the chamber.

"I think someone," He said, locking eyes with Priscilla as he spoke, "Or even more likely several someone's, caused a storm to conceal the sniper who shot the Queen's protector from a distance while someone else collared him so he couldn't warn the Queen. Then one of the Tacet tried to kill him before going after the Queen."

"That's preposterous," Priscilla snapped, all bored theatrics gone now. "If one of the Tacet had been set on your little pet she'd be dead already."

"Actually he was little more than an annoyance to her," Mariana said, unable to keep her silence any longer. "It took her less than a minute to find him, and she would have judged him if he hadn't blown his charge before she could."

"So you do still speak," the old woman said, looking at her like she was something unpleasant. "I was afraid your days of playing with fire had left you mute. What is this nonsense of which you speak?"

"Once she knew he was there, the Queen reached out and found him even though he was cloaked. When he realized she would know who had sent him, he took his own life as his oath demanded."

"And just how do you know this?" Priscilla asked.

"Because I was there," Mari admitted.

"You were outside of Haven in the company of our enemies?" the seer asked dangerously.

"Yes."

"And what exactly were you doing there?"

"Saying my goodbyes," Mari answered reluctantly.

"How touching," Priscilla commented, eyeing her closely. "I wasn't aware that you'd been given permission to consort with the Tuatha dé Danann."

"I wasn't," Mari admitted, looking down in shame.

"Then what could have possibly tempted you to leave the safety of Haven?" she asked.

"Megan was friends with Augustus before his death," Mari answered.

"Even in death that man is still the bane of my existence," the old seer sighed. "I should have known that allowing you to study those moldy old books and scrolls would eventually lead to something like this."

"That doesn't have any bearing on the matter at hand," William interrupted. "Why was one of the Tacet sent without the approval of the council against the Queen of the Tuatha dé? Such an action risks the fragile peace we have with them."

"Marcus was likely working to eliminate what he felt to be a threat to our people," Priscilla answered. "He should be remembered as a hero."

"No one said his name," Mariana said quietly.

"So," William said before the oracle could try to spin the narrative another direction. "Let me get this straight. You didn't believe that the hellhounds had been set against the Queen, and then you knew that a pack had in fact been outside of Haven during the time in question. And that's not even addressing the problematic presence of the collars. Then you said that there was no possibility of one of the Tacet being involved, and now you know exactly which one it was. Let me guess, did he somehow escape too? Was he also wearing an enchanted collar?"

Mariana knew he'd gone so far beyond too far that there might not be any redemption.

"Be careful, half-breed," Priscilla whispered. "You were created to be this child's nemesis. If you are unequal to the task, you and your family might no longer be necessary within these walls. But yes, there is only one of the Tacet absent without my leave. It's not a huge leap to connect that if one of the Tacet is missing and your little friend killed one, that the two must be one in the same."

"And we are to assume that this Marcus worked entirely on his own?" he asked.

"He lost many friends and family at the hands of Emelia. Is it such a hard thing to believe that his honor demanded retribution when opportunity presented itself? Do you remember what that word means, William? Honor? Perhaps his actions were rash and unforgivable. But as he's already taken his own life, this matter is settled."

"She is prepared to leave," William called out before the council could adjourn. "The Queen waits only for her friend to return, and then

279

they will no longer be our problem."

"Our problem, you say?" Priscilla said in a voice that cracked like stone dragging against glass. "It was not *we* who brought her here and forfeited the location of our stronghold. It wasn't *we* who have been working with her in spite of the visions I've seen of her killing us all. This is *your* problem, William. And you had best deal with it soon before we truly begin to question where your loyalties lie. As for the Grimble boy, he has been granted sanctuary. He no longer wishes to remain in the company of this so-called queen. Furthermore, his skills have proven invaluable and it would set our artifact research back decades to lose him now."

"Allow Megan to see him, and perhaps she'll leave," Mari said, hopefully.

"I'm afraid that won't be possible," the seer said with malicious cheerfulness. "He was quite adamant in his desire to not see her again. This business has wasted too much of our time already. Discussion of this matter is ended. Oh, and Mariana?"

"Yes," she said, looking up at the evil woman before her.

"If you leave the gates again, don't bother coming back."

Chapter XXXI: Lost and Found

Megan was still awake when the sun rose the next morning. She'd expected William to come at some point, but as of yet he had not. So she continued to lay there at the center of the web she'd created, waiting for something to come looking for trouble that she'd be more than happy to supply.

Then someone foolishly entered the edge of the land she'd claimed as her own, and Megan slipped through the shadows to where her wards led her and cloaked herself even as she faded into reality.

The intruder was a stout, older woman with short gray hair. Dressed in worn outdoor garb keeping more with something from a department store catalog than something from the fabled Children of Nyx, she walked slowly but with purpose, her eyes sweeping the ground ahead of her as she moved.

"Sure," the old woman muttered to herself, "you can threaten them to leave all you want, but they know you won't just abandon them wolves. I mean, it's not like you could just pack up fifty-three dire wolves and go find somewhere else to live. They're almost extinct as it is and without me, they'd all be gone by the time spring came."

Then the old woman froze where she was and sniffed the air like one of her charges.

"I mean no harm, your majesty," she said. "I'm just trying to find a pregnant she-wolf that didn't return with the rest of the pack."

Megan uncloaked herself.

"Priscilla would be rather upset if she knew that William had taught you to do that," the old woman chuckled.

"I can't say I care much about what she thinks," Megan admitted.

The woman seemed to find that rather amusing as well, and even though her face was wind-burned and hardened, her eyes twinkled with mischief and made Megan immediately think of her grandfather and his friends.

"Me neither when it comes down to it," the old woman said. "I'd like to thank you for not killing my wolves last night. When they haven't been forced into those damned hunting collars, they're really quite sweet."

"You have Mariana to thank for that," Megan admitted. "She stopped me just after an assassin had just tried to kill one of my friends. I wasn't in the best of moods at the time."

"I expect not," she said, nodding in agreement. "She's a good girl. Used to come down to my kennels quite a bit when she was younger, hiding from Antonia."

"Now that's a woman I wouldn't mind killing," Megan admitted.

"Not many would shed a tear if you did," the woman admitted.

"So you lost one?" Megan said, liking the woman more than she should after such a brief acquaintance.

"Yes," she agreed. "Anyone should have been able to see that her time was on her. If I ever find out which sorry lout sent her out like that, there will be one less Child of Nyx causing you problems."

"He took his own life before I could exact any retribution," Megan said.

"Did he now?" the woman asked. "Blew out the back of his head?"

"Mari said he was some sort of assassin," Megan answered. "I didn't know what he'd done until she told me, though."

"One of the younger ones then," the woman said. "The older ones had bigger charges. Wouldn't have been any doubt about one of those. I'm Diana, by the way. But everyone calls me Di."

"And I'm Megan," she said, "Mari didn't recognize the man."

"She wouldn't have," Di explained. "The Tacet keep to themselves mostly. They're an inbred bunch of religious fanatics that think Priscilla is a direct conduit to Nyx. I, unfortunately, have the unpleasant job of working with that nasty bunch from time to time. I'll bet it was Marcus, though. He'd be the type to send out a pregnant wolf to hunt. He's always thought of them as weapons to be discarded afterward."

"So Priscilla was behind this?"

"Nothing important happens in Haven without her personal approval. She'll spin up a yarn as believable as giant birds or dragons, and the High Council will nod and agree. They know she's an evil old fraud, but as long as she keeps them in power they don't care."

"Good to know," Megan mused. "Well, I'm not sure what to do about your wolf. I've warded the whole valley to specifically look for dire wolves. Nothing has tripped them since the pack fled last night."

"Maybe it won't detect ones that aren't a threat," Di suggested, pointing to the tracks she'd been following. "Those are her tracks heading straight for your camp."

"How can you tell that they're hers?"

"She's taking shorter strides to keep from stretching her belly. She was only hours at most away from whelping. I just hope nothing went wrong."

The two of them followed the tracks all the way to camp and then to the small barn where Bruce had stored the cast iron cookware. The door stood partially ajar.

"Stay back and let me check her out," Di asked, "They're very protective of their pups."

So the old woman cautiously looked inside, taking a few seconds for her vision to adapt to the darkened interior.

"We've got a problem," Di warned. "She's nursing her pups in one of the stalls and looks to be okay, but she's still got a collar on her. It's not one that I'm familiar with, and I'm not positive that I could get it off."

Megan reached out with her mind, already familiar with what the things felt like, and broke the lock. Then she drew it through the shadows to her open hand.

"How did you do that?" Di gasped, taking the circle of metal from her hand and looking at it closely. "That thing is made of solid iron."

"Our Queen doesn't share our aversion to it," Bri said, uncloaking next to them.

"And I can see now why my people were so worried when they found out about you," Di said in awe. "Is it okay if she continues to den here? I don't trust the council to not try something like this again."

"We'd love to have her," Megan said. "Is it safe to approach her now?"

"Not yet, but if you were to start bringing her freshly killed game like her mate would normally do, she'd take to you fast enough. She'll be hungry since she won't leave her cubs yet."

"I think we could handle that," Dougal said, appearing as well.

Bruce came back to himself with a wave of nausea, sitting on the edge of the bed in the cell-like room where he'd stayed after leaving the cabin. He tried in vain to remember how he'd gotten there, and quickly realized that it was hard to recall exactly what he'd been doing before now. When he tried to move he found that all of his muscles ached as if he'd been that way for many hours.

He tried to reach out with his extra senses, but it only made the nausea worse. There was something that he was supposed to do, someplace where he needed to go. His thoughts darted from one incomplete thought to another, never staying with anything long enough to make sense.

He needed to get up and start moving. Maybe that would clear the fog in his head.

Reaching out to steady himself on the edge of the table that sat next to his bed, he rose shakily to his feet. He rested there with his back against the wall for support and tried once again to bring his extra senses to bear.

Then the world slipped out from under him and he fell, banging his head on the edge of the table as he went. His hand reached of its own volition to his necklace, hoping that he could reach Megan or perhaps even Emelia through it. Instead he found something unfamiliar that stripped his consciousness away and plunged him back into a future without hope.

Chapter XXXII: The Uneasy Expert

"I'm not sure what's going on with Bruce," William said, sitting at last at the long table inside the cottage. "They've got so much security around that area that some of my students are getting to class half an hour late because they're having to go the long way around. But even so, I don't think they've done anything terrible to him or I would have felt his fear. Every time Cat and I try to find him through his feelings it's like he's asleep."

"Could he be drugged?" Megan asked, from where she was attempting to wear ruts into the flagstones with her pacing.

"It's doubtful," he said. "Alcohol is one of the only things that has any effect on us, so we don't normally keep a store of anything that could keep him unconscious for this long."

"Don't they keep something for interrogations of norms?" Megan asked.

"No," he said, shaking his head. "The Children of Nyx would just break their minds and take the knowledge they want, and both Cat and I would have felt it if they'd done that. Most of my kind consider regular humans like Bruce to be little more than animals. Priscilla and Antonia are some of the worst when it comes to that, which is why we were so concerned about Bruce when we saw him with her that day."

"So the only thing I can do is wait," Megan growled. "I'm not good at waiting."

"And Mariana has been grounded," Bri said sadly.

"She'll start coming back out again when things cool down," he said. "We're pretty sure that we're being watched. So until then, she told me to give you this." He handed her an envelope.

"Wow," Bri said, looking at it and smiling. "Old school."

"I need to think about something else," Megan said. "Is there anything else you wanted to study about us? The minute we get Bruce back, we are going to be out of here. After that you're going to come to Nickelville if you want to talk."

He paused, looking thoughtful as if he had something in mind but didn't want to speak it aloud.

"You're curious about judgement," Dougal said from where he stood, looking out the window. "But it seems wrong to ask about it."

William nodded and shrugged apologetically.

"I'm sure we'd wonder too were our roles reversed," Megan said, stopping her pacing for a moment. "But you'll have to experience that one through our memories unless you can give me Priscilla or Antonia. Then I'd be more than happy to demonstrate for you."

"You know I would if I could," he said regretfully. "Sometimes I wonder what the Children of Nyx would be without Priscilla. But I'm probably just kidding myself. There's a sickness that's taken root in them, and for every good person there are at least five that are evil.

"Wait a minute," Megan said, becoming aware that she knew more than she'd thought through the collective knowledge of the Tuatha dé. "Would you like to speak to an expert on judgement?"

"What do you mean?" William asked, brightening at the idea.

"There's a Tuatha dé scholar who has devoted most of his life to the study of it," she said.

"That would be perfect," William said, rising from the bench where he'd been sitting.

No sooner had Megan summoned the man than he appeared before her, dropping to one knee and almost falling over in his rush to do so. Unlike most of the Tuatha dé that she'd met so far, this wizened old man was distinctly disheveled and flustered.

"I beg forgiveness, My Queen," he stammered in Gaelic. "I was unprepared for your summons."

"No," she replied in his native tongue, knowing without intending to that he didn't speak English. "Forgive me, and please rise. I should have given you more warning. I'm still new to this and I often make mistakes."

"You are too kind," he said quietly, still staring at the floor in front of him.

"Greetings my friend," William said in perfect Gaelic, which earned him raised eyebrows from both Bri and her brother. "My name is William."

"My Queen," the scholar said, realizing who the man before him was. "He's…"

"Not nearly as bad as you've been led to believe," Megan finished for him. "He's a teacher and a scholar above all else, much like yourself in fact."

"And I am Oadh," he said at last. His eyes darted everywhere, like a trapped animal. She wondered how he'd feel if he knew there was a hellhound nursing her pups outside.

"I am honored to meet you, Oadh. Is this your first time away from Tyr Sgodl?" William asked.

Oadh nodded.

"Where are my manners?" William asked, trying to put his new friend at ease. "Would you like to see outside?"

The old scholar looked quickly at Megan.

"You don't need my permission to do anything," she said, trying to make him relax. "And I really am sorry that I startled you with my summons. William is interested in the subject of judgement, and you are the foremost authority in my kingdom."

"Your majesty is once again too kind," he said, puzzled yet flattered all the same by her praise. "But you already know everything that I do by virtue of who and what you are."

"But that knowledge still belongs to you," she explained. "You worked hard for it, and the acquisition of that knowledge has cost you. You've given up a portion of your life in its pursuit. I will not steal the recognition of your sacrifice from you."

"Thank you, My Queen," he said, not knowing what to do in a situation like the one in which he found himself. "I can never repay you for this honor."

"There is no need for repayment, you've already done more than enough of that."

"Just let me get my coat," William said. "We can talk while we walk, but I fear I don't share the hardiness to cold that the Tuatha dé possess. But it is a bright, clear day."

When Megan opened the door for them, she feared Oadh would have another fit of worry over the protocol of her doing such a menial task for him. As William had predicted, it was indeed a bright day outside and the scholar could barely open his eyes against the glare which was so much brighter than anything in Tyr Sgodl.

"Here you go," Megan said, reaching through the shadows and picking up a pair of sunglasses from the dash of her mother's truck. Then she put them on his face, trying not to smile at the comic change that came over his expression. "Lunch should be here fairly soon, and I insist that the two of you eat with us."

"I couldn't," Oadh whispered frantically, slipping back into panic mode. "It wouldn't be right."

"You can and you will," Megan said softly, placing her hand on his arm. "You'd be helping us out. No matter what I tell my cook, he seems to think that there are at least two dozen people staying here, and we can never eat even a portion of what he sends. It would make me feel better if you ate your fill so there is less going to waste."

"As you wish, My Queen," he whispered before positively escaping out the front door with a bemused William in his wake.

"So why is he allowed to call you My Queen, while we are not?" Bri asked.

"I think he might very well have had a heart attack if I'd asked him to call me by my name," Megan chuckled.

"We are going to go and practice sword work," Dougal said. "Would you like to join us?"

"Not this time," Megan answered. "I'm still too aggravated about Bruce. I don't trust myself not to take it out on you. Besides, shouldn't you be resting so that your rib will heal?"

"It feels good to stretch it," he said, rotating his arm to see if he had full movement yet. "And it will take my mind off the damn itching around my neck where the burns are starting to heal."

As soon as the two of them left, Megan poured herself another cup of coffee and went out to watch them all from the cottage steps. A part of her worried about being out in the open like this so soon after the attack, but she knew her wards would tell her if anyone came within sight of the cabin.

She watched Oadh finally start to relax as they walked, and soon they were both talking loudly and making many of the wild gesticulations that only William seemed to understand. The scholar's worry troubled her, and her mind returned yet again to the plight of her subjects and their lack of free will in their service to her. No matter how much those around her tried to write it off with the need to accept what they could not change, it still wore at her like a piece of sand caught in the folds of her skin. The longer she thought about the situation, the worse it became, eventually digging into her heart and leaving her angry with all of her ancestors and the choices that they'd made.

In spite of the privacy she invaded by doing so, she let the thoughts of the Tuatha dé roll over her, not what they were specifically thinking about in that moment, but rather how they felt about their lot in life. She was unprepared for the numb resignation that rose in response. Over and over, she found memories of resentment and fear in childhood replaced by pragmatic acceptance of the unseen force that nonetheless held the reins of life and death over them like the whim of an indifferent and unforgiving god.

Then, without realizing that she was going to do so, Megan began to search the memories of her royal ancestors, looking for any thoughts of the indentured nature of the lives of the Tuatha dé. With the exception of her lifelong companion, The Morrigan, it had never been considered important. For the most part, her ancestors simply considered the sole purpose of the Tuatha dé to be the fulfillment of their own personal desires.

By the time Oadh had answered William's questions, she'd grown sick with the knowledge of what her family had done with the power entrusted to them by The Dagda. For the first time she intentionally made a promise, knowing that it would bind her when she did. No matter what, she would find a way to free her people and give them the choice they deserved.

Chapter XXXIII: Rodent Regret

When Bruce eventually woke again, he found himself back in the bed. His mouth felt as if he'd passed out in that desert crevasse before the flood, and his stomach growled loudly in the quiet room. Ignoring the moment of vertigo it caused when he shifted himself back to lean against the wall, he noticed a bottle of water on the table next to him. He fumbled with the lid and downed most of it before taking a breath.

His head felt clearer than it had been before, and when he noticed his laptop he remembered that he needed to update Sam's portfolio. There were several new projects on the horizon, and the town would need extra capital to stay ahead of the increase. It took him several attempts to sign in. There was something he wanted to get back to, but he couldn't quite make the thought clear.

It took him longer than usual to update the stocks. His thoughts kept jumbling, and then he'd forget what he was doing and have to start over.

"You're up!" Antonia said from the doorway just as he closed the laptop and sat it down next to him. "I think you've had some sort of bug these past few days. You just haven't been yourself."

He noticed that she had a sandwich, and he ate it ravenously before finishing off the last of the water.

"I'm feeling much better," he said, trying to rise. "I think it's time for me to…"

She placed the necklace back into his hand and the visions ensnared him.

Sam led the beginner students through the foundational basics as he'd once done with Bruce and Megan while Jade and Emelia worked with the advanced students. Andrew, of no relationship to the president of the same name had moved up to the intermediate level which currently studied with Mr. Wallace. His eyes were still drawn to the advanced class for some reason.

Sam's phone gave off an unpleasant little trill that he'd never heard it make before. But since moments like that provided opportunities for instruction, he ignored it until it was time for their next water break.

When he pulled it out of his bag, he saw a notification from the investment app that Bruce had installed. When he opened it, he realized it wasn't just one notification. There were several dozen concerning different aspects of his portfolio, but they all said the same thing. In the past half hour he'd lost almost everything.

Now, given that the only real change he'd made in his lifestyle since silently becoming a multi-millionaire was to switch from an all-in-one shampoo to one that had a separate conditioner, it didn't really matter. The rest of the town, however, needed that money and needed it badly. If things progressed as Bruce had predicted, and until now there had been no reason to doubt that it would, the town would be self-sufficient once again in a little over a year. But until then, it simply couldn't have the influx of money that these investments had provided dry up and disappear.

Is everything okay? Emelia asked.

Either Bruce is doing something to throw off suspicion, or something is seriously wrong. He has always warned me before setting anything like this in motion.

I've got a bad feeling about this, she sent. *How much trouble are we in if he doesn't fix it soon?*

I'm pretty sure the whole house of cards is about to come tumbling down, he answered. The stocks have almost zeroed out and most of my capital is tied up in the Baker Hotel.

Here's what we're going to do, Emelia sent while still teaching. *The Tuatha dé are going to buy the hotel from you. That way it stays in the family where we can watch over it. Will that solve our immediate problems?*

Temporarily at least, but we've got to get in touch with our book-loving friend. He's not seeing that Nyx girl again, is he?

If she's got anything to do with this, I may very well have to finish killing off her family line.

I would have thought that she'd back off after the wedding, he sent. I should have left a bigger rat on her pillow.

Chapter XXXIV: Coming of Age

Megan scanned the valley around her from where she perched on the lip of the cottage chimney, looking for someone to take the brunt of her anger. She took another sip of the coffee and once again grimaced that it wasn't sweet enough. No matter how many different scenarios she entertained, she still couldn't think of a way to get Bruce out without putting his life in serious danger.

Heavy snow had fallen during the night, and the entire valley reflected the dim pre-dawn light back up toward the heavens and hushed the morning sounds in a cloak of cold silence. She took a deep breath and tried to center herself like her mother had taught her when she'd been too young to control her abilities. Now it wasn't her lack of control that worried her, it was how much she wanted to lose control, how much she wanted to reduce the mountain before her to nothing more than a faint memory.

The sun chose that moment to clear the horizon in the perfect cleft where two mountains overlapped in her line of sight. It was a magical thing that evoked something in the memories that were slowly becoming her own. It also reminded her, as she suspected sunrises always would, of her grandfather.

What was she supposed to do when they had Bruce back and they went home? Was she going to move into the house on Beverly Road with her mother and Sam? Would she be expected to go back and sit in

geometry and English? Now that her mother was back, would she take driver's ed and pretend she wasn't the queen of a supernatural kingdom?

Or was she expected to move to Tyr Sgodl where her lifespan could easily cover two millennia back here on earth? If so, how would she feel about returning to a world that had moved on without her? One where only

Paul and Luminita remained?

No matter which she chose or had chosen for her, she'd still live with the fear and subjugation of the Tuatha dé digging into her heart and mind. She'd hear the echoes of mothers and fathers warning their children that if they were bad then the Queen would burn them alive.

She was just about to throw the bitter contents of her cup over the side when an eagle passed overhead. Her eyes instinctively tracked its path across the sky and a strange sensation she'd never felt before passed through her, like a tremor passing through the ocean, largely unnoticed until it approached land.

Deep within her something began to break free, shaking the foundations of everything that made her who she was. Caught up in the emotions that followed, she didn't notice that she'd fallen from the chimney, slid down the steep pitch of the roof and landed in a snowdrift.

Dougal was there in a second, cradling her head in his lap. Bri arrived only an instant after that.

Megan, can you hear me? Dougal called.

Her back began to arch as her entire body convulsed, sending out waves of energy that rattled the panes of glass in the windows and melted the snow for several yards in every direction. With each pulse the tension within her grew, breaking chains in dark hidden places where some terrible beauty had been imprisoned.

"What's happening to her?" Bri cried.

"I think she's coming of age," he answered. "She's breaking free of the promise that bound her."

The first of her memories overtook her, flooding her heart for the first time with the emotion her foolish ancestor's promise had stripped from it. She'd been scared and uncertain about this strange new place, that looked and felt too much like all of the ones that had come before. Then Bruce offered to let her sit without being asked. There to protect her and keep her safe, no matter what the cost might be to himself, just as he had been ever since.

They were in the courtyard at the Academy and Chuck Baker had just pulled her through the bushes by her hair. Neither of them had realized it at the time, but Bruce had actually moved partway into the shadows to follow her, going slightly transparent as he leapt after her. Then, in what would become almost a habit for him, he ignored his fear and came to her aid, twisting the bully's arm behind his own back and making him howl in pain.

She reached out with her mind, knocking aside the shields her mother had placed between them to keep Megan safe from herself, and bound herself to him, filling his lungs with air. And even though the promise had bound her conscious mind from acknowledging the fact, it was then that she'd fallen in love with him. But even as it happened, it was stripped from her heart until now.

They were on the field with the great honking beasts when one of them hit her. Then she watched in horror as he chased after her, a skinny boy cast adrift in a tide of chaos. He leapt over the edge of the cliff without hesitation because his fear of living in a world where she no longer existed was far greater than his fear of death, falling or even of the water below.

She'd just yelled at him even though he'd saved her life again only moments before. She'd been angry, she realized, not because she couldn't understand what he felt for her as she'd thought at the time, but because as strong as she was, she couldn't break the promise that bound her, a promise that kept her from seeking the comfort of his arms. Then he fixed her shoe when he could have let her fall...even though she deserved to fall. At the dance he'd used his own body to ground the energy she couldn't control, so she could pretend to be normal for just one night. He had no

298

difficulty hiding how much it hurt to do so, because he loved the sound of her laughter more than he feared the pain.

Then he was standing in the treehouse tower, channeling all the power he could summon through his body in almost perfect reversal from what he'd done for her at the dance while bards played next to him, shaping his storm into something beautiful for her to share with her grandfather on the day he died.

There were more, so many more memories that she relived in fast forward as a thousand locked doors burst open to release what had been stolen from her. The ascension had been nothing compared to this. For even though the vastness of the memories threatened to sweep her away, this incomprehensible avalanche of feeling had been compressed into tiny little boxes and hidden in plain sight all throughout her being. Now they all sprang open at once, filling the empty spaces within her to capacity and beyond. She felt at first as if this feeling, alien to her for so long, was pushing in on her from all sides and threatening to crush her. But that, she realized, was because she was, even in the midst of absorbing so much, still attempting to stay separate from it. So she stopped, instead embracing this strange part of herself that she'd never felt before, and at long last she became whole.

Over the years her shields had been honed and designed to do many things. They hid her from those who followed. They protected her from those who might wish her harm. Quite recently they'd even begun to protect her from the seductive power of sound. But they had never been fashioned to hold something of this magnitude within her, and her shields failed utterly, sending out one giant wave of emotion across the breadth of two worlds.

She began to drift off into dreams of him at once as her mind, body and soul began to find balance once again in the wake of this metamorphosis. And as she did so, the Morrigan whispered that her transformation could now begin in earnest.

"It's okay, My Queen," Dougal said quietly. "We are here with you. We will watch over you while you rest, and we will never let you fall."

He never called her by her name again.

Chapter XXXV: Inferno

Mariana, William and Catherene stood huddled together in the middle of the room, caught up in Megan's ordeal even through the massive shields around Haven. In the first seconds when the emotions drew them in, William accidentally opened the teaching channel he'd implanted in his sister's mind. Even though she'd never shown any empathic sensitivity, she was caught up in his experience of the young Queen's coming of age as if it were her own.

"I have to get Bruce out of Haven," Mariana gasped when the worst had passed. "She was barely keeping herself under control before. She's going to bring down the whole mountain to get to him."

"But what if he doesn't feel that way about her?" Cat asked. "I know he really likes her, but this is something else altogether."

"He does," William assured her. "I was there the night when he left. He always kept his feelings in check around her. I don't know where he learned to hide them so far down. That night when we confronted him about Antonia, he was hoping that Megan would be jealous and thus show some sort of feeling he could take as proof that she loved him. I felt something start to rise in her, then it faded out before it could begin to burn. You know, I've felt that happen with her several times before. But the only part that spilled over was the relief that he might turn his attention away from her. He felt it too, and he finally just gave up."

"That was stupid," Cat observed.

"It's easy to forget that he's just about to turn seventeen," William said. "I wouldn't like to be judged by what I was like at that age."

"I can sneak in and get him," Mariana said quietly.

"You can't," Cat said, reaching out and taking her hand protectively. "If you get caught you won't be able to come back."

"And I'm leaving Haven for good," Mari added.

"But where would you go?" Cat persisted, trying to make her see sense.

"Megan already offered to let me stay in Guarded Wood."

"Where you can study the rest of Augustus's books," William added. "But what about the ones you'll be leaving behind?"

"I won't be leaving any of them behind," his sister answered guilty.

"What have you done?" William asked.

"Antonia would have eventually found out about my interest in them," Mari answered with a shrug. "And you know how much she likes to burn things."

Catherene put her arm around Mari's shoulder.

"It's okay. I started moving them to a cave across the valley about a year ago when Antonia asked me what I was working on these days," Mari explained. "Bri has already taken them to August's cabin with the rest. They're all safely beyond Antonia's reach. And I've been sneaking my stuff to her for a few weeks now when we see each other. The only thing that's left is for me to leave."

"You've been planning this for a while," Cat observed sadly.

"I've never really belonged here," Mari explained quietly. "You and William are the only ones who will even notice that I'm not here anymore."

"And you're willing to abandon this life to start another one with Brighid?" her brother asked.

302

She nodded in reply.

"But what if it doesn't work out?" Cat asked, "In the long run."

"It's okay, Cat, I'm not so gullible as to think that just because we're in love now that it promises anything down the road. I'm okay with that. Megan's offer was to me, not as an extension of Bri. Furthermore, the bards need me to translate all of those books. There's enough there to last me the rest of my life. And I'll be able to read them in the sunshine instead of being cooped up in a cave all of the time."

"You've been my only friend here," Cat whispered, hugging Mari close.

"We're going to miss you," William added.

"Then come with me!" she begged, even though she knew what his answer had to be.

"I can't leave my students," William answered.

"And what if we are right about the boys being off somewhere traveling?" Cat asked, "We have to be here for them to return. They might not be able to find their bodies somewhere else."

Mari nodded, breathing shallowly to keep from crying. Once this was done, she'd never be able to return. And as much as she might like to tease her brother and his wife otherwise, they were dear to her.

After she said her goodbyes to her nephews, silently calling them home again so they could be a family, she cloaked herself and followed William out the door. That way anyone watching wouldn't notice her leaving and would hopefully believe her to still be inside. Meanwhile, William would leave Haven so as not to be accused of what was to happen next. He intended to have several witnesses to back him up later should the need arise.

She left him without saying a word, knowing that he'd be waiting for her at the cottage when she arrived with their young friend. She took her time, plotting her route based on what she encountered and taking advantage of the out of the way places where she could stand without danger of being detected. It was ironic, when she thought about it, that it was Antonia herself that she should thank for her overly-developed stealth skills.

When at last she reached the boy's room, she was surprised that there were no guards present even though she'd already bypassed several others in getting there. Then, suspecting that there might be some well-concealed ward on the door, she studied it for several more minutes until she was sure it was clear. She gently turned the door handle, half expecting it to be locked and slipped inside.

The room stank.

Moving quickly to his side, Mari uncloaked and sat on the edge of the bed, shaking him gently.

He groaned softly, but didn't otherwise stir. She shook him harder and at last he finally opened his eyes

"Bruce," she whispered. "We're getting out of here."

He frowned and started to close his eyes again.

"Bruce," she whispered again, shaking him even harder. "I'm going to take you to Megan."

At this his eyes flew open and he shook his head violently.

"What's wrong with you?" she whispered.

"She's gon kill us all," he mumbled, barely coherent.

"Who is?" she asked.

"Dark Queen," he answered, his eyes starting to roll back into his head.

"You mean Megan?" she asked. "She'd never hurt you."

As he drifted off, he reached up to grip something through his sweat-stained shirt.

Horrified by what she already knew she'd find, she reached in and pulled it free. Then she let out a low moan of despair when she saw the necklace and what it contained.

As if in response to her cry, she heard someone coming down the hall. Frantically cloaking herself, she ducked under the table and reinforced her shields, making sure that none of her distress leaked out.

Her worst fear walked into the room, followed by the seer.

Mari wasn't surprised to note that her childhood bully had reverted to the rich traditional garb she'd worn before Bruce had come. The Seer of course was, as always, dressed in the finest that Haven had to offer.

"I could have sworn I heard him talking," Antonia said, puzzled. "Of course, he's having a lot of nightmares now."

"Wake him," Priscilla commanded.

From where she hid, Mari could see Antonia shake him hard, apparently familiar with how difficult he was to wake. When that didn't work, she reached out and placed a finger on the back of his hand.

He jerked awake with a faint moan, and the smell of burned flesh mingled with the previous stink of the room.

Under the table, Mari absently ran her fingers across the childhood scars on her hand and arm.

Bruce smiled weakly when he saw her.

"It's time to go to work, Bruce," Antonia crooned in the sort of voice one would use with a particularly stupid child. "Can you fix something for me?"

His nod was almost imperceptible.

Priscilla then placed an odd spherical object that seemed to be made up of triangles into his hand. As soon as it made contact with his skin, it started to glow and make strange noises. When it cooled off, Antonia picked it up and music began to play from somewhere within it.

305

"Now this," Priscilla said, holding out what appeared to be an extremely old toy boat.

But instead of passively taking the object from her hands, Bruce's eyes grew wide, and he shook his head violently, managing to shift his body toward the wall in order to get further away.

"No matter," the seer admitted reluctantly. "We'll try again later. It's likely he knows that he needs to rest before unlocking another artifact for us. Even as lost as he's already become, he doesn't want to die just yet."

"We're running out of time," Antonia observed. "His mind could go at any time now."

"Personally I'm amazed that he's lasted this long," Priscilla admitted.

"He was stronger than he looked," Antonia said absently, turning the newly-repaired artifact over in her hands. "It's too bad it wasn't the brother that could do this. I would have much rather seduced that one, enough maybe to have held off longer with the crystal."

"There is a fairly good chance that he'll still be able to unlock the boat after his mind goes," the seer said hopefully as if discussing a promising pet. "From what I've seen his skills are largely unconscious. Have a servant come in and bathe him. It smells in here."

After they left, Mariana spent half an hour desperately trying to think of a way to move him. Any chance she had of getting him to safety required him to be both mobile and in his right frame of mind. Trying to take him this way would only get her caught. Furthermore, it might be better for Megan to be able to remember him the way he'd been and not like this.

Reluctantly, she returned to his side and probed his mind. What little was left was so distant that she suspected he might have already gone.

"I'm so sorry, Bruce," she whispered. "You never deserved this."

She slipped quietly out the door, taking her time and utilizing safe spots as she had before. This didn't change things as far as her leaving was concerned. Megan needed to know what had happened to him, and Mari couldn't spend another night in a place where anyone could do something like this.

Moving in the opposite direction than she'd come, she slowly made her way toward the kennels where she usually exited the city. Although still included in the shield wall, this entrance was keyed to allow her to leave, just as her brother had created it to do.

Halfway down the final corridor, she stumbled into a passive ward and a wave of energy knocked her from her feet, uncloaking her as she fell. Before she could even think to run, Antonia appeared in front of her, blocking her escape.

"Did you really think I wouldn't sense you down on your knees under that table?" the bully taunted. "I'd know that burnt smell anywhere."

Mariana slowly rose to her feet.

"You have no idea how happy I was when my aunt told me I could finally kill you!" Antonia gloated.

"It was a listening ward," Mariana observed calmly. "That's why I didn't feel it. You heard me talking to him."

"Maybe you're not quite as stupid as I thought," Antonia admitted.

"William will know it was you," Mari stalled.

"The half-breed won't be around much longer either," Antonia countered. "A few weeks at most. Should I kill his wife or his half-wit abominations first?"

"They're only children," Mari cried, her anger starting to overtake her fear. "What's wrong with you?"

"Children that might grow up to pollute more of our dwindling race. You're right though. She needs to go first so she can't make him stronger. I am going to miss that about dear old Bruce," she admitted. "It was such a

307

rush when he boosted my power. Tell me, did the fire finger bring back some old memories for you? That's why I did it to him of course. For you."

"Why?" Mari asked. "What did he ever do to you?"

"To get back at that pathetic excuse for a queen and her mother of course. Repairing artifacts was a nice bonus though. I can't wait to find out what that weird toy boat can do."

"You have no idea what Queen Megan will do to you for this," Mari said quietly, getting ready to make her last stand. "There's nothing you can do to me that will even come close to her wrath."

"Oh, I'm not angry with you," Antonia said pleasantly. "I just really like to listen to you scream while you burn. I've always wondered, how many of your toes were they able to save?"

Mariana didn't think, she just acted. Throwing an entire lifetime of fear and anger at her childhood bully, she summoned an inferno so hot that the metal light fixtures turned to slag and dripped onto the floor.

She held no delusion that even fire on this scale would be able to reach Antonia through such powerful shields, but she did know that until she chose to let the fire die, her bully would be trapped where she stood.

Creating an opening large enough for her to pass and close enough to see her enemy, Mariana inched past, pausing only once.

"I'm going to tell her what you've done," Mariana said. "And she'll make you beg for death before she finishes you off." Then she was past, running as fast as her damaged feet would allow. Outside the gate, Megan snatched her up just a few feet from the door and took her to safety.

William was already at the cabin when they arrived, and she knew he could tell from her emotions that the mission had been a failure.

Bri ran forward, and in a manner completely out of character for the light-hearted warrior, she pulled Mari close and refused to let go for several seconds. On the heels of nearly dying, Mari was more than glad to let her.

"Where is Bruce?" William asked, but she wished more than anything that she didn't have to answer. No one deserved the kind of heart break she was about to deliver.

"It took me longer than I'd expected to get to him unnoticed," she said at last. "He was unconscious when I found him and hard to wake." Then she paused for a while, trying to get her own feelings under control.

"You have to tell us," Megan whispered.

"Antonia and Priscilla have given him a memory crystal," Mari said in a rush before she lost her nerve. "They worked it into an old necklace. I'll bet Antonia told him it was an artifact so he'd touch it. He's completely bound to it. Removing it would kill him."

"There's got to be something I can do for him," Megan said, desperation starting to leak past her shields in levels that even Mari could feel.

"It's too late," William said, holding his voice steady in spite of what his sister knew he was feeling from everyone present. "By now he's already gone."

"You can't know that," Bri said, looking at her Queen in horror and demanding any hope that might be given.

"That's what they did to my mother," he said quietly. "That's how they trapped her."

"What do you mean?" Megan asked.

"My mother was a witch, like Emelia," William said, becoming distant as he tried to speak of what had happened without the pain. "But unlike your mother, mine had no interest in the man who was chosen to

309

lower himself and sire a half-breed like me. They gave her a memory crystal and she spent her entire pregnancy in a coma of crystal addiction. Luckily, she didn't survive my birth or there would have been more like me."

"How could you stay here knowing that they'd done something like that?" Dougal asked angrily.

"I didn't know until I was grown," he answered with a shrug that did little to hide how much it really hurt him to talk about this. "And of course, it was dear Antonia who told me all about it."

"But your mother made it at least nine months before she died," Megan said, "he's been affected for no more than a few days."

"The body survives for a long time after the mind and soul have gone," Mariana explained when at last her brother could not. "Priscilla admitted while she was there that she hadn't expected him to make it this long."

"You saw the seer?" Bri asked.

"They had a listening ward on his room that I didn't notice," she said. "I thought they didn't know I was in the room because I'd cloaked myself under a table. The two of them came in after I saw what they had done." Then she explained all that she had seen.

"They've awoken the Dagda's Harp," Dougal exclaimed.

"Megan," William said. "Did you know that Bruce was a greater smith?"

"He made an enchanted barbecue pit for my grandfather that would never rust or break," she said with a shrug.

William shook his head in disbelief and muttered something that sounded suspiciously like "Texans."

"I'm so sorry, Megan," Mari sobbed, no longer able to hold it all in any more. "I couldn't move him by myself after they left. And I could barely feel him in his body anymore."

"You were brave to even try," the young Queen said, looking at her kindly. But there was something in her eyes that was no longer the girl Mari had known.

"I need time alone to think about this," Megan said, and then she was gone.

Bri turned quickly to her brother, but he shook his head in despair.

"She's blocking me," he said. "I have no idea where she just went."

"You said they knew you were there," William said. "How did you get away?"

By the time she was done telling them, Bri looked as if she might go at any minute and storm the gate by herself. Worried for his family, William returned to Haven, and Bri took her to August's cabin where she would spend the night and possibly the foreseeable future.

Dougal stayed behind and continued to search for his Queen, though he knew he had almost no chance until she decided to come back on her own.

Megan walked the shadows to Bruce's bedroom, feeling his wards trip as she entered and for one sweet moment, she convinced herself that he would come at any second to investigate. But as the seconds bled away, so did her hope.

Not wanting to summon either of the newlyweds this close to the boundary, she forged herself a new set of shields, ones that closed her off entirely from the outside, closed her off from the ones who wanted to comfort her. Maybe, if she was lucky, they would cut her off from the flood of might have beens that were gnawing away at her sanity like the rat her mother had left on the soon to be dead girl's pillow.

Inside those shields she wove the emptiness into a shroud like the moonsilk of the old women in Tyr Sgodl, and she prepared a funeral pyre for all the parts of her that had ever been soft and weak. By the time she was done, she'd be...

Exactly the way you were in both my vision and the one from the so-called oracle, the Morrigan whispered.

Get out of my head, or I swear I will find a way to cut you out of my brain, she answered.

Have you learned nothing about what happens when we make promises?

Megan waited for the presence to return, but in this, at least, she was happily disappointed. Then she realized that her ancestor had already accomplished what she'd come for. She saw herself as she'd been in the darker of her mother's two visions, twisted and hungry to feed on the pain of others. And she realized that the first steps down that path were already far behind her.

Even through her shields she could feel word spread of what had happened to the chosen of their Queen. While she mourned, Tyr Sgodl prepared for war.

And just as quickly the Tuatha dé resigned themselves to bloodshed over a boy that most of them would never meet. Resignation turned to fear as they realized that if this generation was lost, there would be none to follow. Yet they had no choice but to fight if she demanded them to do so. If she demanded the life of each and every one of them, they were bound to obey.

The unfairness of it burned her, and she thought about the cleansing fire she could bring down on the Children of Nyx without their help. But she also had to consider what would happen if she were to die in the attempt, taking every single one of her subjects with her. Everyone from her Scathlahm and his sister to the frightened little scholar and the one-woman Tuatha dé tech department. None of them were faceless any more like they'd been when she and her mother had run from the Wild Hunt. She had become their mother, and their future was her personal responsibility.

Someday she would have to produce an heir…

The corner of something stuck out from under his bed. She stared at it for a moment, unable to believe that anything might dare to be out of place in his domain. She'd have to tease him about the next time…

The pain cut her legs from under her, testing the boundaries of her new shields as it sought to erupt out into the minds of her people. She couldn't breathe, and for a childish moment she hoped that if she could just stop breathing it would all be over.

From her new perspective on the floor she could see enough of the dark fabric to recognize the sweat shirt Bruce had brought with him to use as a pillow that night they'd spent together in Guarded Wood with Fang.

It had neither weight nor texture against her numb skin as she crushed it to her chest and wrapped herself around it. But the smell of him clung to it, impregnating the fibers with whispers of fragile immortality.

The light from the window grew dim as she lay there, understanding for the first time what it had been like for him when he thought she'd died. Now she understood what his nightmares must have been like, and what it must have taken for him to wall this pain away from her.

"This is mine," she whispered.

Footsteps drew nearer to the bedroom door, so she cloaked herself there on the darkened floor and waited. The door opened and Mrs. Grimble stood there for a moment, looking hopeful that she might find him there.

I lied to you, Megan mouthed without voice. *I lied when I said he would be okay. I lied when I said that I would take care of him and bring him back safe and sound. For those broken promises I must never be*

313

forgiven. I deserve the curse this life has brought upon me.

When the door closed again, Megan climbed to her feet and pulled sweatshirt over her head. Then she crouched down through the shadows and leaned back against the rough wall of the courtyard, letting her hands trail through the dry leaves of Bruce's hiding spot. She didn't need light to bring the past alive around her.

His family didn't seem to be much for hanging pictures on the walls of their modern home, so she'd never had the chance to see what he looked like as a young child before. *Is this what our son would have looked like?* Megan wondered as she watched him.

Although she could neither see nor sense the Cat Sidhe in the darkened courtyard, his arrival came as no surprise. She held her hand out to him at just the right height and was rewarded with the graze of his fur and a deep purr that drove back a little of the cold within her. Then he placed his paw on her hand and she felt the familiar pull of Tyr Sgodl behind it.

"I don't want to see the bards tonight," she whispered, anchoring herself in her love's hiding spot. "They'll try to take my pain, and I can't allow that. It's all I've got left of him."

His green eyes glowed faintly in the darkness, but she turned away from him and found a more comfortable position. A moment later he crawled into her lap and together they watched Bruce as he read, oblivious to the way it would end.

Mr. Bob followed her back to the cabin when she returned, and Bri rushed forward to embrace her with almost as much concern as she'd had for Mariana several hours earlier. Although Dougal stayed where he stood, Megan found his relief at her return touching.

"Bri, what are you still doing here?" she asked. "You should be curled up at August's place, snoring while Mari reads next to you."

"We were worried about you, My Queen," Dougal said, and she understood what the change in the way he addressed her meant. As her power grew, it became more and more difficult not to hear their thoughts. But perhaps that was as it should be now. Maybe the time had come to leave behind the girl she'd been and become the Queen that the Tuatha dé deserved.

"I'm going to bed," Megan said wearily. "I don't know if I'll sleep, but I don't have the strength to do anything else."

"My Queen," Dougal interrupted, "Please don't take offense."

"Nothing good ever follows that statement," Megan said with a sigh.

"But you've just taken a terrible blow."

"And?" Megan asked, becoming impatient. "I really am tired. Is this something you could tell me in the morning?"

"I fear not," Bri said, picking up where her brother had left off. "When your father went after…"

"My mother and me?"

"Yes," Bri said with all the confidence of someone tap dancing in a minefield. "He accidentally killed several dozen of us when he had a nightmare."

"And you're afraid that I might do something similar," Megan said, catching on at last. "I assure you that there are none among the Tuatha dé that I wish dead. But I already know why you're telling me this. Where do I get this herbed wine?"

"Merely ask your chamberlain," Dougal answered, sighing in relief.

Megan concentrated for a second. When nothing immediately happened, they both looked at her in concern.

"I told him to come when he was ready," Megan explained. "I almost gave Oadh a heart attack, and I'd prefer that the people who serve me to not be freaked out when they show up."

"Your wisdom grows daily," Bri observed.

Megan made a gesture ill befitting a Queen.

When the chamberlain appeared a moment later, he carried an ornate wine bottle and measured out a portion, telling her that the dosage was important because in large doses it could be fatal. She thanked him, making sure to treat him like a person, which she'd come to realize had not always been the case with the royal family. Then he took his leave.

"Now," Megan said after sending the bitter potion directly to the siren's lair where it would do no harm instead of swallowing it, "If you don't have anything else that I need to do, I'm going to go to bed. Bri, please don't stay here tonight. I will be here in the morning when you return."

"As you wish," Bri said with more formality than usual.

"And Bri?"

"Yes?"

"Please tell my generals to stand down," Megan said, feigning sleepiness she didn't feel. "I will not make my personal tragedy into something that endangers even a single one of my people. Nor will I punish the innocents of Haven, of which I believe there to be many. But one day those two women will make the profoundly foolish decision to set foot outside of their dank little cave, and when they do, I will make their deaths last for years."

"Yes, My Queen," Dougal said with enthusiasm.

"And Dougal," she added. "There's no reason for you to stay here and listen to me snore. I wish to be alone in the cabin tonight so that I might properly grieve."

"As you wish, My Queen," he said and then stepped outside.

When she was at last alone, she walked the shadows to August's beach, which was currently in the early hours before dawn. She cloaked herself from prying eyes and shielded herself so thoroughly that not even the guardians of Guarded Wood could feel her presence. There she called back the memory of that night and tried to remember what it had felt like to lay on his chest.

Chapter XXXVI: Royal Spies Everywhere

At first, Emelia thought that Sam must have woken up early and started breakfast because the smell of coffee filled the air. But then she realized that he still slept soundly by her side.

She cast her senses out across the small house, feeling as always, the objects which still held strong echoes of his peoples' power scattered throughout. But of the coffee-making intruder, she felt nothing. More troublesome still, the wards layered on first by Sam and then herself still remained intact.

Missing once again the comforting weight of the Scathlahm's Blade, she crept down the hall toward the kitchen with a huge Buck knife that looked like a toy when her fiancé held it. When she got there, nothing seemed amiss.

Then the air around one of the chairs at the green Formica table shimmered and solidified into her very real though horribly disheveled daughter.

"How did you do that?" she asked, her mind flooded with a myriad of questions, not the least of which included how Megan had bypassed their wards without alerting them in any way.

"It turns out that it's not a genetic mutation like walking in the shadows," her daughter said, in a calm and measured voice. Emelia realized in horror that she could feel nothing of her daughter's presence.

The strain of maintaining shields that rigid should have been unbearable. "Our enemy seems to have come up a bit short on the gifts that their Beloved Nyx bestowed upon them."

"Your speech has changed," Emelia observed.

"I've got at least thirty different languages and the memories of several millennia bleeding into my conscious mind," Megan explained with little interest. "I'm not finished evolving yet."

"So, Megan of great mystery, why are you in my kitchen, drinking my coffee when you have a whole kingdom at your disposal?"

"The Tuatha dé are great at many things," Megan answered with a smile that chilled her mother's heart, "But they make terrible coffee. Are you going to return to Beverly Road?"

"Eventually," Emelia said, putting down the knife and taking down a cup into which she poured some coffee while trying to assess the situation. "Right now there are memories in that house with which I'm not yet ready to reconcile."

"I understand," Megan said, taking a drink from the cup in her hand. She frowned and then steam began to curl up from it again.

"What happened?" Emelia asked, seeing no other way to find out. This whole situation felt dangerous, like walking far out onto thin ice. "Even with those bomb-proof shields you're wearing I can still see the pain in your eyes."

Megan shrugged, and Emelia put the cup down and pulled her little girl into the tightest embrace she could manage with her damaged shoulder.

For just an instant the dam broke, and her daughter's grief tore at her with such ferocity that Sam began to weep in his sleep. It was pain that shredded her defenses in an instant, leaving her mind bare and raw. She clung to Megan even as the girl locked her feelings back up, tighter than before. But even that instant was too much. She embraced the child she'd raised, and it was like holding a statue.

By the time Emelia realized that she was crying, she'd already drenched her daughter's shoulder. When she finally pulled away, her daughter's eyes were still dry and that frightened her more than the brief glimpse into her daughter's pain.

Do you ever wish you could go back and undo something that never should have happened? Megan asked.

"Like what?" Emelia countered.

I don't know, like maybe leaving for college. If you'd stayed, you would have started your life with Sam thirty years earlier. Think about all of the memories you'd have made with him in that time!

Then I'd have never had you, Emelia sent, picking up her cup and sitting back in her chair where she could better study the fresh scars in her daughter's eyes. *And any world without you is not one in which I want to live. Furthermore, unless the Nyx kids have taught you to travel through time, it's an impossible dream.*

I wouldn't have put it past August to have figured it out. The way you shifted from theoretical to declaring it impossible reminds me of the way my people shrug off being bound to my whim as not worthy of consideration since they can't change it.

What has happened? Emelia asked.

I finally came of age. I finally broke free of the damn promise that bound my heart and kept me from loving him the way he deserved. It was terrifying. It nearly killed me, and it was the most beautiful thing imaginable.

But that's not all that happened, is it?

What did August tell you about memory crystals?

He told me that they were worse than drugs or poison for anyone without the heritage of the Children of Nyx. Why do you ask?

Antonia gave one to Bruce when we returned. It was hidden in an amulet.

Dear God no, Emelia sent, horrified by the thought.

And just before we found out, the evil bitch in my head decided to finally turn the key and set me free. I fell in love with him for the first time...

It was at the race, Emelia asked, *wasn't it?*

Megan nodded.

But that was only the first. I fell in love with him a thousand separate times, and that damn promise stole them all from me, only to give them all back at once.

Megan stared at the forgotten cup, which had already begun to cool. She picked it up again. First it began to steam and then boil. A spiderweb of cracks appeared across its surface as the sugary liquid boiled over onto her pale hand.

Without thinking Emelia reached for it before it could cause any more hurt. Her skin sizzled from the heat and she dropped it. Snatching her burned fingers back, she watched as her daughter plucked it from the air as it fell, sending the coffee to the sink and the cup to the counter where it collapsed into several dozen ceramic shards.

Sorry about that, Megan sent. *Maybe Bruce can fix...*

Megan clenched her hands into fists and beat them against her abdomen as her breath escaped in violent expulsions through her clenched teeth. The ring on her thumb left burn marks on her shirt as she did so, giving off tiny puffs of smoke with each blow. When at last the air had leaked from her lungs, and she'd dug her hands into her stomach as if to find the pain and rip it free, an echo of Bruce walked past them, picked up the broken shards of glass that had fallen from the front door and began to fit them into place.

The girl's face softened, and her lips parted with the hint of a smile. But with each small gasp that filled her lungs once again, the expression twisted. Emelia braced for the coming scream and welcomed its coming. Then the dam would break and her daughter would begin to heal.

But at the peak, when her lungs could hold no more, she held it there for a moment, closed her eyes and let it back out during one long hiss. As the air left her body, the image of Bruce faded away.

It's done, Megan's thoughts echoed through her mind. *And now I must move on, because it doesn't matter if I'm okay or not. I am Queen of the Tuatha dé and my life is not my own.*

Oh Megan, Emelia sent, *I know this hurts but you've got your whole life ahead of you.*

Her daughter's eyes began to glow through their closed lids as if she'd somehow turned her gaze inward in preparation for judging herself.

I wasn't allowed to love him while I still had him here with me just because some woman in the past fell in love with a jerk. I'll never be allowed to love anyone else because the cranky lady in our heads lost the man she was allowed to love for a thousand years and across three different worlds. Because one of the Beloved wanted to prevent disloyalty among the Tuatha dé, the next generation will grow up fearing that I'll burn them alive if they do so much as think something I don't like. And then, to put one big cherry on top of the whole shitty sundae, I'll eventually have to conceive a child with a man that I won't be allowed to love even if I could get Bruce out of my soul. Because if I don't, every single man, woman and child who calls me Queen will die when I do.

Maybe we can find a way to do it artificially, Emelia pleaded, trying to find any way past this grief, some way to cut even a small hole into the armor so even the tiniest ray of hope could shine in.

322

Dad tried after we left, Megan sent. *It doesn't work for us.*

"I didn't know," Emelia whispered, the wound of her own grief opening anew.

I'm sorry, I never meant to ever tell you about that. I should go, I'm not doing a very good job of holding it together right now.

"Don't you dare leave when you know I can't follow," Emelia screamed, lunging toward her and holding her as tight as she could, barely noticing the blood that seeped through her shirt at the shoulder.

She felt Sam come awake, but Megan's whispered, "hush," forced him down into slumber again.

I'll be okay, Mom.

You shouldn't be alone right now.

I'm never alone.

You have to promise me you won't do anything...

Haven't you been listening? Megan thought sadly. *Don't you know that I'd never condemn my people like that?*

Stay for the coffee at least, Emelia pleaded.

I'd love to.

So what are you going to do about Haven? She quickly got up and poured her daughter another cup.

You're bleeding again.

It will stop in a few minutes.

I've been thinking about bringing the whole damn mountain down on their heads. Because right now they're looking an awful lot like dinosaurs and I am hurtling toward them like one big fucking rock.

You probably could, Emelia said, picking up her own coffee after giving her daughter a fresh cup and thinking wistfully that she really wished she had something stronger. *I'd understand if you did.*

I can't, Megan sent. *I've met people there. People as good as Antonia and Priscilla are evil. And there are children.*

Emelia nodded in understanding. If she could only get Megan out into Guarded Wood where the bards could play for her...

I'm not willing to risk a single one of my people to get my own personal revenge. I've warded that mountain so tightly that I'll know the instant either of them so much as thinks about coming outside. Then they'll be mine.

I want in on that when it happens, Emelia added.

No.

What do you mean, no? I have every right to want revenge on them.

Your life is here with Sam now. No more battles, no more armor. Just you, him and that child in your tummy.

Emelia's hand dropped to her abdomen, and she knew at once through her extra senses that her daughter was right.

How did you know? She sent. I didn't even feel you pass my shields.

Megan shrugged in response and placed the mostly full cup on the table next to her.

You and the Tuatha dé have officially parted ways. We will owe you for all that you've done to protect us, but from now on you're going to leave them to me. I've lost too many of the people I love already. Plus, I'm keeping you away from that armor, because it likes to stow away in innocents, and that's never going to happen again on my watch.

What about Bruce? They've still got him, don't they?

I'll stay there until I feel his body pass. Everything that made him Bruce is already gone though. Maybe during that time I'll be able to find a way to tell his family what I got him into.

It's not your fault, Emelia told her.

You can't lie mind to mind, Mom.

Emelia found herself alone with only the faint snores of her future husband to comfort her.

Jade wished the patrons a good day as they exited the matinee showing at the Grand Theatre. There weren't anywhere near as many as there had been in the immediate wake of the restoration, but there was still a healthy turnout coming on a regular basis.

She noticed a familiar head of sleek black hair sitting halfway down the main aisle and dropped her broom on the floor in her excitement to go see her. Practically vaulting over the back of the seat next to her best friend, Jade wrapped her arms around Megan and did her best to convey exactly how much she'd missed her through the largely underappreciated art of linebacker hugs. For once, the young Queen just leaned into it and didn't complain.

Oddly enough, her friend seemed more solid than usual, as if the things she'd seen and done had lent their own weight to the girl's slight frame. An instant of irrational fear overtook Jade in which she became convinced that Megan might have started to become the statue she sometimes resembled.

"I've missed you so much," Megan whispered, leaning her head against Jade's shoulder for a few seconds before lifting her head again and looking out across the empty theater.

"Whatcha watchin?" Jade asked.

Megan reached out and took her hand in her own and the room filled with people. It was a scene she recognized at once. Her brother's scout troop filled the seats, and it took her a moment to realize what seemed so out of place before she realized that Paul had still been young that day.

"Ugh," Jade complained when she heard herself thank everyone for their help. "I hate the way I sound."

Megan pointed at her grandfather, who was currently throwing popcorn at his friend, Alan. The Harrises looked happy.

"That was such a good day," Jade said contentedly as they watched the past unfurl around them. "You can hardly tell how much I was afraid that Kate would kill me when she found out."

Then the scene around them changed and Jade found herself looking at some sort of celebration. It took her a second to realize that it must have been some sort of send-off for the troops ahead of the second world war.

"It seems weird that it's not in black and white," Jade giggled and her friend actually smiled.

"Look over there on stage," Megan said, pointing.

"Is that Azarich and Tom?" Jade asked, amazed by how young they looked.

"And that's Alan just behind them."

"This is so cool," Jade whispered.

"Now look over there," Megan said, pointing off into the audience on the side of where they sat. "In the coat. She's got a hat covering her hair."

"Is that Kate?" Jade asked, craning her head for a better look. "She was just a kid. Wait, is this how you knew that they didn't really meet here at the Palace?"

"And this isn't even the first time," Megan confided, reaching out and touching her on the temple where the scene from the Academy played itself out in her mind."

"That's so sweet," Jade said when they were done and the theater had faded back into the present. "They were both hopelessly romantic, weren't they? And speaking of hopeless romantics, where is my bookworm brother, and why isn't he here with you? He hasn't done anything stupid again, has he?"

Megan's smile faltered for such a short instant that it was impossible for Jade to tell if she'd really seen it or not.

"He's a bit under the weather," her friend explained. "But there's something you should know." Then she reached out and gently cupped Jade's cheek in her hand, bringing her forehead against her own.

The love that Megan felt for Bruce flowed across her and made her gasp in surprise.

"Oh my god," Jade squealed, "You weirdo! Who thought anyone could ever fall in love with that nerdy boy!"

"You mean love him the way he's always loved me?" her friend asked in little more than a whisper.

"Does Paul know yet?"

"Would you like to be the one to tell the newlyweds?" Megan asked, smiling faintly at Jade's excitement. "I can't go to see them right now."

"I'm finally going to have a little sister!" she continued, jumping out of her seat in her excitement. "Wait, does that make me royalty?"

"Absolutely," Megan chuckled. "I hereby make you part of the royal family."

Jade babbled on for several more minutes, and Megan looked happy enough to just listen.

"I love you, Jade," the young Queen said at last when Jade paused to catch her breath.

"And I love you sister-to-be! Wait," she said, pausing as she climbed over the seat in front of them to have more room to jump around. "Aren't we already related since my other brother married your aunt?"

"And I pray he never figures that out," Megan agreed, nodding solemnly. "Otherwise he's going to be pestering me to call him Uncle Paul, and that is absolutely never going to happen."

"You're probably right about that," Jade agreed.

"And I'm not going to call you Auntie Jade either," Megan added. "I should probably be going."

"To do Queen stuff?" Jade asked.

"That's right," Megan said, but for just a second, she looked sad. "Tell Andrew he's going to make the second-best librarian the Academy has ever had."

"How did you know?" Jade asked.

"Royal spies," her friend answered. "They're everywhere."

And then she was gone.

Sam had almost finished wiping down the food preparation surfaces at the end of a long day that had started with finding the strongest person he'd ever known quietly crying at his kitchen table. The front door to Gordon's opened, even though Emelia had just locked it a few moments before. Then his fiancé squealed in delight like she had when they were children, and he knew his soon-to-be daughter had returned.

Throwing the dish towel over his shoulder more out of habit than necessity, he strode into the dining area to find not only Megan, but the Tuatha dé siblings that stayed close to her and the young woman he'd seen at the wedding with Bri.

In stark contrast to the smile on Megan's face through which he could detect nothing of what lay beneath, the young people she unconsciously held within her gravity both radiated worry for the young Queen. The young man looked like he'd recently fought someone with a flamethrower, given the newly healing burns about his neck...wounds that on closer examination resembled the ones around Emelia's ring finger.

"To what does my humble restaurant owe the honor of such esteemed guests?" he asked, pleased to see Emelia looking so much happier with her daughter in her arms.

"I told my friends here that the best pizza in the civilized world could only be had in Nickelville, Texas, but I remain doubtful that they are convinced," Megan said, allowing her mother to keep holding her while she spoke. "Furthermore, it would be a shame if I never partook in this family tradition. So mom's going to keep my friends company while you teach me how to make pizza."

"My Queen, I can't let you..." Dougal began.

"Finish that statement, Scathlahm," Megan said, suddenly stern. "And I shall be most displeased with you." He fell instantly silent and her mother glared at her.

"I do not sound like that," Emelia said irritably.

"Why mother," Megan laughed, backing slowly away from the small woman, "I have no idea what you're talking about."

As soon as the two of them were alone in the kitchen, Sam opened his arms and Megan rushed into them.

"What are you doing?" he whispered. "You cannot hold it all in like this. No one can bury their grief so deeply without cost."

"Luminita," Megan answered in a clear voice, devoid of any emotion at all.

"What does the bard have to do with this?" he asked, confused both by her answer and his inability to feel anything of his friend beneath.

"She lost him for two centuries, and yet it hardly shows. She lost everyone and everything she loved, and now she makes sure that she doesn't miss a single second she could spend with the ones she has now. She knows better than anyone that the good parts of our lives don't last. This is how I'm honoring him. Bruce left his whole life behind to make sure I wouldn't become the person my mother saw in her darker visions," she said, her eyes beginning to glow at the mere thought of vengeance, "And right now, I'm balanced on the edge of becoming exactly that. So

I'm going to fake being okay until it eventually takes root." She took a deep breath, centering herself and the light began to fade.

"You promise?" he asked, not sure if what she said was true or just what she wanted him to believe. Behind those shields it was impossible to tell.

"And I really do want to have my father teach me how to make pizza," she added, ginning up at him.

"That's not fair," he whispered, holding her tighter for a moment. "You know how much I've wanted to hear you call me that."

Unlike Emelia, whom he dearly loved but would never in this lifetime allow inside of his kitchen, Megan had all of the makings of an excellent cook. She even made suggestions and showed him techniques he'd never heard or thought of. Of course, from what Emelia had told him, the girl now had the cumulative knowledge of an entire race at her disposal.

When the food was served, they all joked that none of them had ever eaten a meal partially prepared by a ruling monarch. When Sam could eat no more of what even he admitted to be the best pizza he'd ever had, cleanup was easy with so many hands and with so much magic as well.

It surprised him to find that such good fellowship could still be found in the wake of losing so many that they held dear. And even more so, it surprised him that by the end of their meal, he could no longer hear the echoes of sadness in his daughter's laughter.

Chapter XXXVII: Unpacking

A short time later, the chamberlain gave Megan another dose of the bitter herb-laced wine that she immediately sent, like all those before it, to the siren's lair. When she found herself alone, she walked the shadows to the treehouse still cloaked against detection. Then she spent a little while sitting in the tower swing with his memory before climbing down the ladder to where the big duffle bag had remained since that night when Paul had run off into the storm.

She heaved the strap over her shoulder and walked down the spiral staircase with it, admiring the craftsmanship of Bruce's design and listening to the echoes of their laughter as she went. She walked up the path to the darkened porch, and took just a second to enjoy the smells of potting soil and evergreen sap that still permeated everything there.

She passed like a wraith through the silent house with her calves starting to burn from the burden of climbing with the heavy bag of clothing. Once in her darkened bedroom, she unpacked the bag that had been the source of so much teasing. As she mined the layers of her past from its depths, she caught a glimpse of the girl she'd been, the one who'd been so concerned about the way people might look down on her because of her tattered clothes. Then she found the shirt she'd been wearing the day she met him. He'd never cared about any of that, looking straight into her heart and seeing her as no one ever had before.

By the time she was finished, her drawers and closet were overfull, given the amount of clothing she'd bought since packing the duffle that day and the items she'd taken from her mother's room as well. It was hard to close the drawer, but it all worked out in the end, and she was able at last to slide the empty bag that she'd carried during so many escapes under the bed where it belonged.

She spent several hours slowly walking through the silent house, looking at photographs of the past and remembering a time not so long ago when she would have given anything to be where she was now. And she'd have happily traded it all for a chance to tell him the words he'd wanted to hear from her for so long.

Downstairs, she measured coffee out from the last can her grandfather had bought before the end and loaded it into his old percolator.

While she waited for it to brew, she reached through the shadows to her bedroom and brought her school things to her. The backpack reminded her of her grandfather's warmth, as well as the day he'd bought it. She smiled at the notes she'd made for the science test before pulling out pen and paper and sending the rest back to the window bench where it had been before.

She wrote while the kitchen filled again with the familiar scent of coffee. By the time it was finished, so was she. She folded the paper in half and wrote the names of the newlyweds on the outside.

The coffee tasted rich and sweet, exactly the way she liked it. When it was gone, she cleaned out the pot and washed her cup, replacing it in the cabinet where it belonged. Then she cloaked the letter where it lay on the table, trusting that it would reveal itself when her magic faded.

Then she turned off the lights and walked the shadows to Tyr Sgodl.

Bruce opened his eyes in total darkness, too tired to fear it anymore.

His heart raced in a rhythm broken by the single clear vision that had pierced the crystal fog. He understood what had been done to him now, and he'd accepted his fate. Or at least he had until he'd seen where her path led.

He tried to rise from the bed, but his body no longer obeyed even the simplest of commands, and he fell once more to the floor. He gathered his will and magic surged through him, no less powerful than it had been before in spite of his weakened state. Over and over again he tried to bend the world around him and walk the shadows to her side.

At the end of his endurance, he took one deep, ragged breath and screamed a name into the darkness.

Far away in a pocket of space hidden away from the real world, Paul jerked awake. Before the echoes faded from his mind, he sprung from the bed and ran for the front door, snatching his father's coat from the peg where it hung as he passed. Then, without hesitation, he once again sprinted barefoot down the darkened paths and into the heart of Guarded Wood.

Before he'd made it to Guardian Gate, Luminita followed on the path behind him with the enchantment that Emelia had forged into her wedding band leading the way.

Chapter XXXVIII: The Storm

Megan laughed when she saw that her mother had painted the royal bedroom yellow in preparation for its new occupant. The furniture remained the same as it had been, but the bedding had been replaced to compliment the walls, complete with a pillow that looked like a lemon.

"Thanks, Mom," she whispered.

Curious, she explored the room, looking in jewelry boxes and drawers that had been filled with new clothing that, as her mother had put it, befitted her rank and station. In the massive wardrobe hung several dresses for occasions that did not require or were not appropriate for moonsilk. One dress caught her eye, cut long and flowing from a deep green tapestry of fabric embroidered with a powerful intertwining swath of knotwork that faintly glowed with power. Its long hem extended in the hint of a train behind it.

Although she hadn't planned to do so, she took the time to change into it. For the first time she felt like the Queen she was supposed to be. She took the delicate looking crown with its lifelike flowers immortalized in metal and placed it on her brow. It was far heavier than she'd expected, but she'd promised her mother that she'd wear it and she intended to leave none of her promises unkept.

Paul reached the paddock with his wife running only a moment behind him. He hoped she'd stopped to get her shoes. He vaulted onto Shadowfax's bare back and guided the stallion with the sound of his voice. Then he flattened himself against the animal's powerful neck and had him jump the split rail fence that marked the edge of the paddock. Seconds later, he rode at a full gallop down darkened paths never intended for horseback. Branches cut at his face and hands as he rode, but his father's coat protected him from all but the one that snaked past his outstretched arm to cut him across his bare chest.

When he reached the top of the hill and stood upon one of two worn stones within the wide circle of standing monoliths, he began to sing a song lost to the memory of mankind, one that only his wife and perhaps the three Fates would have understood. He sang words of hope and mourning, and before the first echoes began to return, Luminita took her place on the other stone and joined her voice with his. Lightning lit the distant cliffs in silhouette as the bards begged the heavens for courage and speed.

Megan passed unchallenged through the halls of her castle because at long last, she belonged there. The few Tuatha dé she encountered dropped to one knee as she passed, and she touched the minds of each, letting them know that she loved them all through the bond they shared.

The voice of the Morrigan remained silent, possibly banished by the threat of a royal promise. But Megan doubted that to be the true cause. As far as she could tell, the Queen Mother only spoke to Megan when she diverged from the path set before her in the visions. Perhaps this was the path that even the Morrigan had lacked the courage to take.

The frigid air of Tyr Sgodl passed over her without effect, stripped of its power by the numbness in her soul. She followed the echo of Bruce's curiosity all the way to the base of the monument, and wondered once again how it had looked through his eyes.

She stopped only a few yards away, little more than an insect in the shadow of a god. Looking up, she reached back to the shed next to the cottage she'd shared with him for such a short time, and found the javelin-like iron rods Bruce had mentioned. Hoping that it wouldn't disturb the cubs, who were likely starting to crawl around and explore by now, she brought the massive load of pure iron to her.

The air around her crackled with electricity as soon as the rods were in place, and she hurled them with the power of her mind by the score to embed themselves into the likeness of the Morrigan before her, calling lightning from the sky to strike the stone surface over and over again while she watched.

Then, at long last, she shed the shields with which she'd bound herself, and the glow of her power enveloped the monument in violet light. Gathering her magic to augment the lightning which had already fractured portions of the face and hands, she unleashed her pain and her anguish in an eclipsing blast of energy that burned away anything within her that sought to hinder this act, whittling away at her until she was little more than a living conduit of magical potential.

Molten tears ran down the Morrigan's cheeks. Agony pierced the numbness, and Megan could finally feel once again. Then she fed her assault with all of the rage she felt at what had been done to her and at what had been stolen. She squared off against the artifact of a man who was nearly a god, and her pain was such that she almost won.

When the last of it flowed out of her, and she was no more than a husk of who she had been, Megan looked out across the wreckage she had wrought. But even as she watched, it began to heal.

She staggered through the shadows one last time to the cliff where she should have died. Staring out over the edge, she could see the glow of the approaching sunrise in the ocean below.

Clearing her mind lest the exhaustion of her efforts distort her message, she called to the Tuatha dé and as one, they turned to listen.

I never asked for this power to bend you to my will. I never wanted to violate your right to be who and what you wanted to be. So much has been taken from us all just to carry on the dreams of a man who died so long ago. I refuse to be an iron collar around your necks any longer. I refuse to bring a life into this world for the sole purpose of continuing this travesty. I do this, not to be free from my own pain, but to end something that should never have been. Use your lives from this day forward as you see fit without fear of what I or anyone else will do in retribution. Today the Tuatha dé will finally be free.

Brighid had been looking in on the wolf and her cubs when the stack of iron rods disappeared from the stall next to her. Until that moment, she'd thought that the Queen was sleeping off the effects of the bitter potion.

Just as she cleared the barn and the disruptive field that the iron cookware created, she walked the shadows to where her brother dozed against the front door of the cottage. He jerked awake, feeling her approach with his hand already traveling to the hilt of the Scathlahm's Blade.

"What's…" he managed to get out before a horrible, wrenching sensation passed through them both, turning Brighid's knees to water and spilling her on the ground.

"She's broken her bond with the Tuatha dé," Bri cried in horror.

They were still recovering from the assault on their senses when the Queen's words echoed through their minds.

Dougal clawed his way to his feet and faded out only to return a second later.

Iron, he sent, *so much iron. We'll have to land as close as we can!*

Then he was gone, and in the second it took her to follow him, he'd already run several yards toward the horizon where she could see Megan silhouetted against the approaching dawn. All along the edge of the iron's disruptive field, the Tuatha dé burst into existence. From the old and young left behind in the wake of Mag Tuired to the handful who'd survived the Night of Many Goodbyes, the Dagda's children crossed the earth and emptied from Tyr Sgodl to the rusty plain, screaming their Queen's name.

Thunder shook the ground below their feet as a massive storm approached from the mountains at their backs.

Megan reached through the shadows and brought the bottle of herb laced wine to her hand. She pulled the ornate cork from the neck and dropped it on the ground next to her, silently apologizing to Paul for littering. Then she brought it to her lips and began to gulp down the bitter liquid so fast that it ran down the sides of her cheeks and neck.

She clamped her mouth shut and held her breath until the urge to vomit the vile brew passed. Almost at once a blissful warmth rose from the pit of her stomach and silenced her extra senses. Even her sight and hearing began to dim, leaving her perched on the edge of existence in near silence.

The sun cleared the horizon, and in that silence, she thought she could hear voices calling her name. But only one voice held the power to bring her back, and it was because of her that it had faded from the world.

Still straining to reach her, Bruce felt a wrenching sensation of welcome, blinding pain. Then he was free.

He moved, not through the shadows of an alien world that would never accept him, but through the air of his own. Gathering speed, he flew to her side, faster than the sound of a bard's grief.

Brighid knew her brother would reach Megan in time. She'd always known, in spite of what most had said about a Scathlahm without an heir, that Dougal was meant to do something great. He'd always dreamed of great battles and following the path set forth by Emelia. But this, Bri realized, was so much more than anything they could have imagined.

Then, when he was only a few yards away, the Queen disappeared over the edge.

A wail of despair erupted from the crowded plain as the heart of the Tuatha dé broke on the rusty ground that robbed them of their power. The storm overtook them.

Brighid caught up to her brother and hauled him back from the ledge, landing on her back with him just as two massive dark shapes passed scant feet above them. Her eyes tracked them, almost too fast to follow.

Her mind refused to accept the existence of birds as massive as those two, and it was made even harder by the man and woman who rode them. With Luminita shrieking in the voice of an eagle and Paul's rivaling the thunder from the heavens above, both birds pulled up abruptly, halting their forward momentum to hang gracefully for an instant in which Brighid screamed for them to hurry. Then they rolled backward with their riders flattened against their sleek necks and folded their wings against themselves as they plummeted straight down past the edge of the cliff.

Even in her numbed state, Megan worried that she might not be able to find him in whatever lay on the other side. Would he wait for her, when she had never been able to tell him how much he meant to her? Would he still want her after what her love had done to him?

But she needn't have worried. He found her while she fell, pulling her close as the ground rushed up below, holding her just as he'd always done when she needed him.

"I love you, Bruce," she whispered before closing her eyes, content at last in his arms.

Little more than the whisper of a promise, he reached out with what power remained to him in this spectral form and focused his will on slowing her fall. Then, when he'd all but given into despair, he heard his brother's voice, and its wordless cry was filled with promise. It gave him enough strength to thrust her away from him and into the open talons of the bard's mount. He turned his head to watch as, with a shriek of triumph, the massive bird snatched the love of his life away and carried her into the blinding light of the rising sun while he continued to fall.

The storm raged around them, while the whole of the Tuatha dé nation held its collective breath in anticipation of what would come next. Seconds dragged on without regard for their suffering, until at last, Dougal pulled himself from his sister's grasp and crawled to the edge for a better look.

Then he fell back toward her as the first of the two birds burst back into view with Paul on its back, trench coat flapping behind him in the wind. He didn't have Megan, but his boyish grin told them that everything would be okay.

Sliding down from the giant creature's back, he landed in the mud

341

with his bare feet badly lacerated and bleeding. Then the bard and her bird cleared the cliff's edge, buffeted by the strong winds that greeted them at the top. Clutched in one of its claws hung the Queen, frighteningly limp with her arms hanging back and her legs lost in the long green train of her dress.

Paul ran below the creature before the wind could push it back beyond where the world ended, and it dropped Megan neatly into his outstretched arms. Then his wife landed on the ground next to him before her bird fled to calmer winds after its mate.

Laying the girl on the ground, he shook her gently, calling her name over the roar of the rain. Then the smile left his lips, and he reached out to touch the side of her neck, bending low over her to shield her from the worst of the rain.

Bri finally took a closer look at her Queen, noticing that she had dressed herself in a long flowing gown of the type usually worn in handfasting ceremonies among the Tuatha dé. And, as if she had truly been going to such a ceremony, a rough leather cord was clutched in the hand closest to Bri, holding a smooth flat stone to her palm.

"What's wrong?" Luminita cried.

"She's not breathing," Paul yelled. Then he bent low and breathed into the Queen's open mouth, causing her chest to rise and fall in a horrible semblance of life.

"No, No, No," he yelled as he placed his hands together and pushed the heel of his hand into her heart as if forcing it to beat again. "Damn it, Megan," he growled, continuing to work. "We made it this time, don't you dare die on us." The anguish in his voice sent lightning arcing across the sky above.

Bri looked up to find the chamberlain standing next to her with the familiar bottle in his hand.

342

"She drank it all," he cried in despair. "Her soul cannot find its way back now. And without her bond to us, we cannot call her back."

With a look of wild desperation, Dougal dropped to one knee next to her in the sign of homage that his Queen had so hated. Then he drew his knife from the sheath at his side and pointed the blade downward so he could reach out and grasp the blade in his other hand. He ripped it free of his closed hand, freeing a gout of his own blood to flow down across his knee and down his leg to the rusty ground below.

Beating his closed and bleeding fist against his chest, he cried out the words to the ancient oath of fealty, pledging himself to the dead woman before him, binding himself to her in this life and the next. And in that place where the Queen had lived in her heart, Bri felt something stir. Heads rose in recognition from them all, feeling the smallest tremor of her presence within them.

Bri dropped to one knee next to Dougal and did the same, and in doing so opened her mind to the vortex of energy flowing around them. Beating her bloody fist against her breast, she called out into the void, calling her beloved Queen back. She wasn't the only one to do so. Even Adair, who had never taken a knee for the former King, knelt beside them. Soon their voices dwarfed the raging storm and the power of their devotion burned the poison from the Queen's veins.

But still she did not return.

Paul began to chant her name, over and over while wounded fists continued to beat in time with each syllable until the world rang with her name and their blood soaked the earth around them. The earth shook with the strength of their adoration, and her name echoed across this place and possibly into what lay beyond.

"She doesn't want to come back," Luminita called out, looking at something that only she could see. Then the bard began to sing, and everyone present could feel it as Luminita wove their voices together into a new tapestry from which the future could be told.

Megan's eyes flew wide and nearly blinded them with the power she scarcely contained. Her first breath was a wail of despair as the Tuatha dé felt her dominion settle over them, stronger than it had ever been before.

Why? her voice echoed through their minds as she stared up into the storm. *I set you free, why couldn't you just let me go?*

Then, where only the ones closest to her could hear, she sobbed, "I was finally with him."

"You don't understand us at all, do you?" Bri asked, taking her Queen's hand.

Megan closed her eyes and lay there in what was left of the fading storm.

"The price was more than any of us was willing to pay, My Queen," Dougal told her, and for the first time since childhood, Bri saw that he was crying. "So we brought you back. And yes, you still control our lives. Yes, you can bend us to your will."

"But I don't want to," Megan cried in despair.

"And that is why we have pledged ourselves to you," Bri said. "Not because we had to, but because you gave us a choice. You gave each and every one of us a choice, Megan, My Queen, and every damned one of us chose you. Look at us," she demanded, standing up and bringing the waterlogged girl in the beautiful dress to her feet.

Megan looked out across the crowded plain and a sea of violet eyes looked back.

"This is the first time that we've all been in the same place in over two thousand years," Maeve said, coming up and hugging her. "And we came here for you."

Unwilling to look at the crowds any longer, Megan turned to where Paul and Luminita held each other, both on the verge of collapse. Then, noticing the cut across his cheek and looking closer at the rest of his injuries, she froze in recognition.

"That's not possible," Megan said, reaching out and opening his coat to see the cut across his chest. "How do you have the exact same wounds

345

that you did that night?"

"I carried them back with me," Paul explained. "Guarded Wood brought me forward and showed me this future so we could save you. Nita was never the one I was trying to reach in time because she was always at my side. We were always trying to save you together, Little Sister."

Megan winced. "Please don't call me that. He's gone and now I can't even follow him," she whispered, looking back longingly at the cliff. "He was there with me while I fell."

"I know," the bard said, stepping forward and holding Megan's face between her hands to make sure she was paying attention to what she was about to say. "Paul and I could both see him, right up until we caught you."

"I don't know how," Paul continued. "But he slowed you down. You had too much of a head start on us, even with the wingover, and we weren't going to make it. Then all of a sudden Bruce appeared out of nowhere and held you up while you fell, just like before except this time his arm was okay. And as soon as he did, you slowed down. It wasn't a lot, but it gave us just enough room for Nita to catch you and pull out of the dive. As it was, I'm pretty sure your feet touched the water. It was really that close."

"That close?" Megan said quietly, an edge coming into her voice. "And if you hadn't caught me?"

"Then we would have found each other again in the next life," Luminita answered defiantly. "But that's not all that Bruce did."

"What do you mean?" Megan asked.

"It was Bruce that sent me after you," Paul explained. "He's not gone. He called me all the way from Haven. He's still in there, Megan."

"No," she said, shaking her head, not daring to believe.

Paul reached into the pocket of his coat and placed his phone into her hand.

"What am I supposed to do with this?" she asked, frowning down at the wet but functional phone.

"Prove that he's still alive," Bri exclaimed.

"I don't understand," Megan said.

"Judging by your eyes I'd say you should be frying just about everything in the northern hemisphere," Paul said. "Or at least you would be if it wasn't for that ring he made for you. Yes, he could probably have come if he was dead, but he'd have had no power anymore. The only way he could have slowed your fall and the only way that ring could still be working is if he's still alive. And the only way he could call me and work to save you is if he was still conscious inside there!"

Megan brought the ring to her lips and held it there for a moment, savoring the heat it radiated as the rain sizzled across it.

"Now," Paul said, dropping down on the muddy ground. "Now that the adrenaline is starting to wear off, my feet really hurt."

"I still can't believe you made me ride the big one," Nita complained.

"It had to be the lightest load on the strongest bird," he explained. "Otherwise you wouldn't have made it in time."

"So you've known I was going to do this all along?" Megan asked, embarrassed by the thought.

"Only when I slept," he answered. "And it changed every time I figured out how to get here faster. I've lived this day a thousand times. Frankly, I'm looking forward to putting it behind me."

"Yes, this is all great fun," the bard agreed, "but could someone please get our horses?"

"You could always just fly back again," Dougal observed.

"Never again," Nita replied with a shudder. "I've never been so terrified in my life. Besides, I'm a newlywed. I'm not supposed to look like I've just flown a great squawking bird through a thunderstorm."

"You're always going to look beautiful to me," Paul said, happily laying his head down in her lap and looking up at her.

"And I'm always going to think you look tasty," she said, looking down at him and laughing.

"Oh god," he said, cringing. "Can everyone please stop saying that!"

Chapter XXXIX: A Single Stone to Turn a River

Megan dreamed of him, and in those dreams, they found the happiness they'd been denied in the waking world. But even in the potentially perfect world that she created when she slept, there remained unfinished business and debts that had not yet been paid. Even there, a strangeness pervaded them both, as if they'd been disassembled and then put back together by someone not wholly familiar with their design. This new configuration worked, and it might actually be better than the original versions of them, but still felt different and alien.

The smell of fresh coffee summoned her back to the waking world where she found her mother standing at the edge of her bed and Mr. Bob curled against her, purring loudly.

"I hear you had a long night," Emelia said, helping her daughter to sit up before giving her the hot cup.

"Which of my loyal subjects ratted me out?"

"Luminita called me from Paul's phone as soon as they reached the boundary," she answered, running her hand down the cat's soft side.

"She called you?" Megan asked, stopping with the cup half-way to her mouth.

"Yes," her mother said with the air of all mothers who want to scold someone. "Does it bother you that a two-hundred-year-old woman has adapted to the modern age faster than you have?"

"Well, now it does," she muttered, taking a sip and sighing happily.

"I read the letter you left for the bards," Emelia said, taking a seat next to her. "And Brighid told me what you said in your general address to the Tuatha dé."

Megan continued to drink.

"Are you okay?" her mother asked.

"I am now," she answered. "You understand why I had to try, don't you?"

"I understand that in your mind you weren't committing suicide," Emelia said gently. "And there was a certain nobility in what you wanted for your people. I understand why you did it."

"Good," Megan said, relieved.

"But it was also one of the most selfish, destructive things you could have done," Emelia added, somehow merging the power of both mother and former Queen in her tone.

Megan sat there, eyes focused on the bedspread in front of her. She almost walked the shadows to escape what she feared might come next.

"Do you really think any of us could have ever recovered from losing you that way?" Emelia whispered through clenched teeth. "Dougal tried to throw himself off after you, and he would have succeeded if Brighid hadn't pulled him back."

Megan clutched the bedspread in her free hand, and her knuckles turned even paler with the force with which she crushed it in her fist.

"Do you think Sam and I could have ever been happy again?" she continued. "Do you think we would have ever been able to look at each other again without seeing you? Do you think the bards would ever be able to travel through Guarded Wood without remembering the day they tried to save you and failed? And if you had succeeded, you wouldn't have freed the Tuatha dé. You would have just been the last in a long line of royals who took from them without asking. Did you even for a second think about what it would have been like after spending their entire lives tied to the royals, and then suddenly being cast adrift without any purpose? You nearly stole their entire identity."

Megan finally looked up at her mother, not understanding.

"Who would they be without their Queen?" Emelia explained, reaching out to cup her daughter's face in her hand. "You are their heart. You are the one who gives them the purpose they lost when they retreated from the world and stopped trying to guide mankind back onto a better path. In the time since your father's death, they've come to love you more than they ever did him. He was a good man, but what I did broke him."

"Mom, don't" Megan said, releasing her grip on the bedspread and reaching out to her.

"No," Emelia whispered. "I did. And I did it for the most noble of reasons. Furthermore, I'd do the same things a thousand times over again if I had to. But what you did almost made his sacrifice mean nothing. It almost undid everything you and I went through to get here."

"I'm sorry," Megan said quietly, feeling like she had when she'd done something wrong as a child.

"I don't want to scold you," her mother said, likely knowing where her thoughts had gone. "I don't want you to hurt any more than you already do. My god, I only felt it for a second before you locked me out again. I don't know how you stayed sane. But you have to understand that everything we have done, and by we I don't just mean your people. Your Grimbles, Sam, those wonderful old men and women... Everything has been for you, because every single one of us can feel it. You are the one who is going to fix things. You are the one who is going to bring magic back into the world."

They sat there in silence when Emelia ran out of steam and was again just thankful that she had her daughter back safe and sound.

"Would you be a dear and get my coffee from the kitchen table?" she asked and Megan brought it to the nightstand.

"Thank you for talking to me," Megan said at last.

"You'd better believe you should be thanking me," Emelia laughed, taking a sip. "Luminita would have done it if I hadn't, and I'm betting they would have heard her all the way to Haven. She wanted to go free Bruce herself, by the way."

"What do you mean?"

"I think she planned to go full pied piper on the Children of Nyx," Emelia explained. "Her plan may or may not have included summoning a hoard of ants to eat Antonia alive. Apparently, the girl flirted with Paul at the wedding."

"I really love having her around," Megan chuckled.

"I think it's almost time," her mother said, looking around the room.

"To come home?"

"Yes."

"I'd like that," Megan said.

"But first we have planning to do. This will never be a home again until my future son-in-law has been returned and restored."

"I know," Megan replied. "But the problem is, we need Bruce to figure out how to plan how to go and get Bruce. Do you see the problem?"

"No," Emelia said, frowning. "Just use a different seer."

"Somehow I doubt Priscilla will be very cooperative on that front," Megan said, draining the cup and setting it on her nightstand.

"Who said anything about Priscilla?"

Megan thought about how much stronger her bond with her people had become in the wake of what happened at the cliff. In the past, she'd had to concentrate in order to hear them. Now they filled the background of her thoughts with a constant hum of chatter. She thought it would bother her at first, but now that they'd accepted her, she found comfort in their presence, like something soft against her mind at the end of a long day.

She tried not to take offense in the way her entire circle of family and friends didn't want to let her out of their sight. She had, after all, given them quite a scare. And because they didn't have enough horses stabled in Guarded Wood, most carried double riders with only Megan and Dougal riding alone.

"Please don't make me talk to her!" Luminita begged again from where she rode in front of Paul.

"The two of them didn't part on very good terms the last time we were here," Paul explained.

"How bad?" Sam asked with Emelia sitting in front of him, looking almost like a child next to his massive frame.

"I threatened to make her walk off of that cliff," Luminita said, pointing when Roanoke came into view.

"There are worse ways to go," Megan mused, drawing angry glares from everyone around her.

"I am still cross with you for getting me out of bed in the middle of the night," the bard said.

"Let me guess," Emelia said, hoping to distract the bard from combining the ideas of punishment and music where her daughter was concerned, "the seer said something about how good it had felt in the Jubilee Grove."

"Nope," Paul said, snickering. "Nita cured her of that one."

"How?" Megan asked.

"By threatening to make her fall in love with a particularly unpleasant

353

carnie who never mastered the finer points of bathing," he answered.

"You can do that?" Megan asked, impressed.

"Long enough to create some particularly horrifying memories," the bard answered.

"So what did she say that upset you this time?" Jade asked with the boy of no known relation holding on to her waist from behind, "This is almost as good as old guy stories!"

After they turned the corner in the trail but before the bard could answer, they came upon the subject of their discussion. Bundled against the cold, the seer sat within an indention cut into the side of a huge boulder where the sun could reach her but the wind did not.

"I merely noted aloud that her husband was particularly pleasant to look upon," she answered. "And for that I am truly sorry. I thought that with such unwavering devotion on his part that she would not feel threatened, and my foresight provided insufficient warning. I have come to make amends."

"Why all the way out here?" Sam asked. "Surely there were more comfortable places to wait for us. It's barely above freezing out here."

"Because it was the safest place where the Eldest is concerned," the seer answered, looking pointedly at the bard. "As cold as this spot might be, it provides neither the temptation of cliff or smelly man."

"You might have made her get more creative," Paul observed pleasantly, "but it wouldn't save you in the end."

"Stop calling me Eldest," the bard snapped, her temper already starting to rise. "As I recall you're slightly older than me."

"As you wish, oh noble bard, last of your venerable profession."

"I hold you personally responsible for this," Luminita growled, staring Megan down.

"How is the construction going?" Paul asked, trying to diffuse the

354

situation.

"Quite well," the seer answered. "Thank you again, Queen Emelia, for lending us your craftsmen."

"I'm not Queen anymore," Emelia said brightly. "Megan has that burdensome distinction now."

"Gee, thanks, Mom," Megan muttered.

"I assume you already know why we are here?" Luminita asked.

"I wouldn't be much of a seer if I didn't," the young woman observed. "However, I can't see his path directly. He has gone into a place that is shrouded from my sight."

"Inside the protections of Haven," Emelia said.

"But I can see where his path crosses yours," the seer continued, speaking to Megan. "Two days hence, he will be brought out of the darkness for a great festival."

"The Lupercalia," Mari said, perking up and looking over Bri's shoulder. She was still having trouble getting used to the easy camaraderie of the group.

The seer nodded in agreement.

"He will be outside of the protections for this one night, and you must reach him then or he is lost," she declared, sounding mysterious and drawing rolled eyes from the bard. "But I can see nothing of what transpires there. Power to eclipse anything I have ever witnessed will be brought to bear, and I am blind to anything beyond the fact that he is indeed there.

"Huge expenditures of power, you say?" Bri asked.

Everyone turned to look at Megan.

An uncharacteristic lull settled over Caer Sidhe and many of the lost children sired by the other Beloved had moved on. Some used the excuse that they'd come with expectations of wild music and the abandonment of responsibility that looked to remain unfulfilled in the current atmosphere. But for those who looked closer at the tight-knit group that gathered in the furthest corner from the bar, the desire to leave centered around the suspicion that something momentous was afoot. Such matters were best left to the Tuatha dé, thought the young man who preferred to be called Okay.

Watching them from the bar where Maeve had left him, he told himself that what he thought he saw in the patterns of movements and body language was just that, something he imagined and not the hallmarks of a war council. Then there was the oddness in Maeve's behavior. She was not someone to keep a secret, not so much out of malicious intent but rather her questionably charming quality of saying exactly what she was thinking as she thought it.

But the longer he sat there, nursing a flagon of the famous Tuatha dé meade, the more convinced he became that the events that transpired through the gateway of this meeting would indeed culminate in an event that would reach into the darkest corners of the world. He sensed power here, power and potential. And though he would have to be careful, such situations were where his special gift functioned best. Like the Beloved who had given them life, his people possessed a power unlike any other. His mother had described it as the power to turn a river by casting a single stone. He personally thought of it as the ability to identify the domino that started the cascade.

As he sat there, the domino he sought came up and sat next to him.

"Your name is Dougal, right?" he asked.

"And you're Maeve's friend, Okay," the young Tuatha dé responded.

"I've been really curious about something," Okay asked.

"And what might that be?" the Scathlahm asked, turning so he could keep an eye on the Queen.

"I've heard that you carry one of the Beloved's artifacts with you in order to carry out the duties of your order," he said. "Is this correct?"

"Yes," the Scathlahm replied uncomfortably. "But I'm afraid my vows forbid me to allow anyone but My Queen or my successor to handle it."

"Oh no," Okay assured him quickly. "You misunderstand me. Such objects have always been of interest to me, but no one is ever interested in discussing them. Would you mind too terribly much if I were to share some of the knowledge I have about them with you. You don't even have to tell me about yours if you feel it would compromise your ability to protect Queen Megan."

"Whatever you have to say has to be more interesting than what they're talking about over there," the young man observed. "All they want me to do is dance and pray that all hell doesn't break loose."

"Then let me tell you what I know," Okay said, taking aim and releasing his insignificant pebble into the flood. "No matter the purpose of an artifact, there are certain things it can do when the situation calls for it."

It had taken a while for Megan to renew her wards around Haven, which had of course lapsed when she'd died. She shuddered to think of how many tiny enchantments she was going to have to cast anew in the months ahead. But in the case of these new wards, she took her time, trying to recapture the flavor of August's style. If she was lucky, Priscilla might recognize it and think her sister's husband was at last coming for her.

The clang of clashing metal could be heard throughout the valley as Bri and Dougal squared off with swords against the Queen. The exercise provided more passage of time than instruction for Megan, although she could tell that the brother and sister had grown considerably as fighters under her instruction.

She felt the messenger cloak herself as soon as she left the gates of Haven, but decided to let the Child of Nyx make the long cold walk to the cabin before confronting her. It was easier to be patient now. Before the cliff, she'd always turned moments like this into contemplation of the unfairness of what had been done to the Tuatha dé. But now that they'd willingly chosen to put their fate in her hands, she felt free. With that free time, she planned and plotted, reviewing every possible obstacle and outcome through the lens of her ancestors' memories in order to forge a life with him. She would accept nothing less.

Just before the young woman could uncloak herself in what Megan knew would have been a grand entrance, she casually reached out and snatched the unsuspecting Child of Nyx up and brought her to stand before her, uncloaking her as she did so.

"Excellent," Bri drawled, "Another assassin, can I kill it?"

"Wait," the girl wailed frantically, "I have a message from the High Council at Haven."

"Maybe next time," Megan said, still holding her sword in the other hand. Feigning boredom, she put the frightened girl down on her feet. "So what is this message?"

"The High Council wishes to invite you to the festival of Lupercalia, which will be held outside the city when the sun sets tomorrow."

"In the valley on the other side of the gate," Megan asked thoughtfully, pointing her sword for emphasis. "The one with the stone columns around the middle?"

"Yes," the woman answered quickly, looking at the sword in concern.

"Well, at least there will finally be something to do in this dull place,"

Megan observed. "How should I dress for this festival?"

"Traditional dress," she answered, her eyes dropping to the ground as she said it.

"You mean like togas?" Bri asked.

"Yes," the woman answered.

"You may leave now," Megan said, and the girl positively fled.

"She wasn't a particularly good liar with that last part," Bri observed.

"With the exception of our friends, I can't say that the Children of Nyx have proven good at much of anything that doesn't involve fleecing their population so the people at the top can live like the kings and queens they supposedly despise."

"So what are you going to wear?" Dougal asked.

"Exactly what they want," Megan replied.

"I will not wear a toga," Dougal said in disgust, before adding a sullen, "My Queen."

"Oh no," Megan said with an evil grin. "I'm the one that's supposed to be humiliated, not you. But I'm not going to stay that way, am I, Bri?"

"No, Your Majesty, you are not."

"I'm going to leave this part in your capable hands," Megan advised. "Try to stick with what we planned at Caer Sidhe, but feel free to improvise as necessary. That includes my wardrobe."

"Are you insane?" Dougal cried out, horrified by the prospect. "You're not seriously going to let her dress you! Have you thought this through?"

"I'm counting on her to dress me as she would herself," Megan said. "She is, after all, an artist."

"And what a canvas," Bri replied with a grin that made her Queen blush several shades darker.

"Well," Dougal replied, shaking his head, "If seeing you dressed like that doesn't wake Bruce from the dead, nothing will."

That night, in the field where the festival would be held, all of the iron rods that had been driven deep into the earth as a protection against the Tuatha dé disappeared. Inside the shield gate, the Children of Nyx slept on without suspecting a thing.

Chapter XL: Lupercalia

Antonia barely contained her excitement as she walked to the festival field in a dress the color of strong wine, of which she intended to drink much. It covered her shoulders against the cold winter air, but plunged nearly to her waist in the front. And though the hem nearly reached her ankles, the slit on the side exposed her leg to the thigh. It would provide little protection against the cold, but she hoped the queen's anger would keep her warm enough.

She tugged harder on the greater smith's hand, knowing even as she did that he appeared to have only one slow, plodding speed in his current condition. She wasn't entirely sure what had triggered the catatonic state she'd found Bruce in a few days ago, a twisted mass of limbs on the floor of his cell. But to be honest, she preferred him this way. The weeks in which she'd been obliged to cuddle and coddle the sickeningly sweet boy had been hard, but she'd played her part well, and now she was relieved to be free from the restraints that being his friend had placed on her lifestyle.

She just wished that her aunt would see reason with letting them allow the child queen into the city proper so Antonia could torture her in comfort. It was brutally cold outside, and surely, they had nothing to fear from the visions now. After all, Bruce had played an active part in them that would no longer be possible given his current state.

In addition to no longer posing a threat, he was sublimely maneuverable, going anywhere she led him and then staying as still as a statue until someone moved him again. Luckily, even in this mindless state, he retained the full spectrum of his smithing abilities. Well, to say that he retained the ability to repair whatever was placed in his hands might be more accurate. She assumed the rest was somewhere in there too, but without his mind to drive it, her dream of creating new artifacts tailored to her own desires remained regretfully out of reach.

Just last night, shortly after her servant had returned with the news that the pretender queen would indeed attend, Bruce had finally repaired and unlocked the toy boat artifact she'd been trying to get him to restore since Priscilla had seen what he was. It was too bad that he couldn't tell her what it did.

Antonia couldn't wait to see the girl's face when she saw her precious little Bruce. The wind picked up for a moment, whipping through her nearly non-existent clothing and messing up her hair. Why couldn't her aunt see reason and let them hold the damn celebration inside like they always did? But no, the old crone still remained adamant that the girl would never again set foot past the gate. And Antonia absolutely needed for Megan to see Bruce, to see how thoroughly she'd won. By now that little freak Mariana should have told her exactly what she'd done to him. Best of all, the girl would understand that as long as Antonia remained close enough to him that she could take the crystal, his life was in the palm of her indifferent hand. Maybe she'd give into the temptation to do it just so she could watch Megan's reaction. After all, the festival field was staked, so the girl wouldn't be able to bring her own power to bear. It wouldn't be enough to make up for the humiliation the girl's mother had inflicted at the wedding, but it was a start. Now Megan would see exactly how people with real power treated their toys.

Megan walked arm in arm with her loyal Scathlahm onto the festival field, dressed in a simple white stola with a sash of pale green silk to match Luminita's wedding dress. She quite hoped that Antonia would make the connection and think about what had happened at the bard's wedding every time she looked at her.

Dougal had foregone the hooded cloak of the Tuatha dé courtly attire which might have hindered his movements. The high collar of his black leather overcoat hid the partially healed burns that encircled his neck. The sprawling tree of the royal crest covered his chest and marked his oath of service to his Queen. The belt that hung over his hip in tooled knotwork carried the weight of the Scathlahm's Blade in its jewel encrusted sheath as a reminder to the Children of Nyx that he was there as more than just a royal escort.

The stone columns that surrounded the field hung with roses, lilies and amaranth, filling the cold air with their unseasonable fragrances. Bronze braziers filled with incense dripped smoky tendrils that crept in serpentine paths between the feet of the not so festive revelers.

Megan had intentionally arrived half an hour late to make the petty woman worry that she'd changed her mind. She also wanted to make sure that everyone was already there. Antonia would feel safer surrounded by as many of her kind as she could muster. And Megan wanted her to feel safe and untouchable until it was time to strip that misguided belief away forever.

Everywhere she looked, the Children of Nyx stared back at her, dressed and costumed befitting a festival in honor of fertility and ranging from the fantastic to something similar to what Bri had worn the first time Megan had seen her at Caer Sidhe. Apparently, they were all waiting for her to arrive, since there was no music, no dancing and frankly nothing that looked at all like a festival.

363

Megan searched every inch of the field for Bruce without finding any indication of his presence. She wove herself a mask of indifference through which her anger and grief remained hidden. Her best chance of Antonia dropping her guard relied on making the evil woman believe that she did not in fact have the power of life and death over the one-person Megan could never live without.

Her eyes slid over him without recognition when she first found her nemesis. Were it not for the woman's gloating expression, Megan might not have noticed him at all. Although his body remained largely the same, the soul that animated it was absent. Even though his shields were completely gone, she could feel no trace of him in the body before her.

"Oh look, Bruce!" Antonia crooned. "Our royal guest has shown up in her finest."

Megan gave her a practiced look of boredom.

"But where are my manners?" Antonia crooned. "As my guest, you must have a gift."

A young man, dressed much like a butler in a bad movie, stepped forward bearing a white velvet pillow over which a silk cloth had been draped. Holding it up in offering, he removed the covering to reveal a plain iron collar, decorated only with a crudely engraved tree similar to the one on Dougal's chest.

"You simply must try it on," Antonia purred, her hand hovering a fraction of an inch away from the necklace around Bruce's neck. "Your servant can help you."

Her smile never wavering, Megan placed her hand over Dougal's, intercepting it before it reached the pommel of the Scathlahm's Blade. Whispering directly into his mind, she promised him the revenge for which they both hungered.

"You are far too thoughtful," Megan said pleasantly, turning to face him and lifting her hair away from her neck.

He stared at the thing on the pillow, his whole body tensed like the trigger of a trap. Megan could feel the revulsion in him as he lifted it from the pillow, and held it open before the pale skin of her neck. There he froze, unable to commit this act against her.

Filling his mind with soothing visions of violence, she blinded him to the present and used his hands to close it around her neck. As soon as the two halves touched, the collar fused into a single piece of metal. Megan let her hair fall back into place.

"Your invitation implied that this would be a party," she said as if nothing noteworthy had just happened. "Where is the entertainment? Thus far I'm not impressed."

Antonia's eyes flashed with anger and Megan calmly stared back at her, waiting for an answer.

"Seriously," Megan added, nodding toward the crowd, "My high school held wilder school dances for Valentine's Day. I was so looking forward to the things I'd heard about the Lupercalia," she added, leaning closer to Dougal who couldn't stop staring at the thing around her neck.

Reaching into the folds of her dress, Antonia pulled forth the angular orb of the Dagda's Harp. The Morrigan flexed her will, and for a moment, Megan feared the Goddess of War would reach out and take it from this unworthy bearer.

"How pretty," Megan offered, still outwardly bored. "So you plan for us to play Dungeons and Dragons? Bruce had something to do with this, didn't he?"

An undercurrent of laughter passed through those close enough to hear. The muscles along Antonia's jaw stood out prominently as she struggled to maintain her composure. The laughter became louder and more prevalent, making Megan realize that even though the crowds around

365

her shared an ancestral hatred of the Tuatha dé, most of them hated Antonia even more.

They fell silent though when seer's niece began to sing.

Her voice wasn't particularly noteworthy, but the sounds emanating from the Dagda's Harp rang clear and bright. Were it not for the ancestral memories of what the artifact could truly do in the hands of its master, Megan might not have realized how much it resisted the woman's command even though Bruce had unlocked it.

The crowd began to applaud when she finished. Megan yawned.

"Do you think you could do better?" Antonia snapped.

"I don't want to upstage your little gathering," Megan said loftily, "But this whole affair is simply too dull to bear. Let me help."

With a quick gesture of her hand, the Dagda's Harp rose from Antonia's hand and began to glow. The startled Child of Nyx tried to snatch it back, but it burned her.

"She's not terribly bright, is she?" Dougal observed loudly.

"The Tuatha dé can't work magic here!" Antonia cried in dismay and stared at the collar around Megan's neck in horror.

"Oh dear," Megan said in mock worry, "You really should have told me. How am I supposed to follow your rules if no one bothers to tell me what they are? I do hope this doesn't mean you won't be inviting us next year."

Antonia took a half step toward Megan and away from Bruce before realizing what she'd done and moved back.

"Let's adjust the thermostat a bit," Megan taunted. "You Nyx kids are so delicate after all. How can you expect to have a fertility festival if everyone is huddled together with their teeth chattering?"

With a flourish of her hand, warm air filled the field, making fog rise from the ground and pushing away the strange incense. A collective sigh of

366

contentment emanated from the surrounding revelers as they grew comfortable for the first time since leaving the city.

Then, clasping her hands together behind her Scathlahm's neck, Megan began to sing although the words were not her own. Rising to the surface of her thoughts, the Morrigan sang in her native tongue of the day that she and her beloved Dagda had fooled the primordial goddess of night into walking freely to her own death. Although the words were ancient, the music that the Harp provided as it sought out and bonded with the Morrigan within her was not. A full symphony orchestra accompanied the clear, clean notes of her voice and just when Megan's fear that she wouldn't be able to dance reached its peak, the entirety of the Tuatha dé came to her aid and her body flowed with their adoration. Even though she and her Scathlahm were the only ones physically present, each and every one of her subjects stopped what they were doing and turned their attention toward the Queen.

Having been promised a dance in honor of fertility, the Children of Nyx found the magnetism of the pair's movements too intoxicating to resist, and soon all danced to the haunting melody of their enemy. Everyone that is, except for Antonia and her catatonic date.

Megan closed her eyes as she danced, not only to hide their glow, but also to keep her from looking at Bruce and breaking her concentration. When she brought the song to an end the entire valley erupted into applause.

Antonia stormed toward her as fast as she could with Bruce in tow.

"You can't just come here and…"

"I know," Megan said, cutting her off. "It's completely inappropriate for me to come in and give you a taste of a real celebration without doing more. I do, after all, have the resources of an entire kingdom at my disposal."

With an overly theatrical flourish of her hands, the garlands and braziers faded into the shadows to be replaced with knotwork banners that hung down and connected the stone columns. Her crest glowed from each while the designs embroidered in their weave radiated such power that the festival grounds they surrounded were essentially cut off from the surrounding lands and more importantly, from Haven.

Rune carved obelisks appeared between the columns, each holding fuel within its depths that burned in shades of green, towering high above the heads of the revelers.

"My dear Antonia, it really is most crude of you to expect a guest to provide entertainment, and I have much better things to do," she purred, looking at Dougal with such explicit suggestion that he turned three shades darker before he brought himself under control again.

Then she called the glowing orb to her hand and threw it across the mist shrouded space to the waiting hand of Luminita, who had quite clearly been dressed by the Scathlahm's modesty challenged sister.

The bard looked at it for a moment, and it seemed to shimmer and shift in her hand.

"Your Majesty does have the coolest toys," the bard said, her magically enhanced voice reaching everyone present. Then it rose above her, and she began to sing, filling the field with the same intoxicating sharpening of senses that Megan had first experienced at the Jubilee.

From the first notes that the harp played, it became clear the bard had been catching up on all the music she'd missed during her confinement to the Jubilee grove. Her sultry voice spawned emotions of hunger and lust. When Paul faded into existence next to her, his bow evoking a series of notes that danced around the bard's voice and merging effortlessly with the Harp, Megan saw how Bri had dressed him and became truly afraid of what the woman had in store for her Queen.

As she listened, Megan became aware of something embedded in the music, something that brought to mind the hidden carrier tone of Guarded Wood that Bruce had talked about that night. Unlike the rest of the music that the bards had crafted for the sole purpose of manipulating the emotions of the ecstatic Children of Nyx, this thread served a different purpose and it had Paul written all over it.

Hoping that the sudden spectacle of the bards would hide her interest, Megan glanced at Bruce. And while the music didn't seem to be affecting him in any way detectable on the outside, she was horrified to notice that the necklace around his neck had begun to glow.

Terrified that Antonia might notice at any moment, Megan fully committed herself and faded from Dougal's arms for an instant, sending the iron collar to the cabin where it could cause no harm.

It wasn't the sudden unexpected weight of the crown on her brow that startled her the most, but rather what she was no longer wearing under the flowing moonsilk that partially encased her. Of course, given the plunging neckline and open back, anything left underneath on the top half of her body would have shown, breaking the contrasting effect of her bare alabaster skin against the black moonsilk. She feared that the floor-length hem might trip her while they danced until she realized it was slit high on each thigh, giving the liquid fabric room to flow around her as she moved.

Dougal missed his step and almost took her down with him. For some reason he was even more embarrassed than she was. His eyes were everywhere except on her.

What's wrong with you? Megan commanded. *Look at me and dance like it was your last day on Earth!*

"As you command, My Queen," he laughed and obeyed.

Bruce stirred from dreams half formed by the sound of the waves as they struck the rocks around him. The cliff overhead stretched up into the eternity of a star-lit night as he relived the coming of the bards over and over, basking in the memory of Megan's rebirth.

Even though it wasn't all that he'd wanted, he thought she'd told him that she loved him there at the end before the great claws had closed around her. It wasn't possible to be sure. It was becoming difficult to be sure about anything now. He no longer knew if he'd been there for a few minutes or a few hundred years. But he was sure that he'd loved her. He was sure that she'd felt him with her as she'd fallen.

Then a voice whispered through him, a voice that called to him through the blood they shared. Surprised to find that he could still do so, Bruce sat up from where he lay, and turned his head toward the sound of his brother's voice.

Far across the waters he saw a beacon of familiar power, like a lighthouse on stormy seas. It called to him, showing him the way back to her side.

Chancing another quick glance at Bruce when they passed, Megan saw that his mouth no longer hung slack and his jaw muscles were clenched. Antonia let go of his hand and it fell back into place at his side. But she was still too close for Megan to attack without jeopardizing him.

The song came to an end, and the crowd rewarded the bards with thunderous applause as the Children of Nyx began to lose cohesion. Paul faded out and many of the women cried out for him to come back. When he reappeared seconds later, Luminita turned to the crowd.

"Sorry ladies, but the wait time for this ride is two centuries, and I'm not even sure that I'll be finished with this tasty morsel by then," she called out, kissing him hard before laughing along with the crowd that she now owned completely.

She tossed the Harp to Paul before sitting down on a stool that faded into existence next to her and taking the bow and cello that came an instant later. She began a run of what promised to be something classical and completely not in keeping with what they'd just played.

Then the sound began to skip like one of Azarich's old phonographs and the bard looked up, puzzled to find her husband grinning broadly and using the harp to manipulate the sounds she made. She swatted at him with her bow as he danced playfully away and began to sing.

What followed from the harp was an eclectic merging of old and new, delighting the Children of Nyx and working them into a lustful frenzy. Singing in a throaty rumble that reverberated in the chests of all around him, Paul danced in languid, sensuous movements that made Megan blush.

Wondering why they'd stopped trying to free Bruce, she looked over to find Paul under a halo of deceptive illusion, standing just behind his brother, singing in his ear down in the frequency where Megan connected to the Tuatha dé.

Looking quickly back in confusion to where the bard continued to play, Megan realized that Paul had never returned at the end of the previous song and that what she saw there now was an illusion created entirely by the bard with the aid of the Dagda's Harp.

Knowing that Megan could see him, he glanced up and smiled while he sang. Then he became distracted by what his imaginary twin was doing and looked back at her to mouth, *What the hell?*

Now Bruce actively rocked back and forth as his brother called him back from the rocky shore where he'd slowed her fall so Luminita could reach her in time.

Something massive began to move in the space between this world

371

and the next. Megan had one horrified second to think, *this should be interesting*, before hundreds of her people erupted into existence across the field, filling the empty spaces and forcing the children of Nyx aside as they formed the mesmerizing patterns in which they danced.

Caught up in the excitement of their exertions, she and Dougal fell into step with them in the undulating movements through which the Tuatha dé gathered power from the air around them and fed to their Queen.

Even though it was Paul that cleansed the addiction from his brother's soul and cleared a path back, it was Megan's power that led him to her.

Lifting his hand and holding his open palm over the necklace around his neck, Bruce released one brief, but devastatingly powerful burst of energy directly into it. The shockwave of its ending brought Antonia away from her rapt appraisal of Paul's dancing form, and she took a step closer to Bruce.

Megan appeared between them, reaching out and catching her by the throat, binding her motionless before them. Before the Children of Nyx could come to her aid, the Tuatha dé faded from sight and reappeared with their knives pressed to the throats of an entire generation of Nyx's descendants.

"I came here to build peace between our people," Megan said softly in the silence that followed, her voice carried by the bards across the field. "But you chose to harm the ones I love. Twice now, the women of your line have interfered with the Tuatha dé. I would like to think that you and your pathetic aunt would remember to avoid such unpleasantries in the future, but your past doesn't speak well of it."

Megan summoned the iron collar to her hand. She could feel Dougal's anticipation. Moving it partway into the shadows where it became translucent, she passed it through Antonia's neck to encircle her throat. Then she turned it so that the royal crest faced forward.

"Even though it's crude," the Queen mused, "you still aren't worthy to wear my crest."

Megan felt Bri bring Mariana into their connection where she could witness what would come next.

The image faded from the metal as it heated beneath the Queen's gentle touch and Antonia's breathing became ragged.

"Just to prevent future confusion," Megan continued, reaching down and taking her arm. "That collar will not come off as long as I live." She began to walk two of her fingers up Antonia's arm, leaving round blackened footprints that smoked in their wake. Tears ran down the Child of Nyx's cheek to sizzle and evaporate on the iron collar.

"There there," Megan cooed, reaching up to brush them away, leaving the path of her fingertips burned into the woman's face from nose to her ear. "And your feet must be so cold." Then she summoned a pair of boots that fit uncomfortably tight on the Child of Nyx's legs and feet.

Antonia's eyes widened.

"I don't want you to think that I don't like you," Mariana said through Megan's lips, "I just like the way you burn." And then she set them afire.

"Children of Nyx," Megan called out while Antonia whimpered. "Never forget that this woman and her family brought you to this point. The Tuatha dé would be perfectly justified in taking your lives in payment for what Priscilla did to us at Mag Tuired. When my people release you, you will have two choices. Flee back to your cave and give us wide berth in the future, or raise your hands against us and suffer the consequences.

Just keep in mind that I am fresh out of mercy."

Then she released Antonia to fall screaming to the ground, quenching the flames as she fell. Grasping desperately at the collar around her neck, she burned her hands, though not as badly as her feet and legs.

"Help me!" she screamed to her people as the Tuatha dé released them.

Avoiding her gaze, not a single one came to her aid or resisted in any way as they cloaked themselves en masse and fled toward the city.

"Bruce," Antonia pleaded.

"Really?" he asked, tearing what remained of the amulet from his neck. "You have no idea how much I enjoyed watching her do that to you."

"I'll give you as long as it takes for the last of your people to flee," Megan said. "If I can still see you by then, I'm going to give you to Mariana."

Antonia, no longer doubting the Queen's resolve, fled as best she could, considering her injuries. Attempting to cloak herself, she blinked in and out as she tried to run, only to have the agony break her concentration. In the end, she gave up and crawled.

"I've only got a few minutes to fix what I did to Sam's stocks," Bruce said, hugging Megan close. "After that, the damage will be irreversible. People won't trust him in the future, and everything we've done there will be for nothing. I have to go back in."

"There's no way in hell that I'm letting you go back in there," Megan cried. "Priscilla will be after you."

"Not if I cloak myself," he said, "I doubt anyone besides the two of them even know I shouldn't be there. I have to do this."

"Can't I just take you to another computer?" Megan begged.

"It would take me too long to download what I'd need," he whispered. "It has to be now and it has to be my laptop. I'll be right back, and then we can go to Gordons. I'm famished."

"Protecting Sam is one of the only things that could make me let you do this," she said, holding him closer. "We are going to have a long talk when you get back," she whispered and then kissed him hard before reluctantly letting him go. Then she retrieved his necklace and put it around his neck.

Surprised, he staggered back, grinning foolishly and disappeared.

Chapter XLI: The Battle of Haven's Gate

After navigating through the corridors to his room, Bruce uncloaked himself and was overjoyed to see that his laptop still remained plugged into the charger on the table where he'd left it. With a clarity that he hadn't possessed in what felt like months, he quickly selected the series of transactions that he'd memorized before entering the shielded city where his foresight all but dried up. Within a few days the portfolio would rebound and the future of Nickelville should be restored.

He closed the laptop, unplugged it from the wall and sent a huge pulse of raw energy through it, frying it beyond any possibility of repair. He had no intention of bringing anything back with him from Haven. Although he might not have any choice with the strange sense that had settled over him after Megan's incredible kiss. He wasn't complaining, but for some reason he felt like something of her had lingered on in him afterward.

Beyond that, he really hoped he didn't come out of this with a whole new set of phobias. Maybe speluncaphobia? He was pretty sure that was a thing. But maybe not, he sort of still felt curious about caves in general. Just not this one. Was there a fear of crystals?

Outside, he could hear the echoes of all the adults as they took up arms and headed to the front gate. Unsure if he'd be able to get back out that way, he headed for William and Catherene's quarters where he knew he'd find the help he needed.

He was still reflecting on the finer parts of that kiss when he passed through the school's cafeteria and followed his nose to a full tray full of the wonderfully rectangular pizza he'd last eaten at the Academy.

"I guess Andrew was right," he whispered, stacking pieces into his hand. "They really do serve this stuff everywhere. I don't know who was going to eat all of this so late, but it's mine now. And yes, not present Jade, I am thinking with my stomach."

He turned to go, realizing that there was one more piece in the row that he hadn't taken. Not wanting to jinx his escape with such an odd thing, he picked it up and folded it in half before sticking it in the pocket of his tux.

He jogged down the corridor toward his mentor's quarters, leaving bits of sausage in his wake. Just before he reached their home, the air split with a deafening, grinding squeal that made him think of what it would sound like a mile underground when a major fault cut loose and moved. Then the world dropped about three feet and his smith's senses felt the strain on the rock around him. Everything tilted as if the world's largest child had just sat down on the other end of a seesaw. Praying that the whole damn mountain didn't come down on him, he started to run, forgetting to cloak himself as he went.

"Speluncaphobia it is," he muttered to himself. With his foresight so muted, it was easy not to notice that his future had fallen away as if it had never existed at all.

The Tuatha dé were busy moving things out of the cottage and taking them to Nickelville. Megan was eager to go and doubted that she'd ever miss this place. Her only regret in going now was that she still had no idea what the Morrigan had sent her there to do. Whatever it was, she hoped it was finished because she and Bruce were soon to be gone for good.

For that matter, she had no idea what was going to happen when they finally left. But now, with a life together opening up before them, she didn't really care. It would all work out.

A thunderous crack sounded from the direction of Haven, and she felt something powerful yet oddly familiar nearby. Without pausing to wonder what it might be, she walked the shadows to the cliff overlooking Haven, still dressed in the moonsilk dress. Below, a huge cloud of dust billowed out the mouth of the cavern. Knowing that Bruce was inside, she crouched low and waited for him to emerge. Some twenty minutes later, Diana came riding out of the kennel gate on horseback with her hellhounds following behind.

Megan walked the shadows to place herself in the old woman's path.

"What's going on?" Megan yelled when she reined her horse in next to her.

"Something's happened," Diana yelled back. "Word is that there's a huge portion of the cavern that just up and disappeared."

"What do you mean, disappeared?"

"It's like a giant with a great big ice cream scoop just took it right out," she answered.

Megan's memories stirred and the Morrigan became active in her mind as the hellhounds gathered around her, nudging her fondly with their heads.

"There wasn't a toy boat there by any chance?"

"How did you know?" the woman answered. "I guess it's not so strange though. The school was in the part that disappeared. All of the kids are missing too, since that's where we put them when we are afraid there might be trouble. The boat probably belonged to one of them."

"Was the place where Bruce was staying anywhere close to the

379

school?" Megan asked, her heart breaking anew.

"Yes, and your friend William's place too," Diana added.

"I've got to go," Megan said, preparing to walk the shadows to the gate. "Take your wolves to the cottage. My people will take you someplace safe. Ask for Paul when you get there and he'll know what to do."

She could hear screams of dismay through the shield gate in spite of the dampening effect it had. The gatekeeper was there as usual. He hadn't noticed her yet though, probably because she was still dressed in the black moonsilk dress. She lit a flame in her palm to get his attention.

"Go away," he yelled and actually had the audacity to throw a fireball at her, which she deflected with ease. She walked to the place directly across from where he stood, ignoring the rest of his protests.

"It's rude to throw things," Megan said, allowing her eyes to glow. "You should come outside if you want to play."

"I should have known you'd come," Priscilla said, walking into view.

"You made Bruce repair the Ark, didn't you?" Megan asked.

Priscilla looked confused.

"The toy boat," Megan elaborated.

At last she could see that the seer knew what she was talking about.

"You should have left it alone," Megan continued. "It was created by The Dagda to return the Tuatha dé to their birth world should this one prove to be uninhabitable. Instead he used it to take Nyx there so he could kill her."

"How dare you speak such blasphemy!" the old woman cried. "This is your doing, not mine."

"We were on our way back home before you triggered the Ark. Let me in and I'll try to get them back. The Tuatha dé left that place behind for good reasons. The air is toxic, and it's full of monsters."

"Stop wasting my time," Priscilla spat. "We have an emergency to sort out."

"This is your last chance to settle this peacefully," Megan called after her when she turned to go.

When the seer continued to walk away, Megan reached out and took hold of every iron rod embedded in the floor of the valley and ripped it free of the ground in which it lay. Then, twisting it into glowing mass, she hurled it directly into the shield gate.

Both the seer and the gatekeeper dove behind the desk as if the tiny piece of furniture would have stopped the massive projectile if the shield had failed. When the rough metal sphere collided, it sent a shockwave through the mountain, causing small avalanches that Megan swatted away like insects.

"Did you really think that was going to work?" Priscilla asked, pulling herself to her feet. "The entire might of the Children of Nyx powers this shield."

"Who said it didn't?" Megan asked calmly and with a casual flip of her hand, tossed the massive iron ball far over the cliff behind her and several valleys over.

Thunder rumbled across the faces of the mountains and lightning lit the valley. Wind began to howl through the jagged crags overhead, and the deep bray of a war horn announced their coming just as it had in times long past.

As Priscilla turned, the sky flashed again, revealing the Queen standing alone in the same dress that she'd danced in such a short time before. Megan had quenched the flame in her hand, but when the valley plunged back into darkness, her eyes glowed violet in the night.

Rain began to fall, but not loud enough to drown out the bass of the war drums that shook the stony foundations of the city. When lightning lit the field again, the Queen of the Tuatha dé stood at the head of her army.

War had come to Haven.

Bruce met William and Catherene with their twins held in their arms before he reached their home. Both stopped in surprise when they saw him.

"Bruce?" Cat murmured uncertainly, looking at him closely. "How are you up walking around?"

"A bit of tender loving care from my Queen and her bards," he answered. "Any idea what just happened?"

"No," William answered. "But whatever it was felt old and powerful, like an artifact."

"Something else is weird," Cat added. "We can usually feel peoples' emotions even when they're shielded. It feels like almost everyone just disappeared."

"Oh no," Bruce whispered in horror. "Please tell me I didn't restore the Dagda's Ark while I was out."

"What's that?" Cat asked, shifting her stiff child uncomfortably.

By the time he'd explained, they began to realize how dire the situation had become.

"So you're telling me we're stuck in a world that was too much for one of the Beloved to handle?" Cat asked. Then both she and her husband turned toward the direction from which he'd just come as if hearing a distant sound. Screams echoed down the hallway.

Following the sound, they rushed to the gym where they found several dozen children and the three teen helpers from William's classes. The wall had cracked badly, spreading into a dark crevice several inches wide. It was through this opening that a nauseating sulfurous stench spilled, reminding Bruce at once of his nightmares. But it was the mewling things that wriggled through the opening that had caused the children to scream.

Bruce reached out and ripped several steel sheets from a platform near the center of the gym, turning them molten as they flew through the air to seal off the opening.

Beyond what should have been the structural bedrock of the mountain itself, something made a deep series of keening clucks that sounded eerily like human laughter.

William swept the things into a broom closet where they could do no harm, but not before his wife brought one to them and made it hover at waist level. Even before she turned it to where they could see its features, Bruce knew they would be human. Most of its body was covered with the pale mottled skin of something that lives in darkness. Its tangled mass of black hair was broken in places by oozing lesions and its hands, too human to call paws, ended in the bloody remains of the nails it had broken off when it burrowed through the broken wall.

Knowing that he'd regret it even before doing so, he pulled the hair back to look at the thing's face. Pale green eyes glared up at him as it coughed and spat. When it bared its teeth, the ones that remained looked human as well. Cat turned her son's face away.

"I think this is what happened to the people who didn't leave with the Dagda," Bruce said.

"I thought they all have violet eyes," the girl helper said.

"That was after he made them into the Tuatha dé," Bruce explained. They were probably green like this before. I don't think we should kill any of them."

"Are you insane?" the oldest but not biggest of the two male teens gasped.

"Shut up Gaius," the girl said.

"Not now, you two," William said sternly. "We need to work

together. Bruce, this is Clelia," he said nodding toward the girl. "Felix is the big guy with the even bigger heart and the last as you've probably figured out is Gaius, whose mother is on the High Council."

"I don't see any sex organs," Cat observed as she put it into the closet with the others. "I think they're asexual."

Something in the wall shifted loudly, making them all jump.

"We need to get somewhere secure," Bruce said. "I doubt all of Haven came with us, so it's probably open to the outside in any number of places. If Antonia triggered it, she'd probably have done so in her workshop. That place is heavily reinforced, and it's big enough to hold all of us comfortably."

Clelia ran over to one of the side doors.

"What are you doing?" William called after her.

"We don't keep any firearms here, but there is a small cache of short swords and spears," she answered, already starting to pass them to her companions. "Bruce?"

"Not my thing," he answered.

She shrugged in reply, belting on a sword and picking up a spear as well.

Reaching out as far as she could, Megan explored what she could of the fortress city, looking for weaknesses that she could exploit. However, in response to her mother's mischievous taunting, the Children of Nyx had sealed the city up tight. With the exception of two hidden gun turrets on the cliff face high above and the kennel gate which had already been sealed with a large stone block, there appeared to be no weakness. Likewise, the turrets would be invulnerable unless someone opened the embrasures from the inside.

She really wished her mother would have left them alone. But as soon as she thought about it, she remembered that doing so had never been Emelia's idea. Whatever it had been that she was doing had been important enough for the Morrigan to make her miss the death of her father.

Keeping in mind that this taunting had been carried out for the Queen Mother, who never did anything without a reason, Megan studied the defenses more carefully, particularly the way in which the shield wall worked. When she figured it out, she had to laugh at its efficient simplicity.

"What are your orders, My Queen?" Dougal asked.

"I want a two-inch diameter hole opened in the shield," she said, pointing to a place just off center to the left.

"I don't want to question Your Majesty's wisdom," Bri began.

"And yet that's exactly what you're about to do," Megan sighed in resignation.

"But what possible use is a two-inch hole that will remain, at most, open for only a few seconds?"

"Let's just say I'm glad Bruce forced me to watch Star Wars when it was showing at the Palace," Megan answered. If this worked, she'd watch it with him any time he wanted, even if he became as fixated with it as his father was about the motorcycle vampires.

"I was in the balcony when you saw it," her Scathlahm said, looking at the shield. "I rather liked that movie. We're making an exhaust port so you can take out the reactor, aren't we?"

"You and Bruce are going to get along fine," Megan said, smiling.

"As you wish, My Queen," he answered with a faint smile.

Then, as hundreds of her subjects began to bombard one tiny spot in the shield, Megan knelt a dozen yards away and began to gather her power.

"So far, so good," Catherene said, as she and Bruce led their charges to safety. The air had become noticeably warmer since they'd first found the children. The sleeves of Cat's sweatshirt had first been rolled up, but she soon put her son down long enough to discard it entirely.

"I never thought of fantasy tattoos," Bruce said while they walked, looking at the ones not hidden by her t-shirt. "Those are amazing. Do you think William would give me one when this is over?"

"After you turn eighteen," she answered without looking away from the path ahead. "I've already spoken to your mother enough times on the phone to know that I don't want to cross her."

The children had settled down now that they were moving, although they did look at the armed helpers with unease. William brought up the rear carrying their other son.

"Are you sure you don't want help carrying him?" Bruce offered again.

"Don't take this personally, but if things get crazy, I won't be any help if I don't know exactly where our boys are," she explained.

"Fair enough," he said in reply. "You know, I can't help but notice that we're going to pass by the cafeteria. We don't know how long we're going to be stuck in that workroom. We should probably stop for food and water."

"I was thinking the same thing," Cat agreed, relaying the message back to her husband. "He agrees, every kid can carry some of each."

But before they got there, they crossed an intersection from which heat blasted and the sulfurous stench made them gag. Looking to the left they could see an orange glow in the distance.

"I think it's open to the outside," Cat said quietly. "We need to be careful here."

"I'll ward it so we can tell if anything comes through after us," he said, and in a few seconds, it was done.

"You're really good at that," she observed in surprise.

"I had a lot of practice over the summer," he responded.

When they arrived in the dining hall, everything still looked like it had when he'd pilfered his dinner earlier. But when they opened the door, they were greeted by the sight of a crustacean-like thing the size of a grizzly with six heavily armored legs. Unlike the things from the gym that had been sickly and misshapen, this looked like the product of evolutionary refinement. The way that the reds, blacks and purples faded into one another were actually quite beautiful. A somewhat hysterical part of his mind wondered if William could make a tattoo out of it.

Between the segments of its body and the trunk-like joints of its legs, white protrusions waved in the air like sea anemones.

Well, at least that thing was never human, Cat sent.

The protrusions extended like hair under a particularly static laden balloon, and the thing whirled on them faster than should have been possible. Bruce had expected it to have pincers like a crab, but instead he found himself looking into the open maw of a large mammal. It had no eyes that he could see, but there were rudimentary gills, though they were obscured by the heavy chain around the thing's neck.

Cat threw a fireball directly into its face as Bruce slammed the door shut, welding it to the frame as he did so. Before they made it back to the hallway where the others waited, a series of clicking booms reverberated through the surfaces around them.

"Oh, that is definitely not good," Bruce said, "Anything that can communicate in frequencies that low can be heard a long way off. Our vacation is definitely over."

The crescent moon slowly crept across the sky as Megan knelt there, gathering power and waiting while two magical races pitted themselves against one another.

Eyes closed, she felt one of the slots open in the left gun turret high above their heads. She waited patiently while the long barrel of the rifle slid noiselessly out, taking aim at her. With the turret compromised by the opening, she wrapped the entire thing in a shield of her own, before reaching in and igniting all of the ordinance contained inside. Judging from the cloud of smoke that belched from deep inside the cavern, there had been more than just ammunition stored there.

Megan opened her eyes to find Priscilla standing inside the shield directly in front of her.

"That was fun," Megan taunted. Then, looking meaningfully at the other hidden turret overhead, "You should definitely try it again."

The adoration of her people grew. But mingled within that adoration, The Morrigan reminded her again of the second path her mother had sought to avoid. One in which she became everything the Children of Nyx had accused her.

"We must be close to the edge," Bruce said, looking at the cracks that fractured the wall on either side of the corridor.

"What does that mean?" Clelia asked, walking between him and Cat, carrying a spear with a broad steel head and crossbar.

"The structural integrity of the part that came with us will be weakest near the edges," Cat explained, still carrying her son.

"What's that up ahead?" the huge teen named Felix asked after checking the side corridor for movement.

As they approached, the spider web of cracks in the wall gave way to places where chunks of stone had begun to break loose from the ceiling and fall to the ground. It was one such place that had drawn Felix's attention. The sulfurous air grew hot and thick as they approached the harsh orange light that spilled into the corridor from above.

"I don't feel good about this," Bruce said. "Should we find another way?"

"This is the shortest way to the workrooms," Clelia answered. "It's directly ahead a few intersections down."

So they approached in silence with the three helpers trying to keep the children quiet. This close to the opening, Bruce could see that a sort of ash floated down through the hole to dust the floor.

"Great," Cat whispered, watching the opening with mistrust. "Space pollen."

The children began to pile up behind them as Bruce crept cautiously forward to look up through the hole. Something wriggled in the darkness of one of the bigger cracks and a white pill-bug looking thing crawled quickly out then paused, hanging there on the wall as if studying Bruce.

"Rollie pollie," one of the children blurted out, bringing a second one out of the crack.

"Come on," Gaius said, "Let's get moving." Then he reached out with the tip of the short sword he carried and poked the first of the creatures, which did indeed roll up with the exception of a tail-like thing hanging out the back.

"See," he said, pushing past Bruce, "Nothing to worry about."

With a sound like the short blast of an air compressor, the second creature shot from the wall and landed on Gaius's side between the bottom of his last rib and the top of his hip bone. Then its multitude of clawed feet shredded his shirt and the skin beneath, tearing into fat and muscle as it began to burrow into him.

His shriek of terror echoed down the corridor and more of the things began to pour out of the wall.

"Get it off," Gaius sobbed, trying to get hold of it.

Bruce ignored the revulsion of doing so and grabbed it by its blood slickened tail. When he tried to pull it free, the thing lifted the plates of its shell, catching in the torn flesh around the wound. Dimly aware that someone had summoned fire to stop the entrance of the things, Bruce cleared his mind and reached into the boy's side to close the plates before pulling it out and throwing it hastily on the ground where Clelia stomped on it with a sickening crunch before she vomited violently over the floor.

Gaius sagged against Felix, dropping the sword as blood poured from the wound in his side.

Having caught up, William reached out with the hand not holding his son and burned the wound shut.

"My mother will…" Gaius whispered before passing out.

"Your mother can shove a demonic doodle bug where the sun doesn't shine," Cat snapped. "Felix, can you carry him?"

The big boy slung his unconscious friend over his shoulder in response.

"Demonic doodle bug?" Bruce asked.

"She gives silly names to things that scare her," William explained.

"The thing back in the cafeteria?" Bruce asked.

"Phydeaux the angry crustacean," she answered without hesitation.

Bruce's laugh was interrupted by a loud huffing overhead. When they looked up, a huge wedge-shaped snout filled the opening, sending a spray of what felt suspiciously like snot across them.

"Back to the last intersection," Cat said quietly.

Then something hit the roof hard, showering the screaming children with chunks of stone. A blunt claw the length of Bruce's forearm burst through the hole and doubled the size of the opening as something above began to dig.

"Run!" Bruce screamed, as things unlike any he'd ever sensed crossed his ward. Then before he could follow his own advice, orders began to flow from his lips. "Cat, you keep the lead. Clelia you go with her and Felix, try to keep up near the front in case they need you. William, guard the intersection from where we came until everyone has passed.

392

Something is coming. I'll be rearward."

Although surprised to hear him take charge, everyone hurried to do as he'd ordered. But none of them were as surprised as he was because he had no idea where those words had come from. He wasn't even positive that he knew what that last word meant. Soon the children moved away in a surprisingly calm crowd given the circumstances with the big Felix trotting along beside them. Eager to put distance between him and whatever was tearing into the corridor behind him, Bruce brought up the rear.

When he reached the interaction where William stood guard with his rigid son in his arms, Bruce heard a scream from the direction of the cafeteria.

"Is someone still back there?" Bruce asked.

"I don't think so," William whispered so the children who'd just passed wouldn't hear. "It's done that twice already and it's an exact mimic of Gaius."

"They're trying to lure us back," Bruce whispered in horror. "We're being hunted."

Rain became snow and turned the ground white while the Tuatha dé worked to create the hole that their Queen required. But a circle remained clear around Megan who, kneeling in preparation for the breach, radiated stray heat from the energy she'd gathered.

When at last they pierced the shield, her hand shot up, pointing at the hole they'd created. A thin beam of energy shot from her finger, brighter than the sun. It passed through into the bowels of Haven and directly into the flawed heart of the Dark Crystal. Unable to handle this devastating blow, it shattered into the elements from which it had been formed.

Then the energy it stored, along with the tsunami of raw power

Megan had sent into it, surged back into the Children of Nyx. As one they collapsed unconscious throughout the cavern.

The shield gate simply ceased to exist, and the silence within the cavern was ominous to those gathered outside. The Tuatha dé readied their weapons, fully expecting the city's inhabitants to pour out at any second. When they didn't, the Tuatha dé realized what Megan had done, and their cheers echoed into the valleys beyond.

Let it be remembered, her Scathlahm sent to everyone present and through them to all of those not, *That on this day Queen Megan Mackgahe took the stronghold of Haven from the hands of her enemies without losing a single one of her subjects, just as she had promised.*

"Have three score of our people begin evacuating the Children of Nyx from the cavern and be quick about it. This whole place has been destabilized, and it could come down on our heads at any moment. Everyone else starts looking for that damn toy boat. No one can touch it though. I just need to know where it breached the veil so I can open it back up into the same world. Time is of the essence for the people trapped inside. The things that chased our ancestors here are likely still there. And if they were too much for us to handle, then a bunch of Nyx kids have no chance at all."

Bruce ran to beat the front of the line to the next intersection where they'd turn left to get them going in the right direction again. William had resumed his place at the rear.

When he reached it, he could smell once again the sulfurous odor of the outside atmosphere. Unless he was mistaken, the way before him led directly toward the opening and the ward he'd just felt trip.

A familiar series of clicking booms sounded from the darkened corridor before him. More impacts thrummed through the stone from the monstrous brute who was tearing the part of Haven they'd brought with them open like a pinata. Then the emergency lights failed, plunging them into darkness.

The children cried out in alarm, and Bruce hurriedly built a powerful ward of misdirection over the space before him, tuning it to block out light and sound before the things approaching from the other side could see or hear the children. Cat and William lit the corridor around them and Bruce waited for what would come.

Moving quickly now that they understood what they needed to do, the children passed quickly, and William joined him. As they watched, something moved in the darkness beyond the ward. Whether it was the same phydeaux they'd seen back in the kitchen or another just like it, Bruce couldn't tell. But the thing that held the end of the leash was certainly new.

It possessed spindly limbs that ended in long curved claws. Its torso, nearly skeletal in its muscular composition, nevertheless rippled with the flow of muscle beneath the skin.

Although it held the chain that tethered it to the thing on the leash, the newcomer primarily moved on all four of its long limbs, with the hind ones bending back at the knee like a canine. When it lifted its head, sniffing the air through its elongated bone encased snout, Bruce realized he hadn't thought to mask their scent. Like its hind legs, there was something wolfish about the shape of its skull, yet birdlike at the same time.

But even if the loin cloth of some unidentifiable vegetation hadn't already hinted at its intelligence, the luminous eyes that glowed faintly in the dark like the hands of an old clock would have given it away.

Tilting its head back, it screamed in perfect imitation of Gaius then waited, its head bobbing slightly like a bird.

The damaged section of the cavern wasn't exactly difficult to find. Megan soon looked through a perfectly round opening in what had previously been a solid wall. It was tall enough for her to walk through without bending over, but only just. On the other side, a cavernous void roughly a quarter mile long stretched out into the darkness. On the other end, an opening similar to the one in which she stood opened outside.

"It sure would have saved a lot of time if we'd known it made an external opening," Bri observed at her side.

"I didn't bother to look all the way on the other side of the mountain," Megan admitted, shaking her head in disgust.

Maybe it was the way that Diana had described the voided space, but Megan had expected it to be spherical. Instead its ends were stretched out more like a football with each of the tips creating the openings they saw now. That did make a certain amount of sense when she thought about it. Something with that much power would tend to create a strong magnetic field and this particular shape supported that.

Walking down the slick slope of polished stone that the ark had left in its wake, she opened herself to the signature of the damaged veil and found it almost immediately. Born from the familiarity of having spent the last year and a half with one just like it, she realized Bruce was trapped in the nightmare world that Jacob Routh had once sought to enter.

The irony wasn't lost on her.

"Just hold on a little while longer, my love," she whispered, closing her eyes and centering herself. Then, with the Morrigan whispering instructions, Megan began to build the first true gate that the earth had seen in several thousand years.

396

By the time Bruce reached the next intersection, Cat and Clelia had just arrived. The booming clicks of the phydeauxs poured out from within. Clelia summoned a globe of light and threw it down the darkened corridor, revealing a writhing mass of movement rushing toward them.

Stretching his hand up to touch the supports that spanned the height of the opening before him, he began to snap them one by one, glad that the Children of Nyx had only covered the original brittle iron instead of replacing them with steel. Starting at the other end and moving toward where he stood, he collapsed the corridor, crushing as many of the creatures as he could so they wouldn't be able to continue the hunt.

"Damn it!" Cat cried. "That means they've gotten ahead of us in the next tunnel. We have to get back over there if we're going to reach the workrooms."

"I'll run ahead and try to cut them off," Bruce called back, already sprinting away.

He didn't bother with a light, trusting his extra senses to warn him of anything in his path. So it surprised him a moment later when he noticed his shadow cast down the corridor in front of him.

"You didn't think I'd let you go alone," Clelia asked, pulling easily alongside him even though his hands were empty and she carried both a spear and a short sword.

"Either I'm more out of shape than I'd thought, or you're really fast," he panted.

"Fastest in Haven for three years running," she answered, hardly winded at all.

To their horror, two of the spindly legged creatures entered the intersection ahead of them, their glowing eyes fixing on them as they approached.

As if someone had taken control of his body, Bruce sprinted ahead, calling the sword to him from the scabbard on Clelia's hip as he went. Then, casting a sphere of crackling electricity directly into the face of the nearest creature, he dropped low and slid beneath the flailing claws. Reinforcing the edge of the blade with his magic, he severed the leg of the second thing at the mid-thigh, causing it to topple backwards into the corridor from which it had come. Then he threw a shield across the opening they needed to control before whirling to behead the one he'd already hit. The fight was over in less than three seconds.

"Not your thing?" Clelia gasped, still staring down at the creature on the floor. "Where did you learn to fight like that?"

"Emelia," he said, knowing even as he did that it wasn't exactly true.

"No wonder we lost at Mag Tuired," she said in wonder.

The only time he'd ever fought like that was when August had been in control. Something strange was going on, and for all their sakes, he hoped it continued.

August? Bruce sent hopefully.

The only response he got were several of the mimic screams from the darkness on the other side of the shield he'd cast. As they watched, one of the phydeauxs leapt onto the writhing creature on the floor, grabbing it by an arm that it ripped off effortlessly and began to eat before another joined it and together they ripped the rest of the spindly legged creature apart.

Unable to look away, Bruce and Clelia watched in horror as several sets of the luminescent eyes appeared just outside the light. Then they slowly moved toward the shield.

"Keep moving," Cat could be heard, urging the children on. "It's just a little bit further." The ground beneath their feet shuddered, feeling for a moment as if the angle of incline changed, like something heavy had entered from the higher end or perhaps as if something had broken free.

As adamant as Cat had been when telling the children to keep moving, she froze when she saw the creatures on the other side of Bruce's shield.

"The Jabberwocky," she whispered, "with eyes of flame, came whiffing through the tulgey wood and burbled as it came." Then she yelled for the children to run.

"I've always hated that poem," Bruce muttered.

"How long do you think you can hold it?" Clelia asked.

"A few more minutes," he said, watching as a figure left the shadows, walking completely upright. Although it might have once been like the others, the skull had shed its thin layer of skin like the velvet of a buck's antlers, gleaming white in the flickering light of Clelia's flame. Strange symbols had been carved into the skin of its limbs, leaving places where more bone showed through.

As the last of the children fled past along with the silently plodding Felix and his unconscious friend, the jabberwockies across the shield began to bob their heads up and down, uttering the same shrieking calls as before. But now, instead of joining them, the strange one Bruce thought to be the leader pointed one long, claw tipped finger at him. Then it slowly turned its hand palm upward and curled the claw toward himself, unmistakably calling Bruce to him.

"No doubt about it," Bruce cried, pulling Clelia with him as he turned to follow William and the others. "I'm totally getting a whole new set of nightmares to replace the old ones."

As Dougal and Bri stood guard over the opening into the cavern, Megan took a place several dozen feet away from the toy boat that lay almost forgotten on the floor of the cavern. Around her, over a thousand of the Tuatha dé knelt in the vast open space, waiting for their Queen to begin. She was already deep in trance, though her open eyes lit the cavern in a violet glow.

When she began, there was a subtle tug as she began to draw on their power to bridge this world and the one where the man she loved had been trapped. Still clad in the moonsilk dress, the softness of her form contrasted with the rigidness of her body as she worked.

"Did you ever dream in all of those years that you spent searching that she'd be anything like this?" Bri asked from where two of them guarded the entrance to the unnatural cavern.

"Not until I saw her drag that beast of a car through Tyr Sgodl," he answered, looking at his Queen with such longing that his sister put her arm around his shoulder.

"How positively touching," an old woman's voice said from behind them.

They both recognized the seer from Megan's thoughts, and both drew their weapons.

"Why aren't you out with the rest?" Dougal asked.

"You didn't expect me to give up my power to the shield like some common servant, did you?" she cackled. "After all, that damn half-breed didn't even do it properly, or you would all still be outside."

From the shadows four iron monstrosities moved into the light. Both Bri and Dougal recognized them at once as what remained of the Nine, the same artifacts that had nearly wiped out the Tuatha dé on the battlefield of Mag Tuired. And although Dougal did have one of the only weapons that could destroy them, without the Morrigan's armor and spirit to enhance him, he was as doomed to fail as his aunt had been. The best he could hope to do was slow their advance on the helpless Queen.

"Before morning I will finally end any possibility of your green-eyed friend killing me!" Priscilla laughed.

"How many times do you have to be told?" Bri screamed. "None of us have green eyes!"

"Go," Dougal whispered, changing his stance to better meet the expected rush. With the opening so small, the iron soldiers would only be able to pass through one at a time.

"You can't hold them off by yourself," his sister growled.

"I don't have to hold them off for long," he answered. "But you have to go now. We have to give our Queen as much time as we can."

She shook her head violently, tightening her grip on the pommel of her sword.

"Everyone dies if she does," he whispered.

Then, throwing her sword down at his feet, she turned and sprinted past the kneeling men and women that surrounded the Queen and directly toward the opening at the other end of the mountain.

Clelia had taken William's son and run ahead to help Cat when it became clear that the things would likely catch up with them before they reached their destination. Now he and Bruce retreated backward a step at a time, trying to give the children enough time to reach the questionable safety of the workrooms.

It seemed like hours since Bruce had woken on the festival field. As their magical reserves began to dwindle, he found himself relying more and more often on the sword in his hand. But even though his body had sprung into action of its own volition every time it had seemed that all was lost, it was starting to take its toll. His arm and shoulder burned with fatigue, and the only thing keeping him going at this point was fear and adrenaline.

Bruce felt something from one of the side passageways and barely had time to throw a new shield over it before another of the jabberwockies came into view.

"Why isn't Bonehead coming forward?" William asked, seeing the strange creature from a distance yet again.

"I think he's the brains behind the operation," Bruce answered. "And I think he's waiting for something to happen."

"Like what?" William asked.

A loud hyena-like giggle sounded from far behind them in the direction where the children had gone. William's eyes went instantly distant.

"They've reached the workrooms," he said, sighing with relief. "Cat, Clelia and Felix are sending them in and guarding the other side from whatever made that sound."

"Good," Bruce panted, hoping the two of them would make it as well.

"You're taking all of this better than I am," William confided.

"It's not my first rodeo," Bruce answered.

"Speaking of rodeos," William said, "Did you really make an artifact barbecue pit?"

"It was before I knew what the cost would be," Bruce answered.

"Maybe you can dismantle it and get that part of your soul back," William suggested. It looked like the jabberwockies were getting ready for another rush.

"Maybe," Bruce agreed and felt something settle oddly in the back of his mind. Hopefully it wasn't whatever was letting him fight like August.

"The last of the children are almost in," William said.

"Jacob, help me!" a woman's voice called from the massing jabberwockies before them.

402

"That's new," William said in surprise.

"No," Bruce said. "That's very old. I guess Jacob wasn't imagining things when he heard his wife. How fast can you run?"

"Not as fast as those things," William answered.

"You won't have to," Bruce said, reaching down deep and throwing everything he had into a wall of fire that surged away from him in a wave

down the hall to their enemies.

The two of them turned on their heels and began to sprint with Bruce easily outdistancing the older man. At once a series of the eerie shrieks called out after them, letting them know that not all of the jabberwockies had been stopped.

Just up ahead he could see Cat, Clelia and Felix spread out, facing the other direction where he could hear weird chuckling noises coming from nearer than before.

When he reached them, he sent his smith senses deep into the stone around him, locating the places he needed, flexing the stone above them.

"Everyone inside," he yelled as William caught up, "Now!"

Having learned not to question his orders, they quickly retreated back through the huge iron door, just as something huge and misshapen entered the range of his senses. Then he pulled with everything he had left. Clelia yanked him through by the tail of his blood splattered and tattered tux when the roof collapsed and sealed the door shut behind tons of rock.

From where Priscilla watched, she could see the young queen's protector as he held his ground against the automaton that filled the opening before him, unable to see much beyond its monstrous frame. He could not, in fact, see that one of the others had scaled the wall on this side of the cavern wall like the spider that the bottom half of its iron body resembled. There it hung, directly over the opening through which its brethren attempted to pass, waiting for the unsuspecting young Danann to come unsuspectingly within the reach of its scythe-like claws.

But the boy had been trained well and held his ground without advancing for what felt like hours in the face of her need to end this before the smart-mouthed witch queen finished. If that were allowed to happen, the seer knew she might very well lose her last chance to change her destiny and rid the world of these alien vermin.

Then the moment she'd been hoping for arrived.

Working together, the creature in the doorway began an almost imperceptible withdrawal, moving backward no more than a fraction of an inch at a time as the one above flattened itself, moving its torso as close as it could without leaving the hidden protection of the rock's surface.

It happened so slowly that the young man never noticed when he took one small step forward, extending his swing ever so slightly past the opening from which he fought. The seer's breath caught as she waited for the trap to spring, but let it out again when she realized that they were trying to draw him out further yet.

She cursed again whatever twist of fate had given her foresight powerful enough to see into the dark places where others could not, yet not the skill to look on any path at will as she'd sensed in the young smith. Instead, she received clear though disjoined visions of the future without the context through which she could interpret them. Over the centuries she'd learned to use them to the best of her advantage, but at times like this, she'd have given almost anything to know exactly what would happen in the next few hours.

Then the boy took another step, less cautious this time as he swept the curved edge of the Scathlahm's Blade in an arc, severing the arm of the artifact before him. Before the severed piece could hit the ground, the creature above him brought both of its arms down in a deadly arc, impaling the boy through the shoulder and gut. Then the one-armed automaton he'd managed to damage only seconds before slammed the boy with its broken stump, freeing him from the claws of its comrade and sending him flying several feet back through the opening.

Realizing that the path before it lay clear, the damaged member of the Nine surged forward through the opening, intent on finishing off this obstacle so it could move on to the true target of its summoning. But before it could move completely through, the boy was back on his feet again carving off bits of the creature before he leapt through the shadows, leaving sprays of his own blood to fall in his wake before reappearing to strike again.

"That's impossible," Priscilla gasped aloud. *The artifact must be augmenting his abilities,* she thought. Otherwise he shouldn't have been able to teleport within Haven's walls.

Unable to target its foe before the man moved on again, the iron beast began to swing its remaining arm wildly, hoping to catch him again when he appeared. And it did so, many times. But like the berserkers of old, the young queen's protector seemed impervious to pain. At last the brave Tuatha dé appeared directly before the thing just as its remaining arm swept past. Throwing the last of his strength behind the blow, he drove the Beloved's artifact to the hilt in the automaton's chest and the iron beast shattered.

Before the next could take its place, the young man fell to his knees and brought his hands together with the blade of the knife pointed downward between them. A powerful shield sprung into being across the mouth of the cavern, sealing it off from the remaining members of the Nine.

This is taking too long, Priscilla thought as one of the Nine struck its scythe-like claw against the glowing surface of the shield drawing a shower of sparks and melting away the tip of its primary weapon. She wasn't sure how he'd summoned such a powerful defense, or why he hadn't done so before now. But surely, he wouldn't be able to hold it for long, at least not with the mortal wounds he'd already received. In the end, those remaining of the Nine would prevail, but she now doubted that they'd complete the task in time to finish the murder for which she'd sent them.

Leaving the remaining artifacts to deal with the girl's protector, Priscilla turned to go outside the ruined gate and rouse the Tacet from where they lay outside. She'd have preferred to unleash the hellhounds on the girl while she stood there, so gloriously vulnerable, but that traitorous Diana had defected with them early on in the battle. No matter though, when this was over she'd track her down and feed her remains to her own wolves.

But when she turned, she found a large black cat in her path. When she reached out to crush it, she discovered it was protected by shields and protections more ancient than her own.

"I know what you are," the seer sneered. "Oh no, not the Morrigan's feared pet kitty! Are you the best that girl could find in the way of reinforcements?"

The Cat Sidhe looked at her with reproach.

"Judgement won't work on me," the seer warned, suddenly wondering why she bothered to speak with a cat. "I have foreseen the man who will kill me. But by the time the sun rises, none will remain to do the deed. So do your worst."

Valiant as her speech had been, she still screamed when he lept toward her, growing and changing form as he did so. Then he walked the shadows with her to the cliff, holding her frail and struggling form over the edge with fingers that still ended in claws.

"As you wish," he snarled, showing his feline teeth before adding, "Oh Great Oracle."

Then he watched her fall with great amusement, because it is in the nature of cats to do so, even cats who had once been the shape-shifting younger brother of The Dagda. Reverting back to his preferred form, he looked down at the broken body below.

He sniffed his paw in distaste. It would take weeks to get the foul scent from his fur. But before that, he would nap. The sun would be shining through the library window to land on the counter next to where

Andrew currently worked on the new card catalog. Now that his part in this unpleasant business had ended, it was time to move on to more important matters. Soon the new librarian would be comfortable enough to pet him, and then they would get along much better. There would be much to do in the years to come, but the events that had brought him to the intriguing little town of Nickelville were still some years off.

In the silence that followed their arrival in the workrooms, the lost children began to whimper into the shoulders of friends, too frightened of what horrors might hear them if they cried. Felix sat down next to the young ones and they soon packed in around him, feeling a little safer. Bruce thought sadly of the childhoods that had been stolen from them here in this dark place.

William and Cat dropped exhausted on the floor next to the still forms of their boys, whispering words of comfort between them.

Bruce was just about to find his own place to rest when Clelia called out that there was something they should see in the next room. Will started to rise.

"I've got this," Bruce told him. "Rest while you can."

When he reached the next room, the fastest runner in Haven pointed at the space behind one of the workbenches. It was a place he knew well given how many hours he'd spent there over the past few weeks.

As he'd expected, Antonia, or at least what remained of her, lay on the floor. Judging by the position of her rigid hands, she must have held the Ark by both of its ends when she attempted to summon its power.

"Did you really think you could control the weapon that killed Nyx?" he asked, trying to find any sympathy at all for her. The surge of raw power had burned her to ash and charcoal. He could only identify her by the iron collar which had partially turned to slag that still encircled her neck. "You got off easy compared to what my Megan would have done to you." He pulled a packing blanket out of a box and covered her with it more to protect the children from any more horrors than out of any sense of

410

respect.

Then he noticed the medicine blanket artifact and tucked it into his shirt. Sam would likely want it, if by some miracle, they actually made it out alive. As an afterthought, he picked up the amulet he'd accidentally reanimated as well, slipping it into the pocket of his pants.

"Everyone go back to the last room," Felix ordered as he led the children deeper into the workshops, "Find a comfortable spot. We're probably going to be here for a while."

"Where are our parents?" a boy of no more than five or six asked. The dust of so many collapsing walls and ceilings had coated them all in stone grit, but this one had clean trails traveling down his cheeks.

"I'm sure they're okay," Felix said, picking him up. "It might just take a while for them to find us."

"Will we be safe here?" another girl asked.

"Of course," he lied. "Did you see the size of that door? Nothing is getting in here."

Unable to listen any longer, Bruce walked back to the first workroom where Clelia had just picked up both of the twins to carry to the back.

"He's not going to make it," Cat said without emotion, pointing at Gaius. "And we couldn't bring him with us if he did."

"Why not?" Bruce asked, coming over.

In answer, William turned the young man on his side and pulled up the shirt stiff with blood. Several lumps the size of silver dollars were moving just below the skin where Bruce could make out the edges of their shells.

"Apparently the demonic doodle bugs are parasitic," William explained.

"This day just keeps getting better," Bruce said when the urge to vomit finally passed. "We're screwed," he added quietly where the children couldn't hear. "Nothing we've accomplished has been more than a delaying tactic."

"What did you mean when you said that last call was very old?" William asked.

"Remember when I told you that the reason why Megan could hide in Nickelville was the presence of an incomplete gate?"

Both William and Catherene nodded.

"The reason why he tried to pierce the veil was to retrieve his recently deceased wife and infant son," Bruce explained. "He thought they lay within because he said he'd heard his wife call his name from the other side."

"His name was Jacob, wasn't it?" William asked.

"I'm guessing she must have called out to him during labor, and the jabberwockies heard it and mimicked her cries," Bruce finished. "I guess it might be possible to open that gate from this side, but I lost all sense of it when Megan and I closed it completely. Even if we could get out of this room, I doubt that I could find it again. Furthermore, I don't think it ever actually linked the two worlds or those things out there would have come through into Earth."

"I don't see any way for us to get home," William admitted. "But there is something we should talk about in light of this," he said, nodding to Gaius. "There's something I may have to do at the end."

"And what's that?" Bruce asked, finally sliding his back down the wall to sit down. His muscles were already starting to stiffen from all of the unaccustomed activity.

"There's a way to make sure that none of us suffer," he answered quietly.

"What are you talking about?" his wife asked.

"There's a way that I can destroy everything for more than a mile in every direction," William added.

"Why haven't we used this before now?" Bruce asked, but Cat's expression was answer enough.

"It's sort of a one-time trick," William admitted bitterly. "I'll release every bit of life force that I have in one burst of self-sacrifice. What leaves me will be pure unfocused wild magic that nothing can withstand."

"But wouldn't that kill you?" Bruce asked, trying not to look at the expression of horror on Cat's face.

"Losing life force doesn't kill, but I would be extremely weak afterward," he explained. "What would kill me is when it returns. You see, unfocused magic without a purpose always returns to where it began."

"No," Cat said, shaking her head violently. "I won't let you do that."

"I don't want to do it either," he said, putting his arms around her. "But if it comes down to it at the end, I'd rather we die that way than with whatever will happen when those things get to us."

"Hey guys," Clelia called from where they'd taken the children. "Can one of you come back here? Something strange is happening."

Before any of them could go investigate, an unnatural hush settled over their extra senses. Bruce jumped to his feet in excitement, recognizing the way the gate under the Academy had felt.

"Is there a shimmery spot floating in the air that sort of glows?" he yelled, his exhaustion forgotten.

"How did you know?" she called back.

Bruce let out a whoop of excitement and pumped his fist in the air.

"Care to share?" William asked, smiling weakly at his young friend's enthusiasm.

"This, my friends, is what it feels like to be close to an incomplete gate! It has to be Megan. She's bringing us home!"

"She can do that?" William asked. "I thought the Beloved were the

413

only ones who could."

"Megan isn't much for following the rules about things like that," he answered. "I can't wait to see her!"

"She must be awfully eager to see you as well," Cat remarked.

"Oh, it's not like that," Bruce said quickly and just a little sadly. "Well, I mean she doesn't feel that way about me."

"You do realize that Megan is currently tearing a hole in the fabric of time and space to bring you back to her," Cat pointed out, smiling at him. "That's not exactly the sort of thing someone does for a close friend. I mean, I'm not sure I'd do that for him and we've got children together."

"I'll remember that," William said, pretending to be cross. "But Bruce, just in case this doesn't work out, and we don't make it home, I think you should know something."

"What's that?" Bruce asked, dancing around on the spot in his excitement.

"Megan came of age while you were lost to us," he said, watching Bruce's face.

"You mean the promise thing?" Bruce asked.

"We felt her fall in love with you all the way inside the shields around Haven," Cat said.

"It was so strong that I almost fell in love with you myself," William teased.

"You mean she...she really does love me?" Bruce whispered, his fingertips touching his lips as he remembered that last kiss.

Something massive hit the wall where the door stood, buckling it in several inches.

Blood flowed freely through the cuts in the courtly garb Dougal had worn when he danced with the Queen. It pooled on the ground where he knelt, breathing in short, hitching gasps.

It was Maeve's friend who'd saved them in the end, that quiet man in the colorful flowing robes that had told him the secret of the shield he'd summoned to keep them out. It was a power of last resort, one that could ironically only protect the bearer when he or she was dying. Once summoned, it fed off of his waning life force, and the only thing he had to do to maintain it was not die. Unfortunately, that was becoming rather difficult to do.

Each hitching breath brought agony, and agony brought clarity which in turn gave him the strength to hold on for just one more breath. He fortified each breath with the memory of her, the way she'd looked and the way she'd felt in his arms. While he fought for each breath, he could see them, these iron nightmares that had wiped out a whole generation of the Tuatha dé.

He would have liked to say that it was the thought of them wiping out the rest of his people that gave him the strength to hold on, but that wasn't even close to true. He couldn't bear the thought of those monsters reaching her as she stood there, bathed in power. He couldn't bear the thought of a world without her in it, even if he wasn't there to see. So he held on to each breath for all he was worth, and he let it propel him just one more second into the future, just one more second for them to return. After that he'd find another.

Then she was there. The blood that flowed down from a cut above his eye blurred his vision, but he knew her at once.

You are the best of us all. None before have served as well as you. You have done all you can. Rest now, and I will protect her in your place.

The gauntlet closed over the hilt of the Scathlahm's Blade and he let go.

"Thank you, Your Majesty," he whispered, slumping into his sister's arms as they watched the Morrigan Reborn return to the field and finish what she'd started so many years before. By the time she was done, nothing remained of the Nine to show that they'd ever been at all.

When Bri laid him back on the ground, he thought about saying his Queen's name one last time and smiled. But before he could do so, he departed into a memory of her where he could forever remain.

Power coursed through Megan unlike anything she'd ever felt. This was nothing compared to her assault on the Morrigan's Monument. Then it had only been her power, her pain and her grief. It had been a crude, ugly thing meant to destroy. Now the collective might of the Tuatha dé coursed through her, intoxicating her with its vast power. She called on the energies flowing though the earth around her and it burned, this ecstasy of agony, through which she created a framework of energy on which she would build the gate. There came a point, like it had at the Sentinel tree when her creation took on a life of its own and began to pull from her, forcing her to increase what she gave just to keep up. And just like before, she was committed to this path and she would not survive if she failed. But this time there were no fauns to help.

She realized she wasn't strong enough, even with the power that flowed through her like the fires of creation. She still didn't have enough strength to open the veil and set him free. Even recently pierced, it was too thick here, and with the horrified realization that she would take her people with her, she knew she would fail. The place where Jacob had pierced it had been thinner. But thinking of Jacob made her remember that day at the Well of Dreams, that day when she'd called back and received help.

Opening herself to the past, Megan called on her father's ancestors, she called on the Daughters of Crina both before and after they'd taken the name, and just before she lost control of the gate, they answered.

Her back arched and her hands curled into claws. She shrieked in agony as their power flowed through her and into the nearly completed

gate. And even though Azarich and his friends had none to lend her, they still came.

An insignificant speck riding a wave of pure energy, she wielded power to dwarf the Beloved themselves as she forced the Earth to do for her what it did for the Beloved willingly. Even as she did so, she knew there would be a price. The cavern floor fractured beneath her feet, and outside a storm brewed, looking for all the world like a hurricane forming in the mountains of Wyoming.

She held her will focused on the gate, pruning away the branches of time until the only ones that remained were the ones in which she would indeed see him again. She would accept nothing less.

The entire wall and part of the ceiling caved in, forcing the three adults to flee to the back of the chamber as the orange haze of this strange world flowed in. Bruce wondered what name Cat would use to bind this beast with its wedge-shaped head and bony keel protruding from its chest. It had the vague shape of a shell-less turtle, although tortoise might be closer since its front legs appeared to be much longer than the rear. The scales of its chitinous armor were an unpleasant shade of green and its flesh, at least in the few places that it showed, was the non-color of pond sediment.

Focused as he'd been on the brute between them, Bruce hadn't noticed when the collapse had buried Gaius, but he did see the pale creatures that poured out between the openings in the rubble that covered him.

The screaming calls of the jabberwockies almost drowned out the cheers of the children two rooms behind them, calling out that they could see people through the thinning veil of the gate. The young ones, for a little while longer at least, could remain blissfully unaware of the death that reached for them at the very edge of rescue.

Catching sight of its elusive prey, the turtle thing barreled toward them, stepping on the rubble that covered the councilwoman's son and crushing the horrors to which he'd given birth. There was no fighting off or delaying its advance, but Bruce brought the rest of the roof down on it as they retreated through the entrance to the next room.

Hardly slowing, it shook off the debris and exploded through the wall, no longer taking the time to create openings now that its hunting frenzy had begun.

Completely on the defensive, they fled into the last workroom where Clelia and Felix stood, she with her spear and he with the other short sword, prepared to defend the children that cowered behind them. The larger teen looked expectantly at the door as if another would appear, then he nodded to himself, understanding what his friend's absence meant.

Bruce allowed himself one quick glance through the slightly opaque shimmer, recognizing the love of his life in another universe just a few short yards away.

Several of the phydeauxs raced through the final doorway, bearing down on the men and women as they faced off against the creature that was forcing its head and keel through the doorway, collapsing the wall in a shower of dislodged stone blocks.

Cat, her magic almost completely spent, summoned light brighter than the sun and cast it directly into the monster's tiny eyes. It opened its beaky maw, also similar to a turtle, in a silent cry of pain, even as one of its long front legs shot out and snatched her husband from his feet.

While the deafening booms of the phydeauxs filled the chamber as they raced toward Bruce on their armored, crablike legs, he wondered how he should face them. Even fortified by his magic, he doubted his sword would do them any noticeable damage. But just before the closest one reached him, the rubble of the fallen wall took flight.

In a swarm of deadly projectiles, the rubble slammed into the phydeauxs, knocking them from their feet and crushing their crablike shells. Within seconds they'd turned back the way they'd come, but none escaped in time.

Bruce looked back to find nearly five dozen children standing with Felix, identical looks of determination on their young faces. In that moment, they reminded him of Megan when she'd told him that she was finished running, and he forgot about William.

Luckily Clelia did not as she rushed toward the huge beast without regard for her own safety. She shoved the spear directly into its open maw as it descended toward the man trapped beneath its blunt-clawed foot. But as brave as the act had been, the thing simply snapped its jaws shut, cleaving the shaft.

Bruce's body rushed forward once again of its own accord, leaping atop a partially demolished wall and from there onto the thing's back. Terrified that whatever puppet master controlled his movements might leave him to finish alone, he drove his sword into one of the gaps between the scaly armor all the way up to the hilt. But even as he did so, he knew nothing vital lay beneath. Then, much to his surprise since he hadn't known how to do so before starting, he pulled the creature's heat up through the steel and out into the air where it dissipated quickly. Frost began to form on the thing beneath him.

He thought the fight was over until the beast threw him from its back, reminding him that even though it might resemble a reptile, it was something else altogether.

Covering his head to protect it from the expected impact, he instead felt the gentle combination of five dozen young minds catch him and bring him safely to the ground before turning their attention toward the partially frozen beast.

He watched in awe as the stones rose into the air again, becoming a lethal swarm as Felix led his army into battle. Then the beast shifted its weight and William screamed from beneath its foot. The stones dropped and Bruce looked back to find Felix standing confused among a crowd of still, glassy-eyed children.

In horror, Bruce realized that in his pain, William had opened the teaching link, drawing his students directly into his mind. Now they would experience his death as their own.

Cat and Clelia rushed toward him, armed only with desperation. Bruce began to draw power into himself, remembering what they'd said about the end.

William, exhausted both physically and magically, managed one last act in his defense. Summoning the last of his reserves, he threw a fireball directly into the open maw that descended toward him. It tore into the frozen flesh, rupturing the underlying tissues. But even though it clearly hurt the beast, it would take much more than one to finish it off.

Catherene let out a long wail of despair as the sharp beak plunged toward the man she loved. But she was no bard, and her sorrow, no matter how potent, lacked any power over destiny.

Then a fireball flew past her, slamming into the heavily armored shoulder of the beast, followed almost immediately by another, rocking the thing back onto its hind legs as it tried in vain to protect itself from the missiles that now came in a steady barrage.

Seeing their chance, Clelia and Catherene slid in beneath the flailing limbs of the besieged beast and dragged the injured teacher to safety.

Bruce turned, expecting reinforcements from beyond the gate. But all he found were the same frightened though determined children. As he watched, a little girl of perhaps eight cast a single fireball at the beast. Although the skill had come directly from William's mind through the teaching link, the strength to do so had not. She swayed where she stood for a few seconds, watching as her classmates did the same before collapsing unconscious to the ground.

The gate opened at last, and Tuatha dé began to pour through, snatching up children and running back with them to the safety of Earth.

The beast was an unrecognizable, smoking ruin by the time the first energy reached Bruce from his own world, flooding his senses. Now that the shield gate that protected Haven had been destroyed, a multitude of future pathways opened to him. In every single one he saw death.

He'd thought that the jabberwockies were different from the other creatures in this strange world when he'd first seen them, and he'd been right. They were no more native to this world than he was. Nor had they come in search of food as he'd thought. It was the opening of the gate by the artifact that had drawn their attention, and it was the one at his back that drew them now.

Not even they remembered the world from which they'd first come. But they'd stripped and enslaved all that came after.

Even if the gate was closed, the jabberwockies would burrow through like maggots, creating a doorway through which they could bring the rest. Then they would feed as much on the suffering of the human race as they would their flesh.

"No," Bruce moaned. It would have been better if they'd never been rescued at all. The price of this brief extension to their lives would be the loss of all life on Earth and eventually Tyr Sgodl as well.

Feeling the anguish of his friend, William ignored the wrongness of doing so and reached through Bruce's depleted shields to see the vision for himself. Then he took his wife's face between his hands before she could read his intent and kissed her. When he did, a single path opened in the future where all but one of them would survive.

At first, Catherene didn't realize that anything was wrong. By the time she did, it was too late. Using the knowledge that he'd gained from the Tuatha dé judgement scholar, William drained his wife's energy just enough to replenish his own and left her too weak to resist.

"I'm so sorry," he whispered to her, sweeping her quickly into his arms and hugging her to him one last time before passing her to Bruce. "Swear to me that you'll protect them and keep them safe."

"No," Catherene cried weakly, barely able to lift her head.

"And keep trying to reach my boys," he added, looking Bruce hard in the eyes.

"I swear I will," Bruce whispered back, barely able to see past his own tears. He hated this, but he also knew it was the only chance any of them had. "I'll take them to the bards."

"I never thought of that," the doomed man said, smiling. Then he gathered his boys up in his arms and sent one last message out into the universe for them.

Bruce wasn't sure what that message contained, and that was probably as it should be. Then William passed them both into the arms of a man whom he would have considered an enemy just a few months ago.

"Goodbye," Bruce said, his voice breaking. Then he turned to follow the Tuatha dé warrior who carried the twins so they wouldn't be separated from their mother.

Drained past the ability to shield herself, Bruce could see directly through Catherene's eyes as she looked upon her husband for the last time. He was still smiling at her, watching over their escape.

I'll always love you, he mouthed. Behind him they could hear the shrieking cries of the jabberwockies growing nearer as the lure of the gate became too great to resist. Then the brave man turned away and the air around him began to shimmer as he prepared to save them all. The gate closed and he was gone.

Bruce stumbled and went down on one knee under the weight of Catherene's sorrow. His vision narrowed on the twins before him, still carried by one of Megan's subjects. And even though neither of them showed any sign of understanding what happened around them, one reached out behind the neck of the man who carried them and took his brother's hand in his own. Bruce lowered the quiet woman to the ground as gently as he could lest he drop her in his exhaustion. Her eyes continued to stare at the place where they'd been as if she could see what transpired on the other side.

Exhausted beyond measure, Bruce felt Megan's eyes upon him, and he turned to look at her. When her eyes met his through the blinding radiance of her power, he found himself back in the big race when the bond between them had first been forged. But this time, no longer bound by the promise of her ancestor, her love poured into him, so much greater than he ever could have imagined. At last he understood what it meant to be part of something so strong that they would always find each other in the ever-changing pathways of time.

Even as her power burned through him, his amplified hers. Fissures began to form in her skin as at last her frail mortal body could take no more. Her smile never faltered, even when she began to burn.

Chapter XLII: Beloved

Far away in a world almost forgotten by the people of Earth, the shimmering forms of two small boys solidified before Coy, each taking one of his hands in their own. Then, before he could resist, he was ripped from his adopted world to arrive, hands still held by his young kidnappers to a scene of such destruction that it was difficult to imagine what it had been before.

The air reeked of sulfur and the sky overhead burned orange. Everything stretching out to the horizon had been pulverized by some wild and destructive magic, and Coy could almost taste its familiar taint in the air. He'd seen this sort of destruction only once before, and he knew better than anyone that they didn't want to be here when the wave returned.

At the center of the destruction, standing just in front of him and the boys, was a very surprised man.

"Who are you?" the man asked, voice trembling in shock.

"Mom is sad," the boys answered together in one voice. Then they pulled Coy closer and joined their free hands around the man standing awkwardly between them. "It's time for us to go home."

And then, hijacking the Beloved's power once again, the pretentious children did exactly that.

Bruce walked the shadows and caught Megan as she fell, oblivious to the fire that engulfed him. Her mind was a torrent of thoughts, images and sensations that she poured into him as she tried to convey the depth of all she'd never been allowed to express.

The power of the gate's creation and closing began to wane and as it did so, it tugged at the woman in his arms. He clutched her ruined body closer, weaving himself deeper and deeper into her essence, anchoring her fading life force with his own.

"I love you," she whispered through charred and blackened lips. "But it's time to let me go. Not even you can fix me now."

"No," he snarled, shaking his head. "You promised. Either you stay, or you take me with you. We're a package deal."

"I'm sorry," she whispered before going limp in his arms and beginning to recede like an outgoing tide from his mind.

No, he screamed after her. Then he reached out and took hold of the Tuatha dé to which she was bound. They struggled for an instant, then bowed to his will, and their strength flowed into him. He gathered in the power of her ancestors even though his blood gave him no right. Then he pulled her so close that he could hear the voice of the Morrigan whisper in his ear.

All things remember what they once were.

He began to feed her rebirth with his soul.

Ruptured cells began to rebuild themselves, organs became whole, and then her heart took one tentative beat followed by another.

Her eyes flew wide, but it wasn't Megan who looked back at him.

Have you learned nothing from my story, human child? Would you make of her a living artifact, doomed to walk the Earth for eternity, unable to love another? You will not survive this forging. Would it not be kinder to let her go?

"I can't let her die," he sobbed, power burning through him as it had

427

done with her. He needed to finish this while he still could. "My soul will live on in her, just as yours does."

If there were a way, would you share this curse that you place upon her? The Morrigan asked.

"I'm the only one who can do this," he gasped in the agony of his own burning flesh.

Your pride has blinded you. You are an amplifier, nothing more. Why have you never realized that the powers of foresight and smithing were never yours? Think about it boy, I chose you for your mind as much as your gifts.

"I'm not amplifying her," he gasped, "I have these gifts because I've been amplifying you!"

And you didn't lose your power when you crossed into the world of my birth because I sent a part of myself with you. So I ask you again, will you share her curse?

"I beg you for it," he cried.

When the time comes, will you pay my price? Will you do one small thing for me when this is done?

"Anything but live without her."

That will suffice.

Megan straightened in his arms, mostly healed by now, kneeling next to him as she reached out and pulled him yet closer until her cheek rested against his. One of her hands slid up his spine and grasped the back of his head as if she were about to kiss him.

The pain that blossomed at the base of his skull paralyzed him, but still he held onto her, guiding the restoration of her body even as his own changed. His vision dimmed and then sharpened beyond anything he'd experienced before, and even without a mirror he knew that his eyes had turned violet. Her power bleached all color from his skin, even as his hair darkened and his body finished the last of its journey toward adulthood in seconds. His lungs cleared and he knew that the grown woman in his arms would never need to help him breathe again.

Every artifact must have a purpose, the Morrigan told him. *To you I charge the finding of other artifacts so that you might dismantle them and set the souls trapped within free. To this end you will keep the skills of the greater smith of which you will be the last. But you shall never create another artifact.*

And Megan? Bruce asked. *What is to be her purpose?*

She must take up the charge with which we were given at the birth of the Tuatha dé. She will become the hand of justice in this sickening world.

I will not bind her to such a purpose, Bruce told her defiantly. *I will not take any more choices from her when she has already been bound by so many others.*

Do you seek to go back on your word so soon?

No, he answered. *Such a thing might jeopardize our life together, which was what I promised against.*

She is incapable of not loving you, the Morrigan argued. *Your argument is not valid. What is your real purpose in denying my will?*

I love her too much to take more of her free will. I know she would forgive me, but I cannot commit this treason against her. Furthermore, it is my belief that she will follow the path you want without these constraints.

What alternative do you offer?

I will charge her with the containment of the promises that were so foolishly made by her ancestors. As long as she lives, her descendants will be free of them.

How will she have descendants when she shall become immortal and unchanging?

Can even you see what the distant future might have in store for her?

429

he asked.

I accept your offer. It will suffice.

The voice of the Morrigan went silent and like Megan's parents before them, he and the woman who loved him found each other inside the pain and clung to each other, unwilling to ever separate again.

His mind opened and began to fill with the knowledge amassed by all of the Tuatha dé before him. Memories that were not his own settled into place. It terrified him, but Megan held him steady against the flood and the pain fled before her like morning fog in the sunlight.

When silence finally descended, Megan pulled her cheek from his and he saw that she was whole and perfect, a slightly older version of the girl who'd stolen his heart. Then her fingers tangled in his long black hair, and she gave him the kiss he'd dreamed of for so long. When she finally released him, her face was bathed in the violet glow of his eyes.

"Why do you smell like pizza?" she asked, before pulling him down to the floor of the cavern with her and following that kiss with many others.

A short distance away, Catherene rocked back and forth, humming a lullaby that the boys in her arms couldn't hear. A distant part of her observed that she was in shock while she tried to remember exactly where the hole in the world had been in that last moment before it closed and took him away from her.

Her power had gone with him and she planned to take her boys far away where she'd never have to speak again, and where there'd be no chance of awakening any gifts within her. Lost in these thoughts, she didn't notice at first when Ethan and Owen began to wiggle in her arms.

Then they stood up, clasping their hands together as they'd often done in the days before silence had descended. Each of them held up their free hand as if inviting a particularly tall ghost to join them in a game of ring around the rosie.

Then in a much more abrupt arrival than she'd become accustomed to seeing when her friends walked the shadows, a young man not much older than Megan and Bruce appeared, holding each of her boys' hands in his own. And in the open space between the three of them, William returned to her.

Megan would have happily lain there on the cavern floor for another year or so, as long as Bruce remained by her side. How had she never noticed the way that any contact with his skin sent little novas of sensation through her?

"I can't believe you didn't bring me any," she whispered, utterly fascinated by the curve of his jaw where it met the pale expanse of his neck.

"Wait a minute," he said, pulling away from her and reaching into the pocket of his badly burned and too small tux. Like his brother, Bruce had grown into the man he would have eventually become, although with the skin, hair and eyes of the Tuatha dé. She made a sound of displeasure and pulled him back, even as he pulled out a handful of what might once have been a piece of school pizza.

"How sweet," she said, frowning. "Your first gift to me as a couple. Bruce, I love you more than anything, but I'm not eating that."

"Megan," a familiar voice called.

Turning to look, she found her mother standing nearby. But as glad as she was to see her, she immediately noticed that Emelia was wearing the Morrigan's armor in spite of what they'd worried it would do to the child in her womb.

"What are you doing here?" Megan asked, sitting up suddenly. "And why do you have the Dagda's Staff?"

Casting around, she looked for her Scathlahm and found only his sister. The look in Bri's eyes would have told Megan all she needed to know even if his absence in her senses hadn't.

"Things happened while you were rescuing the King," Emelia explained.

"King?" Bruce said. "I'm not…"

"In the eyes of your people," Emelia continued. "What just happened represents a form of marriage more holy than any ceremony. But we'll still have one for the people back home so that no one feels left out. All of that is going to have to wait though. Like I said, something has happened that requires your immediate attention."

Bruce groaned and lay back on the ground. "Why can we never get a moment's peace?" he asked.

"What is it now?" Megan asked, still looking sadly at Bri as Dougal's last moments revealed themselves to her.

"William arrived from the other side of the veil a short time ago," Emelia said.

"That's wonderful news," Megan said, managing to smile.

"How did that happen?" Bruce asked, suddenly rising to his feet. "Are we sure the gate is secure?"

"He didn't use the gate," Emelia said. "Apparently his boys have been exploring a parallel world without their bodies."

"We thought it might be something like that," Bruce said, and Megan realized she could feel his thoughts unhindered in her mind just as she did with the rest of the Tuatha dé. As King, so could he. "But that doesn't explain how he made it back. He stayed behind to make sure none of those things could cross into this world. If that somehow failed, we are in serious trouble."

"Do you feel anything like that in our future?" Megan asked.

"No," he answered, turning inward where she was delighted to realize she could now follow. "There aren't even any blank spots that I can see. We're going to be okay. We can take the boys to Guarded Wood where Paul and Nita can call them back to their bodies like they did with me."

"That won't be necessary," William said, walking up with one of his giggling boys slung over his shoulder. It was hard to recognize the child at first because he looked so different in animated motion. Cat walked behind him, carrying the other one.

Megan noticed that the woman wasn't letting her husband move beyond her reach, and knew exactly how she felt.

"How did you get back exactly?" Bruce asked, smiling at the boys.

"We made our friend Coy bring us," the one in Cat's arms giggled.

"And who is that?" Megan asked.

"That would be me," a stranger said, moving closer.

As soon as Megan saw him, she could feel the power radiating past his powerful, yet poorly constructed shields. His clothing was odd as well.

"You're one of the Beloved," Bruce observed.

"That's what the lady in the armor that talks just called me," Coy said, having trouble adapting to all of this.

"He's from this world," Emelia explained, "But new to his power."

"This is so strange," Coy said. "I'm not even used to speaking English any more. But I really need to go back to where I was before. A girl with short hair just bombarded me with a bunch of interdimensional theory, and the only thing I understood was that time must be moving a lot faster there than it is here. I've been there for close to a year, but only a few days have passed here since I first left."

"We know something about that," Emelia observed. "That's even faster than Tyr Sgodl."

"I have no idea what that is," he said anxiously. "But there are a lot of people back where I came from that are counting on me to end a war. I need to get back, but I don't understand how I got there in the first place, and I'm not sure how these little kidnappers brought me back here."

"You need an army," Bruce said, listening to a vision that had been triggered by the Beloved's words.

"Are you offering to sign up?" Coy asked, surprised.

"No," Megan said, feeling the future open before her. "We are giving you an army of people who are fanatic about the idea of following a new Beloved. They would happily leave this world to follow you. And even though they've been a pain in our backsides, they will serve you well. Even more importantly, there are some among them who could teach you to better use your power."

"That might very well be exactly what I need," Coy said thoughtfully. "But how long will it take for them to be ready to go?"

"You'll have to talk to them about that," Bruce said. "Just watch out for the old seer. You don't happen to have green eyes, do you?"

"No, they're blue," Coy said, confused all over again.

434

Chapter XLIII: The New Capital

In the days that followed, most of the Children of Nyx did indeed follow the Beloved Coy to a world from which they would never again trouble the Tuatha dé. The ones who stayed behind swore fealty to the King and Queen and began to retrofit the Baker Hotel with nonferrous materials so it could become the new seat of the Tuatha dé's government.

The body of Scathlahm Dougal Breathach was laid to rest in a crypt deep within the castle at Tyr Sgodl where he joined many of his ancestors. Brighid took up the staff of the Dagda and became the first Scathlahm of the Immortal King and Queen. She was also hand fasted to a Child of Nyx in a ceremony that had previously been performed only once before. Although the need to bear children was not necessary, it merged their abilities and left them each possessed of the skills from both. As a wedding gift, the King and Queen gave their new Scathlahm some much needed time off to settle into the cabin in Guarded Wood which had been extended by the royal craftsmen.

The former city stronghold of Haven became the new home of Caer Sidhe once the cavernous void was reinforced. But even though the King and Queen were invited on several occasions to return there, they politely declined. Interactions between the children of the various Beloved continued, however, and for the first time, delegations were sent to all the different tribes in hope that a mutual governing body could be formed.

The gifted continued to flow into Nickelville, and it became clear that the town would soon have to extend its borders beyond the Wellspring. Sam's people returned and their numbers soon surpassed what they had been before the accident at the church. He happily ceded his de facto leadership to those who followed so he could focus on the restaurant, the dojo and his new role as mayor. After his election, he declared the Jubilee race open to both girls and boys. In the first co-ed competition, the King's former nemesis suffered a sound defeat to a dark-haired girl named Clelia.

Meanwhile, those with the power to do so restored Josie's Grove and even expanded its boundaries to include the last three houses on Beverly Road where it was rumored the most animated dinner parties continued.

On a blissfully ordinary day in the spring, a small group gathered for a simple ceremony from which anything resembling royal embellishment had been forbidden. Mother and daughter married their best friends while music joined the present with the past, and the Queen's grandmother told her how much better she looked in her old wedding dress. Her grandfather disagreed.

When at long last things began to settle, the Morrigan asked the King to repay the debt she was owed and thus bring to fruition the plan with which she'd guided their steps since the Immortal Queen's conception. On a pleasantly warm day in Nickelville, Bruce used his power to recall the fractured pieces of the Morrigan's soul as he'd already done with the part of his own that he'd so recklessly trapped in a barbecue pit. Then he returned the Goddess of War to the armor she'd forged for herself so long ago, happily sending with her the power of foresight.

The bards played in Josie's grove as they had done once before, but this time it was the enchanted suit of armor that lay on one of the benches. With a single strike Emelia pierced it with the only weapon that could destroy it, the Scathlahm's Blade. In a monumental explosion of power that sounded nonetheless like a sigh of release, she set the Morrigan free at

436

last.

The Dagda looked like nothing more than a man, if anything less remarkable than most. But his smile rivaled the beauty of any god when his wife stood before him at long last. Few would ever understand the need with which they held one another more than the witnesses to their reunion.

A large black cat strolled up to them and waited patiently for them to notice him. When they didn't do so as quickly as he would have liked, he began to wind between their legs, purring loudly as he rubbed against them.

Laughing for the first time in several millennia, the goddess of war snatched up the immortal Cat Sidhe so she and her husband could run their fingers through his thick fur.

Then, close to the end of what time the bards could give them, the Morrigan looked up to find Megan and Bruce holding each other close and watching.

Remember why he made us, she sent. *It's time for magic to return.*

Then they reluctantly put Mr. Bob down on one of the stone benches before giving him a few more loving strokes and fading away.

When the bards stopped playing, he stretched languidly as if nothing had happened only seconds before, and flopped down on his side to better absorb the heat from the sun warmed stone. Then he put his head down and settled in for a good nap.

Chapter XLIV: Epilogue

Unless one knew customized cars well, the one that pulled up to the building's armed checkpoint looked nothing like an armored car. Once past, it was thoroughly searched inside and out before finally being scanned for electronic surveillance.

The process was time consuming, but the man inside took comfort in its thoroughness. Likewise, the armed detail that greeted him soothed his worries. When the elevator opened, his assistant was waiting to greet him inside.

"They've all arrived," the small man in the expensive suit advised him.

"And their mood?"

"Nervous," the assistant answered. "But given the circumstances, they'd be foolish not to be worried."

"Any more intel on what happened to our last rival?" the man asked.

"Our sources at the Bureau say it's exactly like all of the others," the assistant answered.

"Brain aneurysms, fried electronics and no witnesses," the man said, watching as the numbers on the wall in front of him increased. "How is it possible to make that many people have brain aneurysms?"

When they arrived at the penthouse, another armed detail greeted them, all familiar faces. They fell into step with the man and his assistant as they walked down the luxuriously decorated hallway to the boardroom.

The din of conversation greeted them even before they reached the doors, telling the man that things might be worse than he'd expected. Taking a deep breath, he opened the mahogany doors and walked inside.

It pleased him when they fell silent. At least things hadn't deteriorated that far yet.

"Ladies," he said, nodding his head in a semblance of respect to the handful of hard-faced women in the organization. "And gentlemen, thank you for coming. Please take your seats."

In the bustle of movement that followed, he walked over to the well-stocked bar and poured himself a drink.

"Are you sure we're safe here?" someone cried out before he'd even had a chance to sit.

"This room," he said, gesturing with his drink toward the expanse of gold veined black stone, rare woods and bulletproof glass, "Sits atop a fortress. The best army money can buy stands between us and anyone who might seek to reach us. And as you can see from the men stationed both inside and outside of this room, we have enough firepower to end a war."

"But the others were well protected too," complained another.

"No one has ever been protected like this," the man explained. "Our air is filtered, recirculated and monitored. So you can rest assured that we will not fall victim to this fantasy aneurysm gas. Our power is generated on site, and I'm sure you all experienced the new entry protocols first hand."

The power cut out unexpectedly, and the man almost dropped his glass. Cries of panic filled the darkness.

"Please get hold of yourselves," he yelled, irritated that this could happen even after all that he'd spent to assure continuous power. Why weren't the backup generators coming online? "Stay in your seats so our guards can keep track of you," he added. "We don't want any accidents."

This seemed to settle them. No one wanted to be caught in friendly fire.

"Our phones are all dead," someone called out. "I think it's happening."

Suddenly the room was lit by fluttering blue light, casting his shadow across the frightened people at the table who all stared at something directly behind him. Whirling to look, he sent the contents of his glass splashing down the front of his expensive clothing. He found a beautiful woman with pale skin and long black hair staring back at him with predatory interest. Something about the odd color of her eyes made the fear in him almost unbearable.

"I don't know how you got in here but there's no way you're getting out," he said, relieved that he sounded far more confident than he felt. Why should he be so frightened of such a little slip of a girl?

Just then the doors opened and a man with the same strange features entered. For just an instant, the man had thought the newcomer's eyes had glowed violet.

"That didn't take as long as I'd expected, My King," the young woman who strangely enough held a tongue of blue flame in her hand observed.

"Who are you?" the man asked.

"I am Queen Megan Mackgahe of the Tuatha dé," she answered. "And we have come to pass judgement on you for your crimes."

"Do you have any idea who we are?" an older man demanded from where he sat at the table.

"Please be quiet, senator," the King ordered. And when the politician tried to continue, the Queen silenced him with a gesture of the hand not holding the flame.

"Don't worry," she purred. "You'll get your chance to tell us what you know."

441

"We've done nothing wrong," the leader said.

"You mean aside from the human trafficking, the drugs, the illegal arms, the money laundering and all of the horrors I didn't even know existed until quite recently?" the Queen asked.

"You have no right," the man spat.

"Just as none of you had the right to take from those weaker than you," she replied.

Many of those seated around the table gasped when the young woman's eyes began to glow.

"Reinforcements!" the man yelled.

"They're already dead," the King said pleasantly. "And now we know everything that they did. But the real knowledge is here," he said, reaching out to touch the heads of the two men closest to him. "We thank you for bringing them all together in one place for us."

The man looked for the guards stationed around the room and found them missing.

"Why are you doing this?" the once powerful man begged.

"For justice," the Queen answered as if explaining something to a particularly dense child, "For the path that will lead us to others like you, those who prey on those weaker than themselves. And of course for your depraved customers. We can't wait to meet them either."

But just as the King and Queen started to advance on him, they froze. Her hands slipped to her abdomen, and her expression softened.

"I didn't think we could," he whispered in wonder.

"I guess you put me back together better than we thought," she replied, moving into his arms while the silent room began to gauge their chances.

"Don't let any of them escape," she said to no one in particular. Then Megan Mackgahe, Queen of those who walked between the shadows, lost herself in the swirling vortex of her King's eyes and happily dreamed of the days to come while the shadows came alive around her and began to feed.

About the Author

Tom Barnett was a sick kid who escaped into fantasy books at a young age. As he grew, his asthma got better, but his love of reading never diminished. After three decades of leading teens toward a love of reading in which the stories of Nickelville have been percolating in the back of his mind, he's finally set them free.

Tom currently teaches middle school English in the Dallas area where he lives with his wife and children. He is also owned by several cats, one of which may or may not be the oldest creature in the universe.

www.ingramcontent.com/pod-product-compliance
Lightning Source LLC
Chambersburg PA
CBHW030545020726
47494CB00005B/1489